DEAD WRONG

Thorns and Fangs, Book Four

Gillian St. Kevern

To everyone who reached the end of book three and refrained from
emailing me angrily.

It's appreciated.

Nate's no supernatural expert, but even he knows a murdered man coming back to life to kill him can only mean one thing—the necromancer is back and out for revenge.

Recruited by Department Seven in a desperate attempt to stop Peter before he claims new victims, Nate quickly realizes he's in way over his head. His powers are failing him, he's haunted by Peter's ghost, and he can't even remember how he stopped Peter the first time—or why he feels that someone very important is missing from his life.

Ben is fighting for his afterlife. Trapped in the supernatural version of solitary confinement, he knows freeing himself will destroy New Camden's fragile peace—but what choice does he have? The longer he spends in his magical prison, the harder it becomes to resist his inner vampire. But if Ben wants to help Nate prevent Peter taking over the city, he has to prove himself to his sire—Saltaire, a thousand-year-old vampire with no qualms about using his immense power to suppress Ben's free will.

As the casualties mount and the city descends into chaos, Ben and Nate must overcome their worst fears and impossible odds—or be written out of existence entirely.Blurb

A NineStar Press Publication

Published by NineStar Press
P.O. Box 91792,
Albuquerque, New Mexico, 87199 USA.
www.ninestarpress.com

Dead Wrong

Copyright © 2018 by Gillian St. Kevern
Cover Art by Natasha Snow Copyright © 2018

This is a work of fiction. Names, characters, places, and incidents are either the product of the author's imagination or are used fictitiously. Any resemblance to actual persons living or dead, business establishments, events, or locales is entirely coincidental.

All rights reserved. No part of this publication may be reproduced in any material form, whether by printing, photocopying, scanning or otherwise without the written permission of the publisher. To request permission and all other inquiries, contact NineStar Press at the physical or web addresses above or at Contact@ninestarpress.com.

Printed in the USA
First Edition
February, 2018

Print ISBN: 978-1-948608-18-3

Also available in eBook, ISBN: 978-1-948608-10-7

Warning: This book contains sexually explicit content, which may only be suitable for mature readers.

Acknowledgements

Barb and Raevyn at NineStar Press went above and beyond to ensure that we could bring Dead Wrong out fast without sacrificing quality. Sera and Julia kept me on task and focused, and Melissa let me complain at her about rogue characters who refused to do what they were supposed to do. Huge thanks also goes out to my ARC team—Melissa, Meep and Andrea—for their support. I love you all like Aki loves his hair gel.

Chapter One

THE AFTERNOON HAD all the gloom of a funeral. The pavement and the drab external walls of the surrounding buildings extended to the gray sky above. Nate and Aki stood in silence in the alley beside their apartment building and contemplated the dead.

Nate, at six feet tall, had to bow his head to look down at them. "You're sure it's not, I don't know, some kind of vampire cat?" He winced. The question sounded even worse out in the open.

Aki looked up at Nate, his hazel eyes flat. "You're kidding me. Have you ever heard of a vampire cat?"

Nate made a helpless gesture toward the bodies. "Look at them." There were two desiccated rats and, nearby, a shriveled up bird. "Animals don't eat like this." He turned the nearest rat over, noticing what looked like a puncture wound. He crouched to get a closer look.

"Maybe they were sick. Rats are riddled with disease, and pigeons are not any better—don't touch them!" Aki made a disgusted noise. "Ugh. Keep your gross, infected hands away from me."

Nate set the rat down and turned his head, giving Aki a speculative look.

Aki stepped backward. "Touch me and I promise I will dump you."

Nate snorted, turning his attention back to the dead animals. "You can't dump me. We're not dating."

"I can friend dump you—and I will."

"I co-signed the lease. You're stuck with me."

"I'm pretty sure Grant can find me a legal loophole involving pestilence." Aki stuck his hands in the pockets of his plaid trousers. He drummed one foot against the pavement, the movement making his keychain rattle. "Come on. Let's go."

Nate stood slowly, still looking down at the animals. "There's got to be some kind of explanation for this. Maybe we should call Department Seven?"

"They'd laugh in your face. This isn't even a case for animal control." Aki heaved a theatrically loud sigh. "If you're that desperate for excitement, ask George to take you hunting. She'd jump at the chance."

Nate frowned at Aki. "I'm not desperate for excitement."

Aki raised an eyebrow. "Aren't you? This is the longest we've gone without any supernatural mishaps since you got mixed up with the necromancer, and for the last month, you've been glancing over your shoulder, listening to sounds that aren't there, and watching the news for anything paranormal. If that's not desperation, I don't know what is."

Nate shivered. How to explain to Aki that for the last month, he'd had the constant suspicion that there was something there, just on the edge of his awareness? "I'm not desperate."

"Then why are we hanging out in a shadowy alley, acting like revenant bait?"

Nate blanched. Revenants were the most basic form of the undead, recently deceased with a taste for blood and no thought beyond acquiring it. Nate had been closer than he wanted to hungry revenants. "Bait implies I want to find one. I don't."

"Then can we please leave before one finds us—"

Something crunched in the shadows beyond the dumpster.

Nate's breath froze in his throat. He didn't dare turn his head to see what Aki was doing, concentrating all his attention on the shadows.

He heard a second crunch, as if something shifted on the stones beyond the dumpster. Nate stepped toward it.

"Don't." Aki grabbed his arm. "Please, Nate. This is a seriously bad idea."

"Stay here." Nate disentangled himself. "Get ready to call Department Seven."

"And after that, I'll call the funeral home." Aki had his phone in hand. "I'm having them put 'I told him not to do it' on your gravestone."

"Quiet." Nate knew a revenant couldn't kill him. At least he was pretty sure he was safe. His experience with the necromancer had woken Nate's own supernatural side. Being part plant could be inconvenient at times, but it did mean that he was impervious to things that were fatal to ordinary humans. But being a card-carrying psychic wouldn't protect Aki from becoming monster chow. Nate edged his way around the dumpster carefully. If it was a revenant, he'd have to act fast to stop it preying on Aki.

Nate rounded the corner.

Nothing there? The newspaper was spread out as if someone had been sleeping rough—never a good idea in New Camden, the city with the largest monster population in the world—and it crackled under foot. Was the sound just the wind rustling through its pages? Nate turned to leave and caught a dull glow out of the corner of his eyes. He grinned. "Aki, come and look at this."

"Is it more dead animals? Because I can pass."

Nate crouched down. "Here, kitty. I'm not going to hurt you."

"A cat?" Aki snorted, and Nate heard his footsteps on the stone behind him. "All that over nothing."

Nate clicked his fingers. "Come on."

The cat watched him balefully. She stretched, displaying her claws, before taking a step into the light. She flicked her tail, watching Nate out of her one good eye. Her left eye was milky white, with the lines of an old scar above and below. She was skinny, her fur bare in patches, and her tail was crooked. Part of one ear was missing, looking like a tattered flag on a pirate ship, with her prominent ribs the hull.

"Whoa. That's the ugliest cat I've ever seen."

"She can't help that. Poor thing. Who knows how long she's been living out here?"

Aki smacked Nate's hand away from the cat. "Stop risking animal diseases! Look at it. Probably crawling with fleas!"

"It's just an old stray cat."

Aki scoffed. "I was wrong. That's definitely some variety of hell beast."

Nate clicked his fingers, succeeding in drawing the cat closer to him. "You're so mean. Just because she's been on the losing end of a few fights..."

"More than a few. It's probably got every disease in the book."

Nate extended his hand, and the cat cautiously sniffed it. "I think she likes me."

Aki leaned against the dumpster to watch. "Haven't you learned anything from the disaster that was you adopting the last stray?"

Nate looked up. "The last stray turned out to be Grant, who we saved from his evil stepdad, getting you a boyfriend in the process."

"We're not dating," Aki said immediately. "If you're so stuck on Grant, ask him out yourself. I don't want him."

Nate smiled to himself, stretching out his hand to the cat's tattered ears. She hissed, and before Nate could react, sunk her teeth into his hand. He jerked his hand back. "Ow!"

"Ha! Told you!"

Nate sat back on his heels, nursing his hand. "Are you grinning?"

"It's called *schadenfreude*." Aki nudged Nate with the toe of his sneaker. "And you deserved it."

Nate looked back down, but at his exclamation, the cat had darted back into the shadows. She squeezed into the narrow gap between the dumpsters. All he could see of her was the gleam of her dead eye. "You're a bad best friend."

Aki just shrugged. "You should have checked the fine print. It's too late now. You're stuck with me."

Nate stood, dusting off his hands on his jeans. "Maybe Grant will find me a legal loophole."

Aki elbowed him. "Not allowed. It's 'best friends forever.' Not best friends until Aki hurts my feelings."

Nate draped his arm over Aki's shoulders. "Since when is BFF legally binding?"

"Well it is. So it's a good thing I plan on keeping you around." He leaned comfortably against Nate's side. "That's your cue to say there's no one you would rather be stuck with."

Nate paused, guiltily conscious something wasn't right. There was something—someone—missing.

"Nate?"

Nate realized he'd stopped walking.

Aki was watching him with an expression of concern on his face. "I was only joking."

Nate grinned. He leaned over, tapping Aki on his shoulder. "Got you."

"You!" Aki demonstrated his feelings of friendship by trying to kick him.

THEY WERE STILL bickering when they arrived at the apartment.

Nate paused to fish in his pocket for the key. "Grant's nice and obviously into you."

Aki jiggled impatiently. "I liked him better as a dog."

Nate paused, key in hand, to stare at him. "You didn't like him as a dog. In fact, you complained constantly."

"Just open the damn door."

"I'm just saying"—Nate unlocked the door and pushed it open—"that there are a lot of inconsistencies in your story—"

"Surprise!"

Nate's mouth dropped open. Grant stood in the center of their apartment, a smug grin on his face. The werewolf looked relaxed and happy, a big change from their first meeting. While he still looked like a shave wouldn't go amiss, his gaunt face no longer looked starved and his eyes sparkled.

He wasn't alone. Charlotte and Vazul, Nate's friends from supernatural counseling, held up a sign. The difference between angular Charlotte's height and stocky Vazul's lack made it lopsided. Despite the angle, the message was clear: Thirty-one days since Nate started a supernatural event.

Nate looked from the banner to his friends, taking in the decorations strung across the apartment walls. "What's all this?"

George grinned at him from the kitchen doorway. The supernatural hunter was dressed for fun, with dangly earrings and a bright-orange shade of lipstick. She'd ditched her usual headscarf, her curls trimmed to uniform length. If Nate hadn't known where to look, he wouldn't have noticed the damage done by the demonic attack George had only narrowly survived. "You've gone an entire month without a near-death experience. I say you're slacking, but I was outvoted. These wimps consider that an accomplishment."

"Wow. I don't know what to say." Now that the surprise had worn off, Nate saw a lot of effort had gone into the party. Food was laid out on the coffee table—three pizza boxes, a selection of what looked like cakes, a salad, and cupcakes with delicate icing that looked suspiciously like Mandy's handiwork. Nate jerked his head up and saw her standing behind Charlotte and Vazul, nervously picking at her sleeve. "Mandy—Bea?"

Mandy smiled tentatively, but Beatrice just raised her glass in an ironic toast. "Aki told us about it. We agreed it was an occasion worth celebrating."

"I hope that's okay." Mandy bit her lip. "I mean, it's been a while."

"Of course it's okay." Nate closed the distance between them to give her a hug. He breathed in the familiar scent of her jasmine perfume. "It's great to see you." How long had it been? Not since... Not since he'd come out as supernatural. Nate paused. Mandy had made her views on the supernatural clear.

But Mandy squeezed him tightly with obvious relief. "I'm glad."

Nate grinned as he released her. "Wait. If Aki invited you—" He turned his head to stare at his friend.

Aki smirked at him. "Like taking candy from a baby. You've got no idea how many times this week you walked in on us planning this and had no idea."

"Given that we're talking about Nate, I am not surprised." Vazul always sounded superior, but now he was infuriatingly pleased with himself. "Going thirty-one days without incident is more of an accomplishment than I thought."

"Was that what you were doing?" Aki had seemed unusually keen on his coursework, but Nate had put that down to the fact that Grant was brushing up on his studies.

Grant cleared his throat. Immediately the group felt silent, all faces turning toward him. "I think it's time to come clean. Aki?"

Aki slouched on the arm of one of the apartment's two armchairs. "As fun as teasing Nate is, his ability to keep himself out of trouble for an unprecedented thirty-one days—"

"Hey!" Nate protested.

"Was only a front." Aki stuck out his tongue. "The real reason you're all here is because Grant's got some news."

Every head turned back to Grant. He grinned. "My application to live independently of my pack has been approved. I'm a free wolf."

Charlotte squealed, dropping the sign as she clapped. "Grant, I'm so happy!"

"Took their time," Vazul grumbled, leaning the sign against the wall. "I suppose your old pack contested it?"

Grant nodded grimly. "Naturally. They argued that if anything, the extreme circumstances around my first Full Moon proved I was a hazard. The judge wasn't having any of it. He pointed out the extreme events were the result of my stepfather's machinations, and I had shown considerable self-restraint in the face of overwhelming opposition." His grin displayed very sharp teeth. "They slunk out of the courtroom with their tails between their legs."

"You didn't tell us you had your hearing!" Charlotte stared at him with astonishment. "We would have come to support you."

"And risk your final exams?" Grant shook his head. "No. You'd already done so much for me. I couldn't ask any more."

"Congratulations, Grant." Nate held out his hand. "No one deserves this more than you do."

Grant looked at him, light flashing in his tawny eyes. Then it was gone, and he squeezed Nate's hand. "Thank you. This wouldn't have been possible without you."

Nate ducked his head. "At least my tendency for starting supernatural events is good for something."

"Oh god." Aki groaned. "Don't encourage him!"

"We need a toast." George cracked open the wine bottle and Charlotte hastily grabbed glasses. "Gather round."

Grant was perfectly at home as the center of attention. He thanked everyone, even Mandy and Bea who gave their congratulations awkwardly, before planting himself in Aki's chair.

Charlotte immediately sat opposite. "Now that you've got your independence, what are you going to do?"

"He's going to legalize chasing cars." Aki, still perched on the chair's arm, looked sleek and satisfied, like a well-fed cat.

Grant shot him a look, before turning back to Charlotte. "I'm going back to law school. Now, more than ever, it's important for the supernatural community to have a voice in the legal system." His arm settled around Aki's waist, and Aki gravitated slightly toward him. "My experiences of the last month have shown me just how open to exploitation the current laws surrounding werewolves are. I'm sure there are more cases like mine right here in New Camden."

"One step at a time." Aki nudged him with his elbow. "Before you change the world, you have to pass your bar exam. And while you may be able to take on werewolves, you've yet to prove yourself against *lawyers*."

And he expects anyone to believe he's not interested in Grant. Nate shook his head and sipped his drink. From the wine's quality, it was clearly Beatrice's contribution to the party. He made his way to where she leaned against the wall. "Thanks for coming," he said quietly. "How did Aki manage to drag you into this?"

Beatrice cast him an amused sideways glance. "We invited ourselves. We've been listening to Aki complain about the freeloading werewolf in the apartment above for the last month, and well, it's a rare man, werewolf or otherwise, who can hold his attention an entire month."

Nate suppressed his snort of laughter with difficulty. "Now that you've seen him, what do you think?"

Beatrice studied Grant as if she was appraising him for a photo shoot. "Interesting. Very handsome—but with Aki, that goes without saying."

Nate bit his lip. Aki's taste in men was not always so discerning.

Beatrice continued. "He's got something else. I don't know how to put my finger on it... But it's there. I'm not interested at all in men, but I can't deny it. Whatever it is."

Nate studied Grant afresh. Was that Grant's natural charisma, or the latent power of an alpha werewolf?

"He's very good-looking," Mandy agreed. "But he's not the only reason we're here." She looked at Nate. Her copious eyeshadow highlighted the bright blue of her eyes, while her dark lashes made her naturally blonde hair seem even lighter. "You're a very hard man to track down recently."

Nate squirmed. That hadn't been entirely accidental. His memory of exactly what Mandy had done to get him into trouble with Department Seven was fuzzy, but her tearful apology had not been enough. Now that time had passed, he was pleased to see an old friend. "Yeah, well... I've been putting in daytime shifts."

Beatrice took her eyes off Grant to consider Nate. "There's a rumor going round you're looking to leave Century."

Century was the nightclub where Nate and Aki worked—not that nightclub came anywhere close to describing the club. Yes, it had a bar and music and events. The dance floor was nearly always busy, and when it wasn't, it was only because it was too packed for people to dance. But people didn't come to Century to dance.

They came for Century's reputation and for its staff. The club was notorious as New Camden's most well-known brothel, but it was its respectability, not its vice that attracted. Century dressed its staff in designer clothes, gave them protection and a hefty price tag, and encouraged them to employ their charm and their power of veto in equal amounts. The result was a club with an atmosphere unique in New Camden. Mandy and Beatrice were among those attracted by the club's promise of spice and safety, and they'd quickly gravitated to Nate.

Nate was skilled at putting people at ease, and it hadn't taken long for him and Mandy to discover they were both small-town graduates trying to find their feet in the big city. They had enjoyed a low-key flirtation that had continued over months of drink orders and endured Beatrice's pointed remarks. Now?

I've missed Mandy. But the same way as I've missed Bea. Nate frowned. Mandy was lovely, generous, and sweet. More importantly, she got things that only someone who grew up in the country got. *It's great to see her again, but that's as far as it goes.* Nate realized with a guilty start that Beatrice waited for his answer. "Yeah. It's going to be weird not working at Century, but I think it's time."

Mandy tilted her head. "How come?"

Nate shrugged. In many ways, Century was the best thing to have happened to him. How to put into words the nebulous feeling that was behind him giving it up? "I'm not feeling the job anymore."

Beatrice and Mandy exchanged a glance. It was only a second, but it was layered with so much feminine significance that Nate, shameless to a fault, had to fight a blush.

"Did you meet someone special?" Beatrice asked.

It was strange. The answer was no. You didn't meet someone special enough to quit Century over and forget them—but Nate almost thought that there was. "Nah. I think I just reached the point where I want something more from my relationships, and I'm not going to find that while working at Century."

He expected one or both of them to pounce on that, but Beatrice simply nodded, sipping her drink. "Aki's not happy about it."

Nate winced. "No." Not happy was an understatement, and probably behind Aki's recent insistence on emphasizing the importance of their friendship at any given opportunity. "I was hoping Grant living so close to us would be a distraction, but it hasn't worked like that."

"Give Grant time." Mandy looked around. "Who are your other friends?"

"That's George with the pizza." Nate nodded toward her. "She's a supernatural hunter. We met when—" Shit. Nate couldn't tell Mandy that George had been investigating his brother as a suspect in her hunting partner's murder. "She was on a hiking vacation."

Beatrice raised an eyebrow. "Hiking?"

"I met Vazul and Charlotte at my counseling sessions." Nate didn't want to get into this any more than he wanted to get into George investigating him, but at least no one had died during their counseling sessions. "As a newly awoken supernatural, I have to do them."

"Makes sense." Mandy looked curiously at the others. "Are they...newly awoken, too?"

She was taking this way better than Nate expected. "Uh, no, actually. Charlotte's a witch and—" Nate paused. Vazul refused to say what he was.

"A witch?" Mandy brightened, sharing an eager glance with Beatrice.

"Not like a bad witch," Nate said hastily. "She's—" He paused. Mandy seemed interested, not alarmed.

"Would she mind if we asked her about it?" Beatrice asked.

"I don't think so." Nate looked across the room, where Charlotte stood, holding a vegan brownie and looking as though she wasn't quite sure what to do with herself. He caught her eye and beckoned her to join them. "Charlotte, these are my friends Bea and Mandy. They're interested in witchcraft."

"It's not what you think it is," Charlotte said immediately. "Most harmful spells are outlawed. Witchcraft today mostly concentrates on self-improvement. Like yoga, except without the yoga."

"Without the yoga?" Beatrice put her drink down and turned, giving Charlotte her full attention. "Tell me more."

Charlotte looked from Mandy to Beatrice. "Are you interested in practicing?"

Mandy nodded. "We might be. From what I've read, it sounds fascinating."

"Wait." Nate couldn't keep the incredulous note out of his voice. "You've read about witchcraft?"

"An example you could follow." Charlotte frowned at Nate. "You have the makings of a natural witch, if you would only apply yourself."

Nate ignored her, speaking to Mandy. "I didn't think this was something you would want to learn about."

Mandy looked at her feet. "Since learning about you, I had to rethink a lot of my assumptions about the supernatural. I want to learn more. Beatrice and I took a basic spellcraft course at night school."

"Yeah?" Nate grinned. "That's really cool."

Mandy smiled, tucking her hair out of her face. "Well..."

"I was actually thinking of forming a coven," Charlotte said hesitantly, "if you were interested."

The feeling bypassed Nate's nerves and went straight to his fight or flight reflex. *Danger,* it said. *Close and drawing closer. Inescapable.*

Nate's head jerked up. He scanned the room, looking for the source of the threat. In New Camden, danger was never far away. Even daylight was no promise of safety. Vampires were the most well-known of New Camden's population of monsters, but there were many more who hunted during the day.

Instead, he saw Grant laughing at one of Aki's jokes, Vazul busily explaining that whatever Aki had just said was an impossibility and George rolling her eyes as she grabbed another slice of meat lovers. Nate stared. *Am I dreaming?* The feeling was vivid, clinging to him with the same clammy grip as a nightmare. His heart still raced. But not a single one of his friends reacted.

Nate swallowed. Charlotte was an experienced witch. As a werewolf, Grant's reflexes extended beyond the natural world. If anything sinister lurked in the apartment, he would know. Vazul… Nate couldn't speak for his senses, but he was a good ally to have in a fight. And Aki… Nate watched him closely. Aki had the ability to see the future. Foresight was hard to tie down, but it gave him a sixth sense for threats. If there was any danger around, Aki would be the first to know.

Aki leaned forward, helping himself to a slice of pizza. "I'm just saying the sign could have been thirty days since Grant did laundry and have had just the same impact."

Aki couldn't talk. He had only once done the laundry since he and Nate moved in together. But it wasn't his chronic untidiness that troubled Nate.

If there was anything to sense, Aki should have sensed it. Nate looked around the room, from Charlotte, deep in conversation with Beatrice and Mandy, to Grant, trying to steal Aki's pizza, to George, picking up the argument with Vazul. His friends' lack of reaction said it all.

Nate felt sick. *I'm the only one who feels this?*

NATE LEANED AGAINST his bedroom door with a sigh. Excusing himself from the party without seeming suspicious had been a challenge, but finally he was alone. He took a deep breath. The sense of menace was muted but still there.

I know it's nothing. Ruthlessly, Nate faced the feeling with the knowledge that it was only his imagination. *You've got to be a proper Fortune Teller to have precognitions! Someone—people are always telling me that!* He took another breath, this time letting it out slowly. *You're over this.*

By the third slow exhale, some of the feeling of imminent menace had gone. Nate dropped backward onto his bed with a sigh. *Why now? I'm not allergic to parties. I like everyone here. There's no reason for me to be anxious.* He stretched out his hands, absently stroking the quilt Ma had sent in her last care package.

He encountered something cold and smooth. Nate knew what it was even before his fingers closed around the acorn. It hadn't been there when he'd made his bed that morning. *Another one.* He turned it over in his hand, admiring its warm grain. *Just when I needed it... Is that deliberate?*

It had to be deliberate. Acorns didn't appear out of thin air. Aki had insisted that Nate start locking his window at night, but the acorns kept coming. *Someone's behind this.* The thought gave Nate a warm feeling. *Someone's telling me something.*

The door opened. Nate sat up, instinctively hiding the acorn within his fist. "Aki?"

Aki shut the door behind him and leaned on it. He took a moment to eye Nate. Unlike Nate, he was dressed for a party. Nate considered Aki's bright plaid pants, chunky leather belt and boots. *That should have been a major clue.* Aki was dressed to impress, not for a casual coffee with his roommate.

"Are you okay?"

"Me?" Nate licked his lip. Had Aki noticed his reaction?

Aki rolled his eyes. "I'm not talking to your jungle." He gave Nate's collection of plants a glare and then took a step toward him, plunking himself down on the bed next to Nate. "You know the sign was just a joke, right? The only reason we did it because we thought you'd find it funny."

"Because it was." Nate nudged him. "If a bit exaggerated. Still, it was for a good cause."

Aki looked at his nails. "I suppose Grant barely qualifies as a good cause."

"Careful. Werewolves have really good hearing. What if he hears you?"

"I hope he does." Aki glanced at Nate. "So if you're not nursing a sense of injustice, what are you doing in here when you could be making eyes at Mandy?"

It was the perfect opportunity to tell Aki about his feeling. Nate rolled the acorn around his palm as he drew a deep breath. The difficulty was putting it into words—

Aki's eyes dropped to Nate's hand and he froze. "Another one?"

Nate stiffened. "I found it just now. It was on my bed."

"This is getting seriously creepy." Aki stood, tossing Nate's pillows aside as he searched for any further acorns.

"They're just acorns."

"For now. See if you feel this way when it's a disembodied ear." Aki tossed a pillow at Nate and continued his search in Nate's wardrobe.

"An ear?"

"It could be any body part. I don't think serial killers really care."

"It's not a serial killer, Aki."

Aki spun around. "How else do you explain it then? No normal person would spend a month leaving acorns in our apartment!"

"We don't know it's someone," Nate protested.

"They're not getting in here on their own." Aki waved a hand toward Nate's window. "We've both been careful to lock the apartment when we go out. Neither of us are leaving windows open. But this keeps happening!"

"It's no big deal."

"Bypassing a locked door to get into a room is a big deal!" Aki waved his hand toward the door. "Look. One of our friends has to know something that could help us figure this out. Let's ask."

Nate's fingers tightened around the acorn. The idea of sharing something so personal with the group repelled him. "No." The vehemence in his tone startled him.

It startled Aki. He stared at Nate, a faint red tinge spreading across his cheeks.

The doorbell rang.

Thank god for latecomers. Nate nodded toward the door. "Shouldn't you get that?"

Aki shook his head, refusing to be diverted. "They can handle it. Like they'd handle this weirdo if you'd just say something!"

"I don't want to say something."

Aki folded his arms across his chest. "If you don't, I will. This can't keep happening."

There was a knock at Nate's door. "Nate, Aki? Mind if I come in?" Grant's voice had an unusually strained note.

Aki and Nate shared a glance and turned as one to the door. "What's up?"

Grant opened the door. "You've got a visitor, Nate."

"We didn't invite anyone else," Aki started.

Grant stepped out of the doorway. "He insists."

Nate stood, sliding the acorn into his pocket. He stepped into the living room.

The party was not just dead. It had an obituary to prove it. Mandy and Beatrice had retreated into the kitchen, and Vazul looked as if he wished he didn't have too much pride to follow them. Charlotte was doing a very poor job of pretending not to gag on the vaguely sulfurous smell that clung to the air, stifling all the energy in the room. George, never daunted by anything, looked uncomfortable.

The only person, in fact, who looked at home was Gunn, his head tilted as he studied the discarded banner. "Cute," he pronounced. "If wildly inaccurate."

"Gunn?" Nate felt a sense of relief entirely at odds with Gunn's entire existence. Not only was the Department Seven officer's presence a sign that something was seriously wrong, but the man was a *lemur*, a supernatural being Nate didn't fully understand but knew equaled bad news. Despite his better knowledge, he grinned. "What are you doing here?"

Gunn jerked his head toward the sign. "You're going to need to change that."

"What do you mean? I haven't done anything."

"Shows what you know." Gunn bared teeth that were yellowed, jagged, and feral. "You're coming with me, Nate. I got a crime scene that has your name all over it."

Chapter Two

NATE GRIPPED THE side of his seat. His life flashed before his eyes, a fact that had nothing to do with Gunn's summons and everything to do with his driving.

The *lemur* drove like he did everything else, turning a blind eye to the rules when it suited him, or flagrantly pushing them as far as he could. He dived into New Camden's crowded roads with characteristic recklessness. In a good car, Gunn's risk-taking would have been less hair-raising, but Gunn's car took his philosophy of inflicting misery as widely as possible to new lows. Not only was it old, with gears that gasped alarmingly when forced to accelerate, but it seemed to have adopted its owner's carefree approach to little things like signals. It stank of putrefaction and cigarette ash. Nate would not have been surprised to learn someone had died in it.

Gunn charged through a red light, causing a compact sedan to screech to a halt. He hurtled round the corner to a barrage of screeching brakes and horns. "Women drivers."

Nate dared to take his eyes off the road. "Aren't you supposed to use a siren when you're in a hurry?"

"Where's the fun in that?"

Nate bit his lip. "The party was Aki's idea of a joke. I'm not bored or anything, so if this is on my behalf, you don't need to."

Gunn turned his head to grin at Nate. "Don't like my driving?"

"I'm surprised you're driving at all. I didn't think they had cars in your time."

Gunn snorted. "Your education is sadly lacking. I was driving when all you needed for a license was proof you owned the car."

"I'm no longer surprised." Nate shut his eyes.

A few minutes later, after hearing nothing but the screech of tires and the abuse of the other drivers, it occurred to Nate that this was unusual. Gunn was infamous for his terrible interpersonal skills, and Nate was a captive audience. He should be gleefully fanning Nate's fears, not sitting in silence. "You're weirdly quiet. What happened?"

"Don't want to spoil the witness by giving you ideas," Gunn said.

"You've never cared about that before." Nate hesitated. "Is something wrong?" He winced. "Wronger than usual, I mean."

Gunn growled. "Don't push it, Nate."

"What? I'm just saying. You're normally a lot more abrasive."

"I figured I'd go easy on you." Gunn's mouth soured. "After all, the last time you saw me, I wasn't exactly myself."

Nate stared at him. "What do you mean?"

"Jesus, Nate, do I have to spell it out?" Gunn threw his hands up. The car, with no one steering it, lurched dramatically. "You saw the *lemur*."

Nate shivered. A month later, the feeling of sheer terror enfolding him was still very near. He remembered the gaping mouth of the...thing...as it stretched out, all hunger and death. He'd dropped his gaze in the hopes that not looking at it would make it less, but not being able to see it gave its approach the horrible certainty of a nightmare—a living nightmare he couldn't escape. All around him, the werewolves had whined, rolling eyes and baring teeth until their nerves failed them, and they turned and fled. Some had been too petrified to move, and stood shivering, their eyes fixed on the thing as it drew nearer.

And then it had moved beyond them, leaving Nate gasping for breath, surrounded by the werewolves—transformed back into naked men and happy to see the police officers there to arrest them.

"Yeah. I did." He hesitated and then decided that with Gunn's driving, this was hardly going to make things worse. He slapped the officer on his arm. "And I'm pretty sure the *lemur* saved my life."

Gunn snorted. "You've got the worst self-preservation instincts of anyone I know, and that's really saying something." He leaned over, fiddling with the car radio. "How do you feel about jazz, Nate?"

"Hate it."

"Perfect." Gunn cranked the volume up. "Jazz it is."

OLD CEMETERY WAS the most famous of New Camden's many cemeteries. It dated back to when New Camden's settlers innocently looked forward to a prosperous future, untroubled by the knowledge of the supernatural already present among them. Its dead were housed in elegant marble crypts with the expectation they would stay there. Stone angels placed their hands together in attitudes of solemnity, something of their silence extending to the police officer stationed at the wrought-iron gates. He caught sight of Gunn and flinched, snapping to attention as if stung.

"Sir! The—"

"I know the place." Gunn waved the officer aside. "Like old times, isn't it Nate? Can't think of the last time I was here. Oh wait. Yes, I can. You locked me in a crypt."

He should have known Gunn wasn't over that. Nate hunched his shoulders, concentrating on the path. Twilight had been and gone, and the night gave the cemetery even more gravitas. "It seemed like a good idea at the time."

"A good idea. I don't know what happens inside that pretty head of yours, Nathaniel, but it bears no resemblance to thought—" Gunn stopped suddenly.

Nate barely avoided stumbling into his back. He looked over Gunn's shoulders to the path ahead. They were in one of the more modern areas of the cemetery, where marble had been replaced by quartz and crypts and statues by plain slabs. The wrought-iron lamp posts illuminated an orange tent set up over a grave and uniformed officers milling around outside. Nate caught sight of the stocky figure of Kenzies, Gunn's long-suffering deputy, among them. She stood next to another woman in the Department Seven uniform. "There's Kenzies." Nate felt some of his tension ease. Kenzies did not share Gunn's attitude to their work.

Gunn's nostrils flared. He stalked over to the tent, fury evident in every line of his wiry body. "What are *you* doing here?"

Nate gave the Department Seven officer a second glance. She looked just as startled by Gunn's appearance as the others, turning a pale face toward them. Her blonde hair was streaked with gray. Nate would have put her around forty. She looked ordinary, far too ordinary for Department Seven, and Nate frowned, wondering what on earth this mild-looking woman had done to rouse Gunn's ire.

It was then he became aware of the smell of leaves in autumn, and like the brush of a cobweb, the consciousness of a presence that made his skin leap. *Vampire.*

A figure with his back to them turned. Nate saw that what he'd taken for a uniform jacket was actually a navy peacoat. "Evening, Isaiah." Hunter's dark eyes glittered with amusement, and his sultry drawl made his use of Gunn's name sound affectionate, rather than the calculated provocation it was. "You took your time."

Gunn growled. "Kenzies, I gave you orders to boot any spectators."

"ARX was just as involved as Nate in this case." Kenzies bore Gunn's anger with stoic indifference. "Hunter has a right to be here, and we could benefit from his insight."

Gunn grit his teeth. "If you called him in—"

"Give us some credit." Hunter casually rearranged his scarf. Two of the female officers and one of the men slowed what they were doing to watch him smooth his scarf and lift his shoulder-length hair free of it. "ARX has monitored this graveyard ever since the incident. I knew as soon as I woke tonight. I have a right to be here."

"Go about your work," Gunn snapped at the staring officers. He glared at Kenzies. "And I suppose you've been passing the time instead of scouting the scene."

Kenzies smiled at him. "I knew you'd prefer that someone kept a close eye on Hunter."

Gunn dug in his habitual bomber jacket for a cigarette. "A close eye, she says." He turned his glare back onto Hunter. "No flirting with my staff."

Hunter shrugged. "We were merely making polite conversation. I'm aware that 'polite' isn't in your vocabulary, but you might want to try it some time."

"Catch more flies with honey, you mean?" Gunn scowled. "I'll pass."

"There're no flies on your staff," Hunter said. "I haven't even been allowed to view the corpse yet. And I did ask, very nicely." He turned his gaze on Nate, his eyes lingering. "Hello, Nathan. You look well."

Nate gulped. Even with the warning he'd been given, Hunter's gaze was still a shock. It didn't matter how much time he spent in the vampire's presence, it was still hard to think of anything beyond the man's physical presence when he was there. Nate deliberately ran through a list of Hunter's flaws—callous indifference to taking advantage of others to get his own ends, manipulative, questionably honest, way too charming for anyone's good, tried to kill him—and still found himself breathless. "Hunter. I didn't expect to see you." The effort of speaking made his voice sound gruff, and Nate winced. He summoned the calmness of an oak to meet the vampire. "What's going on?"

Hunter raised an eyebrow in surprise and opened his mouth, but Gunn cut him off. "I want Nate to see the scene without any preconceptions. Kenzies?"

"Nothing's been touched," she reported. "The crime scene photographers have been in, but no one else."

Nate looked toward the tent with trepidation. "I'm no expert on investigations. I don't know what you expect me to do here."

The third member of the Department Seven staff cleared her throat. "If he isn't an expert...?"

"Right. Forgot you'd missed the fun." Gunn waved his cigarette toward Nate. "Nathan Granger. Pretty much single-handedly kept the city's police forces occupied while you were off relaxing."

"Hospital isn't exactly what I'd call R and R." The woman's eyes settled on Nate with undisguised interest. "Well, well. I've heard some interesting things about you. Helen Tremaine."

Nate returned her handshake. "I was trying to help." He turned to Kenzies. "I still have no idea what you want me to do."

Kenzies beckoned him to follow her and started toward the tent. "We'd like your opinion on the scene."

Nate followed slowly. "I know nothing about forensics. I don't even watch *CSI*."

Tremaine snorted. "That's a mark in your favor."

"Just give us your honest impressions," Kenzies assured him. "We've got experts for the rest of it."

If they have experts, why are they wasting their time with me at all? Nate was uneasily conscious of the curious glances of the white-coated forensics officers standing around waiting. What did they think of this all? Did they know who—what—Nate was?

Kenzies held the tent flap aside and ushered Nate in. Immediately, he was assailed with a familiar scent. The metallic tang of blood was underlain with a potpourri-like smell of herbs that even the smoke couldn't muffle. Nate felt a cold hand settle on his skin, the rain that fell the night he died running again down his neck. He knew what he would see before he raised his eyes to the gravestone. "No!"

The man sprawled like a puppet with its strings cut. He was shirtless, with jagged red lines carved into his bare chest. With the smooth gray slab of the grave beneath him, he looked like some bizarre entree served at a horrifying feast.

Nate looked helplessly at Kenzies. "He was supposed to stay dead. To be gone for good!"

Kenzies's eyes softened, but her voice remained crisply matter of fact. "Who are you referring to, Nate?"

"The necromancer. Peter de Silver." Nate looked down at the man and immediately wished he hadn't. "You have to see it. Who else worked like this?"

"You're the only person living who saw de Silver's work." Gunn's voice was right behind him and made Nate jump. He turned to see that Gunn and Hunter had both joined him in the tent, watching him closely. "Well, his unofficial work at least." He sneered at Hunter.

The vampire ignored him. "I, too, had the chance to observe his handiwork," he said. "I agree with Nate. This is too much to be coincidence, especially given the location."

The location? Nate knew that asking would do him no favors. Gunn operated on a need-to-know basis, especially in front of Hunter with whom he shared an acrimonious history. Instead, he took a hesitant step toward the body. He looked at the name on the headstone. "In memoriam, Austin Hawick," he read aloud. "This wasn't on the job description." He frowned. "Hawick." The name sounded familiar. Intimately familiar. So why was it coming up blank?

"Former ARX employee," Gunn said. "On whose grave the first of the necromancer's victims was discovered."

"Brook." The memory came back to Nate with a guilty start. Brook had been murdered because of his association with Hunter, an association Nate had briefly shared.

"I'm starting to wonder if old Hawick was the virtuous staff member you took him for. I mean, once is bad enough, but to have two guys murdered on your grave..."

"Austin was a stalwart opponent of black magic, the last person to encourage a necromancer," Hunter said promptly. "I'm entirely at a loss as to why the necromancer would fixate on him at all, unless he was jealous of Austin's position within my household. But even that doesn't make sense. Austin died a year before he made his bid for power."

The necromancer. Nate watched Hunter closely. Odd that he would call him what he was known to the public rather than by his name. When he'd worked for ARX, he'd been "Peter." Or was the name too bitter a reminder? After all, Peter had been an integral part of Hunter's staff.

"There's a lot I don't understand," Tremaine said quietly. "I was reading the case files on the way over here. One of you censored it?"

"I wish," Kenzies said promptly. "It's hard enough getting Gunn to fill out reports at all. I've given up attempting to moderate his language. If I had time to go through them—"

Tremaine shook his head. "Not like that. If you read through the notes, there are large chunks of text missing." She held out a manila file.

"Missing text?" Hunter sounded interested.

Gunn glared at him. "You've seen what you're here to see. Scram."

"Perhaps I can offer my assistance. I was heavily involved in the case, as you might remember."

Kenzies skimmed through the file. "Strange. It seems as though any reference to one particular person has been erased."

"Not just that, but anything that might give us a clue as to what their relationship was to the case is gone with it." Tremaine looked hopefully at Kenzies. "You don't remember?"

"I should," Kenzies said. "I don't." She held the file out to Gunn, who was snapping his fingers for the document.

Gunn's lips moved as he read over the report. His scowl deepened. "Who was the last person to read this?"

"I'll have to check the records back at the Department," Tremaine started.

Nate edged closer to the corpse. Now that the initial horror had worn off, a new one had taken its place. Was this death following the pattern that Peter had established? Hunter had a particular type when it came to men, and Nate had been very lucky not to end up dead like Brook. He had to know. Could this have been him?

The man's hair was a light brown, very different from Nate's short black hair. He was older, with a heavily lined face, and deep purple bags around his eyes. At first glance, Nate had taken him as toned, but looking closer, he could see that the man was merely extremely thin—

The man's eyes jerked open.

Nate's mouth moved, but he couldn't speak. He could only stare, caught by the dangerous glitter in the eyes that should not be working at all.

The man's mouth stretched wide, baring wickedly sharp teeth in a smile that promised violence. He raised himself from the stone, his movements at odds with his body. Little things like pain from twisted muscles or balance didn't mean much to a revenant. They registered only one thing: insatiable hunger. The man growled and leaped.

Run! The thought came much too late for Nate, trapped by the awful certainty of death. He stumbled backward.

Thunder boomed suddenly, unexpectedly. The corpse swayed. A hole appeared in his chest, driving him backward. There was another crack of thunder, and he dropped to his knees. A rough hand jerked Nate away from him, and a storm of gunfire broke out. Nate saw the man twitch and spasm in a gross parody of life and finally fall.

"God."

Kenzies kept her gun leveled at the body. "Hurt, Nate?"

It took Nate a startled second to grasp her meaning. He looked down at himself, registering for the first time that the hand on his arm was Hunter's, and that the vampire was positioned in front of him. "No. Just...shaken."

Gunn lowered his pistol and approached the corpse. "Where were you standing, Nate? Here?" He crouched. "Looks like you were right, Tremaine. A deliberate trap."

"And you let me spring it?" Nate couldn't keep the dismay out of his voice.

"No one else could. We figured knowing who the trap was aimed at would tell us a lot about who set it." Gunn looked down at the body with a frown. "If it helps, Hunter was going to be our next attempt."

"Your manner is charming as ever." Hunter dusted himself off. "Though, I hate to admit your method is not without result."

Nate wrapped his arms around himself. "What do you mean?"

"It's obvious, isn't it?" The tent was thick with the smell of gunpowder, but Gunn still lit a cigarette. "I imagine there's a few people in New Camden who would like to take a shot at you, but only one with the knowledge to rig up a revenant to attack you—and only you."

Nate had felt sick before. Now he felt nauseated. "Peter's back."

Gunn took a long drag on the cigarette. "Back, and it looks like he's out for revenge." He grinned. "It's been far too quiet around here."

CENTURY WAS PACKED. Nate squeezed through the foyer after Gunn. The crowd was so thick that the Department Seven officer, who'd made the unusual decision to change into uniform for the visit, did not raise any eyebrows, any more than Nate did, dressed down in his battered T-shirt and jeans.

When they reached the staff-only staircase, Gunn stopped Nate. "I'd like to talk to your boss alone. Wait here."

"Sure." Nate did not object to the chance to gather his thoughts. He loitered in the stairwell, listening to the music pumped through Century's speakers with a feeling of dislocation. The beat was fast, with an accelerating baseline that spoke directly to the pulse. In any other circumstance, that would have Nate on the dance floor in an instant. Now, dancing was the last thing on his mind.

Nate clenched his fists. *Another guy dead because of me.*

He couldn't stop thinking about the dead man. He had a worn face, the kind acquired through a mortgage, a partner, and kids. He must have family somewhere, people who missed him. Perhaps right now his family was learning that he wouldn't be coming home ever again.

And he was dead, just to set a trap for Nate. *It's my fault—just like Peter's death was my fault.* Nate winced, but he couldn't escape the thought. He leaned back against the wall of the staircase, wrapping his arms around himself. He had a sick feeling in the pit of his stomach. *I didn't know my magic would kill him!* It was the first time he had used his powers on purpose. They were still new. Even now, Nate was unsure what exactly had happened.

I took control of Peter's necromancy, turned it into plants... Nate frowned. That much was clear. In trying to control Nate, Peter had inadvertently linked them, allowing Nate access to the workings of his spells. *But I went too far. Somehow, I turned Peter into a plant—*

"Nate!" Aki barreled into him. "You should have told me you were here! I've been so worried!"

Nate squirmed. He'd hoped to avoid notice by sticking to the staff-only areas. Clothes aside, he felt ill at ease at the club. With everything he'd seen, the idea that other people were having fun, enjoying life, was too much to take. "I sent you a text. Told you I was okay."

"You don't get attacked by a revenant and be okay!" Aki released Nate from his chokehold and stepped back, eyeing him critically. "I know you. You might not be hurt, but there's no way you're not shaken."

Aki knew him well. Sometimes too well. "I'll be fine. I'm just not in a social mood."

Aki snorted. "Reassuring your best friend that you're not going to do something stupid isn't socializing. It's a necessity." He eyed Nate. "Please tell me you don't feel sorry for that thing."

"He was a person until tonight." Nate bit his lip.

"Nate!" Aki stomped his foot. "This is what gets you into trouble! You have to stop feeling sorry for monsters and concentrate on taking care of yourself!"

"This is different. The guy that got killed, it was a trap aimed at me. I can't just shrug it off and say it's none of my business."

Aki narrowed his eyes. "Can't you? Because I can—"

An electronic buzzing sound interrupted him.

They both looked down at Nate's wristband. The sleek black band was standard issue for Century staff, but the technology contained within the seemingly benign device was anything but ordinary. The wristband contained a credit-card reader, GPS system, heart-rate monitor, emergency alarm, and other features designed to keep Century's workers safe. It also contained the in-house messaging system currently being employed.

"Denise wants to see me." It was rare that Denise demanding his presence in her office was a relief. She was notoriously strict when it came to the safety of her workers. There was no way she would take the news of Nate's evening well. But compared to Aki, obviously worried...

Aki narrowed his eyes. "I think it's a really dumb idea," he said. "Seriously stupid and you shouldn't even consider it. But why listen to me? I am only your best friend. Stupid me, for wanting you to take care of yourself!" He flounced off, heading for the club, and within seconds was lost from sight among the club-goers crowding the dance floor.

Nate stared after him. He had no idea what Aki was referring to, only that his friend was genuinely worried. He remembered his feeling of that afternoon, and a shiver crept down his shoulders. *Maybe Aki's right. Maybe I should stay out of it.*

Too late for that, the feeling whispered. Nate remembered the dead man's eyes fixing on him. He began to climb the stairs.

Nate had spent so much time in Denise's office that he found his way automatically. He knocked and pushed the door open. "I'm here."

"Take a seat, Nate." Denise stood at her desk, dressed in the pastel-green suit that was her trademark. She folded her arms across her ample chest as she subjected Nate to an intense examination, very similar to the one he'd just received from Aki. "Gunn has just informed me why you missed the start of your shift. You are not hurt in any way?"

Nate shook his head. "Shaken, but fine."

The first time Nate had met Gunn, he'd been sprawled insolently across Denise's sofa. Now, he sat up straight, his hands resting on his knees. "Nate's safety was never in question. Three Department Seven officers including myself were ready in the event he was threatened."

But sharing that info would have spoiled the witness? Nate looked to Denise for permission to sit and at her nod helped himself to an armchair. "It's not that the revenant tried to attack to me that I mind. It's that it happened at all." Nate hesitated. The necromancer's reign of terror over New Camden had claimed many victims—among them Denise. Broaching the subject was the last thing he wanted to do, but how could they avoid it? "If Peter is back, more people are going to die."

Denise's expression sharpened, like a string pulled tight. "We were told the necromancer was dead."

"Unfortunately, death is not as permanent as it once was." Gunn's eyes flickered over Denise speculatively, but he clearly decided against saying anything. "Especially to someone who specializes in death like a necromancer. It was always a possibility that Peter left behind some means of resurrection. If that's the case, he just had to wait for some fool to trigger it."

Nate stared at Gunn. Denise did not like talking about her death. As a *lemur*, Gunn must sense that. *A prime chance to get under her skin...and he's ignoring it?* Nate looked from Gunn to Denise, conscious that something was off.

If Denise noticed Gunn's restraint, she clearly wasn't impressed by it. "Do you know for a fact that is what happened?"

"No. And that's why we need Nate." Gunn nodded to Nate. "I asked Denise if I can hire you."

Nate froze. He liked Gunn just fine—usually—but this was more than he was prepared for. *I didn't think Gunn liked me like that—liked anyone like that!* The *lemur* gave the impression of being more interested in women. "I, uh...have to think about it."

"Of course Nate needs time to consider." Denise sat on the edge of her desk. "Assisting Department Seven is a serious undertaking. You can't guarantee his safety."

"Maybe not," Gunn conceded. "But he'll be safer with us than he'll be on his own—and your clientele will be safer if Nate's not here." He leaned forward across the coffee table. "If Peter is back and he's targeting Nate, where is he going to go to find him? He knows where Nate works. On the other hand, with Nate assisting us, we can track him down, contain him, and neutralize him much faster than we could otherwise."

Oh, thank God. For a terrified minute, Nate had thought Gunn wanted him for his sexual skills. "What do you mean, assisting Department Seven?"

Gunn smirked at him. "We'll make you a special officer. You'll come with me and Kenzies as we look into this. We need your knowledge and your powers."

Nate looked at his feet. "It's my powers that started this." He bit his lip. "That's why Peter's targeting me, isn't it? Because I killed him."

"Best thing you ever did." Gunn patted his jacket, searching for a cigarette case before remembering where he was. He sat up, trying to pass the gesture off as nothing. "You also tracked him down when the entire city couldn't find him anywhere. It's my hunch that you're the key to this—and maybe you'd cause less trouble if you were in on our plans." He grinned at Nate's discomfort. "Just a thought."

Nate flushed. His attempts to help never worked out how he intended them. "I wouldn't have to have a gun or anything?" As a country kid, Nate knew how to shoot. But the idea of carrying a gun in a city made him seriously uncomfortable.

Gunn shook his head. "No gun, and you would always be accompanied by one of my team. Keeping you safe, the city safe, and trying my patience less."

Gunn has patience? "I don't know. I mean, there's my work here to think about." Nate was indentured to Century. He couldn't see safety-conscious Denise agreeing to the plan.

"Officer Gunn has considered the financial side of things." Denise's tone was cool, giving no hint of what she thought.

Nate looked suspiciously at Gunn. "And?" It was highly likely that Gunn, considering the financial strain that being co-opted by Department Seven would put on Nate, would be even keener to use him.

"The city is willing to foot the bill." Gunn slouched back against the back of the sofa, resting his battered boots on the coffee table. "Can't afford your full rate, of course. But under the circumstances Denise was willing to make us a deal." Gunn suddenly collected himself, sitting up with a speed that would have been comical if he wasn't one of the more terrifying people that Nate knew.

"You approve of this, Denise?"

His boss's gaze rested on him. "If it's what you want to do, then yes. But only if it's what you want to do."

Nate stared at the floor. He wasn't an investigator. He had been completely lost at the crime scene. Yes, he wanted to help people, but his track record in that area was not great. *This is only the start. There are going to be more deaths. I can't get involved.*

But I can't ignore this either. Gunn had come to him for help—and Gunn didn't ask for help from anyone. That meant that he truly believed they needed him. Nate raised his head. "Okay. I'll do it."

Gunn got to his feet. "Good man. I knew—" His phone buzzed. Gunn glanced down at it and his expression darkened. "I have to take this."

It wasn't until Gunn left the room that Nate realized a large part of the tension he felt was the officer's presence. He breathed out. *What have I gotten myself into?*

"Agreements made in the presence of a supernatural with power are not legally binding." Looking up, Nate saw Denise watching him closely. "If you have second thoughts, I'll tell Gunn you are unavailable."

It was tempting, but Nate shook his head. "No. If there is a chance I can stop Peter before anyone else gets hurt, I have to take it."

Denise pursed her lips. Her vivid red lipstick was too close a reminder of her bloody death for Nate's comfort, but Denise refused to let death change her. "Just remember that you're important too, Nate. You're not responsible for the necromancer."

Nate ducked his head. He couldn't look Denise in the eye. "I'll remember." He glanced at the door. "I'd better find Gunn."

Gunn paced the corridor, listening intently to the person on the other side of the phone call. "Yeah. Yeah. I got it. Put all units on full alert and inform the mayor. I'll be there as soon as I can." He hung up as Nate approached. "Ready to roll?"

Nate nodded. "Didn't you say we needed to stop by the department first?"

"No time." Gunn strode down the hall toward the stairway, forcing Nate to jog after him. "Welcome to the life of a Department Seven officer. No rest for the wicked—or anyone else."

"Something's happened." A feeling of dread settled over Nate's chest. "Another death?"

"Not yet—but something tells me it's only a matter of time." Gunn took the stairs two at a time. "Someone's only gone and robbed the Registry."

Nate scrambled to keep up. "You mean the place where all the records of New Camden's supernatural are kept? Why would anyone want to do that?"

Outside in the street, Gunn paused to affix a siren to the roof of his beat-up car. "I can think of a dozen reasons. None of them good."

Chapter Three

THE REGISTER WAS located in a gray stone building with architecture better suited to a cathedral than city hall. Usually, the building was beyond quiet. Tonight, it was host to a scene so chaotic the screech of brakes as Gunn stopped his rust bucket car on the pavement didn't attract any attention.

Gunn climbed out of his vehicle, leaving the key in the ignition. "Stick close, Nate. This crowd is already ugly."

Nate could only agree. Neither the werewolves nor the vampires currently confronting each other on the registry steps were making any effort to hide their supernatural natures. Bared teeth and snarling were the order of the day.

"You leeches are behind this!" The man was powerfully built, wearing a suit slightly too big for him. Nate recognized him as Ronald, one of former Councilor Wisner's two sons. Wisner had been New Camden's security chief, until his ambition got the better of him. He'd orchestrated a takeover of the city, planning to put his werewolves in control. Ronald was clearly continuing his father's work. The men behind him would be Wisner's original pack, still loyal to their pack leader even if he was currently behind bars. "You've never liked the terms of the Register, and now you've decided to get rid of it!"

The vampire's leader stood on the Registry steps, so that he could be seen over the heads of his companions. Nate's heart sank as he saw him. Hot-headed Julian was the newest addition to the Vampire Senate. "Your juvenile attempt to cloud the issue fools no one. You wolves have flaunted your independence of the Register for so long you think you can do as you please. That is no longer the case. Leave now." The last words were layered with the vampire's power of compulsion.

A deep growl broke out among the wolves. Even in their human forms, Julian's imperious treatment raised hackles. "You don't tell us what to do in our territory," an older werewolf snarled.

"Whose territory?" Julian didn't take his eyes off Ronald. "We're not wolves. Your rulings have no effect on us, no matter how many hydrants you pee on."

The growl increased in savagery, and two wolves darted forward, leaping for Julian. The vampires with him immediately tackled the wolves, the fight quickly spreading.

"For fuck's sake!" Gunn pulled a loudspeaker out of the car. "Can't take your eyes off them for five minutes—"

Before he could use it, a female voice barked out from the Registry steps. "Simeon, now!"

There was a strange popping sound. Nate turned toward the source and saw a fire hydrant launch a stream of water into the air. As he watched, the stream twisted, aiming itself directly at the combatants. The snarls and threats turned into cries of alarm. A few minutes later, the vampires and the werewolves crouched on opposite sides of the jet of water, clutching their sodden clothes, and glowering at the Department Seven officer standing beside the hydrant.

Simeon had never struck Nate as attractive, but now, with his eyes bulging and his pale skin gleaming with perspiration, he looked even less appealing. *What* is *he?* Nate looked from the Department Seven officer to the water, now forming a perfect barrier between the groups. *How is he able to do that?*

"Gentlemen!" All heads jerked up to stare at the woman standing before the Registry door. As Gunn's second in command, Kenzies would be known to all present. "We asked you to remain calm and allow Department Seven to look into the situation. Since this is seemingly too much of a strain for you, I must ask you to leave so we can investigate without further incident."

Ronald curled his lip, displaying teeth sharper than any human's should ever be. "You don't tell me what to do! You're no one."

At the same time, Julian scoffed. "We're not going to be told what to do by a wolf! You're all in league—"

"Be ready." Gunn handed the loudspeaker to Nate before sauntering through the wolves to join Kenzies on the Registry steps. "Evening, gentlemen. How very interesting that you're here at the crime scene so quickly. Coincidence? Or prior knowledge?"

The werewolves visibly blanched. It could have been Gunn's particular odor, but Nate thought it was more to do with the last time they'd seen him. Gunn had dropped his human appearance entirely, and the result was enough to have the werewolf pack running with their tails between their legs.

Ronald took a step back and collided with another wolf. The reminder of the presence of his pack gave him courage to snarl, though it lacked its earlier bite. "It's our territory."

"Excuse you. *My* territory." Julian drew himself up.

"*Our* case." Gunn rolled his eyes. "You're obstructing us solving it. Leave."

Julian sneered. "I'll leave when he does."

Ronald's nostrils flared. "Then you're in for a long night, leech."

Gunn heaved an exaggerated sigh. "We don't get paid enough to babysit you. Nate, crowd control."

Nate started, hastily picking up the loudspeaker. "Would you all be kind enough to, uh, settle down?"

Vampires and wolves gave him a cursory glance and then paused. Clearly they remembered him.

Nate resisted the urge to tug his collar. The previous times he'd faced both wolves and vampires he'd had the element of surprise. Now, even if they didn't know what he was, they knew something of what Nate could do. He took a deep breath, resisting the urge to wipe his sweaty palms on his jeans. He couldn't let them see how nervous he was.

One of Julian's companions leaned in to whisper something to him, and Julian smiled, thin and vicious.

Yeah, he definitely remembers me. Nate had humiliated Julian by defeating him before the gathered Vampire Senate, and the way Julian waded through his fellow vampires toward Nate indicated he had revenge in mind.

There's so many of them. Can I withstand so much vampire? Nate sized up the scene. The water from the hydrant had lost pressure and subsided into a trickle that wouldn't deter anyone. He had to do something decisive, something big. But what?

"You fooled me once, *Nate*." There was an unpleasant note in Julian's voice as he planted himself in front of Nate. "But vampires don't take kindly to being fooled."

"That's great. Maybe we can talk this out. You know, over coffee or something." The vampires were moving faster than Nate could keep his eyes on them. He looked up, but Gunn's attention was on Kenzies, gesticulating urgently as she spoke to him.

"You're much less confident without Hunter's power behind you, aren't you? I wonder, how much of that defeat was really you?" Julian continued to fix Nate with his cool stare. "I say we find out."

Someone grabbed Nate's arms from behind.

He reacted instinctively, slamming back against them. But they didn't budge an inch. Instead their grip tightened until he was struggling to breathe.

Vampire strength. Right. Nate struggled to suck in a breath past the crushing pain of his ribs and focused on willing his limbs into heavy, durable wood. *Strength of an oak...*

Julian bared his teeth, getting right into Nate's face. "I'm disappointed. I thought there was more to you than this."

The burning in his chest was urgent enough to drown out his attempt at intimidation. Nate threw himself backward. With the strength of a forest, he rammed the vampire holding him against Gunn's car. He relinquished his hold and fell, Nate landing on top of him. As Nate struggled to stand, someone tackled him. He felt a sharp pain as fangs scraped his skin and looked up to see Julian lick his lips with a smirk.

The sight gave him a moment's horror. Seeing the red, recognizing it as his own blood was bad enough, even without the knowledge that every single vampire and werewolf in the crowd were now aware that he was bleeding.

Think plant! Nate took a step back, aware that Julian's eyes tracked him. There had to be something—

The blood flowed stickily down his arm, curling around his wrist. A memory flashed through his mind. Vine curling around him, seeking the light—

Julian's expression of triumph changed to confusion. "What the hell?"

Nate didn't look down. He didn't need to. The smell of freshly unfurling leaves was strong enough to tell him exactly what was going on. He stretched out an arm, and the vine he had summoned shot out.

The vine tangled around Julian. He tried to dodge, but was hampered by the vampires surrounding them. The vines looped around him, trapping his arms against his body. "Free me at once!" His words were layered with compulsion, and his companions shook off their surprise and hastened to obey.

Grow. Expand. It was hard work without the energy of the sun to give his vines the boost they needed. Nate concentrated on winding his vines around the group of struggling vampires. One stumbled into the puddle of water left by the hydrant. *Perfect.* The water gave the vines a boost and they spread in a powerful burst. Just in time.

The werewolves had waited only long enough to size up the situation before getting involved. As soon as they saw the vampires distracted, they leaped into the fray. Unlike vampires, they couldn't access the wolf's teeth without a physically draining transformation, but they still had their enhanced strength and predator instincts.

Ronald, flanked by two big men, waded through the fray directly toward Nate, tearing through his vines. Nate felt a sudden sharp pain. *I can use that.* The pain directed his attention to the split part of the vine, and he channeled fresh energy through it. Ronald yelped as the torn vine began to grow in his hands. He dropped it, only for the vines to loop themselves around his legs. His next step had him toppling, lost in the sea of struggling bodies.

Grow! Nate sent his awareness through all the vines, urging them onward, putting out fresh vines, even roots. *Why wasn't there any soil here?* A body collided with him from behind, and he was tackled onto the asphalt. His chin stung, bits of gravel sticking to it as he shook his head, trying to clear it. His arm was twisted behind his back and pinned. "Stop this!" Julian hissed. "I order you, let my people go!"

There was a sharp crack, then another. Nate smelled smoke.

"Shit! They're firing at us!" The female vampire sounded worried. "We've got to get out of here!"

"Not even Gunn would fire indiscriminately into a crowd. They're trying to scare us." Julian was contemptuous. "Roll him over. I need to look in his eyes."

She grunted and seconds later, Nate felt himself heaved onto his back. He struggled, but Julian's weight was on his chest before he could rise.

"Let my people go!" Julian stared into Nate's eyes. His voice was low but had weight, and his eyes demanded attention as sharp as his bared teeth.

But Julian could never compel Nate, especially not now with the ripped edges of his vines calling out for his attention. He pushed with his mind, felt the answering surge of growth, the excitement of leaves unfurling and tendrils expanding, searching for more carbon dioxide, more water, and the heat which instinctively they knew was missing. The werewolves were warm, their heat drawing the plants as if toward the sun. Nate didn't need to worry about those. The vampires on the other hand—

He looked up to see Julian almost completely covered by vines. With a grunt, Nate levered himself onto his side, dislodging Julian.

The vampire's arm shot out, gripping Nate. He couldn't speak or even bare his teeth, his jaw completely swathed in green vines. But his eyes locked on to Nate. There was no power in them now, only fear.

Nate stared at him.

Peter had looked like this before he died. Peter, his body half consumed by rot and wood, fighting with all that Nate's magic had not yet consumed of him. Peter had been alive and angry, and then he was dead.

Because of me. My magic—

Nate swallowed bile. His vision blurred. He was no longer sure who he was looking at. Julian beneath the vines, or Peter.

"Nate! Get it together!" Gunn yelled.

Nate jerked out of his daze. He saw Gunn and Kenzies wading through the fighting crowd toward him. Kenzies had a vampire in a headlock, while Gunn casually pistol-whipped a werewolf, using the man's unconscious body as a stepping stone to wade through the vines to Nate. He grabbed Nate's arm, hauling him to his feet. "The situation's a powder keg. We can't have a death. It'd be outright war. I need you to contain this. Now."

Nate sucked in a deep breath. Those few moments when he'd been frozen by the memory of Peter's death, his vines had been all but trampled by the fighters. *I have to stop this. Don't think of Peter. Don't think of what could go wrong.*

But when he reached for the vine there was nothing there.

Gunn wasted no time wading back into the fray. "Come on, Nate. We don't have all day."

I can't! His powers had never failed like this before. Nate struggled to push past the panic, reach deep within himself. *Oak, please. I need you!*

"Halt this disgusting display at once." The voice was awful. Like the sound that precedes an earthquake, it was layered with immediate and certain disaster. Everyone went still before it, rooted to the ground like statues.

Nate forced himself to swallow. It was like being jolted awake from a nightmare, only to find the nightmare had followed you into the waking world. His skin crawled and he could feel each individual hair on his neck tremble. He knew this bad dream only too well. Saltaire was back.

"Brawling in the streets like drunken wretches." Nate didn't want to look at him, but no force on earth could have stopped him from turning his head to look at the master vampire. Saltaire wore a black trench coat over an impeccably tailored suit. The vampire's habitual pallor was emphasized by his dark hair, while his disgusted expression made the sharp lines of his face even more cutting. "You make me sick to look at you. Crawl away like the worms you are."

The combatants dragged themselves over the asphalt on their elbows. Some of the stronger werewolves shook off the command enough to crawl on their hands and knees.

Nate caught a glimpse of Julian, still encased in vine as he began to wriggle his way across the concrete. "You wait, Saltaire. I will not forget this." The sheer hate in his voice made Nate take a step back.

Gunn caught him by his elbow. "You're not going anywhere," he snapped. "Kenzies, heel. Simeon—for fuck's sake, Simeon, get back here."

Kenzies reluctantly stopped choking the vampire she had been fighting. As she straightened, Nate saw Simeon rise to his feet, trying to discreetly brush the asphalt from his palms. *Good to know I'm not the only one Saltaire gets to.* But the knowledge was unsettling.

Nate looked up and found Saltaire looking right at him. The master vampire's lip curled. "Is Department Seven so desperate for help they've resorted to hiring prostitutes?"

"Nate's got skills we need." Gunn snarled. "And you've got no high ground. You've hired him."

Nate winced. Less said about that the better. Though he could no longer remember the exact circumstances—

"It is reckless indeed to put your trust in a man who is both untrained and unknown." Saltaire's voice had lost its momentous edge but still had a chill to it, like a cell door closing.

Nate was glad for Gunn's anger beside him. It provided a counterpoint to the power the vampire exuded. "Everyone's an untrained unknown at the start. Even your own operatives. Now if you don't mind, we've got work to do."

Saltaire narrowed his eyes. "I sensed the disturbance. Something is very wrong. What has happened?"

Gunn sneered. "Department matter. Strictly need to know."

"Tell me."

Nate swallowed. If he'd known, he wasn't sure he wouldn't have opened his mouth immediately. The words went directly past his mind, straight to his brain.

"A robbery. No sign of the thief, or how they eluded the security wards—" Kenzies stomped on his foot, and Simeon gasped, a wet, watery sound. But the damage was done.

Saltaire strode toward the Registry. "What's been stolen?"

"Hey! Watch your mouth around my staff!" Gunn jogged after him. "It's our job to investigate—"

"It's your job to keep order." Saltaire's voice was clipped and cold. "Which you are failing at spectacularly. You are lucky that I came by. But since you won't tell me what has been stolen, I will find out myself." Striding past a gaping security guard, Saltaire vanished into the Registry.

Gunn growled. "Simeon. Stay out here and do your best not to humiliate the department further. Kenzies, Nate, with me."

"What if the others come back?" Nate glanced around. The street was deserted, the combatants having taken advantage of Gunn and Saltaire's verbal spat to get out of there.

"They won't." Kenzies returned her gun to its holster. "Saltaire's good for that much."

"Another statement like that and you're headed back to headquarters." Gunn stormed up the steps.

Nate had no choice but to follow.

THE BUILDING SEEMED incredibly quiet after the chaos outside. The obvious signs of robbery, uniformed officers and distressed-looking staff members, were dwarfed by the sheer scale of the building. Conversations, no matter how urgent, took on the aspect of whispers, against the vastness of the building. And yet, it wasn't that big... Not big enough to explain the feeling of space.

Nate frowned, trailing after Gunn and Kenzies as they headed to the room at the center of the disturbance. It was a library, but not like any library Nate had ever seen. The books were old, with hard, leather-bound covers, and contained in bookshelves with glass fronts. The sense of the room being bigger than its reality was strongest here, but at least Nate could see why. At the center of the room were nine desks laid out in a circle, a book on each one. The pages of each book fluttered rapidly as it cycled through all its pages, reaching the end of the book only to start again. The turning paper sounded like an entire forest of leaves rustling, and Nate stretched out his hand to the cold stone of the building to remind himself where he was.

Now that he wasn't overawed by his surroundings, he could take in more of them. One of the bookcases was cracked, the glass broken. Some of the books were missing, but not gone. The room was littered with tattered scraps of torn pages, whirling in the wind created by the turning pages. A book was wedged in the gap left by the shattered glass, while the other books in the case jumped against the glass, battering it with their bodies.

Trying to break it? Nate gulped. *They're not—they can't be alive?*

"Tremaine!" Gunn ducked through the whirring mass of torn paper, approaching the circle of books. "Report!"

There was a tenth desk right in the middle of the circle, but no book. Instead, Tremaine stood at the center of the storm of pages. Her eyes were closed and her hands flung out. The wind raised by the never-ending turning pages streamed through her hair and tugged at her clothing. She stood firmly, her jaw set, summoning whatever energy was needed to sustain the spell. "The Final Register—the source of energy for the Register spell—is gone! I'm currently acting as the source."

"Are you mad? You're just a sorcerer! You can't keep that up!"

"I only need to sustain it long enough for you to create a solution!" Tremaine's face was white and her teeth gritted. "Do your job and leave me to do mine!"

Gunn gave her a long look before turning to size up the situation. Nate followed suit.

Kenzies had evidently made it her task to keep an eye on Saltaire. She stood a discreet distance from him as he scanned the room. His thoughts were not evident from his set expression, but his mouth tightened as he looked at the desk with the missing book.

A woman was having her statement taken by a uniformed Department Seven officer. It took Nate a moment to place him. Clay, the new recruit who had accompanied Kenzies and Gunn when they'd come to arrest Peter at the hotel. Instead they'd seen Peter die. Clay looked up, tossing Nate a broad grin as he recognized him.

Nate quickly turned his attention to the woman Clay was interviewing. She paired a sedate charcoal trouser suit with a scarf in a shade of pink that was only just shy of being an assault.

"Who is this?" Gunn demanded.

Clay stood at attention. "Ms. Patel is the Registry employee who alerted us to the robbery."

All eyes were on the woman. She flinched, nervously tucking her hair out of her face. "I was working late."

"Late?" Gunn folded his arms. "With your history, I'm surprised to see you out after sunset at all."

History? Nate looked again at the woman. Now that he wasn't blinded by the scarf, he could see that Ms. Patel was very pretty, with melting brown eyes and heavy lashes. Her mouth was as bright as her scarf, but the quick flicker of a tongue darting across it indicated she was ill at ease. "Must have an interesting job," he said.

It was an innocuous comment, but it cut through some of the tension. Gunn shot him an annoyed look, but Ms. Patel relaxed slightly. "I'm fond of it. Being an advocate for the supernatural community, well, it's never dull."

"And that's why you were here?"

"Sort of." Ms. Patel tucked her hair out of her face. It was a nervous gesture, but it drew attention to the delicate lines of her chin. "I was trying to make sense of some incomplete records. It's not something I can work on during work hours since it's not directly related to my job."

"Tell them what you told me," Clay suggested.

She nodded. "I was in my office working on the records when the building seemed to tremble. I thought it was an earthquake. The alarm triggered a second later. I made my way downstairs and found the library like this. I left the building and called Department Seven from the cafe across the road."

"Why did you leave the building?"

Ms. Patel hesitated. "I didn't feel safe. It felt... I kept imagining someone was there."

"The thief?"

She shook her head. "I saw no sign of them."

Gunn snarled reflexively and turned his attention on his staff. "Clay?"

"The thief is long gone. First thing we did when we arrived was scan the building for presences. Tremaine detected nothing—and no sign of forced entry or exit."

Nate looked to Clay. "Could they have left when Ms. Patel opened the door?"

"Impossible," he said immediately. "She would have seen them."

Nate felt very much out of his depth. He looked around the room. The Department Seven staff was photographing the scene. It looked like any other crime scene, except for the books, constantly in motion, and Tremaine, doing...whatever she was doing. Saltaire glowered at the empty desk in the center of the library. Those staff members who could gave him a wide berth.

Nate shivered. Saltaire's expression gave him chills. "What's been stolen?"

"You know New Camden's classification system, honey?" Kenzies caught Nate's question and strolled over to them. "Every member of the supernatural community gets assessed. The rankings reflect their power and the level of threat they pose to the general public."

Having received his Class Three Unknown ranking, requiring regular check-ins with Department Seven staff, only months ago, Nate was not likely to forget. "Yeah, I know. Wait. Did the classification system get stolen?"

"Part of it." Kenzies motioned to the books. "Once an individual has been assessed by us, the Registry staff enter their name into the appropriate book. Each one of those represents a different class."

Nate turned his head to stare at the books. "And those are magic books?"

"Spare me." Gunn turned aside, patting his jacket for his habitual packet of cigarettes.

"The books are both records and components in the spell that keeps, for example, a Class Six warlock with known extremist views from interacting with an unprotected member of the public."

"Huh." Nate looked with interest at the books. "So someone took off with one of the books?"

"Not a book. *The* book—the source." Ms. Patel looked at Tremaine, struggling to sustain the spell. "There was one book that was central to the spell. It was imbued with a lot of magic, enough to keep the classification system going indefinitely."

"Kind of like a magical battery?" Nate asked.

Clay snorted. He turned and walked away quickly, but Nate could see his shoulders shaking.

"Don't feel bad," Kenzies said comfortably. "First night on the job. You can't help it."

"The source should have been better protected." Saltaire's words were quietly furious. Or did the vampire's innate power invest everything he did with dark consequences? "Why were the protections around it removed?"

Ms. Patel blanched. "Former-Councilor Wisner brought in new security measures after the necromancer attacks. He used the source to create the Final Register. This was a list where those supernatural citizens deemed too great a risk would be entered. It was to be the supernatural equivalent of solitary confinement. Anyone on the Final Register would exist only to themselves."

Nate shuddered. "That sounds horrible." Regular prison had been bad enough, but to exist and no one even know…

Saltaire turned to face the room. "I wasn't informed about this."

"You were too busy sulking around Europe."

Saltaire sent Gunn a quelling glance. He took a smartphone from his pocket, carefully pressing the home button to unlock it. He walked past them out of the room, raising the phone to his ear. "Godfrey? We have a situation at the Registry—"

Gunn exhaled noisily. "God, it's a hard life. Having your butler on standby even at this time of night."

Nate nodded absently. A sudden movement had caught his attention, and he'd looked up to see Tremaine, still standing at the center of the spell, sway heavily. "Is Tremaine okay? I mean, she doesn't look so good."

Kenzies and Gunn reacted instantly. Both of their heads snapped toward Tremaine.

"Clay. Chair!" Kenzies ducked beneath the whirlwind of torn pages, to take Tremaine by the arm, steadying her. "How are you feeling?"

"Fine." Tremaine didn't open her eyes. Her face was drained of color, and she let Kenzies support her. "I just need to sit."

Gunn ground his cigarette beneath his boot. "You're getting out of there now. That's an order."

Tremaine's eyes flew open. "The spell's got to keep running. That's all that's protecting the citizens of New Camden from supernatural predators!"

"Not at the cost of your health." Kenzies was not as blunt as her superior officer, but her voice was just as firm. "You're still recovering."

"Where the fuck is the Magic-Users Guild?" Gunn demanded.

"We've called. No answer." Clay was back with a chair from the reception area. "We've left messages."

"How typical. Getting their beauty sleep while the city falls apart!" Gunn looked around, his gaze falling on Nate. "Look me up the address of a spell-caster. Nate and I will go rouse them out of bed physically if we have to."

"No need." Saltaire had returned. He walked across the library, straight for Tremaine. He didn't need to duck to step through the whirling pages that surrounded the spell-circle. As he approached, the books turned to face him, and the wind expanded to rush around him. He took Tremaine's place at the center of the spell, without even the slightest hint of strain. "I will maintain the spell in the interim. Godfrey will arrive soon with the means to create a more permanent stopgap. In the meantime, Gunn, I suggest that you concentrate on finding the thief before news of this leaks."

NATE HAD BEEN to Department Seven many times, but he'd never been in the office before. It was a long, rectangular room, with desks grouped in islands of four. Despite the presence of computers, printers, and even a water cooler, there was no mistaking it for a regular office. Even in New Camden, regular offices didn't do double duty as an armory.

He could almost feel the smooth steel edge of the axe hanging from the wall behind him. *I'm sure that's got to be some kind of health and safety violation...*

"And as a special favor, deigns to tell us how to do our jobs!" Gunn paced the front of the room, a bigger health and safety violation than any of the weaponry attached to the wall or in the racks on the ceiling. He'd moved onto his third cigarette of the evening and was scattering the ash, careless of the loose papers on the desks and floor around him. Fire danger, second hand smoke inhalation, not to mention Gunn was some kind of undead ghost-demon thing...

Not that it matters. I mean, this is Department Seven. How many of these people are supernatural? Nate looked around the room.

Kenzies leaned against the wall, watching Gunn, her expression long-suffering. Simeon stood beside her, looking only minutes away from a complete nervous breakdown, but Nate was starting to think that was just Simeon.

Clay swept a pile of papers off a seat and onto a desk and nudged it toward Nate. "Take a seat."

"Thanks." Nate sat down. He shot a look at Clay, but the man had already swiveled his chair to the front of the room. *Is he human? He seems so...ordinary.*

The harried-looking secretary Nate remembered from reception came into the room, drawing the door closed behind her.

Kenzies raised her voice, cutting Gunn off midcomplaint. "We're all here."

This is everyone? Nate looked around the room. Tremaine sat at her desk, sipping some kind of herbal tea remedy, and there were a handful of others, but compared to the number of supernatural residents in New Camden, Nate felt very outnumbered. *This can't be right...*

"Okay, boys and girls. Listen up." Gunn turned to face the room. "You've probably gathered we've got a problem. Someone decided to steal the Final Register from the Registry, and not only did they get away with it, fucking Saltaire's stepped in to fill the gap. As tempting as it is to leave him there, we need to find out how the thief did it and get the book back before we have a major panic on our hands—and if any of you let the nature of this theft slip to the media, I will personally gut you."

Clay jiggled on his chair. "What's the plan?"

Gunn gave him a sour look. "The same plan we always have. Contain the situation and solve the problem. We've got the support of the police in securing the Registry building, so I'm going to need a volunteer to liaison with our fleshy counterparts. Clay, that's you."

"That's not how volunteering works—"

"Everyone else, you're on investigative duty. Magic-users, you're going to be examining the scene. The rest of you, this is a really good time to visit the usual troublemakers, see who is acting shiftier than usual. You got that?" Gunn looked at the officers. "Then get to it. Kenzies, Tremaine, and Granger, you stay behind."

Nate blinked. He waited until the rest of the room had left before getting to his feet. "I didn't know you knew my last name."

Gunn snorted. "I know a lot of things about you, Nate. Tremaine. How are you holding up?"

Tremaine smiled tightly. "Just fine. You don't need to worry about me. A good sleep and I'll be ready to examine the Registry scene."

"No, you won't." Gunn shook his head. "I have a different assignment for the three of you."

Kenzies frowned. "Sir?"

"The Registry is a subject that produces very strong opinions in the supernatural community as we saw tonight. With the situation so flammable, I'm going to take you off the Registry case."

Kenzies stiffened. "Because I'm a wolf? But you need my strength!"

"I need your experience. I'm putting you in charge of following up on the necromancer's possible return. You're taking Nate to assist—and by assist, I do not mean 'flirt with.' You got that?"

Kenzies smiled. "It'll be a pleasure."

Nate discovered he was very relieved. "Sure. I mean, that sounds fine to me."

Gunn continued. "Tremaine, you'll be joining them as magical expert."

Tremaine's shoulders sagged. "I guess I can't argue. The doctor did say I had to pace myself."

Kenzies frowned. "A murder investigation's not really pacing yourself."

"So you can keep an eye on her. That should satisfy the mother-wolf in you. Any further questions?"

The women shook their heads.

"Come on, poppy." Kenzies signaled Nate to follow her. "We need to get you a uniform and to sign the waiver."

"Not so fast. I want a word with Nate first." Gunn clamped his hand on to Nate's shoulder, steering him out of the office and into the hall. There was an empty briefing room with the door standing open. Gunn shoved Nate toward it. "What the hell was tonight?"

Nate tried to turn and instead stumbled. "What?"

Gunn closed the door and leaned against it, his arms folded. "You're not assisting us so that Kenzies can get her kicks. We need your powers. I've seen you and your vines in action before. You contained a fully transformed werewolf beneath the Full Moon, but you couldn't subdue a crowd of leaderless wolves and leeches?"

"There were a lot of them!" Nate protested.

Gunn was unimpressed. "There were a lot of werewolves the night of the Full Moon too. That didn't stop you then. What's changed?"

Nate flinched. He looked down at his feet, trying to put his concern into words. "When I was facing Wisner, I knew I couldn't think. This time... Well, the vines reminded me of Peter's death. I didn't—I don't want to kill anyone. Even by accident."

"You're serious?" Gunn shook his head. "Killing the necromancer was the single most intelligent thing you've done in your life and you didn't *kill* kill him. The sun and his own ambition did that."

"Yeah, but I made it possible." Talking about it was making Nate feel worse, not better. "And you can't say Peter was happy to have vines growing out of him."

"Look. You've done enough thinking. Let me tell you how this is going to go. I tell you what to do. You do it." Gunn jabbed Nate in the chest with a grubby finger. "Let me worry about the consequences. All you need to worry about is not letting me down."

Was that a pep-talk or a threat? Nate nodded miserably. He was in way over his head.

Chapter Four

"I TOLD YOU this was a bad idea. Didn't I say so? Seriously stupid." It sounded like Aki was leaning against the bathroom door. "How many times do I need to be right about something before you listen to me?"

Nate thought back as his fingers struggled with the buttons of his uniform shirt. "Wait. Last night at Century, you were talking about me joining Department Seven?"

"Obviously! Do I need to explain Foresight to you?"

Nate shook his head and then remembered Aki couldn't see him. "You might want to work on your delivery. You'd be more helpful if you weren't confusing."

"Nate's got a point." Grant was back. Aki had called him over to help tell Nate what a mistake he was making, but as soon as he'd heard about the standoff outside the Registry, Grant had left to get a copy of the morning newspapers.

"No one asked your opinion!"

"Actually, you did, Aki, when you called me—"

"For your opinion on Nate's idiotic decision to join Department Seven." Aki rattled the bathroom door handle. "Aren't you done yet?"

"Almost." The shirt was tight, only just making it over Nate's biceps. Each button was a struggle. Nate conquered the last one and smoothed the shirt down, stepping back to look at himself in the mirror. It wasn't good. The material hugged him in a way that the durable fabric wasn't meant to. "I'm really not sure about this uniform."

"What are you so freaking embarrassed about? I've seen you naked." Aki's fingers beat an impatient rhythm on the door. "Or is this your subconscious trying to tell you how dumb the idea of you as a Department Seven officer is?"

Nate sucked in a sharp breath. That was it. Aki had put his finger on exactly what bothered him. His powers had failed him, he didn't have a clue what he was doing, and he'd disappointed Gunn within hours of starting work. He had no business helping the department. "Maybe you're right." He took a quick glance over his shoulder at his reflection and was not encouraged. The uniform pants were skintight on Nate. Which was flattering and all, but not exactly the image an officer was supposed to project. "But if Peter really is back, then I'm responsible. I can't just walk away from this, Aki."

Aki took a step back as Nate opened the door. He looked up with a frown and paused.

Well, at least it's better than him outright laughing. Nate resisted the urge to smooth his hands down the shirt. "Do you think it's too tight?"

Grant snorted. He was sitting at the coffee table, the newspapers spread out in front of him. "I would definitely ask for the next size up."

"Don't you dare." Aki was circling Nate. "It's perfect."

Nate quirked an eyebrow at him. *What happened to the stupidest thing you've ever done?* He bit his lip. Anything that stopped Aki complaining was worth it—though would Grant agree? Nate shot a look toward the werewolf.

Grant shook his head, holding out a letter. "I saw some mail in your mailbox on my way back with the papers. You've got a letter from a lawyer."

"Really?" Nate took the letter. "Why would a lawyer be contacting me?"

"Only one way to find out." Grant picked up his papers again but didn't go back to reading.

Nate slid into one of the armchairs, tearing open the letter. He scanned it. Bland legalese that told him nothing useful. "They want me to drop by the office at my earliest convenience. No mention of why."

"That is odd." Grant studied Nate. "You've got no idea why they might be contacting you?"

Nate shook his head. "I haven't done anything recently. Besides, you know, wanting to leave Century and assisting Gunn."

"They can't sue you for doing that." Aki folded his arms. "Screw the haters. Do what you have to."

Nate stared at him. "I thought you were against me helping Department Seven."

Aki sat on the arm of Nate's chair, running his fingers over the sleeve barely containing Nate's bicep. "Changed my mind. This is definitely a public service."

Nate rolled his eyes. *Aki never changes.* He looked to Grant frowning as he studied the papers. "Do they say anything about the showdown outside the Registry?"

Grant held up the paper so Nate could see the headline clearly. New Camden On Brink: Theft Threatens Supernatural Violence. "It's the main news item in all the papers."

So much for keeping things quiet. Nate tugged his collar. "What are they saying?"

"That the theft has heightened tensions between the central city vampires and Wisner's pack, and that any violence between the groups could spark a wave of infighting between vampires and werewolves, similar to the sparring over territory we saw in the wake of the necromancer attacks."

Nate felt fear settle in his stomach like a stone. "Any mention of the murder?"

"The one linked to the necromancer?" Grant shook his head. "Looks like that's been kept quiet, for now, at least. What is this 'Final Register' that got stolen?"

Nate's heart raced. "Shit." He reached for the paper that Grant held, flipping through the pages. It was right there on the front page. "'A representative from ARX confirmed that the city's supernatural defenses were still in operation, despite the removal of the Final Register.' That's supposed to be secret."

Grant's eyes narrowed. "And what is it that the city doesn't want us knowing about it?"

Nate glanced at the paper. If it was already out, it wasn't like he was breaking any rules... "Basically, it's the last-case scenario. For beings like Peter that are too dangerous to be allowed contact with people but too powerful for the city to contain. They get written into this Final Register and they exist only to themselves. Like solitary confinement for supernaturals. It was Wisner's idea."

Grant's snarl was reflexive. "Might have known. It has his stench all over it."

"But wouldn't something like the Final Register make sense?"

"If it was properly regulated. This?" Grant stabbed a finger at the newspaper. "The guilty party exists only to themselves. That means there is no chance for appeal. No chance for review. It's entirely dependent on the judgment of the people in charge and people are inherently flawed. No one's judgment is without bias. And given my stepdad's actions..." Grant shook his head. "No wonder people are freaking out."

"You're telling me. There was practically a riot last night, and that was before anyone knew what was stolen." Nate scratched the back of his neck. "Once the supernatural community learns of this, we're looking at big trouble."

"Yeah," Grant said softly. "This is not going to go over well."

KENZIES PICKED NATE up outside his apartment in an unmarked car. "Morning, sunshine!" she greeted him. "Aren't you looking nice."

Walking was not as much of a problem as Nate had feared, but sliding into the back seat reminded him just how closely the uniform adhered to him. "I'm not sure about the uniform. Is there a size up?"

"That's the biggest size we've got. Sorry, Nate." Kenzies did not sound sorry at all. "It suits you. Don't you agree, Tremaine?"

Tremaine looked up from the passenger seat. "What? Oh, yes." She looked tired still, with deep shadows around her eyes.

Nate pulled his seatbelt on. "How are you feeling today?"

Tremaine summoned a pathetic looking smile. "Much better for some sleep, thank you, Granger."

If this was better, how had she felt before? "Just Nate is fine." He looked out the window. "Where are we going?"

"Our first call is de Silver's apartment." Kenzies navigated through the traffic. "Where he spent most of his time, and the most likely place for him to leave a spell."

Nate was glad he was alone in the back seat. The thought of visiting Peter's apartment made him feel as though a heavy weight was pushing down on him.

Being inside the apartment was even worse. It was obviously abandoned, with chains and a heavy metal padlock securing the door. "To prevent atrocity tourism," Kenzies explained as she unlocked it.

Nate was jolted out of his thoughts by disgust. "What, people would actually want to come here?"

"De Silver held the entire city hostage and made international headlines with his killings." Kenzies shut the door behind them and pushed the bolt shut. "You'd be surprised how many people want to see where it happened."

"Or worse. Emulate it." Tremaine looked around the apartment. "These would be his belongings?"

Kenzies nodded. "Next of kin was a distant relative who refused point blank to touch it. Normally the landlord would auction it off, but given de Silver's notoriety, we thought that might encourage thrill seekers. It's being held until Department Seven can come up with a suitable way to destroy it all."

"Given a green light for wanton destruction and Gunn has yet to take advantage of it?" Tremaine snorted. "Is he getting mellow in his old age?"

Kenzies laughed. "We can only dream. No, we've had our hands full with Wisner. I don't know what you've heard about the Full Moon debacle, but..."

The two women were obviously old friends. Nate half listened to them talk, looking around the living room in silence. Thick dust lay over the TV and the DVD collection, and a collection of dishes were left on the coffee table. Had Peter sat here to have his breakfast before leaving the apartment, knowing he would never come back?

He planned it like that. So why does it feel so... Nate fumbled for the right word to capture the emotion churning in his stomach. *So sad?* Peter had lived here. Before he was "the Necromancer," he'd just been Peter. Leaving the apartment every morning alone, coming back to it in the evening—alone.

An explosive sneeze made him jump.

Kenzies rubbed her nose on her sleeve. "Forget defensive spells. The dust alone is a protection against werewolves."

"There's no reason we can't open a window, right?" Tremaine asked. "The apartment must have been checked for magical traps."

Kenzies nodded. "Every magic user in the department's been over it. But you can never be too careful. De Silver was experimenting with new kinds of magic."

Tremaine pushed open the living room window. "You saw his work, didn't you, Nate? What did you notice?"

Nate started. "Uh. That it hurt?" Tremaine turned to look at him, and he shrugged, ducking his head. "I'm not really an expert on magic."

"But you did see Peter at work. How would you describe his methods?" Kenzies prompted. "Haphazard? Methodical? Improvised?"

Nate shot her a grateful look. This he could do. "Definitely methodical. I got the impression he planned everything. He gave me the card with the seal that allowed him to control me days in advance and then got me to buy the knife he planned to kill me with. But when I got rid of the knife, instead of changing his plans, he left me tied to a tree and went to get a second knife himself."

"Definitely sounds like a planner." Tremaine looked to Kenzies. "What happened to the books?"

"ARX confiscated all of them. You can believe the city wasn't happy about that, but they've been dumped in one of ARX's hermetically sealed vaults while the councilors argue over what should be done with them." Kenzies shrugged. "As far as I know, you need level seven clearance to even request to look at them."

"That's something, at least." Tremaine looked around. "I'm getting faint magical residue from over here."

"The office. Makes sense." Kenzies followed her into the room.

Nate stayed where he was. The short conversation with Tremaine had brought back memories he didn't want. He could almost feel the rain on the back of his neck. When he looked down, he half expected to see runes cut into his skin instead of the navy fabric of his uniform.

How long are we gonna be here? He prowled once around the living room, before opening the bathroom and kitchen doors. The rooms had clearly been searched and then left as they were, Peter's life reduced to a scattered collection of objects. Nate began collecting the plates and stacking them. *There was no reason for Peter to do what he did. He was successful. He was earning a decent salary to afford this place... It should have been enough.*

But a nice apartment wasn't enough to make up for a lifetime of loneliness. A lifetime wanting the approval of the one man who wouldn't give it to him. Nate shuddered, the echoes of Saltaire's voice going right down his spine. *I can't imagine anyone I'd want less as a father. Why on earth would Peter fixate on him?*

Did Peter have a choice? Vampires twisted people around them just by existing. Working for Saltaire, seeing him every night, just being in the same building as him... How on earth did you escape that kind of influence?

"You don't." The words were cold, the mocking tone directed inward. "You can fight it for a while, but you don't escape it."

Fear shot through Nate. The plate he was holding slipped from his hand. He started to his feet. In the reflection in the kitchen window, he saw a mouth twist ironically and pale skin standing out in contrast to the raw gash on the neck below. *Peter!*

"Nate!" Kenzies scrambled through the door, her gun drawn. "Are you okay?"

Nate looked from her to the window. Empty glass met his gaze. "He's gone!"

"Who's gone?"

"Peter. I saw him."

Kenzies breathed deeply through her nose. "I can't smell him. Where was he?"

Nate looked again at the window. "I saw his reflection. He must have been standing where you're standing now."

Kenzies looked down at the tiles beneath her feet. "Tremaine?"

Tremaine stepped carefully over the shattered plate to peer at the window. "There're no magical traces. Nothing to indicate a spell or a visitation."

Nate sucked in a deep breath, willing his heart to slow. "I saw him. I really did."

Kenzies raised a hand. "You don't have to convince me. You're as pale as Simeon whenever his phone rings." She looked at Tremaine. "Could it be a ghost?"

"It's too early to say. Ghosts leave an energy signature behind. I don't sense anything, but I'm magically sensitive, not psychically sensitive."

Kenzies growled. "Gunn's going to love this." She pulled out her phone.

Tremaine stood with Nate on Peter's balcony as Kenzies made the call. "You shouldn't have been off on your own. It's one of the first rules of investigating a place like this."

"My bad." Nate sucked in the morning air gratefully. It was warm on the balcony and the air held a freshness the apartment lacked. "Any other first rules I should know? I didn't get an orientation."

Tremaine snorted. "Gunn's policy has always been to throw newbies in the deep end and keep those who float. The high attrition rate is why we no longer have a recruitment budget. But even so, I'd have thought someone would have given you pointers?" As Nate shook his head, she sighed. "First step, when investigating anything that has the potential for possession—ghosts, necromancers, unknown blood magic, cults, warlocks, some witches—you keep your team in eyesight at all times."

Nate turned to watch Kenzies through the glass window of the balcony. "Makes sense."

"If I can ask, why are you here, Nate?"

Somehow, the question didn't seem invasive when Tremaine asked it. "Gunn thought I'd be useful. I've kind of...got involved in every magical emergency that's happened in New Camden since the necromancer, and I guess he figured I'd do less damage working for the department."

Tremaine raised her eyebrows. "You must have considerable magical talent to accomplish that without training. Is that why the necromancer chose you as a victim?"

Nate shook his head. "No. That actually happened later. I thought I was human. Until he killed me and I didn't, well, die."

Tremaine pursed her lips. She clearly had more questions, but instead of asking them, she looked past Nate to Kenzies, pushing the glass door of the balcony open. "New orders?"

Kenzies nodded. "Change of plans. Given Nate's sighting, Gunn wants us to examine de Silver's books. He's put in an official request for ARX's cooperation."

Tremaine snorted. "And you think ARX is going to obey?"

"After the leak to the media? They owe us." Kenzies slid the door shut behind Nate, locking it. She then secured the window Tremaine had opened earlier. "Sorry, petal. You're off duty. You don't have anywhere near the clearance needed to look at those books."

Nate shuddered. "That is fine by me. I've seen more than enough of Peter's magic."

THE MAN AT the desk looked at the papers in front of him, shuffling them into a neat pile. He gave the Department Seven patch on Nate's uniform a hard look. "Nathan Granger?"

Nate hunched his shoulders and nodded. *What did I do?* The office was understated in its furnishings, but he was sure the paintings on the wall were the kind that were supposed to hang in museums, not law firms.

The lawyer hesitated. Abruptly he laid the papers down, resting his hands on his desk. "You're probably wondering why we didn't get in touch with you earlier. This is a most unusual case. Simply put, we needed to consult an expert before we proceeded." He paused, seemingly expecting a response.

Nate nodded in what he hoped was an appropriate way.

The lawyer looked down at the papers. "We received multiple inquiries last month about the status of an apartment in the complex I believe you reside in."

"What, Grant's apartment?"

The lawyer nodded. "You're familiar with the situation?"

"No one knows who the actual owner is, but Grant was obviously invited there. We all were. I remember the rooms, the furniture, just not the owner. We thought magic—" Nate stopped abruptly. Should he be admitting to magic in front of a lawyer?

The man nodded. "The same thought occurred to us. We're used to some unusual requests from our supernaturally inclined clients, but this is very peculiar indeed. We hold the documents related to the apartment building, but the name of the client whose portfolio they belong to is a complete mystery."

Nate saw the lawyer glance again toward his Department Seven patch. *This can't be good.* Number one suspect when anything inexplicable happened was always the supernatural. "I don't understand. What documents?"

"Well, the deed of ownership for one. And the will of who we presume is the current owner."

Nate was about to nod again but caught himself. Pretending he understood was not going to help here. "But you're not sure?"

"The name of our client is missing, but the name of his heir is not. That would be you."

A chill shot through Nate. "Me?"

"Our client—whoever they are—left you the bulk of their property, including the apartment building in which you and Mr. Ferrars reside."

Nate felt a rush of panic. "The entire *building?*" The lawyer nodded. "There's got to be some mistake. I can't take care of an entire building!"

"There is no disputing the intent of the will," the lawyer said drily. "Only the identity is in doubt—and how the records were altered. Obviously my staff would never allow a document in such an incomplete state to be filed."

"Obviously," Nate repeated. His head still spun. *This cannot possibly be right.*

"In light of your...inheritance...I was hoping you'd be able to provide some insight into the identity of our client?"

Nate swallowed. "That's the thing. We've all talked about it. We all agree there's someone that should be here that isn't, but none of us can remember anything definite. It's a feeling. A warm feeling, like seeing the first new shoots in spring. But nothing more. Nothing that could tell us what happened."

The lawyer sat in silence, a frown on his face.

Nate caught himself shifting and forced himself to sit still. A lawyer was only one step away from the police. He had to be on his best behavior.

"We have consulted Department Seven as well as the city's police task force. It seems that until we know the identity of your benefactor, we cannot declare them missing. And since there is no proof that they are in trouble, we cannot at this stage suppose that anything untoward has happened."

"But to vanish so completely people don't even remember you—that can't be normal!"

The lawyer shrugged. "It could be deliberate on the part of your benefactor. In which case, I hope you'll agree to a waiting period before you claim your inheritance."

Nate stared at him. "What do you mean?"

"That for the moment you view yourself interim manager of the property rather than the owner. Unless you want to file to prove that your unknown benefactor is deceased."

The suggestion sparked an immediate feeling of outrage. Nate swung to his feet. "No. No way!"

The lawyer raised his eyebrows in mild surprise but didn't comment on Nate's reaction. "In that case, I will continue my investigations. I leave the decision of whether"—he glanced at his notes—"Grant Ferrars can remain in the apartment to you."

Nate took a deep breath, trying to slow his rapid breathing. "But this is only temporary, right? Until we find the real owner?"

The lawyer picked up the papers once more. "*If* we find them, Mr. Granger. And considering the lengths they've gone to in order to erase themselves from existence, I am not sure that we will."

There was no reason that thought should make Nate feel so empty. No reason. But it did.

"SO YOU'RE MY landlord, Nate?" Grant leaned forward, resting his arms on the back of the sofa Aki was currently occupying. "Does that mean I pay you rent?"

Nate shook his head. "I don't know. And this is only temporary, while the lawyers sort it out."

Grant, who in the third year of his law degree had a much better knowledge of New Camden law, pursed his lips, but before he could argue, Aki interrupted.

"Who the hell would leave you a building? There's no *way* I would miss you having a sugar daddy."

Nate winced. He was thinking the exact same thing, but he wouldn't have put it like that. "Maybe there's a clue here in the apartment." He turned his gaze to Grant. "Have you looked around?"

Grant shook his head, straightening. "I've tried to avoid all the rooms except for the spare bedroom, bathroom, and kitchen as much as possible. It feels weird, being in someone else's space. I can't help feeling like I'm intruding."

"I know the feeling." Even with the lawyer's assurance that Nate had every right to be in the apartment, and the fact that he knew he'd been there before, he still felt like he was doing something he shouldn't be. Nate rubbed the back of his neck, feeling the familiar rasp of his favorite hoodie. To Aki's disappointment, the first thing he'd done after returning from the lawyers was to change into his regular hoodie and jeans combination. "But we need to find out who this guy is. He might need our help."

Grant looked up quickly. "You're sure your benefactor is a 'he'?"

Nate closed his eyes. It was no good trying to scrape up memories, so instead he concentrated on feeling. "Yeah. Besides, the clothes in the bedroom wardrobe are definitely a guy's."

Grant straightened. "If you're comfortable searching the bedroom, why don't you start there? Aki and I can check the study."

Nate expected to miss Aki's irreverent comments as he went through the drawers but instead discovered that he didn't feel alone in the bedroom. Even before he opened the drawer that had the stash of condoms and lube, he could remember lying tangled in the bed sheets—and more. But his partner remained elusively distant.

Nate opened the wardrobe, revealing a row of neat suits. He held one up to himself. The guy was about a head shorter than Nate, slim, but obviously a sharp dresser. He could afford to be. *Who owns an entire building?*

I have to concentrate. He returned the suit to the wardrobe and looked around the room. He'd checked all the drawers. There was nothing left but to rejoin Aki and Grant.

His eyes fell on a rug thrown over the carpet between the bed and the window. *That shouldn't be there.* Nate reached for it and stopped. He had a sudden flash of memory. Waking cold, colder than he had been in a long time. Feeling sick to his core. Rising panic as he realized that someone—someone important—wasn't there. The relief when he found him, and then clammy fear as he realized things were seriously wrong.

Nate stared down at the rug. He sensed what he would see and it took considerable effort to prompt his unwilling fingers to pull back the rug.

The stain was an ugly brown instead of the vivid, accusing red Nate remembered, and the carpet was starting to decay, but Nate recognized it. *Blood. My blood.* He had almost died in this room.

Is that why? Nate swallowed. His memory was imperfect, but the stabbing pain of the despair he'd felt over his failure was as strong as ever. He could remember an answering pain, a slow withdrawal.

Whoever he was, he didn't mean to hurt me. Nate placed his hand on the stained patch. *Is that why he's gone?* He felt things deeply. Too deeply to want to risk causing Nate any pain. *So he just erased himself instead?*

Loss rushed through him, surprisingly strong. Nate felt his legs shake under the onslaught of grief. He sat on the edge of the bed, trying to keep his breathing under control. *What if he's gone forever? What if I never know who he is, what he was to me? What if—*

There was a soft rustle to one side. The jacket Nate had been looking at had slipped off its hanger to the floor.

Mechanically, Nate got to his feet. Ma had taught him to hang up his clothes as soon as he was finished with them. The habit held, even when he was in someone else's apartment. He smoothed down the jacket, absently checking the pockets, and pulled out a letter on crisp, official-looking letterhead with a familiar logo.

The Registry? Nate unfolded the letter.

It was a quick read, if only because so much of it was missing. The recipient's name was absent, but whoever they were, they had an upcoming hearing before the council select committee to prepare for. Most of the letter was concerned with an upcoming appointment with a psychiatrist to confirm that the letter's recipient did not pose a risk to himself or others. It was signed Diya Patel.

Ms. Patel? Now that he thought back, Nate was almost certain he'd spoken to her once before. *In this very room.* They'd both been occupied with helping the letter's recipient, Nate was sure of it. *So why don't I remember anything about the Registry? Is that because of whatever weirdness is going on, or—*

Nate gulped.

The Final Register was created after the necromancer murders to handle cases like Peter's. He'd assumed that Peter's premature death had excluded him from the Final Register, but what if it hadn't? What if he had somehow managed to free himself and now had the power of the Final Register in addition to his own?

The thought was enough to send chills through Nate. He had to force himself to stand, setting a hand against the wall to steady himself. *I have to know.* He took an unsteady step toward the door. *I have to find Gunn.*

Chapter Five

"Jesus, Nate. Is that the uniform you chose?" Gunn was never impressed, but the look he turned on Nate was more disgusted than usual. "You look like a stripper."

"I am occasionally a stripper. Nothing wrong with that," Nate said promptly.

"There is when you work for me." Gunn kicked the door to the briefing room he'd taken over shut and turned to face him. "We got an image to uphold. We're supposed to intimidate."

Gunn's scruffy hair and habitually disheveled uniform wasn't exactly Nate's idea of intimidation. Maybe Gunn's personality did that? He stood straighter, conscious that his instincts were warning him he didn't want to remain in the room an instant longer than he had to. "Kenzies said this was the biggest uniform you had."

"And you believed her?" Gunn shook his head. "How does a fucking prostitute manage to be so naive?" He sighed and stubbed out his cigarette in the overflowing saucer to his right. "Speaking of, showing up when you're not wanted is not gonna impress me with your dedication to your new job, so if you're hoping to get hired..."

The smell of tobacco was welcome, cutting as it did over the more pernicious odor of Gunn himself. Nate breathed it in thankfully. "Actually, I had a question for you. Has anyone ever been put on the Final Register?"

Gunn's head snapped up. His inhumanly yellow eyes fastened on Nate. "What did you say?"

Nate took a step back, colliding with the door. "I just wondered. Do we know if anyone's been put on the Final Register? 'Cause that could explain a lot that's weird about the robbery. Why the thief didn't show up on the security cameras, and why Ms. Patel felt like there was someone there but couldn't explain why."

"Take a seat." Gunn leaned with one elbow against the table, flicking his lighter as he waited for Nate to sit. "I have to say, I underestimated you. I didn't expect you to tumble to that so fast. But you've got to keep your theory to yourself."

Nate's breath caught in his throat. "You mean I'm right?"

"We don't know. Yet. But the possibility has occurred and it's one the council would like to keep quiet until we're in a position to confirm or deny it. We got enough fools spoiling for an excuse to fight without handing them a signed permission slip. Leave this to us experts, Nate, and stay out of it."

"There's just one thing more I have to know." Nate took a deep breath. "Anyone who wound up on the Final Register... They'd have to really deserve it, right?"

Gunn's eyes narrowed to two catlike slits. He was silent a moment. "What do you know—or think you know?"

Somehow Nate didn't think he could trust Gunn with his imperfect remembrances. "It was just a thought that occurred to me. The Final Register could have been stolen by someone with links to whoever's on it."

"You're certain it's been used? Interesting." Gunn kept his gaze fixed on Nate. "There's no way of knowing until we get more information. As the Final Register's creator, Wisner's the only one who might know, and the guy's had a complete mental breakdown following his defeat at the Full Moon. He is undergoing psychiatric treatment in a private hospital and his doctors aren't allowing interviews. But we're looking into this. Matter of fact, I'm expecting the magic-users who worked on Wisner's modifications any moment and I'd prefer to interview them without you cramping my style."

Nate stood. "There's nothing I can do?"

"You can go to the supplies store and get yourself a uniform that doesn't threaten indecent exposure if you make a sudden move. Now, Nate."

THE DEPARTMENT SECRETARY emerged from the supply cupboard shaking her head. "Sorry, Nate. Nothing larger than the uniform you've got."

Nate frowned. "Gunn's not going to be happy."

"He never is," the secretary said. "And I think it looks good on you."

"Can I requisition one or something? Gunn yelled something about a form."

She sighed. "I suppose. Here. Fill this out, though I'm not sure it will get here in time. You're only assisting us temporarily, right?"

"Right." Nate jotted down his measurements on the piece of paper and handed it over. "Thanks."

There was no sign of Tremaine or Kenzies. Presumably they were working on whatever books of Peter's ARX had handed over. Nate walked down the street outside Department Seven, racking his brains for something he could do. Shoving his hands into his pockets, he felt the crisp edge of the letter he'd found.

Maybe Ms. Patel knows something about what's going on? Nate turned his feet in the direction of the Registry.

While daylight kept the vampires away, the contingent of werewolves gathered around the Registry had grown. They mingled in groups on the pavement in front of the Registry building, shooting hostile looks at Nate as he climbed the steps.

"Hey, Nate!" Clay tossed him a friendly salute. "What's the matter? Uniform shrunk in the wash?"

"I don't want to talk about it."

Clay raised an eyebrow. "You know you can requisition a new one, right? What brings you to the Registry, anyway? Here to relieve me?"

Nate shook his head. "Actually, I'm hoping for a word with Ms. Patel. You know if she's in today?"

"She's in her office. You can go on up." Clay nodded to the police officers stationed outside the door. "Nate's with us."

With the Department Seven badge plainly attached to his uniform, the words were unnecessary, but Nate appreciated them all the same. He asked for directions at the reception desk and followed them up a circular stone staircase that emerged on a balcony that looked down at the library from above. Glancing down at the forensics staff scanning the scene for fingerprints and other traces, Nate could see that the empty desk where the Final Register had been was no longer empty. A new book was placed there, its pages spinning like the rest of the books making up the Register.

"A temporary solution." He looked up to see Ms. Patel standing a few meters away. "Fortunately for us Saltaire has in his private collection numerous magical books with properties that make them suitable receptacles for the power required to run this spell and a witch with the knowledge needed to make the transfer of power."

"You don't mean Godfrey?" Nate knew that Saltaire's housekeeper was a witch, but he'd never imagined the benign grandfatherly figure had so much power.

"I don't know his name, I'm afraid." Ms. Patel ran her eyes over Nate's uniform and paused. "Are you here on business, Officer?"

"Just call me Nate. Actually, I was hoping to talk to you."

Ms. Patel jerked her eyes back to his face with what looked like a blush. "Of course. Follow me."

The bright colors of today's scarf, a vivid turquoise, might be intended to draw the eye, but Nate found himself fascinated by the swaying of her hips as she walked. She was graceful but purposeful, with an energy that was very attractive.

Shit. Have to be professional—Department Seven professional. Nate willed himself into a serious mode of thought. He took the chair facing Ms. Patel's desk with relief.

"How can I help you, Nate?" Behind her desk, Ms. Patel was crisp and businesslike.

Nate drew the letter from his pocket and slid it across the desk. "I'm hoping you can tell me something about this."

She pressed it flat and then scanned it, raising an eyebrow as she took in the contents. "I definitely wrote this. It's my signature, and I remember scheduling the appointment with Dr. Wellbeloved. But the who..."

"It's just there, out of reach, but the more you try to grasp it, the more indistinct it gets?"

Her eyes widened, falling on Nate with surprise. "How did you come by this letter?"

"I found it in an apartment that was left to me by someone not even his lawyers remember." Nate took a deep breath. "Ms. Patel—"

"Diya." She looked away quickly, hiding a smile.

Nate blinked. "Diya." Watching the pleased curve of her lips, it was a moment before he collected his train of thought. "You don't remember anything about your client?"

She shook her head. "I've been going over those records. The ones I mentioned last night that are incomplete? They date to a very specific period, ending at the Full Moon last month."

Nate thought back. The Full Moon was when Wisner's plans to take control of the city had ended in his ignominious defeat. "You don't think your client was involved with Wisner's plans? That maybe they ended up on the Final Register?"

"No!" Diya scrambled to stand. Her hand clutched at her throat. "No. I wouldn't—I would never work for someone so dangerous!" She swayed slightly.

"It was just a question." Nate put out a hand to steady her, guiding her back to her seat. "Take a moment. I'm going to get you a glass of water."

It took him several minutes to locate a kitchen unit and return with a glass of water.

Diya was leaning forward with her elbows on the desk and her face in her hands. Nate cleared his throat and she looked up, smiling wanly as she saw the glass. "Thank you." She brushed her hair out of her face, and Nate got a glimpse of a scar, imperfectly healed. "I'm embarrassed. I've no idea why that would upset me so much."

"It's okay. I did the same thing at the lawyer's yesterday. He suggested I might want to get whoever this is declared dead so I can take over his property." Nate hesitated. "The thought... It hurts."

"His property..." Diya sipped slowly at the glass of water. "So my missing client could be a relative?"

Nate shook his head. "My family is all present and accounted for." He could think back to the time spent with Ethan and Ma without any of the worrying gaps. Well, until recently... "Whoever this is, they're important. I know that much."

"I think you're right," Diya said slowly. "I'm...well, as a caseworker for the Registry, I work with a variety of clients. Not all are clients I would necessarily choose. But the fact that I reacted so strongly..." She was silent. "I can't tell you anything about them. But if there's anything I can do to help, I will."

Nate breathed out in relief. "Thank you." If nothing else, he had an ally, one who knew something about the way the Register worked. "Can you tell me more about the Final Register?"

Diya set down the glass of water deliberately before turning to Nate. "You really think...?"

"I don't think I could get involved with someone who was really bad. So now I'm wondering if this is"—Nate shrugged—"some kind of mistake."

Diya's eyebrows drew together in a perfect downward arch. "It's possible. And given the way the Final Register operates, it would be extremely hard to regulate making it open to abuse."

"What do you mean, how it operates?"

Diya leaned forward. "You remember last night I described the Final Register as solitary confinement for supernaturals? It goes even further than that. Anyone whose name is entered on the Final Register would effectively exist only to themselves. They would be unable to be seen by anyone, or heard, or felt. Messages they wrote would disappear and recordings would become inaudible, even to fellow supernaturals. But that's not all."

Nate swallowed. The feeling of dread was back, settling in his chest and sending cold chills all over his body.

"The implications of the Final Register have yet to be truly explored, but it's possible that anyone entered on it would cease to exist legally. Anything that might be able to identify them would vanish, and their name would be erased from records."

"Just like at the lawyer's office. And in your files?"

Diya nodded. "And if there's no proof of who they were or what they did, how is anyone going to know if they deserved to be on the Register?"

Nate stared at her. "Shit. I didn't think of that."

"It was a really hot topic when it was first introduced. Wisner was voted onto the council with an overwhelming show of support for his hardline tactics against rogue supernaturals—in the wake of the necromancer attacks there was a lot of support for introducing tougher controls. He promised to come up with a solution, and the Final Register was it. It was vigorously debated in the council, with opposition from supernatural advocates and human rights representatives, but it was passed in a secret ballot. It was intended to be a last resort known only to councilors. But knowing Wisner..." Diya bit her lip.

"Yeah." That was the thing, wasn't it? Nate knew firsthand just how biased the werewolf leader was. "Not exactly my first choice for being in charge of a supernatural death sentence." He paused, weighing his next question. "Do you know if there's anything we can do to reverse this?"

"Not without the Final Register," Diya said. "Which is significant in itself."

Nate tilted his head. "I don't follow."

"If you were an ally of Wisner's and knew that the Final Register could be overturned, what would you do?"

"Steal it before it could be undone?" Nate's eyes widened. "The werewolves showed up really fast last night. Almost as if they knew."

"There's another possibility. The Final Register is a powerful magic source. It could have been stolen by someone who wants its power." Diya tucked her hair out of her face. "And if our suspect is a magic user, that might explain how they got in and out of here without being seen."

"But if they're that good at magic, would they even need the Final Register? Saltaire made one. Surely they could just do that."

"It's a bit more complicated than that. Saltaire donated his own power to create the Final Register in the first place. He made it back when New Camden was first being built, and donated it to the city when the Registry was still run by the Mutual Co-Existence Society. It's almost as old as the city's founding document."

"Seriously?" Nate turned his head toward the library. "I had no idea."

"Most people don't." Diya paused. "So, Nate. Do—"

His phone beeped with a message. Nate pulled it out of its very snug pocket. "That's a message from Officer Kenzies. I'm wanted back at the station." He stood, holding out his hand to Diya. "Thanks for all the help. I really appreciate you letting me have some of your time."

Her fingers lingered on his. "Here's my number. Maybe you can make it up to me."

Nate raised an eyebrow. Did she mean...? "Could I buy you a coffee some time?"

Diya ducked her head, her hair spilling across her face, but it didn't hide her smile. "Sure. It's a date."

A DATE! THERE was a definite bounce in Nate's step as he made his way back toward Department Seven. *I haven't been on a date since—*

Nate slowed as his mental calculations ended in fog. *The missing person. Just what was he to me?*

Kenzies looked up as he entered the office. "There you are, Nate, just in time." She tore a page out of her notebook and handed it to him. "We need you to take care of this."

"Uh." It appeared to be a list written in some kind of shorthand. Nate squinted at it. "Seven black, four capp—"

"Cappuccinos."

Nate stared at Kenzies. "This is a list of coffees?"

She nodded, already sitting down to her desk. "We prefer Joe's around the block. The coffee's decent and they've got the best food, provided you get there early enough in the day. Speaking of, see what they've got in the way of muffins."

Nate looked back at the list. "But..."

"Keeping the department caffeinated is an important task," Kenzies told him. "And some of us worked through the night. Look at the state of our coffee machine."

She jerked her head toward a bench that was littered with stained glasses, and an empty coffee pot. There was a burnt smell starting to emanate from it.

"Has that been on all night?" Nate turned it off. "Who does the dishes around here?"

"Did you just volunteer? Nate, you're a godsend. But coffee first."

Nate hesitated. "Kenzies... You wouldn't take advantage of the fact that I'm totally new to all this, would you?"

She grinned at him, a hearty smile that showed off every single one of her unnaturally pointed teeth. "Of course not, poppy."

Nate was not reassured. "Okay. Joe's it is. How am I supposed to pay for all this?"

"Almost forgot." Kenzies dug a card out of her pocket. "Gunn's got it covered."

"Gunn?" Nate blinked. "That is way more thoughtful than I gave him credit for."

Kenzies mouth twitched and she gave a muffled snort.

Nate sighed. "Gunn doesn't know he's got it covered?"

Kenzies nodded. "And don't tell him. It's one of the few things that make working with him bearable."

The staff at Joe's was clearly used to Department Seven. The waitress who took Nate's order flirted aggressively with him, and he returned to the Department with all the ordered coffees, muffins, and an on-the-house slice of pie for himself.

At least Gunn's being deceived for a good cause. As he did the rounds of the department, Nate, or at least the coffee he was delivering, was greeted fervently. He noticed more than one officer with shadows under their eyes.

Holding the last coffee, a trim soy latte, Nate wandered through the department, looking for Tremaine. An officer pointed him toward the secure research department. "It seems like she and Kenzies brought back some pretty serious stuff from ARX. They don't want to take any risks with it getting into the wrong hands."

Wrong hands? But this is Department Seven. What could be more secure? Nate followed the stairs down. Instead of ending up in the research department where he'd been tested for traces of vampirism, he found himself looking through the glass panel of a securely locked door into a basement room. There were no windows, and the two light bulbs provided inadequate light. There was a bookcase, much like the ones Nate had seen at the Registry, against one wall, the glass panel securely shut and a metal chain and padlock looped around it. The metal filing cabinets to its side were secured in a similar fashion. The room had one table and three chairs, though only one of them was occupied. Tremaine lay face down on the table.

"Tremaine?" Nate rattled the door handle, but she didn't move. He looked down and discovered the key to the door was still in the lock. *On the outside?* He turned it, pushing the door open and rushing to Tremaine's side. "Tremaine!"

She stirred slowly, looking up at him with a frown. "Granger?" She pushed herself back into her chair, looking around the room. "I fell asleep?"

Nate breathed a sigh of relief. "Guess so." He turned to check the door had shut behind him, his heart still accelerating. He put the latte down. "Special delivery."

"You're a lifesaver." Tremaine reached for the coffee with alacrity. "I cannot tell you how much I need this."

"I found you asleep. I think I have an idea." Nate hesitated. "Do you think maybe you should head home? I mean, you did exert yourself last night."

Tremaine shook her head. "If I clock off, there's no one who can replace me. Department Seven is not so much short-staffed as starved of staff."

So it's not just me. The department really is tiny? "If you're falling asleep at your desk, that seems like a good sign it's time to take a rest."

Tremaine didn't budge. "I'm a little out of practice, but I'll be back up to speed in no time. Especially now that I've got some caffeine in me."

Nate pulled up a chair. "You sure about that?" Either the dim light acerbated the shadows around her eyes, or Tremaine really did not look well. There was no spare flesh on her, and her silvery blonde hair had a limp, uncared for look. "I heard you were sick."

Tremaine snorted. "A little more than sick." At Nate's blank look, she set her coffee down. "I was diagnosed with bowel cancer. It was tough, but it's in remission now."

Nate gulped. He remembered only too well his father's losing battle with that same disease. "I'm sorry."

"Don't be. I'm one of the lucky ones. We spotted it in time that there was something I could do about it." She shook her head. "And here I am. Back at work, protecting the city from the supernatural. Seems ironic, doesn't it? Here we are, with a population of vampires who can pretty much live forever, and instead of trying to harness that power, we're keeping them as far away as possible from ordinary people."

"I never thought about it like that." Nate looked at the books on the table. They were a mixed lot. Musty, leather-bound tomes, ring binders with what looked like printouts, and a stack of Moleskine notebooks, filled with Peter's meticulous handwriting. Nate wrinkled his nose. *Of course Peter would buy the most expensive notebooks.* If he hadn't taken up necromancy, Peter would have been the guy who took an antique typewriter to his local coffee shop so no one could fail to miss the fact he was a writer. "These are Peter's own books?"

Tremaine nodded. "ARX only let us have them on the condition they would be securely contained at all times. Hence the Secure Research Room." She wrinkled her nose. "With the lack of light and how musty it is in here, it's no wonder I fell asleep."

Nate nodded. "When I saw you slumped over the desk, my first thought was that you'd died or been possessed or something."

Tremaine's mouth quirked. "Unfortunately, both are potential risks of reading a necromancer's work."

"Shouldn't you have someone here to spot you?"

"Kenzies was keeping an eye on me, but she got called away to deal with department issues. As Gunn's deputy, she gives the orders when he's out of the office."

"Could I stay? I mean, I don't have clearance, but..."

Tremaine nodded slowly. "As long as you don't try to touch any of the books, I don't see why not."

Nate rested his hands on the table, well away from any of the books. "Sure. So. What are you looking for?"

"These notebooks are where Peter worked out his plans, and these seem to be the reference books he used most. I'm going through, looking for anything that might explain the theories underlying his magic. If I can find anything that looks like a reanimation spell, that would be possible proof that de Silver is connected to the death in the graveyard."

As she talked about the case, the color came back into her cheeks. Or was that caffeine? Nate nodded. "I'll stop interrupting."

Tremaine shook her head. "It's good to have company. Though, Nate—I can call you Nate?—if you wouldn't mind, don't mention my impromptu nap to anyone? Kenzies would worry, and she's already got enough on her plate without me adding to it. And Gunn wouldn't care."

That was too accurate a description of Department Seven's leaders. "Sure. But any time you find yourself working alone or you get tired, you let me know. I seem to be on coffee duty for the department anyway."

Tremaine nodded. "It's a deal."

AKI WAS NOT happy about Nate's date at all. "First you ditch me for Department Seven, now you're joining the opposition? Come on, Nate! Straight people outnumber us a million times over! We need you on our team."

Nate rolled his eyes as he put the groceries he'd picked up on his way home away in the kitchen cupboard. "That's not how being bisexual works and you know it."

"I don't see why you can't just stick to guys."

Nate rubbed his forehead. They had a variation of this argument every single time Nate met a woman he liked. "Withhold judgment till you meet Diya, okay?" On second thought, the idea of Aki meeting Diya was terrifying. In five seconds of opening his mouth, Aki would destroy any good impression Diya had of Nate. "Anyway, we're getting coffee. That doesn't necessarily equal relationship."

"It had better not," Aki said darkly.

Nate shut the cupboard door with relief. "I'm gonna get changed."

He pulled his T-shirt over his head and instantly felt more himself than he had all day. The faded cotton print was more him than the uniform.

Aki was still banging furniture around in the living room. Nate hesitated and then decided that he might as well stay where he was.

He'd watered the collection of plants in his bedroom before leaving for Department Seven, so there was nothing stopping him from stretching out on his bed. Nate settled back, watching the shadows of his plants on the ceiling. The moment his head hit the pillow, however, something hard dug into his shoulder. "Ow!" Nate sat up, shoving the pillow aside. "Aki—"

The book could only be one thing. Nate felt his breath turn to fear in his chest. He struggled to think, to do anything but stare at the book. It was leather-bound with no title. The edges of the pages with gilt, and it had a musty smell of pages and something else. Something that smelled like spice and storm clouds. The smell took him immediately back to the Registry library, and Nate seemed to feel the wind of the spell tugging at his clothes.

The Final Register. It has to be. Nate wiped his hands on his jeans before reaching out to it. *What do I do?*

The instant his fingers touched the cover, Nate felt a sensation like an electric shock. He jerked his hand away, but the electricity remained, making his senses hum. *Fuck me. Is that pure power?*

He had to call Gunn, fast.

Nate pulled out his phone, but the photo that was his lock screen made him pause. He saw it every day, so familiar that he had ceased to notice it. Looking at it now, he felt a rush of sadness. He was standing on the farm at Little River, his arm raised to shade the sun from his eyes. He stood off to the side, as if he'd left room for someone else. But he was alone in the photo.

I don't want to help Peter, or someone like Peter. Nate steeled himself. *This is a trap. Whoever put this here wants me to open it.*

But the absence that wound through his life *hurt*. Nate reached for the book. *I have to know. That's all.*

The book opened stiffly, as if it wasn't opened regularly. There was only one name written on its faded pages.

Bennet Hawick.

Everything seemed to narrow to that pinpoint. Nate stared down at the page. *Ben.*

Memories rushed back faster than he could process them. It was a wave of emotion. The relief to have found his center again, the warmth that always came with the thought of Ben, followed by the slow, terrifying realization that Ben had been forgotten by everyone. That even now he was isolated, cut off from the rest of the world.

Why? There's no way Ben would deserve this!

Memories surfaced. A tense stand-off between Wisner and Grant, ending with Ben coolly asserting his rights as Grant's host. He had remained dedicated to rescuing Grant from his stepfather's machinations, even though he knew he risked the Final Register.

Nate swallowed. *Ben—*

And he'd had no idea. He'd forgotten the man who had changed his life, changed everything.

I have to stop this. I have to get him back. With fingers that shook, Nate tore the page out of the Final Register.

"Ben?" He looked around the room, as if expecting to see him. It had to be Ben who had smuggled the acorns into his room, just as it had to have been Ben who had brought the book to him. Nate flung open the door to the living room. "Where are you?"

Aki shot him a disgusted look. He was sitting on the floor beside the coffee table, his course notes covering the entire surface of the table and some of the floor. "Have you lost your mind? Who is Ben?"

Nate scanned the apartment, but it was definitely empty. "You don't remember him?" Shit. "Aki, this is really bad."

"Worse than you dating a woman bad?"

"You remember how I said there was someone or something missing? That's Ben." A quick glance at Aki's expression told Nate he was wasting his time. "I've got to call Diya."

He paced the length of his room, waiting for her to pick up. He looked at the Final Register, lying open as he'd left it at the torn-out page. Had that been a mistake? What if he'd trapped Ben in that awful state of non-existence—

"Nate? This is a pleasant surprise."

"Diya." Now that he remembered Ben, the attraction was gone. Had it been there to start with, or had it been a subconscious impulse to try to fill the gaping hole Ben's absence left in his life? "Sorry, but I've got a professional question for you. If someone wanted to take a person off the Final Register, how would they do it?"

"Take someone off?" Diya hummed thoughtfully. "Well, I suppose they would make a case and put it before the council. They'd probably need to have the Representative for Supernatural Rights on their side first, to even get a hearing. And then, the legal review would take weeks."

"But assuming it was successful? How would the name be taken off?"

"I'm no magic user, but my understanding is that the power of the spell is in the name. They'd erase it."

"Thanks, Diya." Nate hung up, dropping his phone onto his bed. He returned to the living room. "Aki, I need some whiteout."

Aki watched Nate dump the contents of his pencil case with a scowl. "Don't ask or anything, jeez."

Nate couldn't reply. His heart was thumping so erratically in his chest that it was hard to breathe. He knelt beside the coffee table, spreading the paper flat. *This is never going to work.* Using whiteout on high-level magic? *What if all I'm doing is making this worse?*

But the alternative was leaving Ben in his living prison. Nate's hand shook as he applied the whiteout to the paper.

"Are you okay? You're acting really—" Aki sucked in a deep breath.

Nate didn't dare look up. He finished tracing the last of Ben's name with the correction fluid. *Please, please work.*

"Holy crap, Nate." Aki looked shaken.

"Now do you remember?"

Aki put a trembling hand to his head. "It's Ben, isn't it? He's been gone since—since Wisner came here and threatened all of us."

"That must have been when it happened. When Wisner put him on the Final Register." Nate got to his feet. He felt physically weak, as if he'd gone all day without eating and it had hit him all at once.

Aki gulped. "All that time, he's been alone?"

"Worse than that. All that time, he's been here and we couldn't see him." Nate turned back to his bedroom, hoping against hope that Ben would be there.

"Fail my life. So the creepy acorns were just your creepy boyfriend." Aki's gaze fell on the page and he scrambled to his feet. "Holy shit, Nate, did you—did you just destroy a page out of the Final Register?"

"That's not important now." Nate grabbed his phone, pulling on his coat. "We have to find Ben." Knowing what he knew now, Nate couldn't leave him alone a second longer than necessary.

Chapter Six

NATE PUSHED THE door to the seventh floor apartment—*Ben's apartment*—open. "Ben?"

Grant jumped to his feet and dove behind the sofa. "What the hell?"

Nate barely registered Grant's presence, let alone his words. He scanned the apartment. Every familiar furnishing brought back a memory or an association so strong that it was hard to believe he could have stood there and not known that Ben was absent.

Grant scrambled to his feet, keeping the sofa between himself and Nate and Aki. "Yeah, I know you're my landlord Nate, but you've still got to give warning before coming in here!" He paused, sizing up their expressions. "Something's wrong."

Aki snorted. "Wrong doesn't even start—" He blinked. "Are you naked?"

"It's a wolf thing," Grant said sourly. "We just feel more natural without clothes, and in the privacy of our own apartments—"

If he was here, he should have heard their voices, come to see what was going on. Or had over a month of not being seen by his best friends gotten to him? Nate stepped farther into the living room, scanning anxiously for anything that might indicate Ben's presence.

He got the barest glimpse of white flesh as Grant made for the spare bedroom. "This had better be an emergency."

"Relax," Aki told him, following him to the spare bedroom door. "None of us are particularly interested in your scrawny ass."

Nate strode across to the bedroom. The clothes still hung in the wardrobe exactly as he'd last seen them. He heaved up the fire escape window, but the stairs held only his overflowing plant collection. *Not here. Not anywhere.* Nate took a deep breath. *I can't panic. I have to think clearly about this. Ben is counting on me.*

The bathroom was empty, as was the kitchen. Fighting a growing feeling of nausea, Nate turned to the study.

"Okay." Grant emerged from his room, pulling a T-shirt over his head. His feet were bare, but he'd pulled on jeans. "Now tell me what's going on."

"We're looking for Ben. Nate destroyed a page out of—"

"Ben?" Grant frowned and then his eyes widened. "Ben. *Shit.*"

Nate breathed out, turning from the empty study to Grant. "Yeah." Even though Ben wasn't there, knowing that he wasn't forgotten eased some of the tension he felt.

"How could we—" Grant's sentence transformed to a snarl. "Wisner did this."

The speed at which Grant put the pieces together was impressive. Or would have been, if Nate hadn't been sick with fear. "We have to find him."

"I'll call Charlotte and Vazul. Get them to help." Grant pulled out his phone. "Charlotte might be able to create a locator spell. In the meantime, a list of his favorite hangouts—"

"Nate?" Aki's voice sounded strangled. "Over here."

Nate looked up, spotting him at the door. "What have you found?"

"You hurt yourself recently, Grant?" Aki was staring at something by the door.

"What? No."

"Nate?"

He shook his head, wondering what Aki was getting at. "Why are you asking? You know I'd tell you." His eyes traveled past Aki, to the rust-colored spots on the floor outside the apartment's front door.

Grant breathed in deeply. "Blood," he said with a werewolf's certainty. "I didn't see it."

"None of us did. Until we remembered about Ben." Aki swallowed. For once, his bravado was lacking, and his voice wavered. "He's hurt."

Nate took a step toward the drops of blood. They continued as far as the fireproof door to the stairs. "When was the last time you used the stairs, Grant?"

"When I went to college, Tuesday. I was running late, so I skipped the elevator."

Tuesday morning. Two days ago. He could be anywhere, now!

"Nate." Aki placed his hand on his arm. "It'll be all right. We'll find him."

How bad must he be reacting if Aki was being sympathetic? Nate sucked in a breath, struggling to calm himself. He dug his hands into the pocket of his jacket and closed on something smooth and small—the acorn. "The oak tree." He looked up at Aki and Grant, both watching him with worried expressions. "I have to go."

"BEN?" THE PARK had been eerie the first time Nate visited it at night. Now, with the added memory of his own death in this very clearing, it was downright disturbing. Twilight was just turning into evening, but as he looked around, the shadows seemed to swell before his eyes, filling the park with their implicit threat.

Once Mason Park had been a popular place for New Camden's homeless population to sleep rough, but following Nate's murder, no one dared set foot in there after dark. No one but Nate. Something always drew him back to the place where he'd died. The place he'd woken to his true self.

Ben did not share Nate's fascination with the oak tree that had sheltered them from revenants and had seen Nate's grisly death at Peter's hands. But even though he'd made it clear how much he disliked the memories the place evoked, he'd returned to it in search of Nate. *Not once. Many times.* Nate's hand clenched around the acorn in his pocket. Not every day but most days over the past month he'd found an acorn waiting for him.

He stretched his hand out to the trunk, feeling the rough scrape of the bark beneath his fingertips. The bark had deep furrows in it, but no traces were visible now of the scars Peter's rite had left. Just like there were no scars left on Nate where Peter had carved his spell directly into Nate's skin. No visible scars, at least.

Nate breathed in. A phantom pain pulsed in his chest. Underneath, he was anything but normal. Peter had robbed him of that when he took Nate's life. His new life was entirely unforeseen, unpredicted. At least, Nate hadn't been willing to see it.

Ben showed him not to shy away from the implications of his new life. He'd faced Nate's objections with the same quiet resolve he turned on himself. His sheer determination proved that strength wasn't determined by fights won, but by the getting up afterward, and going forward, even when there was no victory in sight. It was all Ben.

Nate's breath sounded shaky in the night. He sagged forward, leaning against the tree. The oak's strength was comforting, but Nate didn't need comfort. He just needed Ben.

Think! Ben was nothing if not practical. He'd left the acorns, a clear message to Nate. He'd figured out the book. He wouldn't make himself hard to find... *Is there something more to this? Something I haven't seen?* Nate's fingers dug into the bark. *What if the Final Register doesn't work if you're dead?* If Peter had come back remembering Ben, determined to have revenge on them both—

His phone buzzed. In his haste to answer it, Nate fumbled, almost dropping it. "Ben?"

He was answered by a snarl, low and dangerous. "Well. That answers *that* question."

Gunn. Nate sucked in a breath. "You know?"

"All of a sudden, the files we're investigating in relation to the Registry theft have your precious fucking boyfriend's name all over them, and no one can remember the last time they've seen you. Yeah, Nate. We fucking figured it out."

Nate winced. "I told Kenzies I was going home."

"And it didn't occur to you that any of us might like to know you'd found the book that almost caused a riot?" Nate held the phone back from his ear, with misgiving. Gunn usually didn't yell. He didn't need to. He could threaten just by saying hello. "Leaving your apartment is the only smart thing you did tonight because if you'd been here, I would have torn you a new one."

Nate swallowed. "Sorry. You're right. I should have told you. The book—"

"We've got the book. It's in secure custody—which is what I would like to do to you, if it didn't mean I had to deal with your company."

Nate took a deep breath. "Sorry. It's just, when I saw the book, saw there was a chance I could know for sure what was going on, I had to take it."

Gunn snorted. "There's a big difference between simple curiosity and helping the suspect in a murder case evade arrest."

Nate's fingers tightened reflexively around the phone. "What?"

"The murder, Nate. The revenant trap set for you?" Gunn sounded like he was barely keeping himself from flinging his phone to the floor. "Think! Who else saw Peter's work and survived? Only you and Ben."

"Ben would never kill someone!"

"Newsflash, Nate. The guy was a vampire and an ARX operative. He's got blood on his hands and then some."

"Not innocent civilian blood," Nate argued. "You know him! You know he wouldn't do this!"

"Ben in his right mind, maybe not. But we're not talking about Ben in his right mind."

Nate felt cold flood him, his muscles seizing into place. He opened his mouth to protest, but no sound came out.

"He's had a month without any contact with another living thing," Gunn said slowly. "From what I gather from Fujino's rather garbled testimony, he's been present at your apartment, so he's seen you going on with your life without him. Without any memory of him."

Aki must have told him about the acorns. "Ben's strong." The words were scarcely more than a whisper. Nate repeated them, trying to put force behind them. "You know how strong. He stood up to Saltaire."

"He stole the Final Register. That's not the actions of a model citizen. That is desperation. And a month of non-existence... You're besotted, but you've still got to see what that could do to a guy. We need to see him, Nate. You've got to bring him in. For his sake if not your own."

Nate swallowed. "You think I know where he is?"

"You're the most likely suspect. The two of you are practically attached at the hip."

Nate leaned back, feeling the bark push uncomfortably against his shoulder blades. "I can't find him."

"You're shitting me."

"I'm in Mason's Park. The oak tree. I thought for sure he'd be here and he's not." Nate's voice cracked and he winced. Pain was food for an emotional predator like Gunn. "I don't know where he is."

There was a long silence. "And there's no sign of him being there?"

"I can't tell. It's dark. Hello?" The call was suddenly full of static. He could hear voices, but they were muted. Gunn giving orders. Nate felt a new wave of apprehension stealing over him. He could picture the scene. Gunn addressing his subordinates, making plans to capture Ben.

If they can find him. He wasn't at the oak. He wasn't at his apartment, on the fire escape, nor any of the places Ben would wait for Nate in. He wasn't anywhere.

Are we too late? What if— Nate couldn't finish the thought.

"Still there?" Gunn sounded brisk. "I'm sending you home."

"What?"

"For fuck's sake, are you actively trying my patience now? You're going home and you're staying there until I send for you. Not only have you interfered with a legal document, but now that everyone remembers Ben, they remember the part the two of you played in bringing down Wisner. You risk a revenge attack from Wisner's remaining pack, or an opportunistic swipe from any one of the dozens of wolves who saw you take out their leader. Not to mention your history with vampires, and your general inability to—"

"I get the picture. I'm going home, Gunn. There's nothing more I can do here anyway." Nate ended the call. He looked once more around the clearing.

His phone buzzed again, and Nate reached for it mechanically. "Listen, Gunn—"

"It's me. I guess I don't need to tell you that Department Seven's been back."

"Aki?" Nate breathed out. "Yeah. Gunn's not happy, huh?"

"Is he ever happy?" Aki was making an effort, but it was far from his usual tones. "How are you holding up?"

Nate went still. He could put on a front before Gunn, but when Aki asked... "Not good. He's not here, Aki. He's not— He's not anywhere."

"Department Seven's launched a citywide search. They'll find him."

Nate swallowed. Even that felt like a betrayal. Leaving Ben to be found not by his friends but by those who had no cause to trust him. "Search? It's more like a manhunt. They suspect him of..." He couldn't say it.

"Yeah. Look. Grant got enough from the officers accompanying Gunn to have him fuming. He's already on the phone to—I don't know. Some kind of activist group for supernatural rights getting legal advice. No matter who finds him, Ben's going to be all right."

Nate listened silently. He couldn't bring himself to voice the fear that was present in his mind. What if Ben couldn't be found because he was no longer there. *The blood—*

"Nate? Seriously, come home. You are making me stress and I don't like it when I'm stressed."

Nate closed his eyes. He felt tired. Not just exhausted, the tired that went all the way through to bone. "Yeah. On my way." He hung up.

He'd tried Ben's phone multiple times all ready, the call ending with a curt message the number he'd dialed was no longer in use. He wasn't sure he could take even that much disappointment another time.

He looked around the park one last time.

In daylight it was peaceful, even beautiful, the sunlight turning the canopy of leaves a translucent green. The earth smelled fresh with the promise of ever-renewing life, and the wind rustling through the leaves kept New Camden's bustling traffic at a peaceful distance. Now…

Now it held nothing but failure.

AS NATE TURNED onto the block that led to the apartment building, a howl cut across the sound of the traffic, filling the night sky. The two guys smoking on the steps of the neighboring tenement exchanged a look, snuffed out their cigarettes, picked up their beers, and hurried inside.

Nate stayed where he was. The hair on his arms rose, but even the instinctive alarm produced by the howl couldn't dent the depression that had settled over him. He was helpless to aid Ben. Helpless to do anything.

As the howl repeated, Nate's shoulders sagged. *Wisner's pack. Probably calling a meeting to discuss how they can fuck up Ben's life even more.* Did they know he was missing? They must have worked out that the Final Register had been returned. But finding the book had only created more problems.

There's no way Ben's responsible for murder. Nate took a deep breath, forcing himself to unclench the fists he'd made. Even Gunn would have to admit that if Ben was unable to interact with anyone or anything while on the Final Register, then it was physically impossible for him to murder someone. *Only good thing about the Final Register.*

He took a step toward the building, and another. As the apartment grew closer, it became harder and harder to put one foot in front of the other. Nate stopped, looking up.

He'd entered the building for the first time with Ben, just after they'd escaped Peter. In his apartment, their fledgling relationship had taken its first steps toward something more permanent. Even the sixth floor apartment Nate shared with Aki was full of associations with Ben. Now that he knew what was lacking, he couldn't bear the idea of facing that absence all over again.

And he left the building—everything—to me. Nate swallowed. Ben must have trusted Nate to figure it out. Instead he'd gone on with his normal life, leaving him trapped in a living nightmare. Worse than that, he'd forgotten Ben entirely.

Nate's shoulders sagged and he stared down at the cracked pavement before him. *I say I love him and I forget he even exists.* He could never make amends for that. The only thing he could do now was make sure Ben was found. Not return to the apartment building, abandoning his search. *I am the worst—*

A noise behind him made him jump.

He turned. Instead of a starving revenant, he glimpsed the stray cat slink into the alleyway. She held a rat in her jaws. Shooting Nate a wary look from her one good eye, she slunk behind the dumpster.

That explains the mystery of those dead birds, I guess. Probably the cat had lost her teeth or something, and instead of eating her prey normally, she had to suck the blood out of them. A much likelier explanation than vampire—

Nate felt a shock travel through him, rooting him to the pavement. *Fuck me.* He swiveled his head back to the dumpster, feeling a lump of terror form in his throat. Ben had spent a year as a vampire. Even though he was human now, his inner vampire had a way of resurfacing in extreme situations. And what was the Final Register if not extreme? *If Ben died, he would become a full vampire. A vampire would survive a month of starvation.*

But at what cost?

Nate lurched toward the dumpster. Fear clouded his mind, fear of what he might see, but at the same time, he hoped that his hunch was right. *The newspaper that had looked slept on, a cat wouldn't do that.* Nate rounded the corner of the dumpster, his heart pounding. "Ben?"

The eyes that met his were sunken, surrounded by deep shadows—or were they bruises? Hard to tell. There was a layer of dirt over his face, and his tangled hair had been left to fall in his face. His skin was stretched so thin as to be almost translucent, adhering to his bones like Saran Wrap on a skull. He snarled, revealing teeth that were inhumanly sharp and stained.

Nate froze. It was Ben's shape, but it wasn't Ben. He couldn't take his eyes off him, even as the sight caused a chill to travel down the back of his neck. Ben should never look this—this neglected. "Ben." He stepped forward, stretching out a hand. "Ben, I can see you now. Everyone can. We remember everything. It's going to be all right!"

The cat shot under the dumpster and vanished. Ben dropped the rat he held and leaped to his feet, revealing that his clothing was tattered down one side. One sleeve was stained an awful-looking brown, and his arm hung limply at his side.

Dried blood? Nate swallowed. *If no one could see you, no one would avoid you...* Had that been a car? A bike? What? "Ben, it's Nate. You know me."

Ben's gray eyes, hard as stone, showed no sign of recognition. He dropped his gaze to Nate's neck and bared his teeth soundlessly. He hunched down, standing with his legs apart, braced for action.

Nate's breath came hard. He pulled his hand back, taking an involuntary step backward. *This is so messed up. I shouldn't be afraid of Ben.*

As if he'd been waiting for the movement, Ben leaped—straight for Nate's throat.

Nate stumbled backward, bringing up his arm to shield his neck instinctively. Just in time. Teeth grazed his flesh, and sharp pain flared in their wake. Ben's weight was on him. Nate breathed in the sour smell of old blood and panicked. He shoved with all his strength. "Let go!"

Ben had the strength of a vampire. Nate's push only succeeded in freeing his arm, and Ben was back, faster than Nate could anticipate. He felt Ben's cold fingers clamp down on his shoulder as the vampire readied himself for a second attempt at Nate's neck. *Please, no!* "I am an oak."

This time his shove propelled Ben backward. He collided with the wall behind the dumpster and fell—but only for a minute. He snarled, rolling onto his knees.

Nate forced himself to swallow past the bitter taste in his mouth. His hands trembled. His vision swam, seemingly going in and out of focus. A splash of crimson on the concrete caught his attention. Nate stared at the dot. *Blood.* There was a trail of the dots, spreading across the ground—*my blood*—to where Ben crouched. The same crimson was on his lips, dripping from his mouth. As Nate stared, Ben's tongue flicked out, swiping up the red.

Nate's knees shivered, like they were about to give. *Ben would never hurt me, never!* He scanned the creature before him, searching for any sign of awareness, of regret, of...Ben.

The vampire hissed, readying himself for another leap. He bared his teeth, his eyes locked on Nate's with a predator's precision.

Nate felt the world sway around him. He remembered another night, another vampire. *'She hissed at me when she got her fangs out. The last one did, too. That a vampire thing?'*

Ben had glanced at him, his sideways glance not revealing any of his thoughts. 'Instinct. Calls attention to your mouth so your victim doesn't realize you're preparing to strike.'

Nate clenched his fists. *I can't help Ben if I go to pieces!* He willed his knees, locked into place, to bend, shifting to match Ben's movements.

The vampire continued to growl, the sound dropping to a low pitch that rubbed against Nate's flight instincts like nails on a chalkboard. He stalked closer, his movements sinuous and inhuman.

Nate backed away, keeping his gaze locked on Ben. He could barely breathe. His chest felt constricted by the weight pressing down on him. *Is this all that's left of Ben? His shape?*

The memory surfaced faster than Nate could shove it away. *Destroy me. I never want to return to that shadow life.* Nate felt sick. *I can't do this.* He encountered resistance behind him. It took a second to realize he was pressed against the back wall of the alley.

Triumph glinted in the vampire's bared fangs. He gave Nate just time enough to realize he was trapped before he leaped. The force of their impact jolted Nate back against the wall, his skull connecting painfully with the brick. His movements were too slow. As he grabbed Ben's arms, he felt fangs scrape his neck.

Fuck me! Nate tried to push him away, but despite being injured, Ben's small frame had all the strength of a man twice his size. He growled viciously, angling to get better access to Nate's skin.

Nate reacted purely with fear. He reached for the plant deep within him, lashing out wildly. Vines formed instantly where his skin was torn, reaching out with Nate's thoughts to tangle around the vampire.

As ivy wrapped around his face, the vampire staggered back. He relinquished his grip on Nate, tearing at the vine choking him. His fangs made short work of the tendrils wrapped around his mouth, but those looped around his arms gave him a moment of difficulty. Finally, he worked them loose enough to seize the vine and rip it loose.

Nate leaned heavily against the wall, his hand pressed to the ivy at his neck. *He tried to kill me.* Ben would never in a million years do that.

This isn't Ben. The pain rising in his chest made his aching body seem negligible. *This is a revenant with Ben's body. I was too late.*

The vampire threw the last of the vine to the ground. He raised his eyes to Nate, his expression wary. Clearly he had awareness enough to recognize a threat. He darted a gaze toward the street at the end of the alley.

Fuck! If I let him go, he's gonna kill someone! Nate took a step toward the vampire.

Ben immediately backed away, his posture hunched and wary. He felt his way, keeping the dumpster at his back as long as he could.

Aware enough to be scared. Nate forced himself to take another halting step. "I can't let you do that." His voice came out shriller than he wanted, and the vampire paused. Nate could see him weigh the crack in Nate's words against his magic. He had no guarantee that Ben even understood his words, but that quaver in his voice... That told the vampire everything.

I have to do this. Nate steeled himself, reaching for the plants beneath the surface of his skin. *Ben's not going to hurt anyone.* He threw out a hand, and thick strands of ivy shot toward Ben.

His eyes widened and he leaped out of the way of the first but stumbled over the second, low against the ground. Within seconds, the ivy had swarmed around his ankles, climbing him. Ben snarled viciously as he fought against the encircling vine.

Nate drew in a deep breath. His hand trembled as it directed the vine. *It's not a betrayal. It's what Ben would want.* Don't think of this as Ben, think of him as a revenant. Like any other revenant. *That doesn't help!* Nate bit his lip. He felt sorry for revenants, too.

A hoarse whimper was audible over the sound of unfurling leaves and tearing vine. Nate jerked his gaze up to see the vines had reached Ben's injured arm. The vampire slashed at his arm with a pained cry, desperately trying to free himself.

Nate stared. *That sound—*

Curled against Ben's body, pressing a kiss to his shoulders as he adjusted his angle. Ben made a soft sound, halfway between whimper and gasp.

'Am I hurting you?'

'No, it's—god, Nate.' Ben's voice was breathy, and as he turned his head, Nate saw his cheeks were flushed and his eyes dilated. 'You feel so much—'

Not grammatical in any way, but it had sparked a rush of feeling. Nate thrust in, and Ben gave another involuntary gasp—

Nate watched the last of his vines drop to the ground in shreds. *I can't do it. I can't...* His arms were slack at his side. "Ben." His voice cracked. "I'm sorry."

Ben stared at him. His eyes took on a weird gleam from the streetlight, reflecting the light in a way human eyes shouldn't. He kicked aside the last of the vines and stepped backward toward the street.

In a few moments, he'll be gone. Nate willed himself to move but his feet felt like they'd been replaced by concrete blocks. "Ben. *Please.* If there's anything left of you..."

The vampire stopped where he was. He tilted his head, considering Nate.

Does he remember? Nate couldn't breathe, as hope expanded painfully in his chest.

Ben snapped his head toward the street.

Heard something? Nate's heart dropped. A vampire's hearing was far more acute than any human. Was someone coming? If it was Department Seven, Ben would be dead—not undead, really dead—in a matter of seconds.

It was then he heard the footsteps, accompanied by a familiar jangling sound. Nate felt ice stab through him. *Oh god. Aki's keychain.*

Ben's mouth curved in satisfaction. He crouched, readying himself for a leap.

You can't do this! Nate tried to protest, but he couldn't force the words past his mouth. He watched as Ben's lips parted to reveal fangs bared and thirsting for blood. There was nothing in his eyes but the instinct of a predator awaiting prey.

Nate felt his world shatter. *He's going to kill Aki.*

Chapter Seven

THE FOOTSTEPS CONTINUED to come closer, Aki walking at his usual impatient pace. Then, without warning they paused.

Aki's foresight telling him to get out of here? Nate edged carefully toward the vampire. He lurked in the shadow of the dumpster, watching the street. His eyes were fixed on Aki, and he gave a low hiss that made Nate feel dead to hear it.

"C'mon, Nate! Check your damn messages already!" Aki huffed.

Looking at his phone? Nate jumped toward the vampire, knowing that a moment's distraction was all the predator needed.

Once again, he was too late. Snarling, Ben leaped into the street.

Aki yelped. Nate heard something hit the ground. He put on a fresh burst of speed. He rounded the dumpster to see Ben picking himself off the pavement. Aki had evidently only just stepped back in time.

He wouldn't be so lucky a second time. His eyes were locked on Ben, while his mouth hung open. His arms were tucked against his body, and he hadn't even glanced at his phone, lying face down on the pavement. His stare was glassy, and even though his body shook, he didn't try to move as Ben, now back on his feet, stepped toward him.

Petrified. And who could blame him? Vampires, like snakes, could root their prey to the spot with the power of their stare. Nate saw Ben's posture shift as he prepared to strike.

It wasn't a conscious decision to jump. It was all instinct, and then he was crashing into the pavement, Ben's body breaking his fall. They collided with Aki, propelling him backward.

Ben reacted angrily, growling as he tried to shake Nate off his back.

"No, you don't." Nate dug his knee into Ben's back, using his plant strength to keep himself in place, even as Ben did his best to dislodge him. "Aki, get out of here."

"Holy shit, Nate." Aki sucked in a breath but didn't move. "That thing would have killed me!"

Nate grunted as, running out of other options, Ben sank his teeth into Nate's wrist. "Still could. Run!"

Aki's eyes widened as he took in the struggle. "And leave you?"

"Can't kill me." Blood ran down his wrist in thick rivulets. His head swam. *Plant. Roots. Deep. Slow.* A curious calm settled over him, as if he'd been pushed past fear and horror and pain. He saw the roots spill from his wound as if he were watching a nature documentary.

He was calm, but his reactions were slow, a second too late. Ben squirmed free, hauling himself onto his knees. He looked up at Aki, baring his teeth as he sized up the leap.

Since he knew he was too slow, Nate reached out with his vines before Ben leapt. He staggered to his feet, using the vine to pull Ben, kicking and snarling, into a tight hold. He slammed him against the alley wall. Once. Twice. Ben's body went limp in his arms.

Nate continued to hold him.

"What are you doing?" Aki's voice sounded unnaturally shrill. "Make a stake or something! Revenants are base vampires. You have to kill them like one!"

Nate's arms tightened reflexively around his burden.

"I'll do it if you can't. But we have to act quickly. It's stunned, not dead. Well, technically it's dead. But we need to kill it!"

"No." Nate took a deep breath. "We're not killing him."

Aki sucked in an angry breath. "There's a time and a place for sympathy and a revenant is not it. You—" Aki's eyes traveled down to the form Nate held and widened. "Shit. Is that *Ben*?"

Nate met Aki's eyes. He saw his own horror reflected in them and his throat constricted. "I don't know."

AKI HELD THE gauze pad to the mouth of the bottle of Betadine, and the crisp smell of antiseptic filled Ben's living room. The smell made Nate feel like he was seven years old and sitting at the kitchen table, waiting for Ma to clean his grazed knees. It was the one familiar thing in a night that had been disturbing on every level, and Nate clung as hard as he could to the source of comfort.

Aki hummed as he carefully wiped dirt away from Nate's numerous scrapes, giving extra attention to the bites. He knelt on the floor beside the sofa Nate sat on, the contents of a first-aid kit spread out around him. He made sure to avoid the ivy that had settled around the wound on Nate's neck or the roots growing from his wrist. Even focused on his self-appointed task of administering first aid to them both, his gaze kept creeping back to Nate's face.

Nate felt the pressure inside him ease slightly. *Worried about me.* He placed his hand on Aki's shoulder. Aki was freshly showered, wearing a change of clothes. His hair, damp and for once not styled, gave him a strangely young air, while the Band-Aid on his chin made him look downright vulnerable. "Thanks."

Aki's mouth thinned into a flat line and he shook off Nate's hand. "Thank me by not following strange noises into dark alleys. For fuck's sake, Nate, I told you this would happen!"

Aki needed his anger to ward off his fear, so Nate didn't try to talk him out of it. He looked down at himself. At Aki's insistence he'd showered, but the heat of the water and the fresh clothes had done nothing to offset the chill he felt inside, an ache that pulsed like a raw, angry injury.

Finally, Aki sat back on his heels. "There. You're done." He glanced at Nate. "You're not okay, so don't even try to tell me you are."

Nate grimaced. There was a danger to having friends who knew him as well as Aki did. "Being hurt would be easier to deal with than this." He took a deep breath. "Ben... He changed me. He changed my entire life—no, my *world*. Seeing him like this... I feel like the entire universe has come undone. I just— It's thrown me."

Aki clicked the lid of the first-aid kit shut. "You look like you're the one who got slammed head-first into a wall."

Nate winced. Did Aki have to bring that up? "Losing Ben, even when I didn't remember him was bad enough. And when I did... But finding him like this is a thousand times worse."

Aki stared up at Nate, uncharacteristically hesitant. As he sat silently, they both heard a crash from the study.

Nate dug his fingers into the arm of the sofa. That was the sound of Ben throwing himself against the locked door of the safe room. The crash was followed by a second, and then a third, becoming a rhythmic pounding sound until, abruptly, everything fell silent.

Nate's relief was short-lived. *What if he's hurt?* There was nothing in the safe room besides the mattress, but Ben was weak from his month of starvation. He could have injured himself on the walls, or jarred his existing injury—to say nothing of how Nate had hurt him by knocking him out.

Another solid thump echoed through the apartment. Nate breathed out, shutting his eyes. *This is too much.*

A door slammed and the sound of Ben's struggles reduced to a distant scuffling. Nate opened his eyes to see Aki beside the study door.

"It's no good beating yourself up about this." Aki waved a hand toward the study. "You did everything you could—more! Securing him without killing him... There's very few people who would do that, even if they could."

Nate slumped forward, his elbows resting on his knees. "You don't understand. This is what Ben was most afraid of. He did everything possible to avoid becoming a monster." The word tasted sour in his mouth. Nate swallowed but couldn't get rid of the taste. "He lived as Saltaire's prisoner, and he was constantly fighting himself, trying to keep his reactions in check. He was afraid to let himself feel anything because he thought that if he did, he might lose control. So he starved himself of life, of everything. And it made no difference in the end."

Aki climbed onto the sofa beside Nate. He didn't speak, simply placing his palm on Nate's arm.

Nate blinked rapidly. "What makes it worse is we talked about this. About what would happen if he died...because obviously, having been exposed so much to vampires, there's no way he wouldn't become one."

"Right." Aki's comment was muted.

"So he told me he'd never ask me to...to be the one to put him down. At first I was hurt he'd ask someone else. It felt like he was giving up, you know? Not even trying. But then..." Nate swallowed. "I guess I saw a glimpse of what an out-of-control vampire looked like and I understood. But could I do it? No."

Aki's mouth pursed, and Nate winced as if he'd voice the judgment he was sure was in his mind.

"And Ben knew I couldn't do it. So instead he asked me to keep him human. To help him with control." Nate sank his face into his hands. "And that's what makes this really messed up. He trusted me to stop this from happening, and look. I went about my everyday life for a month—"

"That's not your fault!" Aki increased the pressure of his touch. "Think about it seriously. You can't blame yourself for forgetting Ben. I don't fully get how the Final Register works, but that's serious magic. Magic that Charlotte who is an actual licensed witch and all of Department Seven couldn't resist. You're not trained. You don't even know what you are!"

Nate sucked in a deep breath. "Ben—"

"Knows what he's doing," Aki continued. "He knew about the Final Register, he knew Wisner had it in for him, and he was still more worried about Grant than he was himself. He made his choice knowing the risks. We've got to respect that. And by 'respect' I mean not blaming yourself for things that were clearly outside your control."

Nate listened dully. Aki's words washed over him, but he appreciated his friend's tone. "When we talked in the kitchen, just before he left. It was like he was saying goodbye." Nate dropped his head into his hands. "We wasted so much time."

"Beating yourself up over this isn't going to help anyone. Least of all Ben. Just FYI."

Nate smiled tiredly. It meant a lot that even after his own terrifying near-death experience, Aki had stuck around to make his opinions on Nate's disastrous love life known. "Are you okay?"

Aki snorted. "You're asking me?"

Nate sat up, turning to look at his friend. "You're not being as caustic as you usually are."

Aki leaned against Nate's side, settling his head against Nate's shoulder. His fingers absently skated down Nate's arm. "You saved my life tonight. Quite literally. I was frozen to the spot. If you hadn't stopped Ben, I would have been dead in a matter of seconds."

Nate's arm tightened reflexively around Aki. "Don't think about that."

"I can't help it. Nate. You—" Aki's tongue flicked over his lips. "I've got all this adrenalin coursing through my system. It's almost like I'm high or something. I feel more conscious of everything I do." His hand dropped to loop around Nate's chest. "Every breath, every touch… I want to celebrate not being a bloody smear on the pavement. I want to be wrapped in someone else's arms and fucked into the ground."

Nate smiled tiredly as he stroked Aki's hair. "Ben told me about that. It's a common psychological reaction to near death and one vampires, in particular, like to use to their advantage." It was strange to think about the conversation in the barn now. It felt like it belonged to another lifetime, not just a couple of months ago. *Why did we waste so much time fighting?* Nate's jaw locked, and he had to force himself to swallow.

"So." Aki's voice was pure invitation. "If you need to recover from your near-death experience, I'm right here."

Nate's chest constricted, but with warmth this time. It was rare Aki put anyone's needs above his own, and he ruffled his friend's hair. "You don't have to do that, Aki, but thanks. I appreciate it. You're such a good friend."

"Yeah." Aki's voice sounded choked. "That's me. A real good friend."

Probably angry that he'd been caught out being nice. Nate thumped him on the back and then stood. "I'm going to get something to eat. I think I'm a bit light-headed still."

"Light-headed is one way to put it." Aki sounded annoyed. Definitely feeling better.

Grant returned as they were finishing off their cup ramen. He held a plastic grocery bag. "Sorry I'm late. It took me a while to find a blood-vending machine that hadn't been vandalized."

"Vandalized?" Nate set his noodles aside. "Who in New Camden would want hungry vampires roaming around?"

"Werewolves," Aki said immediately. "People who hate vampires. Dumb teenagers. Drunk idiots—"

"The important thing is that we got the blood." Grant held out the bag to Nate.

He took it, looking inside. The blood was in several pouches, each medically sealed and labeled. There were instructions on how to use them. Nate frowned. "Heat first?"

"Apparently it's better at body temperature." Grant took the place Nate had just vacated on the sofa.

Aki scowled. "Can we not talk about blood while I'm eating? I was very nearly vampire chow an hour ago."

Grant's attention was immediately fixated on Aki, and Nate made his way into the kitchen, a pack of blood in hand. They could probably do with some alone time, and well, he needed to do this himself.

When he emerged with the pack of warmed blood, he was surprised that Aki and Grant were not tangled on the sofa. Aki was still eating his noodles. Grant watched him closely but looked up as Nate walked toward the study. "Do you want help?"

"No." Had that been too sharp? Nate ducked his head in apology. "No. I know Ben would hate anyone to see him in the condition he's in now. And I can handle him."

Grant nodded slowly. His yellow eyes were thoughtful. "Yell out if you need us."

Nate took a deep breath, his palm resting against the door to the hidden safe room. One breath wasn't enough to steady himself for what he was about to do, but it was all he had. The blood pack was warm in his hand, but it wouldn't stay warm for long. And Ben—

I can't leave him trapped like this a second longer than necessary. Hunger had a really bad effect on vampires, forcing through their facade of control. Maybe if they removed Ben's hunger, he would come back.

Nate pushed the image of Ben's fangs, stained and sharp, from his mind. *I have to try. If I don't...* He pushed the door open.

Ben must have heard him coming. As soon as the door opened, he leaped at Nate, trying to force his way through the doorway. He had recovered from their scuffle, his nails sharp as they dug into Nate's flesh.

Nate shoved Ben away. He turned quickly, slamming the door behind him.

Ben growled. He dropped into a fighting position, his teeth bared. If he'd possessed hackles they would be raised. His eyes were wild and fixed on Nate.

"It's all right. I'm not here to fight you." He wasn't sure Ben even understood the words, but maybe the tone would reach him. Nate held out the blood packet. "We got this for you. Yummy blood."

Ben's eyes flicked over the packet and back to Nate.

He doesn't recognize it? Taking his eyes off Ben even for a second felt like a huge mistake, but Nate needed to read the instructions printed on the back. *Remove sticker?* There was a flap on the front. Nate peeled it off, revealing two neat puncture marks that immediately began to ooze blood.

The metallic smell of blood filled the small safe room and had an instant effect on Ben. His hands clamped onto Nate's arm holding the blood pack, and he growled, fixing Nate with the stare he'd turned on Aki in the street.

Nate swallowed. *Now* he had Ben's attention. The vampire's stare wasn't enough to petrify him, but seeing that gaze without Ben's knowledge and fondness behind it was chilling...

His stillness seemed to satisfy the vampire. He bent his head to the packet, starting to lap up the blood. In no time at all, his mouth was sticky, blood dribbling down his chin, but he continued to suck ravenously.

Starving. Nate swallowed. The Final Register wasn't solitary confinement. It was a death sentence. Ben had been unable to get food for himself, and he must have become weaker and weaker until the vampire emerged...

Is he dead? The thought sent a wave of terror through Nate. If Ben had starved, then this was all there was left of him. He reached for Ben's hand, intending to feel for a pulse.

The vampire jerked away from him, snatching the blood packet away from Nate.

"Easy! I just wanted to check something." Nate took a step toward him, but Ben backed farther away. He kept his eyes locked on Nate, even as his mouth worked hungrily at the blood packet.

It was almost empty, but Ben showed no sign of stopping. "You want another one? I'll be right back." Nate slipped out of the safe room. This time, the vampire made no attempt to follow him out. Was the blood already having an effect?

Aki joined Nate in the kitchen as he began heating the second blood pack. "Please tell me that's not your blood."

Nate looked down at his arm. Ben had splattered him with blood in his feeding frenzy. "I'm fine. He wasn't exactly happy to see me at first, but once he figured out what the blood pack was, he was all over it."

Grant leaned in the doorway. "We need to talk about what we're going to do in the long-term. It's a criminal offense to harbor a revenant."

Nate spun around. "He's not a revenant! I know what it looks like, but he's still Ben!"

Aki placed his hand on Nate's arm. "You said it yourself earlier. The last thing Ben would want is to hurt people, and he hated being a vampire. If he has gone full vampire, maybe the best thing to do is honor his wishes."

And put him down? Nate swallowed back a wave of despair. *I can't! We can't give up on him!*

"I know it's a difficult thought." Grant watched Nate carefully. "Which is why we're here. We want to help you, Nate, and while we also care about Ben, we're not so involved with him that we have trouble seeing the broader situation."

Nate shook his head. "It's not that. You—" He couldn't tell them they didn't know the full story without telling them the full story. "Ben... Vampires aren't supposed to come back to life—be alive again, right? But even when Ben was living and going around in sunlight and everything, there were times when, if he was pushed, the vampire would come out."

"Wait. He's some kind of day-pire?" Aki glanced in the direction of the study.

"I don't know. And neither did he. Being a vampire was so traumatic for him that he wasn't exactly keen to explore it. But this—it doesn't prove anything. You've got to remember that he was a vampire before. And there was nothing wrong with his control then."

"His control, or Saltaire's?" Grant's voice was firm, even as his eyes were sympathetic. "I know it's hard to face this possibility, but if we want to help Ben, we can't shy away from the facts. Ben spent most of his time as a vampire in the company of a master vampire. That's not necessarily proof of his control."

When had Grant learned so much about Ben's vampire past? Nate looked to Aki, fidgeting with the bandage on his arm. Is that what they'd been doing instead of making out?

"Ben spent time as a vampire outside of Saltaire's control and he was in command of himself."

"But he'd been a vampire for over a year at that point, right? This... It's like the clock's rolled back and he's starting from scratch. He's not a vampire now. He's a revenant."

"He'll get control again." Nate turned back to the pot of water in front of him. The thermometer lay on the bench from where he'd been using it earlier. He checked the temperature and added a second blood pack.

"We can't be sure of that." Grant's voice was calm. "Very few revenants survive long enough to gain enough control to be recognized as vampires. Just because Ben's done it once is not necessarily an indication he can do it again."

"You don't know Ben." Nate took a deep breath, gripping the counter. "You don't know what he's capable of. He was leaving acorns for me to find up until a few days ago. Hell, he stole the Final Register! That's something you've got to plan for. Proof that he was in control of himself until really recently. He's just hungry and hurt."

There was a pause before Aki spoke. "You don't know that, Nate."

"Does he have a pulse?" Grant asked. "If he does, we can be sure."

Nate swallowed. So Grant's thoughts were going along the same lines his were. "I'll find out." He snagged the blood pack out of the pot and headed back to the safe room.

He stepped into the narrow room and looked around. "Ben? I brought you another." As his gaze took in the empty room, Nate's heart constricted. *He can't be gone!*

A movement called his attention too late. Nate looked up, only to be met by Ben's full weight. He stumbled, crashing to the ground. The blood pack spilled from his hand and Ben dived after it. He snatched it up. Instead of ripping off the sticker, he sank his fangs through the plastic, puncturing it, and sending a copper spurt through the air.

Fuck me. Nate rolled to a sitting position, his head ringing. Ben had literally gotten the drop on him. He looked up to where Ben had positioned himself above the doorway, using the narrowness of the room to suspend himself, waiting to ambush Nate. *That shows planning, right?* He leaned over, pulling the door shut.

Ben shifted as Nate moved, but stilled as soon as he realized he wasn't threatened. His mouth continued to work hungrily, lapping up the spilled blood.

Vampires are not tidy eaters. Nate tried to look past the blood. Was it his imagination or did Ben's face not look quite so hollow, his skin not quite as glassy? Nate rubbed his shoulders which had taken the brunt of Ben's attack. *Well, he's definitely stronger.* But did he have a pulse? He reached for Ben's wrist a second time.

Ben snarled. His fangs were even more horrifying with the blood smeared around his mouth.

Nate gulped.

"I COULDN'T TOUCH him." With Ben and his blood pack securely locked inside the safe room, Nate slumped at the kitchen table. "I tried, but he was having none of it." His shoulder ached and Nate suppressed the urge to rub it. He hadn't told Aki and Grant about Ben's ambush.

Grant frowned at Nate across the table. He looked as though he had questions he very much wanted to ask.

Aki plunked himself down at the table. "There's a much easier way to find out if he's alive or not. Just wait." He jerked his head toward the window. "It's going to be dawn soon."

Nate looked out the window above the sink. New Camden's night was broken by the light spilling out of countless apartment buildings, even at this late hour. He couldn't tell if that was dawn creeping above the horizon or light pollution. His throat constricted. All vampires, including revenants, revealed their true nature in the light of the sun.

Dawn would be Ben's salvation—or his death sentence.

SUNLIGHT FILTERED THROUGH the forest of plants on Nate's windowsill, producing a collage of green and light on his walls. The sight usually made him feel comforted, the plant within him responding to the sun's rays with a feeling of content. Now, he simply felt cold.

There was a knock at his door. "You awake?" Aki asked.

Nate bit his lip. Tempting as it was to fake sleep, he'd been lying in his room for hours without relief. Perhaps it was time to face his fear. "I'm awake."

"Grant and I wondered if you wanted us to check. I mean, this is going to suck for you no matter what, why not spare yourself having to be the one who checks?"

"No!" Nate sat up. "I'll do it."

"Suit yourself. But if you're going to do it, you want to do it sometime today?"

Nate peeled the blanket off himself. His skin felt clammy, and he'd spent most of the night bathed in a cold sweat. He pushed back his curtains, but the sun seemed unusually muted today.

The safe room smelled stale. Nate pushed open the door cautiously, braced for another surprise attack. Instead, Ben lay perfectly still in the center of the room. He was positioned on his back, his arms folded across his chest, medieval-crypt style. His eyes were shut. Without his mouth in motion, his face looked not just still but empty. The fact his cheeks had color and some flesh had returned to his bones did nothing to relieve Nate's dread. That didn't prove anything. Instead, he looked at Ben's chest. Was it rising? He couldn't tell.

He swallowed, wiping his sweaty palms on his T-shirt as he knelt beside Ben. His hand shook as he took Ben's wrist.

His skin was cold, as cold as the marble it resembled. Nate clamped his fingers around Ben's wrist.

For a long time, he felt nothing. *Maybe I'm not doing this right.* Nate shifted the position of his hand and tried again. This time he felt it, a faint beat under his thumb. *That could be my pulse.* How to know for sure? Nate hesitated, trying to dredge up the barely remembered first-aid course he'd taken in high school. He held his hand just above Ben's mouth. This time he felt a faint tickle.

"Aki? Can you get in here?"

Aki must have been right outside the door. He stepped over to Nate, looking down at Ben's unmoving form. "Well?"

"You tell me." Nate's fingers dug into his jeans. He had to be sure he wasn't imagining this.

"The things I do for you." Aki didn't quite pull off the complaint successfully. He crouched beside Ben, positioning his index and middle fingers on one side of Ben's throat.

Nate swallowed, his eyes focused on Aki's face. *Please—*

Aki's eyes widened. He placed his palm flat on Ben's chest. "No way."

"What's the matter?" Grant stuck his head in the door. "Is he—"

"Alive." Aki removed his hand. "This shouldn't be possible. Ben feels and looks like death, but he's breathing, he's got a pulse..."

Nate shut his eyes. *He's alive.*

NATE SAT ON the end of Ben's bed, watching as the late afternoon sunlight illuminated the shadows and hollows of the still figure lying on the bed. He reached out his hand, brushing Ben's hair out of his face. He'd given him a bath, washed his hair and put him in clean clothes. Through it all, Ben had not so much as stirred. He lay as limp as the corpse he resembled, even as Aki had carefully probed his injured arm.

"Broken," Aki said at last. "Or it was."

"What do you mean, 'or it was?'" Grant leaned against the far wall, his arms folded.

Nate resisted the urge to snap at him. Grant wanted to help. It wasn't his fault that Grant's help consisted of turning everything into a collection of facts that could be assembled into a case and argued over.

Aki lifted his gaze to Grant's. "I could swear I felt bone shifting beneath my fingers, putting itself back together."

"You mean he's healing?" Nate looked down at Ben, trying to find the scratches he'd acquired in their fight.

"Don't ask me! I'm training to work on humans. And I'm only a physical therapist, not a doctor! There's a really big difference!"

"You're doing fine," Grant assured him. "I'm pretty sure I read something about vampires having unnaturally heightened healing." As he spoke to Aki, his posture changed. Grant dropped his arms to his side, taking a step toward him.

Yeah, he's not subtle at all. Nate was willing to bet that if he hadn't been in the room, Grant's hand would have been on Aki's shoulder. He dropped his gaze down to Ben. It felt wrong for their friends to be flirting while Ben lay unnaturally still. *Like a corpse.*

Nate reached his hand to Ben's neck, seeking again the reassurance of his pulse. He needed the reminder. The longer Ben lay without stirring, the harder it was to believe that he was waking up from this.

The sound of a phone ringing made him flinch.

"Jesus." Aki took a deep breath, trying to pretend he hadn't started. "Answer it, Nate."

Nate put the phone to his ear. "Hello?"

"Done anything stupid today?" Gunn didn't make a habit of pleasantries, but this was next level direct.

Nate forced himself to breathe out. Gunn wasn't psychic and his ability to read emotion only worked in person. There was no way he knew about Ben. "Don't know about 'stupid'...but I haven't left the apartment building since last night."

"That's a start." Gunn sounded grudging. "The council's called an emergency meeting to decide what action they're taking to contain the Final Register situation, and they want to see you."

"What situation?" The sour taste was back in Nate's mouth. "You got it back, didn't you?"

"Yeah. Minus its one and only occupant." Gunn did not sound impressed. "Take that in combination with the fact we got a necromancer-style killing on our hands. How do you think that looks, Nate?"

Nate struggled to his feet. "Ben's got nothing to do with that death! And you know as well as I do he didn't deserve the Final Register!"

"Easy there, tiger. I've got no interest in you relating your ongoing obsession with the whiniest vampire. The council, on the other hand, are very interested in hearing what reasons you have for finding yourself in possession of the most powerful magical source in New Camden, failing to turn it over to the authorities, and promptly vandalizing the city's supernatural defenses."

Nate took a deep breath, trying to digest what Gunn had told him. "I'm in trouble."

"*Nate.*" Gunn's tone was almost gleeful. "I knew you wouldn't disappoint me. *Trouble.* Members of the council are out for your blood!"

"And I have to talk to them?" Nate dragged a hand over his face. Just what he didn't need.

"I've been charged with issuing you an official summons. You don't want to skip out on this. The council tends to take that really personal. You'd find yourself slapped with a warrant for your arrest."

"You've made your point. I'll come."

"Tremaine's already on her way to pick you up. Do us all a massive favor, and try to dress like you've got delusions of being a well-behaved citizen. I had to vouch for your character, and if you show up dressed like you were yesterday, my credibility is going to be in the dirt."

No one in the city believed in Gunn's credibility, not even Gunn. Another warning? "Anything else I should know?"

"Is Wisner's stepson around? It might help your case if you brought a friend that wasn't a complete train wreck."

"I heard that." Grant's reply was immediate. "I'll be there."

"I'll try to contain my excitement. And Nate, for the love of whatever you believe in, don't start anything on your way to the Registry." He cut the call before Nate could muster a defense.

Nate lowered the phone. He looked to Aki and Grant. If Grant's reply hadn't already indicated they'd heard everything, their worried expressions would have given it away. "So."

Grant stepped forward, putting a hand on Nate's shoulder. "The council might be unhappy, but they've still got to follow due process. Due process that was not applied in Ben's case. You'll be able to put that fact before them."

Nate took a deep breath. "Right." That was what they wanted—the chance to expose Wisner's machinations and remove the limitations on Ben. He looked down at the still figure on the bed. Leaving Ben felt beyond wrong, but what choice did they have?

Nate felt his throat tighten. None.

Chapter Eight

TREMAINE PULLED THE police car she was driving over to the side of the road. "Good luck."

Nate realized guiltily that his thoughts had drifted back to Ben. He looked out the window and saw she'd parked across the road from the Registry building. "You're not coming with us?"

She shook her head, motioning to the building. "You'll have a better time of it if I'm not with you. Department Seven isn't popular at the best of times, but now..."

Nate followed her gaze. A crowd had assembled outside the Registry, holding placards that said things like "Transparency not Invisibility," "We respect your laws. Respect our rights!" and "What else is the council hiding?"

"Protestors?"

"Can you blame people for being upset?" Grant leaned forward. "The Final Register was pushed through in secret to appease the fears of the council. How did anyone think it was a good idea?"

"Don't ask me," Tremaine shot back. "I was in the hospital. All I know about this is from my colleague's report."

Standing between the Registry and the chanting crowd were several individuals in dark blue. Nate caught a glimpse of Kenzies standing on the top steps, her expression rigid. "But Department Seven is staffed by supernaturals. Why would the protestors target them?"

"When tensions get high, people tend to jump to conclusions." Tremaine shrugged. "Department Seven is associated with the status quo. Basically, they don't trust us." She caught Nate's worried expression in the rearview mirror and smiled. "This is hardly the worst situation we've ever faced."

Despite the smile, Nate couldn't help but notice that she looked worn out. He swallowed, resting heavy palms on his knee. *This is my fault. I fucked up big time.* If supernaturals clashed with Department Seven, there would be no one free to deal with actual supernatural emergencies. *All I've done is make the city more dangerous.*

Grant drew in a sharp breath. "That's Wisner's pack."

Nate turned his head. Standing separately from the protesters, in a huddle down the street, was a group of men. Some looked familiar, but that might just have been their beards. "They came back?"

"And as soon as the sun sets, you can bet we'll have the central city vampires back as well." Tremaine sounded exasperated. "Like I said. Tensions are high and both groups smell an opportunity to manipulate the situation for their own gain."

Grant's growl was surprisingly loud in the small police car. "Our rights are too important to be collateral in a power struggle." He opened the car door. "Ready, Nate?" His expression was set. No need to ask if he was sure he wanted to do this.

Nate nodded. He looked to the third member of their group. Aki had been uncharacteristically silent the entire drive. "You don't have to come. Tremaine won't mind if you stay here."

"Are you kidding?" Aki scrambled out of the car. "I've been telling you for months that you should listen to me and stay out of trouble. Now I'm about to be proved right. No way I'm missing this."

Nate couldn't fight his smile. Aki's bluster hid a very real concern, and Grant had spent the entire car ride rehearsing arguments in Nate's defense. If he had to do this, he couldn't hope for better support.

He slid out of the car, looking up at the Registry building. In the daylight, it had all the weight of the church it so resembled, its stone walls and towering roof suggesting more than moral judgment.

Grant put an arm around Aki, maneuvering him so that he was screened by Nate on one side, himself on the other. "Let's go."

NATE STOOD BEHIND a podium, not "in the dock," but in every other respect he felt like he was being tried in a court of law. The room, with its wooden paneling, rows of seats around the wall, and long table with the members of New Camden's Council around it had all the weight of a courtroom. He tried to calm his quickened breathing, using the smooth wood surface of the podium to steady himself. *Deep breaths.*

"That's the mayor," Diya said in a low voice. She stood beside Nate's podium, dressed in a charcoal gray suit. She'd reined in her choice of accessories, limiting her use of bright color to red lips and nails. Nate was really glad that he'd followed Gunn's advice and worn a suit. "Diane Chandler. Career politician. Adept at escaping getting pinned down. Will side with whatever gets her most points with the public."

Nate saw a blonde woman with a hard jaw seated at the center of the table. Her face was a mask, and she studied Nate absently, listening to the rat-faced man leaning in to talk to her.

"Brownlee, New Camden's acting Head of Security after Wisner's ignominious dismissal," Diya continued. "On her other side is Roger Hartman, the Council's Advisor on Supernatural Rights, and I can tell you he is furious about this. He wasn't a fan of the Final Register to start with, arguing that it was open to exploitation of entirely this sort, and well, circumstances have pretty much proved him right."

The man was an ally? Nate felt some of his tension ease. Grant and Aki were seated on one of the benches surrounding the room, and Gunn had snarled at him in greeting as he'd arrived. He now sat with the councilors, at the very end of the table. His neighbor leaned away, trying to create as much distance between himself and Gunn as possible. Nate recognized New Camden's chief of police. "Everyone's here."

"Don't think about the crowd," Diya told him. "You'll get the chance to speak, and then the council can ask you questions. If you want advice, I'm right here."

He nodded slowly, his eyes continuing to search the crowd. He spotted a familiar shock of white hair in the front row and his eyes widened. "Is that Godfrey?"

"You're talking about the ARX representative? They've sent an observer and their legal team." Diya patted his arm. "Looks like they're ready to start. Remember, you haven't been formally charged with anything yet."

If that was meant to reassure him, it failed. Nate sucked in a deep breath, willing himself ready to meet his questioners.

Brownlee stood. "Your name?"

"Nathan Granger."

"Class Three Unknown?"

"Yes."

"Care to elaborate on that 'unknown'?"

Nate stared helplessly at the man. "If we knew, it wouldn't be 'unknown.'"

Someone snorted and tried to muffle the sound. Aki? Nate didn't feel quite so alone.

Brownlee scowled. "Your occupation?"

What was the point of this? "I'm a host at Century."

Brownlee's lip curled. "A host." He gave the members of the council a pointed look. "Hardly an occupation that would give someone insight into the supernatural."

The guy's attitude riled Nate. "You're wrong. You'd be surprised what people share when they're, uh, relaxed. I'd say my job is half sex-worker, half therapist."

A startled laugh rippled through the court. Brownlee's mouth tightened. "You're here to answer questions, Mr. Granger. Unless a question has been directed at you, stay silent."

Nate swallowed. "Yes, sir." He pressed his palms flat against the oak stand, seeking the reassurance of feeling wood under his hands.

"You are accused of endangering the safety of all New Camden's citizens by not declaring your possession of the Final Register, vital to the security of New Camden's supernatural defenses, and indeed vandalizing the same in order to help a man of dubious reputation elude justice." Brownlee paused dramatically. "You have nothing to say for yourself now, Mr. Granger?"

"That wasn't a question."

Again a snicker broke the tension of the courtroom.

Gunn leaned back in his chair, kicking his feet up on the table. "You tell 'im, Nate!"

Brownlee shot him a look of dislike, his face transforming into a dull red.

Before he could speak, Hartman turned to the mayor. "Perhaps a more informal style of questioning would better suit Mr. Granger?" As she nodded, he stood. "Mr. Granger, you know why you're here. Would you care to tell the council, in your own words, exactly what happened?" He reminded Nate of his fifth-grade teacher, kindly and encouraging. He'd never minded that Ethan wasn't an attentive student, encouraging both twins to do their best, whatever their best might be.

"Sure." Nate took another deep breath. "I'll try." He looked down at the podium surface. The polished wood showed clearly the grain of the tree it was made from, and the warmth of the wood reminded him of the acorns Ben had left for him even when he didn't remember him. "The last time I saw Ben was the night of the Full Moon. We were preparing the safe room for Grant." Nate stopped. Was this really his story to tell?

He looked across, finding Grant in the crowd. He nodded, his expression encouraging. Nate pressed on. "Wisner showed up to try and scare us out of helping Grant. He made a comment to Ben that was basically 'if you help him, you're going to regret it.' I didn't know then what that meant, but Ben did. Right after that, he got a call to come to the Registry. I knew he was having some problems with his application but I didn't know what."

"This would be his application for the revocation of his supernatural listing?" Hartman said. At Nate's nod, he gave the mayor a significant look. "I remarked at the time that Wisner seemed to be bringing undue pressure to bear on Mr. Hawick. There were several instances where Wisner overrode proper protocol for Hawick's hearing, including having him under surveillance by members of Wisner's own pack, bringing the time of Hawick's final hearing forward without informing him or myself, and finally forcing a decision on Hawick's case when only two of the three members required to reach a unanimous decision were present."

There was a snarl from the back of the room. "These allegations are slanderous!" Nate recognized Wisner's son, Ronald. "My father acted only in the interests of New Camden's safety."

"Your father's actions are a matter of public record," the mayor shot back immediately. "You'll be able to speak later." She looked back at Hartman. "At the time, Wisner claimed to have made an attempt to contact you, and to have sent a car to fetch you. It's now been proved no such attempt was made. That was blatant manipulation of the facts, and I want it on record that I cannot be responsible for a decision coerced in such circumstances."

The mayor was regretting her decision to add Ben to the Final Register? Nate breathed out. That had to be a good sign.

"Perhaps we should hear the rest of Mr. Granger's account?" Hartman suggested, fixing Nate with an encouraging smile.

It was easier to pretend he was speaking solely to Hartman. Nate slowly and carefully related the entire story, from Ben's disappearance to the lingering sensations of being haunted, to the mystery of the empty apartment, to his discovery of the Final Register, and his realization of just what had happened to Ben. "I had to do something. The thought of him being alone for so long...well, I panicked." Nate hung his head. "I wasn't thinking clearly. I wouldn't have ripped the page out if I'd known."

Brownlee sneered. "You're an expert on magic, Mr. Granger?"

"You know I'm not."

"A legal expert?"

Nate shook his head. "No, sir."

"Then what makes you think you are qualified to make legal judgments that impact the security of the entire city?"

"I don't think that at all—sir." Nate looked Brownlee square in his eyes. "I know I don't know much about due legal process and all the rest of it. But I know Ben." The thought of Ben's quiet strength gave Nate new determination. "I was there when the necromancer tried to use him for his plans. I've seen him living as a vampire and working for ARX and doing his best to find his place in the world on his own. And I know that if you'd seen how far he's prepared to go to keep people safe, you'd know, just like I do, Ben never belonged on the Final Register."

He looked around the room. The mayor's expression was thoughtful, while Hartman leaned forward. The chief of police looked grave, but the majority of the council leaned forward, interested.

Nate gripped the edge of the podium and continued. "Ever since we first met, Ben's primary concern has been helping others. He hated being a vampire, and he wanted nothing more than to put his past behind him and make a new life for himself. But the moment he knew Grant needed his help, he was prepared to sacrifice all of that and more to help Grant get the justice and freedom he deserves." He looked down, struggling to put all of Ben into words. "I don't know if I could have done that, knowing that I risked something like the Final Register. But Ben knew and he did it anyway. That's how little he cared about himself, and how much he believes in doing what is right. Knowing how hard he'd fought for other people's safety—well, you see why I had to help him. The Final Register... It's worse than a prison. It's total deprivation. I couldn't leave him like that a second longer than necessary."

Hartman stood again. "You are Mr. Hawick's primary heir?"

It took Nate a moment to understand the question. "You mean the will and everything? I don't know about that. I mean, he left me the apartment, but I don't want it."

Hartman's smile was kind. He spoke not to Nate but to his fellow council members. "If Mr. Hawick trusted Mr. Granger enough to leave him in control of his property, I think we can interpret that as Mr. Granger having power of attorney. Who better qualified than Mr. Granger to lodge an appeal on Mr. Hawick's behalf?"

"But he didn't lodge an appeal." Brownlee balled his fists. "He took matters into his own hands!"

That was unfair. "What else could I do?" Nate asked. "No one but me remembered Ben!"

Hartman held up a hand. "As Mr. Granger states, it is impossible to lodge an appeal on behalf of someone who doesn't exist. Which is why when we instated the Final Register, we came up with a series of checks and balances to ensure that no one was entered onto the Register without every precaution taken to ensure they had full right of appeal. In Mr. Hawick's case, these checks were discarded. Therefore, I consider that Mr. Granger acted properly in respect of the law."

Nate breathed out.

"Mr. Hawick remains an unknown!" Brownlee slammed his fist down on the table, making several councilors jump. "And the recent murder—"

"Took place while Mr. Hawick was entered on the Final Register." Hartman removed his glasses, polishing them on his sweater. "Surely you see that it would have been impossible for Mr. Hawick to commit a murder?"

Brownlee's lip curled. "He stole the Final Register, didn't he?"

"Removal of an inanimate object is possible under the terms of the Final Register. Interaction with another person is not. The only way Mr. Hawick could have been involved with the unfortunate death in the cemetery is if the deceased were already dead." Hartman's voice was mild and scholarly, but there was a stern note in it. Nate half expected him to turn back to the council and suggest that if they didn't want detention, they should quietly open their textbooks. "In any case, we are not currently discussing the issue of Mr. Hawick's character. What we need to discover is whether or not Mr. Granger was justified in his actions." The councilors shuffled the papers in front of them like children caught talking when they should have been working. "Now. Are there any further questions for Mr. Granger?"

Nate dug his fingers into the podium.

There was silence.

"In that case, I suggest, we hear from the next speaker."

As Diya took the stand in her capacity as Ben's caseworker, Nate walked on shaky legs to the benches. Aki and Grant squeezed along to make room for him on the bench.

Aki reached for his hand. "You did fine. There were a couple of moments where you looked like you were going to throw up, but you kept it together."

"Barely." Why had Aki mentioned throwing up? Now Nate was acutely conscious of the pressure settled in his stomach.

"Hartman's good," Grant said in an undertone. "He's not letting Brownlee employ scare tactics, and he shut down Ronald perfectly. But the real test is going to be when they get the stand."

Nate felt his heart lurch into his throat. "Ronald's going to speak?"

"Probably trying to protect their father's reputation by defending his actions in placing Ben on the Final Register." Grant's eyes were fixed on the interview unfolding before them. "I wouldn't worry about that. From the sounds of things, they don't have a legal leg to stand on."

But if there were no legal grounds for Ben to be placed on the Final Register, how had he ended up there? Nate looked at the councilors. Dressed crisply in suits, they looked like the epitome of respectable citizens. If any of them were supernatural, there was no sign of it. He didn't know how familiar they were with the laws governing the supernatural, or how sympathetic. *Wisner managed to use fear to get his way once. What is to stop it happening again?*

"You okay? You're looking like you're going to hurl."

Nate stood. "I'm gonna go get some air."

As he slipped out of the room, Kenzies came to meet him. "You can't leave, sunshine. You're being held until the council comes to a decision on your case."

"My case?"

She nodded, leaning against one of the stone pillars. "Whether to charge you with obstructing justice."

How did things go this wrong? Nate ran a hand through his hair. He looked up to see Kenzies watching him.

"You okay?"

Nate shook his head. "I am so out of my depth, it's not funny. I know I messed up, but... Is it bad that I would still do the same thing now?"

Kenzies shrugged. "While I do think you could have handled it less dramatically, what else could you do? If it was my mate in trouble..."

"But all the protestors—"

"They're upset the Final Register exists at all." Kenzies narrowed her eyes. "Wisner got his position by promising to take a hardline against supernatural offenders and then used his popularity to force the council to vote for his Final Register despite the objections of legal experts and supernatural activists. The mayor was able to keep it secret knowing that if word got out, we'd see exactly the kind of reaction that's going down now. This is nothing to do with you, everything to do with the council not liking the bed they've made for us to lie in."

Nate nodded slowly. That explained the mayor's anxiety to distance herself from her decision. He leaned against the stone wall. It had the strength of wood, but while it lacked wood's warmth, the cool stone was refreshing in the way he'd hoped a breath of air would be. "You sure? Gunn sounded pretty pissed at me."

"When is Gunn not annoyed?" Kenzies slapped Nate on his arm. "If you ask me, he was mainly furious at himself. After all, we got back the Final Register before the city's defenses were seriously threatened, and without harm to the Register."

"Why would Gunn be mad at himself?"

Kenzies snorted. "Should have seen this coming. The fallout was entirely predictable. If we'd had one inkling Ben existed, we'd never have allowed you to go off on your own once the Final Register was stolen."

Was that a good thing or bad? As Nate tried to work it out, the doors to the assembly room where the council's emergency hearing took place flew open. Wisner's son Ronald appeared, kicking and snarling as he was hauled from the room by Gunn and the stony-faced chief of police.

"I demand to be heard!" Ronald's face was mottled with rage. He bared his teeth, snarling like the wolf he became on the Full Moon. "You can't treat me like this! It's an insult!"

"Warned you that if you continued to interrupt we'd throw you out." Gunn was cheerfully vindictive. "Not our fault you are apparently incapable of following basic instructions." He gave Ronald a shove toward the door.

"You can't eject me! My father has a right to representation!"

"But not to interfere with the hearing of another individual." The last time Nate had met the chief of the police, he'd been trying to persuade him to turn Grant over to Wisner's justice. He was clearly not much happier with the current situation. "If you want to challenge today's proceedings, you'll have to do it like any other citizen. Through the courts."

Ronald glared at the two men. "You'll regret treating me this way. Werewolves are not to be treated like second-class citizens!"

"You want to be treated with respect? Stop acting like a first-class asshole." Kenzies's voice was cold. "Don't imagine you speak for all wolves with your demands. The majority of wolves in this city want nothing to do with you and your blatant fear-mongering."

Had he ever heard her swear before? Nate kept his face blank, trying to hide his shock.

Ronald's eyes widened. Apparently being told off by another werewolf, and a female one at that, was a shock to his entire existence. "You don't know what you're talking about! Look me in the eyes and say that!"

Kenzies stepped toward him, her eyes fixed on his. "I was protecting this city when you were still a pup, yapping at your father's heels. I've walked its streets while you were sitting within the walls of your compound, congratulating yourself on your plans for the city. I've fought vampire, I've fought wolf, I've fought witch, and sorcerer, and ghoul, and things you couldn't even name." Her voice was low, barely above a growl.

Nate felt his skin prickle with every word. He couldn't take his eyes off Kenzies. It was like watching someone peel off a mask to reveal an animal beneath. Gunn was silent, and the Police Chief stood still, his hand resting on the holster of his gun.

Ronald's eyes bulged. He desperately wanted to flee, but he couldn't move, couldn't look away.

Kenzies continued to advance. "I've shed my blood for the people of New Camden. I've laughed with them. I've cried. They're my pack. All of them, in all their ugliness, in all their fear, in all their glory, and their fight, their triumphs, and tragedies. And until you're part of that struggle, you can't speak for it." She jabbed Ronald in the chest with her finger. "Howl at the moon and tell your wolves how strong you all are all you want, but you won't ever be master of this city. Are we clear, little wolf?"

Ronald bared his teeth. "You're nothing! A bitch from a pack without a proper leader—"

Kenzies's snarl was vicious and deep. "Are we clear?"

Ronald stumbled backward. He dropped his gaze, his breath coming in heaving gasps. Without looking at any of them, he turned, slinking out of the Registry doors.

"He won't be coming back again tonight, sir." Kenzies's tone was her usual crisp report. She looked after Ronald, her arms held tight at her side. Her fists clenched and unclenched.

"Nicely done." Gunn looked pointedly at Jacobs. "Still think having a werewolf on the payroll is a liability?"

"Officer Kenzies's handling of the situation is commendable." Jacobs tone was curt. "But we've still got the problem of crowd control to deal with." He looked toward the door Ronald had just exited. "It's not long until sunset."

"If we can wrap Nate's case up before then—and with the blowhard ejected, that shouldn't be difficult—the crowd'll have no reason to stick around." Gunn dug a tattered pack of cigarettes from his pocket.

"You know as well as I do that Granger is only part of the problem." Jacobs eyed Gunn's cigarette with dislike but made no comment. "They're here because of the Final Register."

Nate felt incredibly unnecessary. "Should I go?"

If anyone heard him, they didn't respond.

Gunn flicked his lighter. "Funny that. It's almost like the crowd wants to know they're assured of a fair trial and the protections afforded to them by the law."

Jacobs took a step toward Gunn. "All right already, you've made your point! But what else were we to do? The necromancer was claiming fresh victims every day, and the city was terrified. If we hadn't done something, the army would have been called in." Snapping at Gunn? Surely Jacobs knew it only added to a *lemur*'s power.

"You don't have the necromancer as an excuse now. And what you do now counts big time." Gunn breathed out smoke. "Think very carefully, Jacobs. This time the city is watching."

Without a word, Jacobs marched back to the hearing.

"You should go," Gunn said. His voice was dispassionate. For a moment, he didn't even sound like Gunn.

Nate blinked. "You mean me?"

"Things were getting really interesting." Gunn's smile was pointed. "Trust me on this. You don't want to miss it."

Nate took a step before he realized Gunn wasn't following. "Aren't you coming?"

Gunn shook his head. "I can feel the room from here."

Nate slid back on the bench next to Aki to find Jacobs on the stand. "Where's Grant?" he whispered.

"Shush." Aki waved Nate to be silent. "I'm listening."

"For the security of the city, our laws have to be enforced and seen to be enforced," Jacobs told the gathering. "No one can be above the law. No human, no supernatural citizen—no matter how good their intentions. Mr. Granger acted in the way he thought right. He is charged with breaking our laws, but his actions have brought to light a deeper injustice. Does the result of his actions justify his means? That question will be put to the vote. I don't propose to tell you how to vote, council. What I will say is this." Jacobs took a deep breath. "Outside the Registry we have several hundred citizens gathered here to see justice done. We have a duty to them, to the rest of the city, to the world, to see that we make the right decision. We cannot afford to let our own biases, our allegiances, even our past mistakes influence us now. Whatever decision we make, we must be prepared to stand by it. For the good of all our citizens." He stepped down.

Brownlee looked to the podium. "Is that the last?"

"There is one more speaker." Hartman said. "With the mayor's permission, Grant Ferrars wishes to take the stand."

It was just as well Ronald had already been thrown out. The reaction from the remaining wolves was immediate and intense.

The mayor grabbed the ceremonial mallet, banging it on the table to drown out the howls. "Silence! Anyone who continues to disrupt the hearing will be thrown out!"

"Mr. Ferrars is not a legal expert," Brownlee said. "Why should we listen to him?"

"He has been in the unique position of having the laws created for New Camden's protection manipulated against him," Hartman said. "And he was acquainted with Mr. Hawick. I think his perspective should be heard."

"Let's hear him then." The mayor leaned back in her chair, folding her arms.

If Grant was rattled by his reception, it didn't show on his face. He took the podium as if making a speech at a moment's notice was simply how he rolled. "I'll be brief. You already know me. You heard me state my case against my stepfather's abuse of the law he was elected to uphold in this very room, and you saw blatant evidence that New Camden's laws governing the supernatural are, although groundbreaking in many respects, still open to abuse." Grant's gaze travelled across the room, his expression grim. "Today you learned that

I was not my stepfather's only victim. The chief of police has made a strong statement in defense of the integrity of our laws. For the security of our city, it's necessary that our laws be enforced. Before we enforce our laws, however, we must first ask this. Are they just?"

The room was silent.

"When the might of the city is directed in an unjust vendetta, not only its officials, but its laws and the integrity of its officers are called into question." Grant leaned forward. "You saw yourselves how the media, the police force, and the law was arraigned against me by my stepfather. It was all legal, despite the fact there was no basis to his allegations. There were no checks. There was no appeal. The system is flawed. Until it is fixed, enforcing it sends a clear message to New Camden's supernatural citizens that they have no right to protection, no right to safety, in short—no rights." Grant paused to catch his breath. "Is that the message you want the supernatural citizens who have come here today, exercising their right to peaceful protest, and demonstrating their faith in the very system that excludes them, to hear?"

He stepped down from the podium.

The hush grew louder. In a moment, someone was going to clap—

Brownlee stood. "And that concludes the speakers. The council will adjourn for the final decision on Mr. Granger's case."

"HOLY CRAP, GRANT." As the last councilor filed out and the room erupted into discussion, Aki sidled up to Grant. "Where were you hiding that?"

Grant turned away from his conversation with Diya. "Hiding what?"

"That air of authority." Aki placed his hand on Grant's arm, deliberately stroking it. "When you get legal, you get *hot*."

Grant's face flooded pink. "Supernatural rights are something I feel strongly about. I couldn't not say anything. Not after what Ben did for me."

Nate turned aside, wanting to give them privacy. As he did, he caught Diya's eye. Her smile was rueful. "I guess we'd better take a rain check on the coffee."

He'd entirely forgotten. "Yeah. Sorry."

She shook her head. "No need. It's good to know that Ben has your support. He's a remarkable person."

"He really is," Nate said fervently.

"Is it true he's missing?"

Nate swallowed. This felt all sorts of wrong. "Yeah. I guess—"

Diya held her hand up. The council was filing back into the room.

"No way they've reached a decision," Aki said, his arm around Grant. "Is there?"

Nate felt his chest constrict. He had a really bad feeling about this.

The mayor climbed the podium. "We've reached a conclusion. In light of the serious flaws in Mr. Hawick's assessment and hearing, we cannot in due conscience find Mr. Granger guilty of the charges against him. We wish to warn him of the dangers of acting hastily and suggest that he acquaint himself thoroughly with the city's legal process."

Nate tried to make sense of the words he'd just heard. *I'm not being punished?*

Aki whooped. "You're okay!" He threw his arms around Nate.

Nate put his arm on Aki's shoulder, but he couldn't make himself smile. The pressure in the room hadn't abated.

The mayor shot a dirty look their way and continued. "The council will now consider the case against Mr. Hawick. In the meantime, Hawick is to be considered a potential danger, and the police have recourse to all powers they consider necessary to secure him. In addition, I hereby authorize a citywide advisory to the effect that anyone harboring Hawick or concealing knowledge of his whereabouts will be considered guilty of criminal behavior with intent to obstruct justice."

"But that's all wrong!" Nate took a step toward her. "Ben's the victim here! You're treating him like—like he's a criminal!"

The mayor looked directly at him. "Mr. Hawick has been subjected to a period of extreme duress and his mental state is unknown. In view of his past and the fact that he has resorted to extreme measures detrimental to the safety of the city, making every effort to secure him as quickly as possible is in the best interests of Mr. Hawick and the city. We will resume our deliberations in one hour."

Ben, a wanted criminal. Nate swallowed, remembering the manhunt that had been launched to find Grant. *This is a disaster.*

Chapter Nine

NATE HELD HIS phone to his ear, his back turned to the people still milling around the Registry entrance. Outside he could hear the crackle of a loudspeaker as Chief Jacobs tried to persuade the crowd it was in their best interest to leave before sunset. *Come on, Ben. Pick up!*

There was a click as the call transferred to the recorded message. "The number you have dialed is not—"

Nate cut the call and immediately hit redial.

A hand reached out, covering his phone. "Just go home, Nate."

He looked up to see Grant's eyes on him, steady and sympathetic. "I can't do that. Ben's hearing's about to start. If I'm not here, how's that going to look to people?"

"After your performance this afternoon, I don't think anyone on the council has any doubts about how you feel about Ben." Aki rolled his eyes. "Ugh. Hearing you talk about him was enough to make me want to date him. And I have *actual* standards."

"We'll be here," Grant said simply. "And you'll do more good *at home.*"

Nate felt his throat tighten and he nodded. Grant and Aki weren't saying it, but like Nate, they were worried about Ben. Was he still asleep? Had he woken up to find himself once again alone and abandoned? "You'll call me if anything happens?"

Aki waved him away impatiently. "You'll get all the exciting updates. Councilor yawns. Aki almost falls asleep but doesn't."

"Thanks." Nate thumped him on the back and turned for the door.

On the way he passed a cloud of tobacco smoke. Nate paused, waving a hand in front of himself to avoid breathing in as much of the fumes as possible. "Gunn? Can I go home now?"

Gunn exhaled slowly. "Tough call. Is the frustration holding you here would cause worth the aggravation of putting up with your presence?" The dim light in the Registry was suddenly augmented as, with a neon crackle, the streetlights came on. Gunn's eyes narrowed. "Sunset."

"What's so bad about sunset?"

"Just wait." Gunn gripped his current cigarette, turning to face the door.

Nate turned with him, wondering what the problem was. And then he felt it. An impending disaster, drawing closer to the building, as inexorable as death itself. One by one, every hair on the back of his neck stood up, alerting him to the building pressure in the air. It was like a hand reaching down from above, intent on crushing the life out of all of them.

Nate heard a hush outside as the thing approached and saw a blankness form on the face of the police officer stationed beside the door. The man reached out an arm to open the door, stepping back to let Saltaire enter.

The vampire didn't even glance at him. Did he know he'd just commanded the man to open the door for him? Nate couldn't tell. *Whether he's aware or doesn't care, it's the same.* Nate took a deep breath, fighting to push back the need to placate this powerful force in human shape. *Saltaire's influencing everyone around him.*

How on earth did I miss this? It was impossible to think that he'd spent time in the man's presence and not been aware of the command he'd wielded. *What has changed?* It hadn't been this bad when Saltaire had made his unannounced appearance to quell the riot. *Is this Saltaire with the gloves off?*

A grating sound beside him called his attention to Gunn, his body wound tighter than a guitar string. He ground his teeth and stalked forward, brandishing his cigarette like a weapon. "You're too late. The Final Register's been restored to its place as power source for the Register, and Nate's been cleared of criminal wrongdoing. Your own legal team was there to observe, and they can tell you there was no undue influence, nothing you can object to."

No undue influence? Was that why Gunn had chosen to wait in the lobby?

Saltaire looked at Gunn coldly. "I am merely here to observe." He raised his head, finding Nate unerringly, even in the shadows of the Registry building. "Is it true that Bennet survived?"

"Yes." Nate heard his own words before he realized he'd spoken. *Fuck me!* That was the worst of Saltaire. He had a way of making people do what he wanted. "No thanks to you." Taking a deep breath, Nate stared back at the master vampire. If Saltaire thought Nate had forgotten that he left the both of them for dead, he was very much mistaken.

Saltaire's eyes rested on Nate the same way he'd look at a fly that had landed on his plate. Nate half expected to be swatted aside, but instead, Saltaire spoke. "He did not have the qualities necessary for survival in the night world. I allowed my fondness for his father to blind me to that fact. It would be better if he had died." He moved down the corridor toward the assembly room.

Fury rose in Nate, sharp and immediate. He shook his head, trying to rid it of the sense of heaviness that clung to his thoughts, dulling his senses and making his body feel like concrete. "That's not true!"

Saltaire stopped. He looked back over his shoulder at Nate.

"That's not true." Nate fought the urge to lick his lips. He was not going to show weakness in front of Saltaire. "You held Ben up against a measure he could never achieve. You didn't see him for who he was. You saw him for who he wasn't. And when you didn't succeed in bending him entirely to your will, you discounted him entirely!"

"You speak of things you have no knowledge of." The words were talons on stone, ancient and powerful. Nate saw those people still in the corridor flinch back. "You would be wise to curb your impudence. I owe you no favors, Nathan Granger, and I have not forgotten your role in Bennet's ill-judged rebellion."

That's utterly wrong! Nate tried to protest and found that his mouth didn't work. As he battled his own locked muscles, he was aware of Saltaire turning aside again. *Fucking master vampires!* No wonder Gunn hated the guy so passionately—

A mild cough announced a considerably more benign presence. "I thought I detected your presence. I've made notes for you." Godfrey passed Saltaire a file. "My summary of the afternoon session." As Saltaire began to flip through the pages, Godfrey turned to Nate. "Congratulations, Nathan. I must say, I was pleased by the decision. A well-deserved result."

"Thank you." His voice was still hoarse, but somehow Godfrey took the edge off Saltaire's existence. Nate discovered he was able to swallow. "Here's hoping Ben is just as fortunate."

Godfrey tilted his head as he studied Nate. "You're worried? From the impassioned defense you delivered in Ben's favor, I'd have thought that you, surely, would have no doubts about the outcome."

"I'm sure of Ben. But after what happened with Grant, I know innocence alone is no defense. And...I don't know. I got a weird vibe from some of the council members. Almost like this is personal. That Ben's not being judged on who he is, but something else entirely."

The sudden blaring of a phone made him jump. Gunn, scowling, pulled out his phone. "Tremaine. This had better be worth it," he snarled as he turned aside to take the call.

Nate was startled to remember there were people present besides Saltaire. He tugged at his collar, wondering if Gunn had found any ammunition in Nate's unguarded reply to Godfrey, his gaze roaming across the room. As he did, he noticed how quiet the corridor was. People slowed down as they stepped into the hall. Those who had been there the longest had a glassy look in their eyes and slack jaws. *Is this Saltaire's effect in person?*

As Nate watched, the mayor strode down the corridor, returning from a briefing with her aides. As she saw Saltaire, she blanched, wavering in the doorway of the room. She caught herself almost immediately, her face stiffening as she steeled herself to meet him. "Back from Europe early, I see."

"Your Honor." Saltaire inclined his head just enough to meet the minimum requirements of courtesy. "I had some interesting reports from the city. I thought it best to return."

The mayor sneered. "Here to protect your protégé, I suppose."

"I am here merely in the role of observer."

"Very likely." The mayor squared her shoulders, seemingly finding fighting Saltaire's presence an uphill battle. "Well he will be found and held accountable for his actions. New Camden has no future so long as it is shackled to its past."

Saltaire's expression didn't so much as flicker. "The past is New Camden's foundation. Take it away and you are left with a very precarious basis for a city."

"Don't talk to me about precarious." The mayor drew herself up. "This Final Register debacle has shown only one thing. New Camden has made a serious error in investing all of its magical defenses in one method. I intend to make sure that the city never again finds itself reliant on one source of power." She deliberately walked past Saltaire down the corridor to the assembly room, her aides chasing after her.

Saltaire looked after her. His gaze was flat. If the mayor had offended him, he gave no sign of it. With the file Godfrey gave him in hand, he prepared to follow her.

"Why didn't you say anything?"

Saltaire's head swiveled back to Nate, his expression sour. "Excuse me?"

"You heard me." Focusing on his anger made it easier to push past the overwhelming dread surrounding the man. "The mayor basically insinuated Ben was still under your protection. That makes him a target for anyone with a grudge against you. If you tell them that you've parted ways, then he'll be able to be judged without his association with you."

Godfrey tried frantically to catch Nate's eye. "Perhaps we should discuss this another time—"

Saltaire held up a hand and his servant fell silent. He looked at Nate. "I cannot do that."

"Of course you can."

"For me to state that Bennet has chosen his own way implies my belief in his ability to carve a path for himself without posing a risk to the citizens of New Camden. I cannot vouch for his success outside of my command."

Nate felt as if he was arguing with a wall. "But—"

"I know how Bennet struggled to come to terms with his vampire nature, even under my control. I cannot in good conscience vouch for his ability to retain that control surrounded by all the temptations of New Camden and without even the slightest supervision. Once we find Bennet, I will request that he be returned to my keeping."

The way he spoke. It was as if the matter was entirely settled. It took all Nate's willpower to form his next sentence. "Don't you see how wrong this is? Your influence—it warps people! Controlling them—it's like bonsai! Yeah, you're making nice, neat, controllable plants, but at what cost? You're reducing them to nothing, when they should be forests!"

Saltaire's eyes glittered dark. "To continue your most novel metaphor, restraint is sometimes an aid. Think of the sprawling bean. Without the support of a frame, it cannot attain any heights at all. No, I know what is best for Bennet."

Nate swallowed. "But your way will kill him!"

Again Saltaire's eyes glittered. "Better that than Bennet becoming a danger." He walked down the corridor.

Nate shut his eyes. He swayed on his feet, feeling suddenly dizzy, as if he'd lost a lot of altitude suddenly. He wouldn't have been surprised if his ears had popped.

"Whoa. That was the vamp-daddy?"

After the conversation with Saltaire, Aki was his own special kind of whiplash. Nate turned to him, discovering that his neck and shoulders were a mass of aches. "Yeah. That's Ben's sire."

"You really did not exaggerate the nope-factor." Aki shook his head. "I didn't even hear what you guys were saying and I wanted to curl up and die—and not in the fun way."

"There's a fun way?" Nate noticed Aki craning his neck as he looked around the corridor. "Looking for something?"

"I thought that if the big bad vamp was here, maybe Hunter would be here too."

Nate winced. He'd almost forgotten about Aki's crush on Saltaire's second-in-command. "Stick with Grant," he said shortly. "I'm going home."

"Not so fast." Gunn ended his call with Tremaine. "Cancel your plans for tonight people. We got another murder."

THIS TIME THE victim was a woman. She was in her midthirties, well dressed in a sleek skirt and puffy, exaggerated sweater. Her blonde hair was cut short. Her skin looked very pale, though whether that was a result of her death or a side effect of being entirely drained of blood, Nate didn't know, and he didn't really want to ask.

I'm going to be sick. He pinched his arm, hoping that the pain would take his mind away from his rolling stomach. The victim lay on a magical circle, and Nate didn't need to be an expert to know there was a distinct resemblance between it and the circle the first victim had been found in. Just like the one Peter had carved into Nate's own skin. *There's no doubt about it. Peter is back.*

Gunn finished prowling the side street the woman had been found on and stood next to Nate, looking down at the dead woman. "A vampire combined with necromancy. Yeah, great job giving Ben the ability to run around and interact with the world again."

Nate shuddered. "What do you mean, vampire?"

"Come on. It's obvious." Gunn motioned to the victim. "Take a closer look. It's fine. The forensics crew has already done their thing."

Nate bit his lip. It wasn't the fear of forensics holding him back from examining the body.

Fortunately, Kenzies came to his rescue. She crouched beside the woman, pulling the puffy neck of her sweater down so that Nate could see the two puncture marks at her neck. "Vampire," she reported. "Not that it wasn't obvious from the fact our victim is entirely bloodless."

Nate swallowed. "That doesn't mean it's Ben. There's a ton of vampires in New Camden." And how many of those vampires knew about Peter's experiments combining the power of a vampire with necromancy? "Kenzies, you know Ben's scent. Does this even smell of him?"

"I'd have to get a second smell of him," Kenzies said slowly. "But the entire scene has been doused with wolfsbane. It's very hard for me to smell anything right now."

"There you go." Gunn waved his cigarette at Nate. "Ben knows about Kenzies's nose. He's smart enough to take precautions."

"But so is Peter." Nate forced himself to speak through the feeling of nausea. "Peter was an ARX agent. He'd also know about Kenzies and what precautions to take."

"Peter's dead," Gunn informed Nate. "If this is him, he's got no need to disguise his actions."

"He could be hoping for the element of surprise, or maybe—" Nate felt dizzy. Surely not? "Maybe he's hoping Ben will take the blame for all this."

"You forget Bennet was on the Final Register. No one remembered him."

"But does the Final Register even work on the dead? I mean, I know vampires are on it, but Peter—he's not currently classified, right? So if he has come back..."

"It's just possible," Kenzies allowed.

"But only just. And why do mental gymnastics to arrive at Peter when we've got the obvious answer right in front of us?"

Nate felt a wave of despair. "Did anyone here see anything?" He looked to the surrounding houses. It was a nice suburb, with neat homes and tidy lawns. The curtains were all resolutely drawn, as if that was enough to ward off New Camden's dangers.

"So far we're drawing a blank, petal. The officers going door to door to see if anyone heard or saw anything suspicious are coming up blank. Until Tremaine called it in, they had no idea anything had happened."

"Where is Tremaine?" Nate looked around.

"She wasn't feeling well. Made her report to the first officers to arrive on scene and took herself home."

Nate couldn't blame her. He was feeling more than a little sick himself. Drained of all blood, the woman's skin had a waxy look. It reminded him of the way Ben had looked when he found him in the ally, after a month of starvation. The memory of Ben tearing into the blood pack flashed into his mind and Nate shuddered. Ben was hungry. But hungry enough to kill?

No! I can't—don't believe it! Nate took a deep breath, trying to find something to focus on. Instead, he looked up to see that Gunn's gaze was fixed on him.

"That's a very interesting cocktail of emotion you're mixing there," Gunn said slowly. "I can taste horror, repulsion, and a good amount of fear. And since we both know you're invulnerable to these creatures, I'm going to guess that fear is directed toward a certain fanged individual we both have the misfortune of knowing."

"There's lots of reasons I could be afraid for Ben," Nate said stoutly. "With his hearing underway, the last thing he needs is to be accused of a crime he didn't do by a Department Seven officer with an obvious vendetta against him."

"It's been twenty minutes," Kenzies reported. "And no signs of an appearance. With the amount of wolfsbane in the air, I'm not surprised. If our perp is out there, no way he's going to be able to pick up Nate's scent."

Nate gave her a startled glance. "Wait. *I'm* bait?"

Kenzies shook her head. "Well, you're not here for your forensics knowledge, honey."

Nate felt for the support of Gunn's car, parked haphazardly half on the road, half on the pavement. *If I'm bait, it's bait for Ben.* "Ben didn't do this. I know he didn't."

Gunn kept his eyes fastened on Nate. "Where is he?"

It took all of Nate's willpower to keep his eyes from widening. "Um, what? You know I don't know."

"That's a really interesting reaction for someone who doesn't know." Gunn's nostrils flared. "I think we need to pay you another visit, Nate."

No! The reaction was immediate. Ben couldn't be discovered now!

Before he even had time to process it, Nate watched a triumphant grin break out across Gunn's face. "Bullseye. Kenzies, you remain here. I'm going to get me a vampire."

NATE HAD NEVER imagined wanting to spend more time in a car with Gunn, but the drive to his apartment was far, far too short. He jogged up the apartment steps after Gunn. "You're wrong about Ben. I know you are!"

"Forgive me if I don't find your hunches convincing." Gunn pressed the call button for the elevator. "You're infatuated with the guy. You want to talk about biases, start there."

"Maybe the reason I like Ben so much is because he's a genuinely nice guy. Did you ever think of that?"

Gunn snorted as he stepped into the elevator. "Newsflash, Nate. There are no nice guys in New Camden." His eyes widened and a grin broke out on his face. "Speak of the devil. That's saved us some time."

Nate whipped around. *Ben!* This was the worst that could happen!

But the reception area was entirely empty. As Nate looked up and down the room, wondering what he'd missed, the elevator doors shut behind him. He pressed the up button, but it was too late. Gunn had a head start.

I know he has no morals, no qualms, and will totally kick a guy when he's down. And I still fall for it ever time! Nate pushed the fire door open and ran up the seven flights of stairs to Ben's apartment.

By the time he reached the top, he was breathless and his knees shook. He staggered through the open door to Ben's apartment, sagging against the sofa as he looked around. "Gunn?"

There were sounds from the study. Presumably Gunn was investigating the safe room.

Sucking in a fresh breath of air, Nate made his way to the master bedroom. He pushed open the door with a feeling of trepidation.

But where he'd last seen Ben lying on the bed was only a slight hollow. *Gone.* Nate looked from the bed to the open window and felt a stab of confusion. *Why?* And more to the point, where was Ben now? *He can't have left.*

"Interesting that you'd come here first." Gunn spoke directly behind Nate's shoulder. "He's been here, then?"

Nate stepped back to face him. "I figured this would be the first place he came. He's got strong associations with this room."

Gunn shot Nate a suspicious look. He threw open the closet and looked under the bed, but he didn't need to search the room to know Ben wasn't there. "If you warned him…"

"How could I? You sat next to me the entire drive here. I needed both my hands just to keep myself in my seat."

Gunn gave Nate a sharp look and stepped toward the window.

Nate dug his fingers into his arm, but it was too late to ward off the alarm he felt.

"Interesting. You got a special reason to be protective of these plants, Nate?" Gunn leaned on the windowsill, looking down at the fire escape

"They're cool plants," Nate said immediately. "Aki's constantly on my back to get rid of them. I don't need anyone else telling me they're a fire hazard."

Gunn snorted, shutting the window. "Tell Grant to keep his windows shut when he goes out. Yeah, the apartment stinks of wolf, but he's got to maintain a secure place to stay as part of his independence contract."

Was it possible that Grant's presence in the apartment had drowned out any scent of vampire? Nate followed Gunn back into the living room, doing a quick mental summary of all the places Ben had been. Once daylight had arrived and Ben had sunk into his sleep, Nate had cleaned the safe room out. Ben's old, bloodstained clothing was in the trashcan under the kitchen sink—

Gunn immediately turned into the kitchen.

Fuck me. Nate wiped his palms on his jeans and took a firm grip on himself. *Think. There's got to be a reason for the clothes, a good reason. Old clothes maybe that I'd kept to use as cleaning rags—*

Gunn stuck his head out the kitchen door. "There a reason you keep your fridge full of blood, Nate?"

"I, uh. What?"

Gunn held up a blood pack. "I find this really interesting for a vegetarian."

"I'm not vegetarian. I eat meat and stuff just fine. Just not when I've been doing a lot of plant stuff." Nate shook his head. "Anyway. This isn't my fridge. It's Grant's. And you really want to say that a werewolf might not want blood on hand?"

Gunn looked down at the packet and raised it to his nose. Whatever he found, it wasn't what he wanted. He threw the blood pack onto the table and started for the door.

Nate hastily returned the pack to the fridge before jogging after Gunn. "Where are you going now?"

"You think I would forget that your apartment is right beneath Ben's?" Gunn shook his head. "I mean to find him, Nate."

Oh god. It was the only other place Nate could think Ben might be. He hurried down the stairs, pushing past Gunn to reach the apartment first. He used his plant magic to call to the wooden door to unlock itself, rather than waste precious moments fumbling with his keys. "Ben!" He hurried through the living room, not waiting to turn on lights. He threw open the door to his bedroom, scanning the room for any sign of Ben.

His plants rustled as the breeze caused by the door ruffled their leaves, but that was the only movement in the room. Nate looked at the window which connected to the fire escape that led to Ben's bedroom. *I was sure—*

The light flickered on. "Interesting reaction."

Nate did his best to summon indifference as he turned back to Gunn, but it was so hard. The day had taken a heavy toll on him. "You know how I feel about Ben. Why is it any surprise that I want to find him?"

"If you want what's best for Ben, you'll hand him over to the department." Gunn's gaze summed up Nate's room, pausing as they came to rest on his plant collection.

Nate's hands balled into fists. "So he can be put on the Final Register again? There's no way I'm going to let that happen. You saw the mayor, heard her conversation with Saltaire. She as good as said that she's going to see Ben punished to get at Saltaire. And you're just as bad!"

Gunn shook a cigarette out of the packet in his pocket. "It's my guess that it's very unlikely anyone'll be using the Final Register again. There's talk of a high court injunction to determine the very legality of its existence, and we all know how those things drag out. Until it's settled, the Final Register will be off-limits."

Nate swallowed. "You really think so?" At Gunn's nod, he let out a breath, sitting on the end of his bed. "What do you think will happen?"

"Ben's hearing takes place. He's examined, found to be a potential risk to the city, but no one can prove intent." Gunn shrugged. "Best case scenario, he founds a police department integral to the security of the city, making himself so valuable that they can't get rid of him, no matter how much they want to."

Nate tilted his head. "Is that what you did?"

"Worst case scenario," Gunn continued, "they remand him into protective custody. There's only one person in the city strong enough and stable enough to do that."

Nate gulped. "Saltaire?" At Gunn's nod, he dug his fingers into the blanket draped across his bed. "But that would be just as bad as the Final Register. Maybe worse!"

"Nothing's worse than the Final Register, Nate. And Ben stuck with Saltaire for an entire year. He can do it again. Given the choice between the Register and Saltaire, I can tell you now which one he'd choose."

Nate winced. "Ben told me the reason he was applying for humanity was because if he got his supernatural status removed, Saltaire wouldn't come after him. Implying that Saltaire would come for him if he was supernatural."

Gunn paused flicking his lighter to nod slowly. "It's likely. Saltaire's not exactly a model of respecting other people's autonomy. Chances are he'd see Ben's defection as a sign he'd lost his mind and needed to be reined in. For the good of the city, of course."

"So if Saltaire gets custody of Ben, basically, he's as good as dead."

Gunn's grin was immediate. "And we could slap him with a murder charge! Good thinking. Guess that optimism of yours has its uses."

Nate stared at him. "But Ben would be dead."

"Glass half-full. I know, I get it." Gunn waved him aside. "I'm going to continue the search. I'd take you with me, but we both know you're a massive liability where Ben is concerned. Stay here, and for the love of whatever you consider holy, don't do anything, Nate. Any. Thing."

Nate trailed after Gunn to the door. "If you find him, call me? Please? I really want to see him." His voice cracked on the last words. Wherever Ben was, Nate needed to know he was all right.

"Spare me." But Gunn hesitated. "Sure. Why not? We could all use the entertainment."

It was as good as he was going to get. Nate decided not to risk annoying Gunn with a thank-you. He shut the door. After a moment's deliberation, he made his way to his room, opened the window, and climbed out onto the fire escape.

He sat on the step, feeling the slight evening chill echoed in the metal beneath him. He breathed in the night air, the soft scent of his plants mingling with burnt rubber and exhaust. After being in close quarters with Gunn, it tasted sweeter than honey.

Sitting still was hard. He wanted nothing more than to make his way down the stairs, looking for Ben in the shadows and hidden alleys of New Camden. What had possessed him to leave? Had he been tipped off to Gunn's presence? Had he heard about the warrant for his arrest and turned himself in? Nate pulled out his phone, but there were no new messages from either Grant or Aki, nothing that would give Nate any clue to what was going on. He sighed, stretching out a hand to the nearest plant.

The morning glory inclined toward him. It was happy to share the sunlight with Nate and the memory of the breeze lifting its tendrils, or unfurling fresh shoots. It couldn't tell Nate when Ben had climbed down the ladder or where he'd gone afterward. *If only plants could see.*

There was an angry splutter from the street, followed immediately by slamming brakes. As a chorus of angry horns sounded, Nate heard the engine of Gunn's car rev, making its way down the street. *Gone.* Waiting to see what Nate did?

He couldn't think of that now. He had to find Ben.

Nate made his way down the fire escape, hoping that retracing Ben's steps would give him the clue he lacked to Ben's location. *He's got to be somewhere...*

But where? Nate couldn't imagine anywhere in the city Ben would chose over his apartment. *And if he's chosen to hide, what chance do I have of finding him?*

He clambered onto the ladder that was the end of the fire escape and dropped the last of the way, landing with a thump in the alley.

A startled yowl was immediately silenced.

No way. Nate swallowed. It wouldn't be that easy. He moved carefully toward the dumpster, pausing after every step. As he rounded it, he held his breath.

The cat eyed him balefully, her one good eye a clear warning. The milky eye stared through him as the cat hissed. But it wasn't the cat that made Nate's blood run cold.

Ben held the cat on his lap, an arm curled protectively around her. He mirrored her actions, hissing at Nate. The fangs he bared were stained, his face and throat messy with blood.

Nate saw again the still form of the woman lying dead in the street, the two puncture marks in her neck. *No. It can't be.*

Chapter Ten

NEW CAMDEN'S POLICE force maintained a regular updated roster of missing people on their website. Nate scrolled past photos of missing citizens, scanning for a last known location in their neighborhood. *Please, no.* As he hit the bottom of the page with no results, he groaned, covering his face with his hands. Just because the result was negative, didn't mean Ben hadn't killed someone. That blood had to come from somewhere.

A thump from the safe room caused the cup of coffee next to him to tremble. As Nate shifted it away from Ben's laptop, the sound repeated. "All right, already. I can take a hint." He stood, taking the mug with him. As he stepped into the kitchen he took a sip and grimaced. Cold.

He no longer needed to check the instructions on the packs of blood. Instead, he set the water to boil and automatically set the blood pack on the counter ready. The thermometer was waiting beside the cooktop. Nate swallowed the cold coffee and tried to will his brain to think. Instead, it was locked on one thought. *If Ben's killed someone...*

The pot was bubbling. Nate took it off the heat, added cold water from the faucet in the sink to bring it to body temperature, and then dropped in the blood pack. When it was ready, he returned to the safe room.

Ben no longer tried to attack him. He stepped back as Nate opened the door, his gaze going immediately to the blood pack. He snatched it, sinking his fangs into the plastic.

Nate flinched. "Ben, snap out of this. Please." He took a step toward him, but Ben didn't even look up. "Come on! I know you're not a vampire! You've got to shake yourself out of this! Now!" He put his hand on Ben's arm.

Ben growled in warning, batting his hand away.

"Listen to me." Nate grasped his arm firmly. He wouldn't let Ben get out of this so easily. He couldn't. "It's me, Nate. Come on, Ben. I know you're in there."

Ben's eyes flashed. He snarled and, with one vicious swipe, sunk his fist directly into Nate's stomach. As Nate staggered back, he followed with a powerful shove that slammed Nate into the wall.

Nate slid to the floor. His head swam. It was a moment before his vision cleared. He staggered to his feet, putting himself between Ben and the open door, but satisfied that Nate wasn't going to try to remove the blood pack, Ben paid him no attention. Nate backed out the door, securing it behind him.

Holy fuck. He shut his eyes, pressing a hand against the back of his head that pulsed where it had connected with the wall. *Definitely got his strength back.* That wasn't all Ben had regained. He'd never had anything resembling extra flesh, but his face no longer looked painfully thin, and his eyes were bright, the shadows around them vanished. In the struggle to get Ben out of the blood-soaked clothes and into fresh ones, Nate had discovered that his arm wasn't even bruised. *Is that from the blood we've been giving him? Or—*

He didn't want to finish the thought.

None of the websites he scrolled through were geared toward taking care of vampires. The information seemed to fall into three different categories: how to defend yourself and your home against vampires, how to identify vampires, and how to seduce them. Nate bit his lip as he scanned yet another thinly disguised supernatural matchmaking site. *I need an expert.*

Luckily, although it'd been months since he'd done any yard work for Godfrey, he still had the man's number in his phone. Nate dialed. As he waited for Godfrey to pick up, he glanced at the phone and winced. It was very late to be calling anyone.

"Nathan. This is an unexpected pleasure." Godfrey sounded as unruffled as if it was midday. "How can I help?"

"How do you train a vampire?" Nate winced. The question sounded even worse out in the open. And Godfrey was right there at the hearing, he would guess.

"Train a vampire?" Godfrey's voice held only polite surprise.

"Yeah. You know, when Ben was a new vampire. How did he go from being basically a revenant to, well, him."

"You want to know about Ben's early days?" Godfrey's tone was thoughtful. "Are you sure? It is not a pleasant matter to contemplate."

"I'm sure. I am...trying to get what the difference between a revenant and a vampire is."

"A vampire has self-awareness, knowledge, and some measure of control. A revenant has only hunger."

"But not all revenants become vampires."

"Most simply do not survive long enough. It is a question of feeding." Nate could picture Godfrey pushing his glasses up his nose. "When Bennet first awakened, he was contained in the crypts here. Hunter and Saltaire brought him revenants to feed on over the course of several nights. When he had consumed enough lives, his reason began to return, but it was many, many weeks before he was able to master his vampire instincts and could trust himself around people."

Nate swallowed. "What do you mean, consumed enough lives? Vampires drink blood, don't they?"

"It is not blood alone, but the magical properties of blood. Drinking blood, especially that of the living, feeds a vampire's power as well as their hunger. Being dead, what power a revenant's blood has depends on how recently they fed, but if they are killed, the consumption of their undead life is enough."

"Blood alone's not enough?"

"You refer to synthetic blood or transfusions? No, while that blood will satisfy the vampire's hunger, it has generally been stored in a way that removes the living magic from it, and it will not restore their power or consciousness."

So the blood packs were doing nothing? Nate felt acute disappointment. "Right. I get it."

"Has something happened, Nate? Has Bennet returned?"

Nate was glad the call was voice only. "I really don't like the idea of Ben out there alone. I guess my mind is stuck on all that could go wrong. If something happened..."

"Yes," Godfrey said simply. "It is not a welcome thought. If it helps, I can tell you that Hunter has been sent to search all of Ben's hunting grounds from his time as an ARX agent, and I am ready should he return to the house here."

Now Nate felt an entirely new kind of guilt. "What will you do if he does come back to the house? Saltaire basically wants to make him a prisoner!"

"Under Saltaire's control, Ben would not pose a risk to anyone. He would be free from that responsibility, and as a vampire, that is a constant responsibility. He would be able to recover from his ordeal with the confidence that he will not be allowed to endanger anyone."

Nate swallowed. "But Ben left. Do you really think Saltaire can forgive him that? He won't just destroy him?"

"That would depend on whether or not Bennet retains himself. Not all revenants can become vampires, no matter how many lives they consume. There has to be a certain quality an individual possesses, a strength of character that remains even after death. It's rare. I do not believe that Saltaire would easily destroy that."

Nate swallowed. "Thanks." He ended the call quickly, before Godfrey could ask any more questions. The guy sounded so concerned that lying to him was difficult.

There was a thump from the safe room followed almost immediately by another. Ben was hungry again.

Nate put his head in his hands. *I can't let Ben kill!* But what other options did he have? No vampire in the city would see Ben as anything but the chance to steal some of Saltaire's power, and Saltaire...

Do I just not want to admit that he might actually be best for Ben right now? Nate bit his lip. Saltaire would rein in Ben's vampire instincts and give him the help he needed to get back to his old self. The problem would be extricating himself from Saltaire's control a second time. It was not an encouraging thought. *But compared to putting others at risk, I know which Ben would choose.*

The bookcase shuddered as Ben launched a prolonged attack on the door hidden behind it. Nate turned to watch a book slide to the ground. *I have to face facts.* Aki and Grant would go a long way for Nate, but he didn't think either of them would be cool with finding revenant victims for Ben to consume. *Saltaire is my only choice.*

"No." He took a deep breath, stealing himself. "I'm not giving up." He reached for his phone. He had one option left.

GEORGE LISTENED TO Nate's plan as she leaned against Ben's father's desk, sharpening the blade on her axe. Her expression was blank, but if Nate had to guess, she was furious. His explanation of his plans came to a halt, letting the silence hang between them.

Right on cue, the bookcase shuddered as Ben slammed into it again.

Nate winced. "You see why I'm asking for your help. I can't do this alone and Ben—I know Ben has a lot of respect for you."

George cocked her head at him. "You're aware Ben made me promise to kill him should he die and raise as a vampire a second time?"

Nate's stomach dropped. "You don't think there's any hope?"

"I didn't say that." George returned to her task. After a few seconds she spoke again. "You said he has a heartbeat?"

Nate nodded. "I know it doesn't make sense, but I think, somehow, he tapped into the vampire and it kept him alive the month he was on the Final Register. He's not dead. I know he isn't. We've just got to get him out of this."

The thumping was replaced by a scuffling sound, as if Ben were trying to claw his way out of the room.

George raised her head toward the door. "As long as we're clear. If I think that Ben's gone for good, I am going to end him, Nate. I owe him that."

"I know. I don't want it to come to that, but—" If it did, would he be able to stand by and let it happen? "We owe it to Ben to try everything we can first. No one else is going to help."

"Agreed." George slid off the desk, tucking her sharpener back into her backpack. She held up the axe, admiring her handiwork before returning it to its holder. "You got a place in mind for this plan of yours, Nate?"

"Actually, I do. You ever been to Old Cemetery?"

George drove them there in her RV. It took all Nate's concentration to restrain a furious Ben in the trailer, and by the time they parked outside the cemetery gates, George's mobile home was littered with pieces of vine and torn leaves.

She looked from the mess to the vines growing directly from Nate's skin and shook her head. "Just when you think you've seen it all." She grinned, slapping Nate on his arm, narrowly avoiding Ben's fangs. "Good thing I like variety."

It might have been Nate's imagination, but he thought Ben fought slightly less as they bundled him through the cemetery and into the crypt once used by Saltaire's family as a second sleeping place. He looked around constantly, seemingly fascinated by their location. Nate got only a brief glimpse of the inside of the crypt as he shoved Ben inside, but it didn't seem to have been altered since he last saw it. Had Saltaire's family abandoned it now that its existence was known to others? If so, that was a massive point in their favor.

Old Cemetery was well named. Established shortly after New Camden was founded, it was imperfectly maintained. Nate found a block of marble that he could lean against the crypt door to prevent Ben from escaping. He looked to George. "Ready?"

George adjusted her infrared goggles. "Yeah. You want first on pickup duty?"

Something about her matter-of-factness was supremely reassuring. Nate nodded. "Sure."

Wandering the cemetery alone allowed ample time for his doubts to creep back. Nate carefully followed the paths, concentrating on keeping his footing on the uneven stone. He couldn't help but remember the night he'd come dangerously close to dying in that very cemetery. *Ben didn't let me down then. I can't—won't—let him down now.*

Behind him came the sound of a footstep crunching on loose stone. Nate swung his flashlight up, the light catching a man with hungry eyes and a ravenous mouth.

A revenant. Nate hit speed dial on his phone. "George? I got one. I'm heading your way."

The revenant was fast. Once he realized Nate had seen him, he threw caution to the wind and charged after him. Nate had to scramble to avoid his jaws. He ran for the circle of light before the crypt, skidding to a halt as he reached it. "George?"

"Got you covered." George's voice sounded from above the crypt. She crouched, her crossbow balanced on a protruding piece of gutter. "Everything is fine on this end."

A growl indicated that the revenant had caught up with him. The glow of the streetlight beside the crypt gave him a moment's pause, but as Nate removed the stone, the scrape of the crypt door opening drew the revenant's attention to Nate. He sized up the leap and went for it.

I'm a tree. He no longer needed the words, not exactly. He knew where to find the well of power and how to draw out what he needed. The revenant struggled, but Nate's hold was as firm as the towering willows that grew throughout the cemetery.

Ben appeared in the doorway. His eyes flashed as he saw the revenant and he growled low.

Nate felt the revenant tense. He released it with a shove and saw it turn immediately to face Ben. In the presence of a fellow predator, the revenant placed defense over feeding. With a growl of his own, he launched himself at Ben.

Jesus. Nate desperately wanted to look away but couldn't. The fight was vicious, more like a scrap between dogs than anything human.

"Hey, Nate?" George's voice sounded above. "Question for you. What do we do if Ben looks like he's going to lose this fight?"

Nate swallowed. "I hadn't thought of that."

"If you hold the guy a moment, I can clip him, but I don't want to risk hitting Ben if I can avoid it."

He turned his attention back to the fight. It was hard to tell who had the upper hand. Both combatants snarled, struggling viciously for advantage. They seemed to be trying to go for the other's neck. The revenant was bigger than Ben and had the advantage of weight.

An advantage that did him no good against Ben's strength or speed. The revenant's snarl ended in a gurgle as Ben's teeth tore through his throat. Before the man had hit the ground, Ben was on him, bent hungrily to the man's neck.

Nate reached out his hand for the crypt wall. He swayed, afraid he was going to be sick.

"Wow. Hope he doesn't kiss you with those teeth."

Nate winced. "George!" Her comment was the last thing he needed. Or maybe not. Jarred out of horror, Nate found himself wondering about the revenant. "Hey, random question. You ever wondered why New Camden has so many revenants?"

"Isn't it obvious?" George shifted, moving into a crouch to better survey the surrounding area. "New Camden's got a high population of vampires. Not everyone who gets fed from declares it."

"Why wouldn't you declare it?"

"Tons of reasons. There's a stigma to getting bitten, and you could lose health benefits and insurance. Not to mention your rights. I mean it sucks, but there's a reason a lot of people don't want to be open about it. And of course, if you're not open about it, how is anyone going to know to take precautions when you do die?"

The revenant's corpse had stopped its spasmodic twitching. That was something at least. "But the risk to other people…"

"Denial is a powerful thing, Nate. Speaking of, you got any idea how many revs Ben has to eat before we know if he's coming back to us or not?"

Nate shook his head. "I don't want to ask my source for an exact number. That's got to look incredibly suspicious."

"I like the fact that you think you're not already incredibly obvious, but your call. Want me to get the next one?"

"Sure." Nate took a deep breath. *Come on!* He was tougher than this. *I need to get my head in gear.* They weren't going to solve this problem by standing around having feelings!

He heard the thump as George slid off the crypt roof, and the clatter of her army boots over the stone paving surrounding the crypt. "I think I caught some movement near the pond. Hopefully, I'll be back soon." She tilted her head. "You're not going to wish me good hunting?"

Nate started. "Uh, good hunting?"

George snorted as she turned aside. "Just wait. I'll make a hunter of you yet."

As the trudge of her boots faded out of hearing, Nate felt himself even more alone. The sound of Ben feeding had slowed to an unpleasant gurgle, and it seemed to lack its earlier urgency. *He's getting full?* That was a relief. Nate wasn't sure how much of this he could take. Seeing anyone he loved become a revenant would be bad enough, but for it to be Ben, who had fought so hard to retain his mind, his self...

Ben let the revenant's corpse fall. He stood, his back to Nate, his head lifted as he sized up the surrounding cemetery. In contrast to his earlier actions, he stood stock still. Waiting.

Nate swallowed. "Ben?"

He turned toward him, the glow from the streetlight above them catching in his eyes and giving them a sharp, inhuman glint. He was still a moment, sizing Nate up. When he moved it was calm, unhurried. He stretched out his hand, placing the palm flat against Nate's chest, his eyes looking into Nate's. Searching for what?

Is this...? Nate didn't dare breathe. He waited, his heart in his mouth, scanning Ben's expression for any clue to his thoughts. Had he remembered? Or was he merely trying to will Nate into lowering his guard so he could strike? As Ben continued to look, Nate felt himself tremble. *Please, Ben. I miss you so much.*

His phone blared. With shaking hands, Nate answered the call. "George?"

"Head's up! You got incoming." George sounded as though she was running. "I had two on my tail. I was hoping to lure them into the light so I could wound them before we turned Ben on them, but all of a sudden they took off in your direction. I think they sensed Ben."

Nate could hear crashing sounds as bodies fought their way through the cemetery plantings. "I hear them." He returned his phone to his pocket, summoning the strength of an oak. *Calm down. You've got this.*

Ben had already turned toward the sounds. He saw them before Nate did, baring his teeth in a vicious promise.

The revenants slowed as they drew near, sizing up their opponents. There was an older man with a beard that was badly bloodstained and a younger woman. They seemed only peripherally aware of each other, all their attention focused on Ben and Nate. The man put on a sudden burst of speed to close the distance between them. Ben launched forward to meet him. He had accuracy the man didn't and grazed his neck with his teeth.

As they closed in a vicious struggle, the woman leaped, not to her fellow revenant's aid, but toward Nate. No teamwork here, just opportunism. Nate was able to hold her at arm's length, toughening his skin like bark to withstand her teeth, but this meant he couldn't see how Ben was managing. "Ben!"

The scent of copper filled the air. The woman's hunger-filled eyes locked on Nate's own, and she snarled, making a renewed effort to reach him. Nate summoned the vines of the ivy crawling over a neighboring grave to help him. The earthy tendrils melded with the metallic tang of blood. The streetlight caught the white of the revenant's face, making it look like bone. She looked up at him with Peter's eyes.

Nate recoiled, snatching his arms back.

Peter's grin was as mocking as always. "Took you long enough, but I see you've finally come round to my point of view." He stretched out his hands, swaying as he swiveled to face Nate.

Nate took another step back and felt the crypt behind him. Trapped. "What the fuck are you talking about?"

"Blood magic." Peter's smile was sardonic. His eyes glittered with his habitual disdain. "Wake up, Nate! You're taking their lives to feed Ben. How is that any different from what I did and died for?"

Nate felt a rising sense of panic. "That's completely different. You wanted to hurt people!"

"I wanted what I was entitled to. Hurting people was never my goal. It was an unfortunate side effect. But tell me, how many people are you prepared to see hurt for Ben? At what point does this stop being justifiable?" Peter's grin stretched as he stepped toward Nate.

"You're trying to confuse me." Nate struggled to contain the growing sense of panic within him. "You're supposed to be dead!"

"So is Ben."

"Stop talking!" Nate threw his fist wildly. It connected and the female revenant staggered backward with a human-sounding grunt.

Nate stared after her. His shoulders heaved, a tendril of blood slowly trickling down his knuckles. As he watched, the revenant regained her balance with a snarl. She sized him up. There was no sign of Peter now.

Did I imagine it or— No time to wonder. She leaped, and Nate only just brought his arms up in time to catch her. He gasped, finding the revenant's superhuman strength forcing him against the crypt. *Come on!* He dug deep, trying to reach his roots, but he came up empty. *Oh fuck. What did he do to me?* His powers were gone. Nate was on his own against the revenant.

The woman bared her teeth. She could taste his fear and knew as well as Nate did that this was it. She leaned in for the kill.

And was jerked roughly back by her hair. She screamed as she tried to pull free, but Ben didn't relent. His mouth, smeared with the blood of the two previous revenants, bared in mute threat. A second later, they were buried in her throat and the scream became a liquid gurgle.

Nate leaned back against the crypt. The cold marble wasn't any cooler than his own clammy skin. He felt shaken through and through, unable even to stand without the crypt's support. *Come on! You have to do something!* He reached again for the protection of his plants, but all he touched was fear.

Ben let the woman crumple. His eyes were fastened on Nate with a predator's awareness, but he approached him without any hurry.

Like he knows I'm not going anywhere. Nate pressed himself against the crypt wall. Did Ben know that Nate's supernatural defenses had failed? *If he rips into me now, that's it. I'm going to bleed out. It'll be over in seconds.*

Ben halted in front of Nate, his eyes searching Nate's like before. He frowned, lifting Nate's hand so that he could see the trail of blood across it.

What is he waiting for? Nate didn't dare breathe, in case a too-loud exhale triggered the vampire's destructive instincts.

A movement in the shadows alerted them to another presence.

Ben moved before Nate could react, slamming Nate against the crypt as he pivoted to face this new threat. *"Mine."*

Nate's mouth ran dry. *He spoke.*

"And they say romance is dead." George stepped into the light. "I see you took care of both revenants."

"Don't get too close." Nate reached out a hand to Ben's arm. "Ben, do you remember me?" Ben turned his head to look at Nate's hand on his arm but didn't remove it. "Please, Ben. Do you remember who you are?"

Ben raised his head to look at Nate. His eyes, obscured by the shadows, were dark. "Mine." He planted his hand on Nate's chest and pulled him close. His tongue tickled Nate's neck, cold and sticky with congealing blood.

"Wow. Like, I don't want to judge—whatever floats your boat—but that seems really unsanitary—"

"I appreciate the assist and all, George, but you're not helping." Nate tried to step back, but Ben's hand tightened warningly on his arm and he obediently stayed where he was.

George snickered. "You want me to look for another rev?"

Peter's words jumped into Nate's mind. "No. I don't know. I got to figure this out. I—" He flinched as Ben's tongue explored the blood on Nate's knuckles. "Stop that!"

"Need backup?" George kept her tone conversational, but she hadn't missed Ben's actions. Deliberately playing it cool to avoid startling him.

Nate hesitated. Bizarrely, Ben seemed calmer now than he had the entire time since he'd found him in the alley. He reached and discovered the surrounding ivy leaned toward him at his call. "I think I have this. You mind giving me a moment to try to talk to him?"

"Some private time, huh." George nodded. "I'll take the RV around the block. I'm pretty sure I saw a diner on the way here."

"Sounds good." Nate watched George go. Was he making an even bigger mistake?

AS SOON AS George's footsteps faded, Ben tugged Nate toward the open crypt door. Nate let himself be guided inside. He watched as Ben examined the door, turning the key and then tugging it to make sure it locked. *He didn't even remember door handles earlier.* Ben was remembering. But how far did it go?

The industrial-strength flashlight George had lent him illuminated the crypt. Not that there was much to see. The crypt was a simple square design, with coffins built into three of the four walls like a macabre window seat, with one grander coffin in the center. Nate was pretty sure he remembered seeing a first-aid kit in the crypt. He lifted the lid of the coffin on the right, revealing a vampire's emergency kit: a bundle of twigs, candles, salt crystals, herbs, a mirror, chalk and, incongruously modern, a first-aid kit. "Thank god." Nate pulled it out and turned to find Ben standing only inches away from him. "Jesus!" The kit leaped out of his hands, and Nate scrambled to catch it. "You scared the shit out of me."

Ben didn't smile. His expression didn't flicker as he continued to watch Nate.

"This is nice. Companionable almost." Nate fumbled with a plastic-wrapped alcohol wipe. He carefully cleaned his banged knuckles. "Much nicer than you trying to bite me." Ben didn't try to stop Nate as he applied the plaster to the cut.

Nate tried to gauge his mood. Ben dragged his tongue over his mouth, but he didn't seem hungry. "Cleaning yourself up?" He hesitated but decided that even if it hurt, this couldn't kill him. He grabbed a wipe from the packet in the first-aid kit and dabbed at Ben's mouth.

Ben snarled reflexively, catching hold of Nate's wrist in retaliation. Nate switched to the other hand. "I'm not hurting you. Just getting some of this blood off. Man, you are really not a tidy eater." Then again, was there a tidy way to eat something doing its best to murder the shit out of you?

Nate saw Peter's grin in his mind and gritted his teeth. *Revenants are the living dead! It doesn't count. They don't count!* It wasn't like they were ever going to make vampires. Most of them would be destroyed by Department Seven or ARX operatives, or picked up by vampires and werewolves as a meal. Any that survived posed a threat to New Camden's living population. "Really, we're doing everyone a favor."

"My human."

Nate's hand jerked back in shock. That was two words. And what words they were! "Ben?"

Ben turned his face, nuzzling against Nate's wrist. "Mine." He purred the word, sounding supremely pleased with himself. And then he tugged Nate toward him, jerking him off-balance. "Please me." The words were breathy, layered with invitation, but in case there was any confusion over Ben's intent, he released Nate's wrist, placing a hand on his shoulder and pushing him onto his knees. His hand tangled in Nate's hair, holding him in place as he thrust against him.

Oh god. Over the musty herbs and the tang of the antibacterial wipe, Nate could smell Ben's arousal, and the scent brought on an instant chain reaction. He could feel his heartbeat increase, as his body pulsed with new awareness of his danger—and his lust. *I shouldn't even be contemplating this.*

Ben's fingers tightened in his hair and Nate knew he was lost. Nothing got him hotter than a guy who wanted him and wasn't above using a little force to get his point across. Add in the undercurrent of danger that was part and parcel of fooling around with a vampire and Nate was incapable of resisting. "Fuck me." He gripped the waist of Ben's jeans, swiping his tongue across his cloth-covered erection, before wrestling with the zipper. He knew from prior experience that when Ben was in vampire mode, he did not appreciate being kept waiting.

Vampire mode. Is that what this is? Nate caught his breath as he eased Ben's fly down and freed him from his boxers. He'd encountered Ben's inner vampire before. *Blood magic isn't just worked through blood. It's blood, sex, and bonds.* Like the bond between him and Ben.

Freed from its cloth restraints, Ben's erection bobbed up to meet him. He was hard, his tip glistening in the light of the flashlight.

Nate steadied his hands on either side of Ben's hips and leaned in to swipe up the dribble of precome with his tongue. He tried to ignore the vaguely metallic undertaste, but the memory of blood and danger made him even more acutely aware of his own heartbeat and the need pulsing in his groin. *Fuck me. I am totally getting off on this.*

Ben's cock butted against his mouth, seeking admission. As Nate's lips parted, Ben pushed inside, pausing only to get a better grip on Nate's hair. Fingers painfully tight against Nate's scalp, he thrust, holding Nate in place.

Ben was never this forceful. Was it bad that made it hotter? Like he was playing with fire, dancing with a great big dangerous unknown. Yeah, some of his clients liked to use him forcefully, but he'd always had the security of his wristband, known safety was a few seconds away. This... Even if things got bad, Nate wasn't sure he'd want to call for help. It was rough, and as he got used to Ben's rhythm, anticipating it and moving to meet his thrusts, he felt the thrill of it. Of living right on that edge between ecstasy and death.

Yeah. Come on, Ben. Fuck my mouth—fuck me hard. He hummed, putting all his want into it. He felt an answering reaction in Ben, felt the shudder build within him before his come splattered across this throat. Ben sagged back, leaning against the central tomb.

Nate pulled back to suck at his tip, intent on capturing every last drop of come. His senses were full of Ben, his taste, his smell, the coolness of his thigh against Nate's cheek, his fingers, trembling as they skated over Nate's hair. And then, abruptly, they tensed, and Nate felt himself tightly gripped and roughly lifted against the tomb. He flung out an arm to balance himself and caught the flashlight, sending it tumbling to the floor. The crypt plunged into darkness.

Fuck me sideways. This was really, really bad. Nate's chest heaved as he tried to work out where Ben was in proportion to him. He lay on his back on the tomb, Ben's hand planted firmly in the middle of his chest. He felt the vampire's other hand fumble with the waist of his jeans and heard a fury-choked snarl.

"Want me to get the zipper?"

Ben snarled. "Mine. I want—" He fell silent, continuing to grapple with Nate's pants.

"Let me." His hands tangled with Ben's, but eventually Nate managed to undo his zipper. He scooted up, pulling his jeans down, praying that he'd correctly interpreted Ben's intentions. *I'm fucked either way. Just got to hope it's the good fucked.* If he died with his pants down, Ma would be furious.

Ben hummed, a curiously fierce sound, even though it wasn't threatening. He ran his hand over Nate's exposed flesh, lingering over his hard cock. He seemed to take personal satisfaction in the evidence of Nate's need, though Nate was sure he was an open book to Ben. Every gasped breath, his heightened pulse, the way his entire awareness was centered on the movements of Ben's fingers over his heated skin. And then he was swallowed, a cold tongue swiping the underside of his cock, even as he felt Ben's fangs against his length. *Yes.*

It was more intense than he could have believed possible for something this rushed, this careless, but god, did it feel good—the threat of the fangs, the coldness of Ben's mouth, and the heat building within him. He heard a pained whimper and didn't recognize his own voice, his hips bucking urgently.

Ben growled, pulling back. He took firm hold of Nate's hips, pinning him down.

"Ben." Nate couldn't keep the whine out of his voice. He tried desperately to move and got a warning squeeze. Only when he was entirely still, did Ben go back to work. His tongue trailed its way down Nate's thigh and then darted across his tip.

Nate grunted, as his body jerked in thwarted longing. Ben could have released him and it would have made no difference. He could not have moved if his life depended on it. "God, Ben. You're killing me here. Please—" The part of his mind not totally focused on the burning need noted that Ben had not had the capacity to tease him earlier. *More control? If sex is like blood in magic then is this helping?*

"Oh god." Ben had tired of teasing and swallowed him whole. Nate kicked his heels out, searching for purchase, but only found thin air. Ben's hands held him firmly in place as he took what he wanted—Nate moaning incoherently, his fingers locked on the marble of the tomb lid as he tried to resist moving as he came.

"Jesus. We got to do that sometime when you're not..." Nate felt himself hauled into a sitting position and reached for Ben's mouth.

Instead of the kiss he wanted, Ben's teeth nipped at his neck. A playful warning rather than a bite. Nate was tugged off the tomb and hastily caught the lid to keep his balance as Ben pressed against him. He felt an erect cock pressed against his bare cheeks and grabbed the tomb's edge to steady himself. "Fuck. We're—we're really doing this."

Was that a warning or a promise Ben growled against his neck? Nate didn't care. He leaned against the tomb, one hand lazily stroking Ben's length as he felt in his pocket. "I got a condom. Let me just—" He had to let go of Ben to peel open the packet.

Ben took firm grip of his hips, lifting him bodily as he positioned Nate hard up against the tomb. Nate felt the cold night air on his skin as Ben's fingers urged his legs farther apart. "Pushy, aren't you?" He twisted, swiveling awkwardly to take hold of Ben's cock with one hand, and slide the condom on with the other. In the pitch dark, he had to navigate by touch, a task made more difficult by the fact that Ben was obviously unimpressed by Nate's maneuvers. No sooner had Nate smoothed the condom over Ben's length than he felt Ben's teeth close on his skin—no playful nip but a definite warning—and Ben's hand between his shoulder blades shoved him flat against the tomb lid.

The lack of light was no inconvenience to Ben's vampire senses. He obviously felt the condom was concession enough and intended to waste no more time. Ben's cock bumped against Nate entrance, and then it was pushing past the tight ring of muscle, burying itself deep inside.

Nate grunted. *Fuck yeah.* He liked it rough, liked it wild and fast. His cock twitched, trapped between Nate's stomach and the cold stone, but he knew better than to try to reach for it. He needed all his attention on Ben's next move.

Ben hummed in satisfaction, his fingers stroking their way down Nate's spine.

What is he doing? Nate's body trembled with the difficulty of holding himself still. "Fuck, Ben."

And then Ben moved, driving into Nate. He paused only to readjust his grip on Nate's waist, slamming into him with a month's worth of hunger.

Fuck me. Nate scrabbled to steady himself against the marble tomb, but Ben wasn't giving him any breathing space. His attack was relentless, every thrust going deep, sparking Nate's need even more. "God. You—"

Ben squeezed Nate's hips in warning, pulling Nate against him. His thrusts were shallow and frenzied, but even in his rush he had a vampire's accuracy for Nate's weak points.

White spots danced in his vision, as Nate felt the need building in him in a rush. "Ben!" It was all he could do to keep his grip on the stone as release crashed through him, an incredible, overwhelming wave.

He heard Ben grunt as if from a distance and felt his rhythm become even more sporadic. The grip on his hips tightened as Ben shook against him and then relaxed as Ben's weight rested on him.

Nate breathed out. His body still pulsed, pleasure dancing in every nerve ending. He shifted, finding no resistance from Ben as he pulled them together into a loose hug. Ben leaned against him, and Nate felt his eyelashes tickle his neck as Ben shut his eyes.

Nate pressed a kiss to Ben's forehead as he stroked his hair out of his eyes. "Fucking hell, Ben. That was incredible."

But was it enough?

A PHONE BUZZED.

Nate had the feeling it had been doing that for some time. He stretched, finding his body stiff. Opening his eyes, he saw the marble walls and tombs of the crypt, illuminated by the daylight creeping through the crack beneath the door.

Morning. He frowned at the time on his phone. *We were out all night?* He sat on the floor, his back against the central tomb. Ben was curled in his lap, resting his head against Nate's chest. His eyes were shut and his skin was cold.

Nate bit his lip. *What is it going to take?*

The phone buzzed again. George was calling. "Hello?"

"You survived. Good. I was getting worried."

Fuck. Had George been waiting all night? "Sorry. I totally forgot."

"I figured either things were going really well and you wouldn't want me, or really bad, in which case there'd be nothing I could do until daylight."

"We're fine, I think."

"Want me to pick you up?"

"Please."

"Meet you by the cemetery gates."

"Thanks, George." Nate ended the call. Looking up, he froze.

Ben had raised his head and was looking directly at him.

Nate swallowed. *Please—*

Ben's mouth turned up at the edges. "Hello, Nate." His eyes fluttered shut, and he sank back against Nate's side.

Nate's arms tightened around him. *Oh my god.* Ben—Ben remembered.

Chapter Eleven

SUNLIGHT FELL DIRECTLY into his eyes. Nate flung a hand up to shield himself. Instead of the shapes of his plants as they were ruffled by the morning breeze, he saw bare ceiling above him. *Where are my plants?* Turning toward the window, Nate was met by an unexpected but familiar sight. *Ben's room?*

Ben! The events of the previous night came rushing back. Nate struggled to sit up.

A hand tightened around his arm. "Not yet." And then, as if ashamed of the movement, the hand relaxed. "Please?"

Nate rolled onto his side, looking over his shoulder. Ben lay on the bed next to him. His face was still gaunt but no longer had that starved look. The shadows around his eyes were still marked, and he looked like a week of sleep would not be enough, but he smiled as Nate's eyes met his. The fear had gone, replaced by something that made Nate's heart constrict painfully.

The night came back to Nate in a rush. Their tryst in the crypt. Ben going limp in his arms as they stepped into the sunlight. George smirking the entire drive back to the apartment building. "Ben. You. I." Nate choked on the words. "I am so sor—"

"I don't want to talk about it." Ben shut his eyes. "I don't even want to think about it." He shuddered, and Nate could not stop himself reaching out to place his hand on Ben's painfully thin shoulder. "Please, Nate. I just want to feel again."

Nate wrapped his body around Ben's. Immediately, Ben wriggled so they were closer together, his back wedged tightly against Nate's bulk. "How are you feeling?"

"Cold. On the surface, I'm thawing, but the center of me... I'm still frozen." Ben's fingers found Nate's hand and wrapped around it. "Hold me."

Nate drew Ben even tighter against himself. "I've got you."

"It's not enough." The hurt he felt at Ben's words was startling. Nate sucked in the pain, floundering for words of apology. But Ben continued. "I need more." He turned his head, so his mouth rested against Nate's neck. He sucked at his flesh, drawing an immediate surge of pleasure from Nate. "More of you."

Fuck! Nate body's tightened around Ben. He had to force himself to relax. Ben was so frail, he had to be careful not to hurt him. "You're not yourself. You've had an ordeal, you're still recovering—"

"I'm fine. Trust me, Nate. I know what I need." Ben's hands ran across Nate's skin, constantly in motion as if he were devouring Nate through touch. "You don't know how it felt. To reach out and not touch you. For no one to see me." His fingers trembled. "I need this. I need to feel I am real, that you feel me."

"You're real." Nate rolled onto his back, tugging Ben on top of him. "God, Ben. Even when I couldn't see you, I knew something was missing. You—this—" Ben buried his face against Nate's shoulder, and he felt something that felt suspiciously like tears. "This entire time, I was missing you."

"I couldn't be near you. Not being able to make you see me... It hurt too much. But I couldn't stay away." Ben lifted his head, seeking Nate's mouth. "I don't want to remember."

Nate tipped his mouth up, capturing Ben's lips, but only for a second. Ben kissed with a hunger that was as unlike him as his behavior of the night before. His tongue, flicking over Nate's mouth like a cool breeze, sought for more. Nate shut his eyes, so Ben wouldn't see his alarm. *He's fed, but he's still starving.* He felt for the drawer of the bedside table and the lube he knew was there. The only thing he could think of was to give Ben exactly what he wanted.

As Nate's hand settled experimentally on the waist of Ben's sweatpants, Ben relinquished Nate's mouth. He sat back on his heels, whipping his T-shirt over his head.

Nate's eyes went immediately to the injured arm. The bruises had almost entirely vanished, and the scars he remembered seeing were barely there. Ben's ribs were no longer visible, and while Nate wanted nothing more than to sit Ben in front of a heaped plate of breakfast, some of his worry eased. *If this is what he wants...* With Ben on top, he had more control over what they did, but Nate would still have to make sure they didn't overdo things. As Ben wriggled out of the sweatpants and resettled himself on Nate, he skimmed his hands down Ben's back.

Sheer proximity had him hard, and he could feel Ben's erection against his own. *A month's absence?* His body had known even if Nate had forgotten. He'd not had a reaction like this for any of his clients.

Only Ben. Nate felt for the lube lost somewhere in the sheets. He found the tube and carefully coated his fingers. Ben waited patiently, his head resting on Nate's shoulder, his body rubbing against Nate's.

"Hey." Nate turned, seeking Ben's mouth, even as his hand searched for Ben's cock. He slicked Ben and then himself, lazily pumping their erections to the slow rhythm of Ben's movements.

Ben's earlier hunger had gone. He kissed Nate leisurely, his eyes closed.

Nate felt a flood of warmth that had nothing to do with the heat building in his stomach. Ben felt so right in his arms that it was a struggle not to hold him tighter, or simply press him into the mattress. The slow rhythm of his strokes was quickly becoming torture, but Nate ignored the ache and kept the slow pace. *Got to take it slow. Ben...* It was all about Ben's needs.

Ben broke away from this kiss with a gasp. A shudder went through him, and he tightened his grip on Nate, thrusting desperately against him. Nate relaxed his hold on Ben, allowing him to dictate the pace. Instead, Ben came to a halt, raising his flushed face to look at Nate.

"I need more," he said, his voice no longer shaky. "I want your weight on me, to feel totally surrounded by you. I want you inside and out." Ben swallowed, his eyes locked on Nate. From Ben, that level of explicitness was a big admission. "Nate—"

Nate knew it was game over. He couldn't refuse Ben anything when he asked like that. "I don't want to hurt you."

"Then let me feel you." Ben tightened his grip on Nate's arms. "I need to feel—and only feel." He gave Nate a preemptory tug.

Nate let Ben guide him on top, pressing him down into the mattress he'd just vacated. It felt good, like Nate was a barrier between Ben and the rest of the world. He planted a kiss on Ben's neck, and Ben gave a breathy moan that traveled like electricity all the way down Nate's cock.

Fuck. Nate bit back his moan, but with nothing between them but air and not much of that, he was pretty sure Ben had noticed his reaction. Ben's hands were busy, travelling over Nate's shoulders, down the length of his back to cup his ass, gliding over his cheeks and urging him to move against Ben. There was an obvious message there, and Nate fumbled again for the lube.

He could feel Ben's eagerness from the way he tightened his grip on Nate's ass as his finger slipped inside. "More, Nate. Please." Preparing him was an ordeal for them both. Ben made a needy sound that touched something deep in Nate, sparking the desire to be deep inside him. He gritted his teeth and continued his slow, careful stretching, not aware that he was trembling until Ben placed his hands firmly on Nate's shoulders.

"I'm ready. And so are you."

There was no hesitation in his eyes, just confidence. Nate felt his heart ache as something that made him blink rapidly welled up inside. "Ben." It would have been easier to sit back to line himself up, but Ben didn't seem keen on letting go of him, even for a second. Nate guided his cock to Ben's entrance, watching Ben's face as he slid inside.

Ben's lips parted, his mouth opening soundlessly. His fingers tightened around Nate's shoulders. There was no fear on his face, no reservation. Just feeling.

Nate paused to readjust his grip on Ben and began to move. Locked this tightly together, his thrusts were shallower, but Ben was not complaining. He broke his silence to hum, his hands once again settling on Nate's ass, pulling their bodies closer. "Nate—"

Nate felt his fear start to shatter. He buried his face against Ben's neck, planting a kiss to it. Ben was here. This was real. The events of the last twenty-four hours would always haunt him, but they began to take on the insubstantiality of ghosts, next to the reality of Ben's cool skin beneath his, the heat of his cock, sliding against Nate's stomach, and the incomparable feeling of being deep inside him. He sucked Ben's skin, trying to take in as much of Ben as he could at one time.

Ben responded by hooking a leg around Nate's waist. "More. Please Nate. I'm so close—"

Nate slipped his hand between them, intending to find Ben's cock, but Ben caught his hand. He laid it on the bed beside them, his fingers linking through Nate's. His other hand found Nate's hand on his shoulder and did the same. The simple action brought back the memory of their first time in Ben's apartment, their first time free of Ben's vampire family and the machinations of the necromancer. Nate's fingers tightened around Ben and he swallowed as he stared down at him, knowing that this battle was already lost. "Ben."

Ben looked up at him, his eyes absolutely clear of anything but expectation. His mouth, long and flat, held the suggestion of a smile, and his hair, falling in his face, looked positively gentle. He was vulnerable without being weak, his quiet strength present in the firmness of his grip on Nate, the intimacy of their clasped hands.

There was no conscious decision to move, but as Nate did, he found his erratic rhythm matched by Ben. It was somehow a huge relief to know that a month of nothing had not destroyed their synchronicity. Nate thrust urgently, unable to hold back the tide of what he felt, but Ben's face did not show anything but exultation. He rode Nate's wave as expertly as a surfer, and it was he who found his release first, the heat of his climax splattering Nate's chest. Nate followed immediately, and they lay locked together, their breathing mingling.

Nate pressed a kiss to Ben's shoulder. "I never want to move. This..."

Ben's arms tightened around him. "You just found me. Promise me you won't let me go."

Nate shifted so that his arms could wrap more securely around Ben. "Never," he promised. "Never again."

AKI FOLDED HIS arms against his chest, leaning against the wall of the lobby before Ben's apartment. "I don't know. Ben's normal? That's a pretty high bar where he's concerned."

Nate kept his hand on the door handle. "Just go easy on him, okay? He's had a really rough time and he's still processing it all."

"But he is processing it?" Grant also had his arms crossed. He watched Nate closely.

"Well, yeah." They hadn't discussed it, not in those words. Or in any words, really. But Ben was using sentences again. That was something, right? "Just no sudden moves, loud noises, raised voices, that kind of thing. He's a little on edge." Nate led the way back into the kitchen.

Ben sat at the kitchen table, exactly where Nate had left him. He hadn't touched the plate of toast, and Nate could only hope he'd had some of the coffee. He looked up as Nate entered and his body tensed as he took in Grant and Aki.

Aki snorted. "Having breakfast at sunset. Yeah, that's really normal."

Nate squeezed Aki's shoulder in warning. "Baby steps," he hissed. "Hey, Ben. You remember Aki and Grant?" He placed his hand on Ben's back.

Ben swiveled his head toward Grant and said nothing. He held his body rigidly, as if he thought he was going to have to move quickly, but Nate thought he wasn't as tense as he had been.

"So, Ben." Aki was incapable of staying still, and this was no exception. He helped himself to a seat, his leg jiggling. "It's really cool to see you being your usual cheery self—ow!" He shot Grant a dark look.

"Hello, Ben." Grant didn't seem bothered by the lack of response. He took the seat next to Aki. "Good to have you back." He deliberately turned his attention to Nate. "You heard the latest news from the Registry?"

"No. There's been a decision?"

Grant shook his head. "After talking themselves into a frenzy, the council realized that there's no way they can try Ben without knowing what kind of state he's in. His hearing's on hold until he's found and a proper assessment done. They're now debating the legality of the Final Register."

Aki leaned across the table to snag a piece of Ben's toast. "You know, if you turned yourself in, you'd probably get massive bonus points with the council."

Nate tensed, but Ben didn't react to the theft of his toast. "Aki."

"It's not a bad suggestion. After all, you can't hide forever. And the sooner Ben meets with his legal representatives, the better case they'll be able to build," Grant said.

Nate shook his head. "We need more time. Ben's had an ordeal. You don't recover from that in a few days. He needs to work up to it."

Aki chewed his piece of toast with a frown. "Realistically, how much time do you think you have? You've brought Ben back to his own apartment. It's the first place anyone will look for him."

"They looked. They didn't find him."

Aki's expression turned thoughtful. "I guess they're looking for Ben, not you. Ben's smart enough to have a safe house bought under a fake name. They're probably hunting for him out of state by now. If they were looking for you on the other hand, then you'd be in trouble..."

Nate leaned back so he could see to kick Aki under the table. "Shut up."

"You're mad because I'm right."

Grant rolled his eyes. "Is there any coffee going?"

"Yeah. I made a pot. You want some?" Nate patted Ben's arm in apology before walking over to the counter. He took out two mugs. "Aki?"

"Sure." Aki ran his hands over the table. "So much for going two months without supernatural occurrences."

Nate hesitated. In his delight at Ben's progress he'd almost forgotten. "I haven't had the chance to catch up on the news. Anything happen?"

"Anything?"

Nate nodded. "You know, missing people, murders, stuff like that. How do you take your coffee, Grant?"

"Black. Like my soul."

"I didn't ask you, Aki." Nate looked at Grant.

"Milk. Thanks." Grant shifted. He was careful not to look at Ben, but Nate thought he was very aware of him. A wolf thing?

He put the two coffees on the table. "There. So, no recent deaths?"

"It's New Camden. There's always deaths." Aki slurped his coffee happily.

"The feud between the Central City vampires and Wisner's pack is continuing to grow. There was a scuffle last night and a civilian got injured in the fray. The humanist media picked up on the story and are having a field day with it." Grant's hand clenched the handle of his mug. "This is exactly the sort of situation where we need to pull together, and instead, they're making it worse to exploit the panic."

Nate pulled out his seat slowly. *What kind of crap person am I?* Grant was worried about the city, and all Nate thought about was himself and Ben. *That really doesn't say much for me at all.* He frowned, remembering Peter's appearance in the cemetery. *Is he right? Is there really no difference between us?*

"Jeez, Nate. You're not really Department Seven. You've got no excuse for looking that grim." Aki rolled his eyes. "Though on that note, you got a package. The woman who drove us all to the Registry dropped by with a new uniform for you."

"Tremaine did?" Nate stared at his friend. "You mean, they still want my help?"

"I was surprised too, but I guess when you're as chronically underfunded as Department Seven, you have to commit an actual felony before you get fired, and maybe not even then." Aki scowled. "Fucking Gunn." He shoved the last piece of his toast in his mouth and walked into the living room, returning with a paper-wrapped bundle. "Here it is. You know, you can stick with the old one if you want—"

Nate snorted. "No thanks." He reached out to take the parcel.

Ben's hand shot out, batting the parcel away. It hit the ground and he ripped into it, scraps of paper going flying as he systematically shredded the wrapping paper.

"Hey!" Nate caught Ben's arm, pulling him back from the bundle. "What's the matter? You were fine a minute ago!"

Ben ignored Nate's words, scanning the kitchen. His eyes locked on Aki and he threw himself across the table, directly at him.

Aki yelped. "What the—" He staggered backward, half rising from his chair, but he wasn't fast enough to prevent Ben grabbing him by the collar. Coffee cups and toast went flying as Ben seemingly attempted to strangle Aki—

No! Nate grabbed Ben, ignoring the snap of his teeth as he hauled him back. He wrapped his arms around Ben as he fought, summoning his power. Instead of the vines he asked for, supple branches shot from his arms, wrapping around Ben in a hold he could not break.

Nate took a moment to steady himself. Ignoring the snarl as Ben continued to fight against the branches that contained him, he raised his head. "Aki? Are you—"

"Unhurt." Grant had leaped into action at the same moment as Nate, pulling Aki against his side and out of Ben's reach. He still had an arm clamped protectively around Aki, who, dazed with wide-eyes, did not seem to be objecting.

Nate breathed out. "Thank god." If anything had happened to Aki...

The same thought seemed to occur to his companions. Aki narrowed his eyes. "Ben is normal?" His expression was flat and angry. Nate turned to Grant and saw the same lack of sympathy. His heart sank. *This can't be happening.*

THE STUDY WALLS shook as Ben launched himself at them over and over again. It was the most depressing sound Nate had heard in his life. He sat on the floor against the door, his head in his hands, listening as the man he loved most fought like a caged animal.

The study door clicked open. He looked up to see Grant carefully close the door behind him. He was alone.

"How's Aki?"

"I think he's more scared than anything else," Grant said. "I persuaded him to take a hot shower and try to relax." He leaned against the desk. "You?"

Nate lowered his gaze. "Take a guess."

"Look." Grant's voice was even. "Neither of us want to have this conversation, Nate, but we have to. I owe Ben my freedom. There's nothing I want more than to have him back with us. But his current behavior… That's not what recovering from a traumatic experience looks like."

Nate winced.

Grant paused, but when Nate didn't respond, continued. "We need to make a call about what's best for Ben, and the people around him. I think it's time that he got expert help. For his own benefit as much as ours."

"You're giving up?"

"Nate—"

"Expert help? What expert help is there? Department Seven's too busy to play psychiatrist! They'll imprison him, which has the exact same result as keeping him here, until the council can review his case. And with how he's acting now, he'll just get slapped straight back on the Final Register. No one cares about his recovery. They just want this problem solved!"

"There is another alternative," Grant said. "I'm not as familiar with vampire society as I could be, but I understand Ben's maker is still around."

"Absolutely not."

"But Nate—"

"Saltaire's just as bad as the council. He doesn't care about people. He just sees them as tools. And once he has Ben, he won't let go. Bringing Ben to Saltaire is… We'd never see him again."

Grant walked across the room to crouch beside Nate, placing a hand on his shoulder. "At times like this, we can't afford to make selfish decisions. We can't think about what we want. Only what is best for Ben."

Nate's shoulders drooped farther. *Even my friends think I'm being selfish?*

Grant stood. "I'll come back to see you at dawn. If you haven't made a decision by then, I'll make it. One way or another, we can't leave Ben a threat to his fellow citizens. Or his friends." He hesitated. "I'm truly sorry."

Nate didn't respond. He waited until Grant left and then buried his face in his hands. *I can't be selfish. I have to do what's best for Ben.*

And Ben would do anything to prevent himself becoming a monster.

"I UNDERESTIMATED YOU." Saltaire's voice was frost on a winter's morning, a bitter chill that gradually numbed everything it came into contact with. "You have more sense than I gave you credit for."

Nate's skin crawled. It was all he could do not to pace the room. Saltaire's mere presence made the stately drawing room a prison. Even breathing was hard work, the pressure extending to his chest. He felt clammy all over. But this time it was not because of Saltaire's proximity.

Ben.

He cowered in the corner farthest from Saltaire, crouched in on himself like a terrified animal. And he was very clearly terrified. His skin had drained of all the color he'd gained over the last few days, and he made a soft, despairing whimper, his eyes fixed on Saltaire, like a rat transfixed by the snake about to devour it.

Nate's heart tore. *I should be doing everything I can to stop this.* Instead, he'd called Saltaire and dragged Ben across the city, delivering him to the man he feared most.

This is a mistake. Even if Ben does regain control, he'll never be free. I have to get him out of here.

But as his eyes fell on Ben, Nate's heart sank. His fangs were prominent, and his shirt splattered with blood. He'd caught Nate off guard as he struggled to get Ben up the stairs and inside the house, slicing Nate's arm. The cut would heal, but the damage was done. *If I can't stop Ben from hurting me, how I can I protect anyone else? And I know Ben would choose the safety of others over his own freedom, without any doubt.*

But would he choose this living death over a complete end? George had offered—

No. Nate squared his shoulders. *Not while there is a chance that Ben might come back to his senses.* Ben had returned to himself, if only for a few fleeting moments. *That has to mean something.*

"My demands are few and I think straightforward," Saltaire said, drawing Nate's attention.

"Demands?"

"In order to ensure that Ben's cure is complete." Saltaire's eyes glittered with a light that made Nate feel supremely uncomfortable. "You will not contact him. You'll say nothing to Department Seven or the council about Ben's location, and you will not reveal how he came to be under my protection."

Nate swallowed and nodded, returning his gaze to Ben's huddled form. He slipped his hands into the pockets of his jacket, searching for the acorn. He needed the reminder of its strength more than ever.

"And finally..." Saltaire paused, until Nate looked back to him, fixing him with a piercing glare. "You will forget him entirely."

Nate felt a chill sweep over him as Saltaire's full force of will turned on him. That wasn't a suggestion, or even a command. It was compulsion, the vampire's ability to force their will upon another. The power was stronger the older the vampire and the more victims they had to their name. Saltaire's power was almost irresistible. Nate struggled to think, to even remember who he was. His fingers locked around the acorn, and he found the strength to speak. "What? No!"

Saltaire's expression flickered, showing his disapproval. "You will forget."

"Never." Nate wasn't sure how he was able to push back against the immense pressure being brought to bear on him. "Ben is—I will never forget him!"

Saltaire's nostrils flared. "You are unwise to test my patience. I am doing both you and Ben a considerable favor. You are in my debt, Nathan Granger, and it is up to me how you will repay it."

That was a threat, Nate was sure of it. "Believe me, I know." Probably best not to risk ticking him off any further. Nate sucked in a hasty breath, clenching his fists. "But I'm not going to forget him."

"Have it your way then." Saltaire lifted his shoulders in a careless gesture. "I admire your mettle, if not your choice. You will find it harder than you think to live with the knowledge nothing you did could prevent Ben from lapsing into the lowest form of monster. Indeed, your entire association has caused nothing but harm."

The words stung, but Nate could not protest them. Not when he stood on the brink of abandoning Ben to a fate worse than death.

"Leave him. You have harmed him enough." Saltaire pointed to the door. "Just remember this the next time you are tempted to interfere with my family. I know what is right for me and mine. I always have."

Nate had no resistance left to offer. He shuffled toward the door, his head bowed and his steps heavy.

As he reached the threshold, Ben gave a pained cry. As Nate looked back, he launched himself across the room, clinging to Nate. Even in his regressed state, he clearly associated Nate with safety.

I've failed totally. Ignoring the way Ben's body shook, Nate peeled himself free from his grip. He looked into Ben's eyes and saw clearly the pain and confusion at this, the ultimate betrayal.

"Go." There was no room for argument in Saltaire's command, or even choice.

Nate turned. The moment had the feeling of a nightmare, but he knew all of this—the hallway beneath his feet, the sound of the door closing behind him, the scrabble of Ben's fingers against the door, desperately fighting for a way to follow him—was real.

He'd ruined everything.

Chapter Twelve

THE REVENANT BARED his teeth and snarled. His eyes were full of hunger, but the vampire could taste the undercurrent of fear beneath it. The revenant was a stupid thing, a collection of flesh, muscle, and instinct, but he knew he faced a superior predator. He knew he didn't have a chance.

The vampire gloried in that knowledge. His fangs pressed against his cheeks as he smiled. There was no need to hurry. The doors of the crypt were closed. The revenant wasn't going anywhere.

A discordant presence caught his attention. The vampire was not alone with the revenant. There was another, one like him. He was conscious of the other's power, even contained, as it was, at the far side of the musty crypt. The other vampire leaned against the wall, quite still. His expression was distant.

Having his back to the other vampire felt wrong, but somehow the vampire knew he had nothing to fear from his presence.

The revenant's eyes flicked toward the distant figure. Did he think of turning the two vampires against each other, or was even that too much for him? He darted to the side and the vampire intercepted him smoothly. They had played long enough. The revenant's fear woke the hunger in him. Time to end this.

It was a brutal but efficient killing. One jerk broke the revenant's neck, and the vampire's teeth were buried in his flesh before the creature began his death throes. Blood ran down his flesh, and the vampire lapped it up, savoring the thrill as he felt its power fill him. Rich and warm and coppery, but most of all, it was life.

Someone else's life. Now that the edge was off his hunger, a small part of him registered disgust. *If you were any better than an animal, this would be murder!* He realized his fingers had dug into the revenant's skin in a way that would be painful—were the man alive to feel it. He let the man fall, staggering back. His first impulse was to seek out a fresh victim, and let the disquieting thought be drowned out by the thrill of the hunt. Instead, the vampire shut his eyes. *Hold on to that feeling.* The disgust was what separated them from the revenants and worse, those that retained their knowledge but gloried in the brutality of their new natures. *This is what makes us different.*

They weren't his thoughts, but they resonated within him. Memories, perhaps? Someone had spoken them here in this very room, someone whose memory turned the stolen blood in his veins to marble. Someone—

"How do you feel?" The other vampire spoke slowly, forming his words with care. "Still hungry?"

The vampire stood still, digesting the flood of emotion the sound of the voice raised. Relief, fondness, excitement. "I've got the oddest feeling of deja vu." Ben raised his head. "I thought we finished my training?"

Hunter didn't need to breathe, but his breath caught in his throat, a startled, strangled sound. "Ben!" He crossed the crypt, throwing his arms around him.

Ben patted his arm awkwardly. "Did I say something wrong?" *Wrong? Shouldn't that be right? Hunter was—* Ben had an unrequited crush on the vampire for his entire adult life, even earlier. Being caught up in Hunter's arms was everything he'd ever wanted. So why did it leave him feeling cold?

"Ben." Hunter's voice shook with feeling. He stepped back to better look at him. "I have missed you."

Ben smiled automatically, even as he tried to digest Hunter's statement. Missed him? *Where have I been if not here?*

THE GRANDFATHER CLOCK in the hall struck the quarter hour, its echoes reverberating through the Victorian townhouse. As the last chimes faded, Ben still hadn't moved from the doorway to his bedroom. He'd been standing there fifteen minutes. *What is wrong with me?*

His belongings were exactly as he'd last seen them. His classic monster movie posters hung on the wall in frames—*Dracula, Nosferatu, House of Frankenstein*—while the bookshelves held his extensive collection of comics, games, DVDs, and figurines. Cautiously, Ben stepped inside.

The unease persisted. He looked around, mentally cataloguing his possessions. Nothing was missing or even out of place. *So why do I feel on edge?* The room was Ben's sanctuary, where he came to bury himself in his favorite series, where he could forget, if only temporarily, that he was one of the monsters he devoted his waking life to destroying. It was the only place in the house where he could be himself. But just standing there sent a prickle of cold across his skin.

This isn't me. It was like looking into a mirror and seeing a reflection that wasn't your own. *But why? What had changed?* Ben paused, patting his pocket for his phone. He'd check the date, see how much time had passed—

But his phone wasn't there. He pulled open the drawer of his desk, but his laptop wasn't there either.

He should have been alarmed. Instead, Ben found a sense of calm, even as his heartbeat kicked up a notch. *I knew something was wrong.*

He left his room, making his way down the stairs in the dark. Light spilled out from under the door of the dining room, and Ben knew immediately who was within. Three of the house's four occupants had perfect night vision, leaving only one possibility. He pushed open the door. "Evening, Godfrey."

"Bennet." The elderly witch's eyes roved over him quickly. "You have found everything you want?"

"Yes." Even Godfrey was being oddly polite. Treating him like a guest and not as if he'd lived there since he was nine. "You've redone the wards."

Godfrey tilted his head, considering Ben. "You noticed that?"

Ben nodded. "The house feels different." There was a lot more energy in the walls than he remembered. Godfrey had added a second layer of defenses to those he'd employed before. "Did something happen?"

Godfrey pursed his lips. "Saltaire and Hunter are in the office. You must ask them."

Not ominous at all. Ben made his way down the hall, his steps growing slower and slower the closer he got to the office. With every step, the weight of Saltaire's presence increased.

Was this the reason I was so uneasy? It was hard to imagine a time when he wasn't conscious of Saltaire. The master vampire had so much sheer power that his very existence was like having a powerful magnet present, both drawing and repelling Ben. As part of his bloodline, Ben felt an inner awareness each time Saltaire moved from room to room, and had, even before he became a vampire. Most of the time he wasn't even conscious of it. But now—

It feels heavy. Like I'm not used to it. Ben stood still in the hallway, trying to summon the strength of will to step through the door. There was nothing he wanted to do less.

"Both victims remain unidentified!" It was impossible for Ben not to hear Saltaire's words. He was tuned to the master vampire's presence. "What is Isaiah doing?"

"Give him the credit he is due." Hunter's habitual boredom masked a wealth of feelings. "You know most of his supposed incompetence is a ruse. He is very good at what he does. If he hasn't found their names, it is a good indication the killer made sure they wouldn't be found."

"Impossible. You saw the state he was in when the male whore brought him here. He was no more capable of planning than Isaiah is capable of mercy." Saltaire's statement made Ben flinch, laced as it was with his iron-clad certainty.

"Have the dental records been circulated yet? That usually works—"

"A complete blank. It is like they don't exist. Which, when you take into account the fact that the Final Register was in his possession—"

"But as you said yourself just now, the state he was in precludes any—"

"We will speak no more on this matter." Saltaire's tone was final. Inevitably so. Born of Saltaire's blood, Hunter would not be able to argue with his maker without considerable effort. "Bennet has joined us."

Ben steeled himself and pushed open the door.

Saltaire and Hunter sat in the study. The fire was lit, purely for aesthetic value. Although vampires were constantly cold, even in the lingering New Camden summer, fire alone could not warm them. Instead of the electric light, Saltaire had lit a candelabra. The flickering candles illuminated the papers spread on the table between himself and Hunter. In one motion, he swept the papers into the desk drawer. "Bennet. Hunter informs me that you are feeling your usual self."

Ben bowed his head before he was aware of what he was doing. Saltaire was accustomed to respect from his subordinates. That Ben had unconsciously adopted a gesture abandoned at least a century before his birth said less about his manners, more about the influence Saltaire exercised on everyone around him. "I am."

"I hope your rest refreshed you." Hunter's smile was much more natural. "How do you feel?"

"Fine." Ben took a deep breath. It was so hard to speak in Saltaire's presence. "I'm ready to get to work. What is the case you were discussing?"

Saltaire shook his head. "It is of no interest to you."

Ben's mouth parted. "But—" He struggled for words. Hadn't he proved himself as an ARX agent over and over again?

"You have been ill," Saltaire continued. "Your control has been compromised. You will stay within the house until it is proved that you can command yourself."

Ben felt his body tense as, entirely against his will, he responded to Saltaire's command. It didn't matter that he fought it. Saltaire spoke to the blood that beat in Ben's veins, the very core of his existence. "I will stay." He would never be able to disobey him. He was worse than a prisoner, he was a puppet.

Saltaire nodded, turning to Hunter as he stood. "I will leave his recovery up to you. I have a meeting to attend. We will speak again before dawn."

Hunter inclined his head. "The mayor again? I do not envy you."

Ben clenched his fists. Through sheer force of will, he was able to find his voice. "What would you have me do?"

Saltaire paused in the doorway to consider him. His face was blank of expression, as it nearly always was. Saltaire was too guarded to express himself, even in the company of his family. "You will focus on your recovery." And then he was gone.

Ben felt the tension in his bones fade the moment the front door shut behind Saltaire. There was another corresponding release when the master vampire moved beyond the outer boundary of the property. Only then could Ben expel the breath he was holding.

"Let us return to the crypt. There is a revenant waiting for you." Hunter settled a hand on Ben's shoulder.

Ben felt a wave of disgust at the hunger that jolted through him. "What did he mean, I've been ill? I don't remember anything like that."

Hunter's hand remained on Ben's shoulder as he steered him down the hall. "Do you remember everything?"

"No." Ben frowned. Had they discussed this? "There are a lot of gaps in my memory. I remember my own death. Dad—dying." He swallowed.

"I remember the early days, and then working the night shift for ARX, with you at first and then on my own. Then—" He shook his head. "Nothing recent."

"That might be for the best. There are things I would prefer never to recollect again, but they are burnt upon my mind like a brand." Hunter shrugged, his mouth twisting at his own words. He pushed aside the rug that concealed the trapdoor that led to the basement and tugged the metal ring that unlocked the door. "I've often thought that memory may be a vampire's greatest punishment."

Ben bit his lip. At any other time he would be flattered by Hunter's admission. It was rare that he confided in anyone. These moments were precious.

And it's my professional opinion that Hunter's noticed that you're not a kid anymore. He's into you.

The words jumped into Ben's head, unasked for and unrecognized. Ben frowned. He'd definitely heard them spoken, here in this very house. But the speaker's identity escaped him.

"Coming?" Hunter's tone was amused. With a start, Ben realized Hunter already stood at the base of the stairs, waiting for him.

The basement doubled as a wine cellar and had originally seen service as a dairy. Now the disused icebox disguised the entrance to the crypt. It was built from Italian marble, a luxury at the time of the house's construction. Now, the rock had the appearance of a much older edifice. The carving deliberately resembled that of a church or monastery, and the rectangular tombs were deep and impressive. A home any vampire could be proud of.

Between the columns that supported the crypt, iron grating had been inserted. As they entered the tomb, a snarl indicated the revenant Hunter had promised, locked in the cage. This one had been a woman.

Ben's heart sank as he looked at her. "This is entirely unnecessary. I should be out there, hunting!"

"Patience." Hunter seated himself on the nearest tomb in a manner that would have been disrespectful had it been in use. "It will not be for much longer."

"I hope not. The city needs you out there protecting people, not capturing revenants I'm perfectly capable of handling myself."

"I do not complain. Not if it means that the city will have another of her protectors restored."

Ben swallowed. This close, he was very much aware of the revenant, her fear, her blood. She was a fresh creation and would taste sweeter for it.

I hate this so much. The instant he came close enough to her, he would be taken over by the same animalistic instinct to prey or be preyed on.

Unless I act before the hunger builds to that point. Taking a deep breath, Ben twisted the key.

As the door swung open, the woman recoiled—but only for a moment. She leaped for the open space, but her movements were loudly telegraphed by her stance, even if she'd had a choice of places to go. Ben caught her quickly, swinging her arm around her back and pressing her against the grill. He sank his fangs into her throat, expertly slicing through her carotid artery. Her blood bubbled up in a jet, quickly filling his mouth.

Ben swallowed. It was impossible to get every drop of blood, but it was disrespectful not to try. The revenants were pitiful remnants of living things, but they had once been people, and their deaths should not be trivialized. He drank as deeply as he could before lowering the woman's still form to the ground.

"That was well done," Hunter said. "You kill efficiently, causing the minimum of distress to your victim. A night ago, you were not capable of that much thought."

Ben felt sick. Already the blood was congealing on his lips. "This is wrong."

"Every revenant we remove from the streets makes the city safer." Hunter's touch on his back startled him. He hadn't heard his approach.

"And isn't that convenient for us?"

"Convenient or not, it is the truth."

Ben looked down at the woman. She would not rise again. With her blood, he'd taken the unnatural second life passed to the woman by her creator. She was free in a way that he was not. He looked around the dim crypt with something like panic. *Is this all I have to look forward to?*

A movement caught his eye. The crypt was located, not beneath the house, but the garden. A few discreet grills provided air and occasionally light. The breeze passing through one of these grills disturbed the roots of a tree that had tunneled through the ceiling, inserting itself between the blocks of marble above their heads.

"Dawn approaches." Hunter did not need to look at a watch. Like all vampires, he knew instinctively the movements of the sun. "We should retire."

Hunter didn't command him, but if he wanted to, he could. Ben's senior by many centuries, he had consumed enough life to make him almost as formidable as Saltaire. And with Saltaire's blood in his veins, he could summon his power if necessary. Ben obediently turned toward the stone tomb that was his usual shelter. He did not feel the dawn, but if Hunter wished him to rest, he would.

As he settled in his tomb, Hunter placed the stone lid above him. "I think, Ben, that we will leave it ajar."

"Why?" Vampires preferred their tombs tightly sealed, even if it made him feel claustrophobic.

"Trust me. I think you will sleep easier."

Ben settled himself, listening to the scrape of stone as Hunter arranged the tomb to his liking. Something was off here. All right, *many* things were off. This was hardly the most concerning.

Perhaps he wants to be sure that I stay here and don't try to overhear his conversation with Saltaire? But if that was the case, there was nothing stopping Hunter from commanding Ben. Nothing except Hunter's knowledge of how strongly Ben resented being the prisoner of his blood. *At least that hasn't changed.* But why, when Hunter's regard was the only bright spot in an unwanted afterlife, did Ben not feel anything?

Whatever happened must have been bad. That would explain the precautions Saltaire was taking, and Hunter's unusual concern. For a moment Ben's heart sank as he contemplated how bad a loss of control would have precipitated his return to little more than a revenant... Then he steeled himself. *If I take that attitude, I'll never get to the bottom of this.* And get to the bottom he would. *I'm not giving up what little freedom I have without a fight.*

EVENING. BEN LEANED against the metal grating that had contained the revenant. He couldn't hear the voices of Saltaire and Hunter's dinner guests but knew they were present. He was aware of the presence of the living, tracking their heartbeats like others might track footsteps. He heard them reach the edge of the property where another heartbeat, presumably the driver's, waited for them. In another moment, all three had gone.

Ben sighed for the lost meal—and immediately winced. The vampiric instinct went deeper than he liked to admit.

The sound of well-oiled metal preceded the crypt door opening. Hunter crossed to the cage, a heavy iron key in hand. "You're making excellent progress," he assured Ben. "Even last night—"

Ben raised his eyes directly to Hunter's. "What happened?"

As Hunter hesitated, Ben allowed a pained note to enter his voice. "Not knowing—whatever I have done, it can't be worse than speculation. Please, Hunter, tell me."

Hunter shook his head. "Saltaire has forbidden it."

Freed from the cage, Ben placed his hand on Hunter's arm. "Did I kill an innocent? Tell me that at least."

"I do not believe it," Hunter said immediately. "Not you. There is more to investigate before the truth is known. Please, do not ask more until we have the answers. It might wound you more than necessary."

Ben felt himself unable to move. Cold rooted his body to the spot. He knew without any doubt whose case Saltaire and Hunter had been discussing. *Saltaire believes me guilty.*

And who would know better than Saltaire? He was Ben's sire, and no matter where he went or what he did, he would never be free of the vampire's influence.

"Ben, you must believe me. There are inconsistencies to the case."

"Saltaire doesn't think so." His voice sounded hollow. Was the unease he'd felt since waking a manifestation of his known guilt? How could he ever imagine that he might roam the city freely if he had succumbed to the temptation to kill while under Saltaire's supervision? Saltaire was powerful, his command centuries old. If he could not repress Ben's killer instincts, nothing could.

"Saltaire feels keenly his guilt at not protecting you from...certain events," Hunter said. "His guilt fuels an already pessimistic nature. You know that anything unexpected is a disaster to him. Put him from your mind and concentrate on your recovery. You can accomplish nothing by needlessly worrying."

It was all right for Hunter to say his worries were needless. He knew what Ben faced. For Ben, his vampire brother's words were only further proof that he had to investigate.

Fortunately, Saltaire had meetings of an urgent nature to attend, and Hunter was charged with finding Ben sustenance. Ben kept his face a blank mask, suppressing his impatience as he waited for both vampires to depart. Finally, Godfrey was occupied in the kitchen, and Ben found himself at leisure to pursue his curiosity.

He opened the door to the office cautiously, but the room was not locked. *For once I'm glad for Saltaire's arrogance.* Saltaire did not believe a member of his household would dare snoop into his affairs. He hadn't even locked the drawer. For a painful moment, Ben feared this was because he'd taken the papers with him, but he was in luck. The file was there. Spreading its contents out on Saltaire's desk, Ben began to read.

The file consisted of three different reports. The first was a murder, the report made by Hunter. A middle-aged man, found dead on—Ben swallowed—his own father's grave. *'Needless to say the location, and the presence of necromancy, call to mind de Silver's work.'*

Peter? Ben frowned. Peter had been one of Ben's donors, and served Hunter in the capacity of personal assistant. It was very strange he hadn't been by the house, if only to bring Hunter his evening reports. *But if Peter was practicing necromancy on the side?*

That would be instant dismissal, and imprisonment or death, depending on whether he was discovered by Department Seven or ARX. Saltaire was notoriously intolerant of any evil magic, particularly when practiced by his subordinates. *Is this connected to me losing control?* His mind came up blank.

Ben concentrated on the report. The sketch of the victim (vampires were unable to be recorded on camera and passed this trait to their victims, an aspect which made reporting vampire deaths even more difficult) did not ring any bells. Ben was prepared to state that he had never seen the man in his life. *But is that a side effect of whatever is wrong with my memory, or actual proof I've never seen him?* The man was drained of blood, and the manner of his death indicated that he'd been used in some form of spell.

Ben gave the photo of the scene a hard look. The man wasn't familiar, but the runic circle in which he'd died was. *It looked just like that, only carved into flesh—*

For a moment, he tasted the thick copper in the air, mingling with the heady smell of decomposing leaves. He felt the rain on his cheeks and hands, and the disturbed soil turning to mud beneath his feet.

A man lay dead in the clearing before him. His eyes were shut, but his mouth was open in a gesture of surprise that seemed ludicrous paired with the gash across his neck. It gaped black in the moonlight, and Ben hastily turned his eyes away. Even dead he makes his emotions clear. *He didn't need to look at him to know there was no chance of life. He could hear the lack of heartbeat—*

Pain flared in Ben's chest, so sharp it startled him out of the memory. He pressed a hand to his chest, surprised at the strength of it. Just thinking of that man hurt.

Who is he? There was no name, just the stirrings of something deep and disturbing. Ben closed the file and picked up the second.

At first he thought the burglary at the Registry must have been included as a mistake. Only when he saw Saltaire's scrawled note—*possible motive: acquisition of power source?*—did he realize the significance. *Necromancy is traditionally concerned with controlling the dead, but if the murderer had decided to take out the middle man and simply acquire power...* But no, that didn't explain the vampiric aspect to the deaths.

Unless the necromancer is also a vampire? Necromancy was one of the few forms of magic able to be practiced by the undead. Ben sat stock still. *I wondered, of course. I never tried it, but—* Had his curiosity gotten the best of him?

He shook his head. Speculation without fact was simply speculation. He turned to the next page and began to read the description of the investigation. The report had been made by Department Seven and was, like most of the department's documents, extremely brief. Ben gathered that the burglary was determined to have been carried out by one person entered onto the Final Register with the intent of removing himself from it. Ben raised an eyebrow at the brief description of the register's function. *Who would interfere with something so vital to New Camden's defenses?* No one really knew much about how the Register worked. That was the province of the Magic-User's Guild, and they simply kept up a system laid out by the city's founders.

Then Ben's eyes fell on the name of the presumed burglar and he choked. *Me?*

That's impossible! That sort of punishment went beyond manslaughter, though that would have been bad enough. This implied deliberate criminal intention, enough to pose a credible threat to New Camden's defenses. *Never in a million years would I do something that bad!*

But he'd managed to extricate himself from the Final Register, risking the city's well-being in the process. Ben let the file slip from his fingers. He felt stunned. The enormity of it was so great that it was some time before he picked up the third document.

This was another murder, resembling the first in terms of method, but lacking the melodrama of the location. The cul-de-sac where the woman was discovered meant nothing to Ben, and her image did not raise any memories. He frowned at the terse note indicating the problems of identification and studied the diagram of the runic circle. It took a few minutes to ascertain that while differing in intent, it was worked by the same person who'd created the circle found with the first victim. *What purpose could it have?*

Ben restored the files to the drawer and went to the library. It hadn't occurred to Saltaire to remove the treatises on necromancy any more than he would lock his drawers. Ben flicked through the pages, quickly finding what he wanted. *Just as I thought. An improvised spell of transference.* The circle blended elements taken from blood magic and necromancy with an overlay that originated in witchcraft, a hodgepodge that spoke of eclectic magic tastes if nothing else. *Is that why it hasn't been recognized?* Ben returned the reference books to their shelves thoughtfully. The only reason he'd identified it was that before his untimely death, he'd been studying living magic with the intention of becoming a practicing witch. Once a vampire, unable to access the magic he'd studied, he'd hoped to find in blood magic an adequate substitution for what he'd lost, but found its crudities uninspiring. *Necromancy...* Ben bit his lip. He didn't remember ever acting on his interest in it, but there was so much of his memory missing.

"No speculation." He had to focus on what he knew. And what did he know? That a necromancer who found some way to harness the power amassed by a vampire would be extremely powerful—

Ben's blood ran colder. It was a disquieting thought, but it was familiar. *Is that what I did?* No wonder he'd been entered on the Final Register. That was a threat to New Camden, all right! *The only wonder is that I'm still walking around. Saltaire should have killed me on the spot!*

That was a good point. Saltaire did not hesitate to kill even those he considered family, and he clearly believed Ben's guilt. That he'd chosen to leave Ben alive was puzzling. *Unless I'm not guilty of the necromancy?* Did Ben have an associate? Peter? But then, where was he? Ben turned aside from the bookcase, raising a hand to his rapidly pounding temples. *If only I could remember!*

A movement made him start. He looked up. "If I'm to be stuck here, I don't see why I can't—"

It wasn't Saltaire's disapproving eyes he stared into but his own, wide and startled.

Ben swallowed. He took a step toward his reflection, holding out his hand. His reflection echoed the movement. Ben shook his head, seeing his complete confusion thrown back at him. *A vampire doesn't have a reflection.* And he was a vampire. He had the teeth, the blood lust, even the memories to prove it.

But this... "Hunter!" In a flash, Hunter's odd insistence that he leave the lid of his tomb ajar came back to him. Ben pressed his fingers to his wrist. It took a moment, but he felt it. Beneath his fingertips there was a faint but steady pulsing.

Ben stared into his own astonished face. *I'm alive.*

IN DAYTIME, SALTAIRE'S commands were weaker, but they were still in effect. Ben sighed as he turned away from the front door. He'd been hoping to slip from the house, but Saltaire's command kept him trapped within. *There must be a way to undo that.* As a vampire, resistance had been impossible, but now he knew he had the potential for living magic, there were other options before him. *The wards perhaps? They're made to keep people out, not keep people in...*

A wooden *creak* caught his attention and he paused. It was midmorning, as far as he could tell. Godfrey, exhausted by an evening's entertaining, would still be asleep. After a long moment without any further noise, Ben relaxed. *Just the house shifting.* All the same, he should be careful. It wasn't a good idea to let Saltaire know he was aware of his dual nature.

A living vampire... How on earth had it happened? Clearly necromancy had been involved, but was Ben the target or the caster? *Does it matter? I benefited, so I must have been involved in some way.* And how did this tie in to the two murders?

The doorbell sounded, followed by the sound of something hitting the floor. Ben spun around to see the daily newspaper on the floor behind him. In other cities, newspapers might be delivered ready for breakfast, but with New Camden's population of monsters, no paperboy would stir before dawn. Receiving a paper before noon was a rarity. Ben preferred to read the news online, but this was a stroke of luck he couldn't ignore. He grabbed the newspaper and retreated back to his tomb.

He skimmed the headlines. *Fear Continues: Will Necromancer's Revenge Claim Further Victims?* The reporter believed Peter was behind the killings, but the account did not provide any evidence Ben hadn't already seen. *Department Seven Officer Threatens Reporter with Bodily Harm.* Slow news day—Gunn threatened everyone. *Mayor Vows City Won't Be Held Hostage by Special Interest Groups.* That was worrying. Ben frowned as he read the mayor's statement in full. The Final Register's destruction was being lobbied for by supernatural right's groups. Two other groups, the Central City Vampires and Former Councilor Wisner's pack, had both made claims to be in a better position to defend the Register, citing the burglary as proof the Registry building was not secure. The article continued onto a new page and a new headline—*Civilian Injuries as Werewolf and Vampire Fight Spills into Public Places.* Ben frowned. A city divided, fear rising and warring groups of supernatural. No wonder the mayor was annoyed and Gunn lost his temper. The city needed a prompt solution.

On the third page he discovered a grainy photo of himself pre-death, accompanying a terse paragraph to the effect that the police wanted to interview him and that he should not be approached. Ben frowned at his photo. *Should I even be contemplating trying to escape and investigate? If I'm guilty... Saltaire's hard, but he's not as hard as Gunn.* The thought of being the officer's prisoner was not appealing at all.

But staying here— Ben swallowed. That was the problem, wasn't it? In the daylight with the full pressure of Saltaire diminished, he could think clearly. He could feel the stirrings of outrage. He hadn't done anything wrong, he knew it... He hadn't even been tried for his crimes, and here he was, a prisoner, his guilt already decided.

But Saltaire believed him guilty. And as soon as he awoke, Ben would once again be carrying the full weight of Saltaire's belief in his guilt. And what Saltaire thought generally happened. *His influence...* Ben's eyes widened. *Was I ever actually a monster, or was that his influence, believing me to be a monster?* It was telling that he'd regained more memories of himself when Saltaire was out of the house.

The sound of footsteps in the hall above indicated that Godfrey had woken. Ben climbed into his tomb. He shut his eyes, but it was not to sleep. He had a lot of planning to do. *If I don't extricate myself from Saltaire's control soon, I'll end up believing in my guilt.*

Chapter Thirteen

"WHY DO THESE things always come in threes? You never win the lottery three times, do you?" Gunn had steeled himself for entering the yoga studio by lighting a cigarette before he went inside. The tobacco and sulfur scent mingled oddly with the herbal notes of the incense lingering in the room, but even that couldn't mask the smell dominating the studio—death.

Kenzies snorted. "If our perp sticks to only three we'll be lucky." She turned to Nate. "You okay, blossom?"

Nate swallowed. The victim's eyes were open, and she stared at the ceiling. Her short hair was buzzed on one side and spilled into vibrant green-purple-indigo curls on the other, but while she'd obviously gone to a lot of effort to get the cut, she hadn't maintained it. Her brown roots were showing.

Why am I focused on her haircut and not her death? Nate felt bile at the back of his throat. The woman was dead, the third victim in this ongoing case. She lay on her back on a runic circle that even to Nate's untrained eyes looked exactly like those the previous victims had been found on. The two fang marks in her neck stood out against the paleness of her skin like a brand. Just like the others, she had been entirely drained of blood.

With a start, Nate realized Kenzies was still waiting for an answer. "Yeah. Uh. Fine."

"There's something really suspicious about your reactions," Gunn remarked conversationally. "I can taste shock, but we've already established you don't know the victim. Has this convinced you that Ben's responsible?"

Nate gulped. That was it, wasn't it? If Ben was in Saltaire's custody, he couldn't have done this. *I need to talk to Godfrey ASAP.*

"How long has she been here?" Kenzies asked.

Clay stepped forward. He was far, far too cheerful for anyone who worked with Gunn. "The yoga studio closed at six. Sunset was at 7:02 p.m. The corpse was discovered by the cleaner at—when did you say, Tremaine?"

Tremaine looked up from her inspection of the studio's supply cupboards. "I got the call at 8:17 p.m. I arrived here ten minutes later."

Nate was relieved to see that she no longer looked ill. She didn't even look tired. Having a case to work on was clearly more to her liking than crowd control.

Tremaine cocked an eyebrow at him, and Nate realized he was staring. "I see you got your uniform without problem."

"Yeah, thanks for dropping it off." Nate tugged the shirt straight. The new shirt didn't adhere to his skin. "I feel much more comfortable." He cast around for a way to change the subject. He didn't want to remember what had followed the delivery of Nate's new uniform: Ben snarling as he launched himself at Aki in an entirely unprovoked assault.

Am I sure that Ben isn't guilty? He has all the killing instinct of a vampire... I have to talk to Godfrey. Nate slipped his hand into his pocket, gripping his phone, and took a step backward toward the door.

Gunn spat out smoke. "What are the odds we can't identify this one either?"

Clay grinned. "Bad news."

Gunn glared. "Security footage only shows victim?"

"Not even that. It's a complete blank from the owner leaving to Tremaine arriving. Also, we had the owner in to ID the victim, and she says she's never seen her before."

"Do you think they're doing this just to annoy us?"

Kenzies sniffed. "It would explain the wolfsbane."

Nate was startled. "You can't smell anything?"

"I can smell too much. Even despite the best efforts of him"—she jerked her head toward Gunn—"and the goddamn patchouli this place is drowning in, I can barely make out the smell of the rite. And you know how much necromancy stinks!"

Nate did not, but he filed that away for future reference. Evil equals smelly. "And the wolfsbane?"

"Overkill. Then again, the fact they used it at all is a good indication, if one were needed, that our perp is not a wolf."

"Or a vampire. Don't they have sensitive noses too?"

Kenzies looked sadly at Nate. Out of respect for Nate's feelings, she referred to the killer as 'the perp' when Nate was in earshot, but he suspected she shared her superior's views of Ben's guilt. "I caught a whiff of vampire when we approached the building."

"We gotta go," Gunn announced. "Another night, another demonstration scheduled outside the Registry. You'd think people would have better things to do, but there you go. Kenzies, I leave the rest to you."

Kenzies saluted. "I'm going to sniff around here. Clay, you monitor the Forensics team, and make sure they don't accidentally set off a necromantic booby trap. Tremaine, take Nate back to the station. I want you to figure out who these victims are."

DEPARTMENT SEVEN SEEMED unnaturally quiet. Nate, who'd been there long enough to get accustomed to the chaos, found this ominous, but Leanne, the secretary, shrugged. "It's either dead quiet or pandemonium. There's not a lot of in-between. I say enjoy it while it lasts. And I'll have a regular cappuccino."

Coffee delivered, Tremaine parked Nate at a desk in the office that had been cleared of most of the papers on it. She brushed dust off the screen of the aged desktop and logged into the Department Seven database. "This is how you access the missing people reports. I want you to read each one, looking for anything that sounds like one of our victims."

Nate nodded, sitting up straight. *Look at me! Doing actual police stuff!* "How far back should I go?"

"As far as you can get." Tremaine patted him on the back. "I'm going to be down in the Secure Research Room continuing my work."

Nate obediently settled into his task. *Man, Aki is going to eat his words. He said I wouldn't be doing anything useful.* He worked his way through the files, glancing at the printouts listing the identifying details of each of the three murder victims beside him.

A missing person's report with the last seen location a store in Nate's neighborhood. He felt a chill settle over him and glanced at the date. Three weeks ago. *Ben's not responsible.* The relief was immediate and followed by a rush of guilt almost as strong.

Department Seven is depending on me to help. Instead, I've got my own agenda. Nate looked down at the mottled surface of the desk, his shoulders sagging. *Should I be here at all?*

But if he wasn't, who would be helping Ben? Nate wiped his clammy palms on his uniform trousers and turned back to the computer. *I can look into Ben's activity at the same time I look for the victims.*

But there was no one missing or dead in their neighborhood and, when Nate figured out how to check the police reports, no reports of any disturbances or increased levels of magic.

Nothing. Nate sat very still at the desk. *Does that mean—Ben didn't kill anyone?* He remembered the blood staining Ben's mouth and front, his teeth bared as he lunged toward Aki. Hope battled with the fear inside him, making his chest feel uncomfortably tight. *If he didn't kill anyone and he's Saltaire's prisoner for nothing...* He had to know.

Nate pulled the door of the supply cupboard shut behind him. It smelled unpleasantly damp. Did Simeon use it? Nate dug his phone out of his pocket and dialed. His hand shook as he waited for an answer. "Godfrey?"

"Nathan." Godfrey's mild tones gave no hint to his emotional state. "I understand that the terms of your agreement specified there would be no contact."

"I know. But this is important. You've got to tell me. Did Ben leave the house this evening?"

"He did not."

Nate shut his eyes. His throat was so tight he could barely breathe. "You're sure?"

"Absolutely. Not only have I the assurance of knowing he has not passed through the protective wards around the house, but I have seen him."

"Thank god." The relief was dizzying. Nate leaned against the wall, letting it rush over him. Ben was clear.

"Did something happen?"

"There's been another victim. But now we can prove Ben's not involved—"

"I do not wish to be the bearer of bad news, but there are such things as copycat killers."

"Not in this case. The work—it's the same. And all the details are right, even those that weren't shared with the press."

"I see."

There was a brief muffled sound and then a new voice spoke. "What details would those be?"

Nate's mouth fell open, the phone almost slipping from his fingers. "Ben!" And Ben sounding like himself. Analytical, focused—Nate could picture his frown as he held the phone to his ear, waiting for Nate's reply. He readjusted his hold on his phone, putting his hand out to brace himself against the wall. "Is it—you're really, you're you?"

"I'm me, as far as I can tell." The reply was wry. That was Ben all right. "Hello, Nate."

There was a warmth in the way he said Nate's name, a warmth that Nate in no way deserved. "You're—you remember?"

"Most things, not all. There are still gaps—Godfrey, this is important. I don't care if Saltaire approves. I'm the main suspect, aren't I? If I'm going to clear my name, I need to know what happened."

He sounded just like his usual self. Collected, cool, in control. Nate felt sick. *And I abandoned him to Saltaire.* Knowing what Saltaire's presence would do to Ben, he just surrendered him, without even a fight. "I'm so sorry. I know—"

"Give me the situation."

Was Ben angry? It was hard to tell. He sounded focused, and he listened without comment as Nate reported on everything that had happened, from the first victim's reaction to Nate's presence, the discovery of the second, and the circumstances surrounding the latest victim. "Just like the two previous killings, the necromancer took the precaution of dousing the scene with wolfsbane. No one knows that except for the Department Seven officers, so you see it's got to be the same guy."

"So either there is a leak in the department and someone is trying to frame me for the third victim, or I'm not the killer."

Nate gulped. "You don't think you could—"

"My opinion is biased, but I don't think I'm guilty." Ben's tone was ironic. "Neither of the victims whose pictures I've seen rang a bell, but I'm afraid you'll have to take my word for it."

Nate let out the breath he was holding slowly. "I know you're not behind these deaths. You wouldn't, even if you could have..." He didn't want to go there, not when Ben was finally sounding like himself again.

"Could have?"

"It's not important. I'm at Department Seven now, looking up the missing persons reports to try and find anyone who looks like the victims in this case. It's a complete blank. I've hit last year's reports and there's still nothing."

"Victims wouldn't be in ARX reports or Saltaire and Hunter would have said something, not that they're confiding in me about this case." There was a pointed note in Ben's voice. "Godfrey?"

After a moment's delay, Nate heard Godfrey's reply. "Nothing. Either they are from out of town or the killer took special steps to prevent his victims being identified."

"How are we supposed to find them then? If Department Seven and ARX can't—"

"We keep looking." Ben's tone was matter-of-fact. "It's possible the victims are from out of town, which would explain why they haven't been reported missing. Godfrey and I will start calling hotels and hostels, looking for anyone who might have made a booking they didn't show up for."

Nate hesitated. As an out of towner, he knew from experience that if you went to New Camden and failed to update your family regularly, they were inclined to assume the worst. The amount of times his mother had nearly reported him missing because he'd overslept and missed their regular call...

"Nate, I'm going to need your help with this."

He swallowed. "Sure. Whatever you need."

"You've seen all three crime scenes. Do you think the work is Peter's?"

Nate nodded, forgetting that Ben couldn't see him. "Yeah. I mean, I'm no expert, but it's got to be him. There's no one else who mixes vampires and necromancy, and well—it's just got to be him." He finished up unhappily, aware that this was not convincing.

He could sense Ben's frown. "There's more to this, isn't there?"

Nate shut his eyes. "When we went to Peter's apartment, I saw him. And then again at the—the other night. He spoke to me."

"He was physically there?"

"No one else saw him. But I know he was there. He said—" *You're taking their lives to feed Ben. How is that any different from what I did and died for?* "It doesn't matter what he said, but it was exactly what Peter *would* say."

Ben's voice was muffled. Had he turned away from the phone. "A shade?"

"It is possible," Godfrey allowed thoughtfully. Was Nate on speaker phone? "If Peter's magic is working again, it would be a strong call to his spirit—as would the media focus on his case. But a shade could not kill."

"No. But if Peter has successfully worked a possession..." Ben paused. Nate could practically hear him thinking. "Nate, you remember the spell he left in my apartment?"

"The one under the rug that you almost stepped on?"

"It's possible Peter left others and that one of those is successful. He could be working his magic through another person."

Nate swallowed. "He could be anyone?"

"Right. And it's possible that the victims will give us a clue to their killer, whose identity Peter has taken."

New meaning to identity theft. Nate pinched the bridge of his nose. He needed to stay focused. "But if we can't identify the victims—"

"All three had vampire bite marks, correct?" Ben said. "I want you to look at the register of recent deaths. I'll do the same."

Nate stuck his head out of the cupboard but the hall was clear. There was no one in the office, and he sat back at the desk, clicking the mouse to get rid of the screensaver. "Okay. Ready to go."

"I'll take this month. You take last month."

Even though Ben was halfway across the city, knowing that they were working together on this gave Nate a feeling of relief. "What are we looking for?"

"Your victims. It's just a hunch, but if it is Peter behind this, then the victims might not have been killed by vampires. They might *be* vampires."

"But they were drained of blood," Nate said, even as he navigated to the deaths tab.

"A consequence not of hunger but of the spell?" Godfrey sounded speculative. "An interesting theory. I will consult the texts in the library and determine what spells might have that effect."

They didn't speak after that. Nate put his phone onto speakerphone and set it down on the desk, working his way through the reports. Ben worked faster than he did, announcing that he was starting the next month. Shortly after that, he found a recent death, a woman with mermaid hair.

"Alison Cooper. From the description, she sounds like tonight's victim, but you'll need to confirm. You've seen her, I haven't."

Nate left the file he was looking at and opened a fresh tab. "How far through the month is this?"

"Now we have a name, you can go right to her file. Type Alison Cooper into the search bar."

Nate did. "No results found."

"Are you sure? How did you spell it?"

A few minutes of deliberation justified Nate's spelling and revealed that her file was not in the computer system. Neither was Tim Hyatt, a good match for the first victim, or Olivia Barnett, who sounded very similar to the second.

"ARX gets the majority of its missing people and recent death information directly from Department Seven's files," Ben said slowly. "I can think of only one reason that they wouldn't be there."

"Deliberate sabotage?"

Ben hesitated. "I might be jumping to conclusions, but this feels personal. Like it's a grudge against me. Only three people have ever hated me enough to do something like this, and one of them runs Department Seven."

Nate's heart sank. "You really think Gunn—"

"That's the weird part. I don't. Gunn's unrepentant in his biases but at his heart, he's got his own code. He wouldn't pervert the course of justice out of spite. But if public safety was an issue, I'm not sure what he wouldn't do...but he needs his code. Otherwise, he's a monster and I don't think he would be able to process his existence without it."

Nate nodded slowly, relieved. Despite the many, many reasons not to like Gunn, he did. "What does that leave?"

"Before we speculate, let's be sure that the files have been removed. Department Seven must have paper copies of all these files, right? See if you can find them so that we know they were deliberately removed from the databases."

"Right." Nate bit his lip. "I'll call you back."

It felt wrong to press the button and end the call. Part of him wondered if that was the last time he'd talk to Ben. After all, he'd given his word to Saltaire not to contact him... *Fuck Saltaire. Ben's himself. He's not a killer.* Nate dropped his phone in his pocket and stood. *The sooner we clear this mess up, he can be free, away from Saltaire's influence.*

Nate swallowed. It was under Saltaire's influence that Ben had made his startling recovery. *Is he going to go full-vamp the moment he's released?* He stood motionless before the desk, hesitating. Then with a deep breath, he squared his shoulders and walked toward the reception desk. *I have to have more faith in Ben than that.*

LEANNE DIRECTED NATE to the filing cabinets. "They're in the basement, next to the Secure Research Room. You'll need to get Tremaine to unlock it for you."

Nate knocked on the glass doors but made no attempt to enter. Tremaine looked up from her work, closing the book she was reading before walking over to the door. "Found anything, Nate?"

"Possibly. Leanne said there were paper records down here in the basement. I want to look at those."

"Technically accurate, but—well, I'll let you see for yourself." Tremaine led Nate to a metal door with a padlock on it. She unlocked the door with a key on the same chain as the one she was using to get in and out of the Secure Records Room. She coughed as the door swung open. "I don't think anyone's been in here since I went on sick leave."

Nate was getting used to Department Seven smells, but this was a new one. Moldering pages, with a distinct undertone of rust and rot. He felt for the light switch and turned it on, revealing three lopsided filing cabinets, and a series of wooden shelves attached directly to the wall, what looked like a section of high school lockers, and an actual chest of drawers looking incredibly out of place. There was also a chair missing a leg, a fax machine that seemed to have been involved in a fire, and covering every available surface including the floor, a sea of loose paper.

"Is this the junk room?"

Tremaine sighed. "It might as well be. Gunn's not exactly the most systematic of people, and the rest of the department is too busy to have the time to tidy up down here. Coming up with a proper filing system is one of the things Kenzies and I plan to do someday, but something always takes precedence."

Nate eyed the mess of papers. "How do you find anything in here?"

"You get lucky." Tremaine patted his arm. "Yell if anything moves that shouldn't move."

Nate opened the first filing cabinet and was met with a collection of handwritten notes on yellowed paper. The date said 1878. *Man. Before Gunn?* He shut that drawer and went to the next. These were considerably more recent—the 1960s—but nowhere near what he wanted. Worse, as Nate continued his search of the cabinet, there was no order to the papers. They appeared to have been jammed in wherever there was space. There was no order, no theme, and no chance of finding anything among the mess.

Nate shut the third filing cabinet, his mind racing. He hadn't been able to find the recently deceased reports but that itself was no proof they'd been tampered with. *We're no further along.* Absently he began to scoop up the papers resting on top of the filing cabinet. He cleared a space on the floor and began placing the papers into piles according to what type they were.

Aki would have laughed at him, claiming that Nate's passion for cleanliness verged on the excessive, but Aki had only once done the laundry in their entire acquaintance and thought leaving things on the floor was a valid means of storage. Nate found that tidying was soothing, particularly when he had a lot to think about.

I have to help Ben. That was uppermost, followed shortly by the knowledge that every second they didn't catch the real murderer was a second that Ben spent in Saltaire's custody. *Would he try to bring Ben under his control again?* Stupid question. Saltaire came from a time when leaders were accustomed to their men dying for them at the least provocation. He wouldn't allow Ben to escape a second time. *Not unless we can prove beyond any doubt that he's innocent.*

Nate continued his sorting. His piles of paper stood wrist high, and he'd succeeded in clearing the floor before he stood. Nate stretched, looking around the room. With the sea of paper removed, it was obvious that mushrooms were growing out of the carpet. There was a vent above them, no doubt the source of the moisture. Nate wrinkled his nose. He didn't think much of his chances of persuading Gunn to run repairs, but the least he could do was make sure there weren't any more loose papers. He shifted, accidentally brushing against one of the piles, and their slow descent was like the whisper of leaves. *And they were leaves once.* Nate reached out to them. *I know I can feel wood. What about the trees in paper?*

It was faint, but there. He couldn't wake it, but it was a mild tickle. Nate shuffled the papers together and turned toward the door. *How to break the news to Ben? I found fuck all...*

There was a slight tickle as he reached the door. Nate turned his head. The bookcase held dust-covered bottles of specimens and boxes that smelled even mustier than the papers—evidence from old cases? Half were clearly labeled, half had no label whatsoever.

The tickle came from a box labeled *"Zombie Outbreak '88."* Nate pulled it down and discovered that in addition to a few jars contained samples of what looked like body parts, a shorn-off shotgun, and a hazmat suit mask and gloves, there was a manila file.

Nate picked it up and opened it. *Recently Deceased.* His hands felt clammy. *Deliberately hidden.*

The girl with mermaid hair was there, right at the top of the file. The reason for the file's disappearance was immediately visible. Attached to her file was a post-it note saying simply "vampire."

"You were right, Ben. The files were hidden—and they're all three of them vampires." Nate sat on the carpet, gripping his phone, the file in front of him. "They died in the last few months."

"Recent vampires. Old enough to have reason, young enough to be hungry—and reckless." Ben sounded thoughtful.

"But the vampires have been here every night harassing Gunn about the Registry. Why wouldn't they tell us vampires were missing?"

"No vampire worth their fangs would admit to Gunn that someone's picking off members of their entourage. They're not likely to mention it, even to their allies."

"But three vampires—"

"Three relatively recent vampires. At the exact age where they are likely to get into trouble. Their masters might be looking into their disappearances, but if they've made the connection between their servants and the necromancer killings, they're unlikely to announce it. No one wants the stigma of being associated with Peter."

The way Ben said that... "Have you remembered the—um."

"Circumstances that led to me being placed on the register? Not entirely. The gaps in my memory are so persistent, and so specific, that I suspect this is deliberate."

Nate's heart leaped into his throat. *Saltaire. He could order Ben to forget, and Ben would have no choice.* What had he done, handing Ben's future over to a mono-maniac control freak?

"At any rate, I think we can confidently say this is Peter back to his old tricks with the help of an unwilling accomplice. Tell me how you found the files, Nate?"

"There's this record room that's pretty much been neglected for years. It's—well, you don't want to know how bad it smells in here. But I started putting a few things in order—"

Ben snorted. "As you do."

Those simple three words gave Nate a rush of feeling. He blinked quickly, glad there was no one there to see his wide grin. "Anyway. The file was shoved into a box of zombie stuff."

"Suggesting that Peter's got an ally in the department."

Ben's statement sliced through Nate's elation. "But everyone in the department wants him found ASAP."

"I didn't say willing ally, Nate. And who would be more at risk of accidentally triggering one of his traps than the staff investigating his crimes? He might have been biding his time for months, waiting for a chance to put this plan into operation."

"And then you disappeared and he decided it was time to act?" Nate bit his lip.

"If he made his first move while I was still on the Final Register..." Ben's voice hardened. "Then I'm not his only target."

"You mean—"

"That first revenant responded to your presence," Ben said. "And now that you're working with Department Seven, Peter's agent has access to you. You've got to be on guard, Nate."

"I can't believe it. No one in Department Seven—" A breeze touched the back of Nate's neck. The door was opening. He turned his head, but before he could glimpse more than a hand in a plastic glove touching the light switch, the room was plunged into darkness.

Shit. Nate scrambled to his feet. He had a thought of tackling the mysterious figure in the doorway, but before he could, he heard a hiss and a chemical substance was sprayed at him, connecting with his eyes. Immediately they started to burn. Nate screamed and stumbled back.

The next blast went into his mouth. He made the mistake of swallowing and felt the fire travel down his throat and into his lungs. He choked, staggering into the table and sending the papers flying.

He heard the metal door slam shut, and forcing himself to ignore the pain, leaped for the door. Unable to open his eyes, he was still searching for the door handle when he heard the click of the key turning. "Let me out!"

"Nate? What's happening?" Ben's voice sounded tinny from the phone.

Nate sank to his knees. Moving so fast had not been a good idea. He'd breathed in more of the air, and it had settled in his lungs, a painful, pulsing mass. "Locked in. Someone sprayed something in my face. It burns."

"Can you cover your mouth? Try to breathe in as little of the stuff as possible."

Nate undid the top buttons of his uniform shirt, pulling his undershirt up to cover his mouth and nose. His throat rasped painfully with every breath, and dizziness warred with nausea.

"We need to identify what you've been sprayed with."

Nate grunted. With his back against the door, he used his legs to push himself upward. They shook wildly, but they got him level with the light switch. It took two attempts, but the light flicked on. *Now the hard part.* He had to force his eyes open. They didn't want to obey and the pain was enough to make Nate think twice. As the dizziness came over him in a wave, Nate swallowed.

"Weed killer." That wasn't accidental. That was someone who knew him, knew what he was—

"Nate! Focus! Summon your energy. You need to break down the door." Ben's voice was calm and commanding. "Godfrey's calling for help, but you need to get out."

It was easy for Ben to talk about focus. Nothing hurt like he hurt now. The stinging had increased, feeling like actual flames. "Trying." But when he reached for his magic, it shrank back, wilting beneath his touch. "Not...not working."

Ben was speaking again, but Nate couldn't take in the words. He swayed, the room dipping wildly around him. He felt himself start to fall.

"Nate!"

The collision with the floor left him stunned. Nate listened to Ben call him. He needed all his energy to fight to breathe, even though every mouthful of air was another stab in his burning chest. "Ben..." There was something wrong with the lights. They were fading fast, darkness enveloping him. "Sorry. I didn't mean—"

And then there was just the burning.

Chapter Fourteen

"NATE?" BEN GRIPPED the phone to his ear. The only sound he heard was Nate's labored breathing—and labored was generous. Every breath sounded like Darth Vader's last gasp. *Please, Nate. Survive—*

He placed a hand on the stainless steel counter of Godfrey's modern kitchen to steady himself. A confused rush of memory swept over him, similar to the one he'd experienced when he heard the faint echo of Nate's voice through Godfrey's phone. He'd acted without thinking, grabbing the phone at once. Hearing him speak directly had brought a rush of warmth and tears to his eyes, and he'd forced himself to focus on the facts of the case rather than the depth of emotion Nate awoke within him—and the worrying question of how he'd forgotten a man who clearly meant everything to him.

Now the emotional roller coaster was rapidly plummeting down a steep drop. Ben felt himself paralyzed with fear at the thought of Nate's danger.

Nate's nothing if not a survivor. Ben took a deep breath. Godfrey had left to call an ambulance from the landline. He needed to think.

Weed killer. The word set off a chain reaction of dread. Nate had survived all sorts of things that would have been fatal to a human. This weapon was chosen by someone who knew exactly what Nate was. And that was a very small field.

Gunn. Kenzies, hell, any member of Department Seven. Gunn must have records of some sort. He complained enough about paperwork. *And if this is a member of Department Seven, they could still be there. What's to say they're not just waiting for the spray to take effect before going in and personally finishing the job?*

Ben heard the door open behind him. Godfrey must be back. "We have to go. Nate needs our help!" He felt the chill too late.

Saltaire stood in the doorway. His face was impassive. "You will not leave this house."

Ben stood stock-still as Saltaire's presence crashed down on him with all the force of a rockslide. He fought just to hold his ground and not cringe as Saltaire approached. He snatched the phone from Ben's hand, glancing at the number before ending the call.

Ben was unable to repress a cry of horror. "You—"

"Godfrey informed me of Granger's situation. That does not alter the conditions under which you remain here."

Ben's hands balled into fists. He forced them to relax. He could not fight Saltaire if he was fighting himself. "What do you mean, conditions? Am I a prisoner?"

Saltaire looked at him as others might look at a cockroach. "You are not to leave until I have satisfied myself to the extent of your misdeeds—and depending on that result, you may never leave."

"You could have said 'yes.'" Ben took a deep breath, steeling himself against the pressure bearing down on him. "What grounds do you have for holding me?"

"The grounds of being responsible for making you." Saltaire's tone was flat. "As your creator, it is my duty to ensure you do not become a threat. You know me better than to think I would cast aside an unpleasant task, no matter how it pains me."

There it was—the combination of duty and pain. Ben remembered how much he'd been impressed by Saltaire's dedication to his perceived duty, until he realized how narrow his application of it was. "You don't expect me to be impressed by your pain while Nate is lying in agony at the mercy of a person already responsible for three deaths, do you?"

Saltaire snarled. "That man is no loss. His reckless ways have endangered the city and damaged the reputations of all associated with him!"

"You care more about your reputation than the people you're sworn to protect!" Ben shot back.

"I'm sworn to protect the lives of innocent humans." Saltaire's laugh was scornful. "Granger is not an innocent. He's not human, and he barely qualifies as benign."

"You despised him even before you knew he wasn't human." The memories were still patchy, but they were resurfacing fast. Ben felt his nails dig into the skin of his palms as his fists clenched. "Nate was attacked because whoever is behind these murders sees him as a threat—and the longer that person goes unpunished, the more innocent lives are at risk." Saltaire's expression didn't so much as flicker, and Ben, who knew better than to expect anything from him, was still outraged. "And you refuse to act?"

"The situation is volatile," Saltaire said, his voice a chilly rebuke. "Largely thanks to your own actions."

"You'd like to believe that, wouldn't you?" His pulse pounded in his head, either an excess of adrenaline or the start of a killer headache. "It would justify the control you keep us under. Well, I'm not going to stand by and do nothing while people are in danger."

Saltaire's eyes flashed. He took a step toward Ben. "My control is the only thing separating you from a monster right now. You may despise it, but you need it. You need me." Saltaire fixed him with a hard stare. It had the full weight of his personality behind it. Ben, glaring back, didn't realize what a mistake he'd made until Saltaire moved several seconds later, and Ben suddenly realized he could think again. "You will remain here until I decide you are fit to leave."

Just like a criminal. Ben felt himself shaking with a mixture of exertion and fury. "I'm innocent until proven guilty, a concept which is after your time, but one you have agreed to obey. But you're very anxious to prevent me from standing trial."

Saltaire's movements were usually measured. Now he looked up sharply. "I aim to prevent a further disturbance. The city's security is perilous enough without throwing its justice system into disrepute."

"Are you afraid they'll find me guilty or innocent?" Ben sucked in a deep breath. "I don't remember how you captured me, but I demand that you set me free to face the consequences of my actions."

"I did not capture you." Saltaire sneered. "A so-called friend handed you over to me. He could not deal with the reality of your existence."

"You're wrong." Saltaire could lie and did when it suited him, but Ben was willing to bet this was willful misunderstanding. "You can't stand the thought that I can and did exist outside the umbrella of your control. Newsflash. We're not your puppets. We have thoughts and minds of our own and sooner or later you will not be able to hold us back."

Saltaire stood very still. And then he smiled. Ben couldn't remember seeing him smile before. Forgetting a smile like this wasn't possible. It was stiff, as if the muscles around it had not been used in centuries, and bared his fangs in an expression more suited to a snarl. "You wish to exist without my control. Very well. I will show you how false your accusations are by granting your misguided request."

Ben swallowed. *He's really going to take his power back?*

Saltaire had done this once before, and rather than a benevolent gift, he'd intended it to end in Ben's death. Saltaire removing his control effectively reverted Ben to the mindset and power of any fresh vampire. Hungry, wild, and little more than a revenant.

"Twice you have drunk my blood. Twice you have slept in my house. Twice I have freed you from your obligation to me." Saltaire moved fast, faster than Ben was expecting. He grabbed Ben's arm, his nails raking across his flesh. A red drop splashed to the ground. "There will be no freedom the third time."

What does he mean, third time? It was Ben's last conscious thought. The pulsing throbbing in his head increased, drowning out any thoughts but the uppermost instinct—fear. He was trapped in the room with a dangerous predator.

He hissed as he stepped back against the kitchen cabinets, instinct telling him to make himself look as big as possible. His peripheral vision narrowed to the other predator and he blundered into the arm of a saucepan left on the stove as he backed away. It clattered to the ground, making Ben jump. He saw another saucepan beside it and snatched it up. It would not make much of weapon, but if he could only convince the other that he was more trouble than he was worth—

Saltaire moved so quickly Ben didn't even see him. The saucepan was knocked aside and the master vampire simply backhanded him into the wall with such force that Ben's breath was knocked out of him. His fangs grazed his lip and he spat out blood.

"Pitiful." Saltaire seized him by the back of his collar and flung him into the hallway.

Ben skidded over the polished wood before coming to a halt on his knees.

There was a cry of alarm. "Is this really necessary?" Godfrey had retreated up the stairs at the sound of the disturbance.

"It is what he wants." Saltaire's tone was smug. "Perhaps he will not try my patience a third time." He paused, looking down at Ben. "Well? Will you try to attack me again?"

Ben cringed. He hissed, but his only thought now was escape. He glanced toward the door. Even in this state, he was aware of the presence of the wards. *No escape—*

"I think you begin to understand." With a single lunge, Saltaire grabbed Ben again by his neck. He was held, choking for breath, as Saltaire unlatched the hidden trapdoor to the crypt and forced him down the stairs. He locked Ben in the enclosure Hunter had used to store the revenants.

"You will have time to come to your senses," Saltaire told him. "And when you do, I hope you will understand what a risk you take, seeking to free yourself of my protection. It would be wise not to try my patience a third time."

Ben whimpered, pressing as far back against the stone walls of his cage as possible.

Saltaire's lip curled in disgust. He had never tolerated any sign of weakness, in any circumstances. He turned the key in the lock and made his way out of the crypt.

Ben took a deep breath. He held it until he heard the crypt door close behind Saltaire and then let it out in a gasp. He breathed in again, releasing this in a more measured fashion. The air was thick with the stench of revenant, and he felt a momentary wave of nausea. *Is how I look to Saltaire the same as how the revenants look to me?*

Hold that thought. If he was getting out of here and helping Nate—and he was—then he needed a calm, focused approach. Ben concentrated on calming his breathing. The first time Saltaire had withdrawn his protective control, Nate had physically contained Ben until he'd come back to his senses. This time, he was entirely alone, but he had precious time spent outside Saltaire's control and the knowledge that he'd escaped once before. Even if he didn't entirely understand how that had happened.

I got out once. I'm getting out now. None of the revenants had figured out the key. Saltaire clearly didn't think that Ben was capable of even that much reasoning and had left it in the lock. Ben simply reached through the bars and turned the key. The door clicked open. *Like taking candy from a baby. An evil, controlling vampiric baby.*

He paused on the threshold of the crypt, listening carefully for any sounds from above. The trapdoor wasn't shut. He could hear Godfrey's voice raised in mild reproach and the sound of a door banging loudly—their version of an argument. Godfrey never raised his voice, but when Saltaire was in a bad temper, he reverted to the ways he was accustomed to, such as flinging belongings about and leaving them for his menials to pick up later—like the open trapdoor.

Ben quickly slipped up the stairs and into the kitchen. No one blocked his way to the back door, and—as he was hoping—with Saltaire's power removed, he encountered no compulsion to stay in the house. *Saltaire didn't see that coming.*

But as Ben scrambled over the fence and into a neighbor's garden, he felt a twinge of misgiving. *Am I making a big mistake?* There was a big difference between retaining control in a locked crypt on his own and when confronted with an emergency situation—or even other people. Ben hesitated, straddling the wall. *Do I have any right to endanger others?*

He could almost hear Saltaire's disapproval. *You cannot deny the truth. You're a ticking time bomb. The moment you come face-to-face with a situation that calls to your hunger, any illusion of control you have will be gone.*

As he hesitated, the evening breeze stirred the leaves of the ivy that grew over the fence. *Nate!* Ben swung himself over the wall without any hesitation. *If Saltaire even knows what a time bomb is I will be very surprised. And even if I am a threat, the only person who needs to watch out is whoever harmed Nate.* Ben slunk through the garden, breaking into a run as he reached the road.

THE WHITE FLASHES of the ambulance parked outside Department Seven alternately bathed the street in light and then plunged it into darkness. Ben dropped silently from the roof of the building he had climbed and approached the scene on foot. One technician stood guard near the vehicle. Her colleagues were presumably inside. As he drew nearer, the reception door was flung open, and a stretcher carried by the two EMTs emerged.

Ben found himself rooted to the spot. His eyes sought the form on the stretcher. Nate lay still, an oxygen mask over his mouth. His hand moved slightly.

Thank everything. Ben shut his eyes, grateful Nate's unnatural luck had not deserted them.

"I'll tell Gunn and Kenzies what happened." A woman in a Department Seven uniform shut the door behind the stretcher. As the EMT staff supervised the lowering of the ramp that would enable them to move Nate inside the ambulance, she continued to speak, touching Nate's arm. "Don't worry, Granger. We'll make sure whoever did this to you doesn't try it on anyone else."

Who was this woman? Ben felt the vampire's proprietary feelings stir. He stayed where he was until he was sure he was not going to do anything that might prove Saltaire's actions justified.

There was another woman with them, one who obviously didn't share her colleague's appraisal of his condition. She drew her arm across her eyes and sniffed. "I don't see how this could have happened."

As the uniformed woman turned to reassure her, Ben approached the EMT standing guard. "What happened? Is he okay?"

The woman turned, sizing him. "He inhaled a poisonous chemical. We're taking him to the hospital for urgent care."

"But he'll be all right, won't he?" Despite his best intentions, his voice cracked.

The woman tilted her head. "Do you know him?" As Ben hesitated, she frowned. "You seem familiar."

Ben remembered that his photo was plastered across the New Camden newspapers in an attempt to find him. "Just curious." He gave her a tight smile and turned and walked back the way he'd come. He kept his steps even—nothing said suspicious like running away from the authorities—and listened for sound of pursuit. There was none. Instead, he watched from the roof as Nate was loaded into the ambulance and it drove off.

At least he'll get proper treatment at the hospital— Ben caught sight of something left behind in the street by the ambulance. In the dark, his eyes saw perfectly. It was a single, withered leaf.

The leaf had not been there before the stretcher had emerged, and a quick look around the street confirmed there were no trees in their vicinity.

Shit. Nate's magic! Ben swallowed. It was hard to imagine he could forget that Nate occasionally bled leaves or sprouted roots. His manner of healing was as original as he was, and he could only imagine the reactions of the hospital staff. *He'd be a sensation—or the newest evidence of New Camden's many dangers.* Either way, Nate could forget all about privacy. He and his brother Ethan would be subjected to an intense amount of attention.

There will be new restrictions. Ethan will definitely not be allowed to keep farming. And while Ben didn't feel overwhelming concern for Ethan, he could imagine the effect his brother's misery would have on Nate. *Not to mention danger to them both.* He didn't want to think about the Final Register.

I have to get him out of the hospital before his nature is discovered.

Breaking into a medical facility was all kinds of risky—not to mention illegal. There was no way Ben could walk in. Even if he was willing to trust his untested control over his inner vampire, the city wouldn't. All hospitals were specifically warded to keep vampires out. Even if his dual nature gave him a loophole, Ben knew he couldn't expect to get away unrecognized.

I need help. Someone who doesn't care about breaking the law for a friend... The choice was easy. Ben scaled the roof, working his way in the direction of the nearest facility. "Hey, George."

"Ben?" Her surprise only lasted a second. "Good to hear you sounding like you. You're back?"

"Tell me about it. And yeah, I guess." Ben sucked in a breath. "Are you busy?"

"Nothing that can't wait. You need my help, huh? Men." George snorted. "You only call when you want something."

"Nate's in trouble."

There was a pause and then George sighed. "Tell me where you are and I'm on my way."

THERE WAS A police car parked outside the emergency entrance. It could have been coincidence, but Ben thought it was far more likely that knowing their relationship, Gunn had urged the staff to be on the lookout for him. *Better that than Nate's secret is already uncovered.*

"The plan is simple. I create a diversion drawing security after me, allowing you to sneak in and find Nate."

George looked away from the squad car and back to Ben. It was hard to read her expression. "You're gonna be in big trouble. The whole city's looking for you."

"That's what I'm counting on." If he delayed, he would only psych himself out of this. Ben shoved his hands into his pockets and made his way across the street. In case Saltaire had reported his disappearance, he'd taken the liberty of borrowing a few personal items from an unattended clothesline, including a hat. Knowing New Camden's nocturnal population, anyone who cared about their possessions being borrowed wouldn't leave them out overnight. He hoped the disguise would be enough to get him inside.

It was. Ben approached the reception desk where a harried looking woman was catching up on paperwork. "Excuse me. I'm looking for Nathan Granger."

Her eyes widened, and her hand went immediately to the underside of her desk. *Yeah, they were warned.* Ben turned his head to see the security guard approaching, a police officer with him.

"Excuse me, sir—"

Ben ducked under the security man's outstretched arm and ran down the hospital corridor. He shouldered his way through the wide doors. He caught a whiff of a strong, leafy smell and wavered in the doorway. *No. George has got this—I have to trust her.* He turned away from the Emergency Room and down the hall to his left, hearing someone collide with the door behind him. His pursuit was clearly not far behind.

As Ben sprinted down the hall, he heard a deafening crack and felt something graze his leg. He ignored the stinging pain, forcing himself to weave as he continued to run. *Who takes their gun out in a hospital? Seriously!*

He hurled himself up the stairs to the right, the smell of blood rising in the night air.

Pitiful fools! His inner vampire snarled. *They will rue the day they messed with me! They are no match for me. Why should I run?*

Ben dug his fingers into the skin of his arm. *Now is not the time.* He continued to haul himself up the stairs. *I've got to be in control—not my instincts.*

The third floor was high enough no one would expect him to go out the window. Ben slipped over the ledge, lowering himself carefully from it. He took a deep breath, hoping against hope that his vampire strength would come through for him, and let go.

He stumbled but staggered to his feet. His feet and knees protested but he managed to take off in a shambling run.

"There he is!" Another round of gunshots peppered the pavement. Ben shot across the road into an alley and clambered up onto a wall. He ran lightly across the wall with a grace no one who looked at his skinny form would suspect him of possessing.

The wall allowed him to put distance between himself and his clumsier pursuers. Ben jumped from the wall into a parking lot and from there to the street. He had lost the police, but it was still a good idea to put as much distance between them as possible.

"Cut him off!"

Ben put on a fresh burst of speed. As he ran down the street, assessing his surroundings for new escape routes, part of his mind was in shock. *How did they find me?* As he ran, he heard an echo, the sound of footsteps keeping pace with him.

No. Catching up. Whoever this was, they ran faster than a vampire. Ben sprinted with all he had. A form crashed into him. He collided with the pavement, their combined momentum dragging him along the pavement. He could smell his blood, even as his body registered numerous scrapes. *How dare they!* He snarled, furious, as he kicked off his pursuer's bulk—

And heard a deeper growl in response.

Shit. Ben suddenly became aware of the smell of rotten meat that always seemed to hang around werewolves. He pulled himself into a crouch, turning—and found himself face-to-face with a rust-colored wolf, also picking herself up. She bared her teeth, revealing a jaw of sharp and unusually well-cared-for teeth.

Fight it! Fight! The vampire was not happy about this. Ben took a deep breath, trying to push past the instant fear response. He saw a wall to the side of them. *I can haul myself over that. Kenzies can't.* He snarled, adjusting his stance as though he was preparing to leap at her, and at the last moment dashed toward the wall. He jumped up, grabbing the top of the wall, but before he could get a firm purchase on the brick, he was hauled back by his foot. He fell, the pavement knocking the breath out of him. Before he could recover, Kenzies settled her weight on top of him.

A fully grown werewolf weighs a lot. Ben shut his eyes, fighting to keep himself in check. He'd caused enough trouble for one night. He'd bought George time to go to Nate's aid. No reason to add to his problems by scrapping with the deputy head of Department Seven.

Kenzies took a deep sniff at him but seemed to sense he wasn't going anywhere. She raised her head. Her howl brought forth another wave of panic from the vampire. *The beast glories in her capture! I cannot let this go unpunished!*

Ben knew better. *Calling backup.* He could hear the crackle of a radio as Kenzies's companions cautiously approached them. He shut his eyes. *Please, Nate. Be all right.*

THE DANK CELL could only belong to Department Seven. It was poorly lit, had no ventilation to speak of, and only the hinges on the wall gave any indication that there had once been a bench there. The biggest clue, however, was the smell. Ben sat on a patch of floor near the door, carefully not breathing through his nose. *How does anything smell this bad?* He could identify the ripe smell of werewolf, the fresh graveyard smell of ghouls, something damp and unpleasant, and the usual whiff of brimstone, tomb, and tobacco that indicated Gunn's presence.

With a start, Ben realized that smell was fresh. He got to his feet to find Gunn studying him through the cell bars.

Gunn removed the cigarette between his lips. "Oh, Benny. You bring more drama than an entire teenage sitcom."

"I'm not doing this for my own amusement. Or for yours."

"Good. Because I'm not amused." Gunn stepped forward, adding stale breath to the list of crimes against olfactory senses. "I can see why you'd want off the Final Register, and, now the entire city isn't on me wanting the situation fixed yesterday, I got to admit what you did was clever. I hope Wisner recovers long enough to hear about the loophole in his precious weapon. But why not turn yourself in?"

Ben snorted. "Would you have any respect for me if I did?"

"No," Gunn said readily. "But if you imagine I have any respect for you anyway..." He took a drag of his cigarette and stepped right up to the bars. It was all Ben could do not to take a step back, even when Gunn exhaled, the smoke from his cigarette stinging his eyes. "I taste fear. You're only tenuously keeping yourself together."

Ben felt a spike of panic—*Why did I think putting myself in contact with an unscrupulous lemur was a good idea?*—and gripped the bars of the cell. "We need to talk about Peter."

"Not you too."

"The evidence points toward him."

"There's more than one suspect. Peter's been killed and preemptively exorcised. You on the other hand are still here."

"I was in Saltaire's custody for the third murder," Ben shot back. "I know you only have a scant regard for the investigative process, but I'm sure you can see I can't be in two places at once. Which leaves one alternative."

"I don't want to hear it."

"You can't ignore this. Peter's successfully possessed someone, Gunn—and it's someone in your department. The attack on Nate proves it. He found something the killer didn't want anyone to know. Wondered why your victims didn't show up on any missing persons report? They were all dead. At least three months previously."

Gunn's scowl increased. "You're sure about this?"

"Nate saw the files. He was telling me about them on the phone. That's when he was attacked." Ben took a deep breath. "The files were not in the Department Seven database. They were deliberately erased. Who could do that but a member of the department?"

"We share some computer access with the police."

"Would the police know what makes Nate so…unique? Would they be able to pick the one weapon that could seriously harm him?"

"Enough! You're barking up a dead tree. No one in my department is possessed."

"But—"

Gunn put his face right up against the bars. His tawny eyes stared into Ben's. "Have you forgotten what I am, Benny? You don't think I couldn't smell a possession? I would know the second anyone tried it on with one of my people."

"But the facts—"

"Let me worry about the facts. You need to worry about what's going to happen when the council stops hyperventilating and gets down to discussion." At Ben's frown, Gunn cocked an eyebrow. "You missed the fact that they've been itching to try you? Soon as they can assemble, they're gonna be deciding your fate. I was coming to inform you of that fact and ask if you've got anything in the way of legal representation."

"Diya's on the job?" At Gunn's nod, Ben sat. "I'm satisfied with whatever she thinks best."

"You're putting a lot of trust in a woman with no reason to like vampires."

Ben rolled his eyes. Gunn was barking up the wrong tree there. "I have every confidence in Ms. Patel's professionalism."

"Suit yourself. But if I were you, I would be second-guessing my judgment right now."

Ben paused. Ten to one, Gunn was just trying to get to him. The *lemur* fed on negative emotion. Unease and doubt were bread and butter to him. "What do you mean?"

"How did you end up in Saltaire's custody?" Gunn's eyes glittered.

Ben frowned. "You didn't hand me over to him?" As soon as he said the words, he knew how unlikely that was. If Gunn ever secured a prisoner that Saltaire wanted, he would hang on to them, determined to annoy Saltaire as much as possible.

"You were eluding us, just as you were eluding everyone else in this damn city. Then I got a call from your boyfriend's roommate, saying they had you in the werewolf closet in your apartment. By the time we got there, you were gone. And so was Nate." Gunn's grin was sharp.

Nate? Ben took a step back. *Nate would never—he knew how much Ben hated Saltaire!* "You're lying."

"That's got to sting. After you just gave up your freedom—possibly for good—for him too." Gunn bared yellowed teeth in what was possibly a smile.

He's lying. He lives on pain. He wants you to hurt! Ben tried to suppress the thoughts, but he couldn't do anything about the pain rising within him. It felt like a Band-Aid had been torn off his soul, leaving an already sensitive part of him exposed and vulnerable and raw. "Nate wouldn't. You know how he feels about me."

"Which is why I wouldn't make this up. I wouldn't believe it if I didn't know it was true." Gunn's expression was definitely gloating. "Either there's some hope for him still, or your precious relationship's not as strong as you think."

Ben clenched the bars of the cell. He took control of the pain, forcing it down, forcing the thoughts into silence. "Stop talking."

"Have it your way, Benny." Gunn shrugged, sauntering away. His personal odor lingered, and his voice floated back from the shadowy corridor. "But everything I told you just now is the truth."

The cell bars rattled. Ben forced himself to exhale slowly, releasing the bars. He breathed in again, but the lessening of tension made way for a rush of feeling. He leaned his head against the bars. *Nate handed me over to Saltaire?*

Saltaire's parting words came back to Ben. *A so-called friend handed you over to me. He could not deal with the reality of your existence.*

Ben shut his eyes. *Nate.* It was Nate he'd believed in while on the Final Register, his confidence in him that kept him going even when the obstacles seemed too insurmountable. When he'd been injured and felt himself slipping back into the vampire's mindset, he'd come up with the plan to steal the Register, trusting that Nate would stand by him while he recovered. *This... I believe in you, Nate. Why don't you believe in me?*

Chapter Fifteen

THE SUN'S DEPARTURE woke him. As its warmth faded, Nate, who'd been basking in its glow for an indeterminate amount of time, rolled over, hoping to keep its light. As he did, he lay on something grainy. Other discordant sensations began to register. He wasn't lying on a mattress, but on a thin mat on the floor. The air smelled thick with herbs and smoke. There was a faint musical tinkle in the distance. Nate frowned. *I don't know anyone who owns a wind chime.* He opened his eyes.

From the collection of magical reference books, to the herbs growing in window boxes, and the earthy bent of the decorations, the room belonged to a witch. Which explained a lot about the circle he was sitting in. It was formed from salt interspersed with rose petals. Seven candles surrounded him, all but one having burned themselves out. The circle was loosely formed, with the candles placed at uneven intervals. *So not a necromancer then.* But if not a necromancer, who? Waking up in a magical circle was not usually a good thing...

I don't feel like I've been cursed. He wore a hospital gown, which was itself a mystery, until Nate moved his head too quickly, setting off a chain reaction of nausea. *That explains it.* He swallowed and discovered that his throat ached like the worst sort of cold. His eyes were irritated, but to his left he found a towel that had obviously been used to bathe his eyes. After pausing to wipe them, Nate saw an item that made him blink. Standing in the circle with the candles was a bottle of his favorite brand of vegetable juice. *That's got to be deliberate.*

Not until he'd drunk half of it did it occur to Nate the drink might be drugged. He considered tipping the rest out, but it felt so good on his throat he reasoned that he was in enough trouble anyway. So what if he was drugged? The drink not only cooled his skin but made it easier to think. He looked around the room, searching for further clues to his location.

On a wooden chest at the foot of the room's single bed, there was a stone bowl containing a bundle of twigs and herbs, the source of the smoke. As Nate carefully levered himself up for a closer look, he discovered the bowl contained sand and had been used to extinguish the bundle, the ends of which were blackened with flame. Beside it stood a watering can and half a candy bar.

The vegetable juice might have been coincidence, but Nate could think of only one person who would bring him a candy bar and then eat half of it. "Aki?"

He wasn't consciously aware of the voices in the room beyond until they stopped. The bedroom door was flung open, and Aki stood looking down at him. His eyes lit up. "He's alive!" Immediately, Aki scowled. "Not that I was worried or anything. Like I told you all, Nate's too dumb to know when he should call it quits."

You all? Nate wasn't left in suspense long. Aki stepped forward, allowing Charlotte to slip through the doorway and make her way to Nate's side. "How are you feeling?"

"I've had better days." Nate gingerly felt the skin around his eyes. It was painful and he quickly abandoned the experiment. "What happened?"

"You took weed killer to the face." George leaned in the doorway, looking down at him with an expression of smugness, though what on earth she was smug about was beyond Nate. "Looks like someone really doesn't like you."

"Peter." Nate swallowed. "He's back. I was on the phone to Ben—" He paused, scanning the faces in the doorway. He saw Grant, Vazul, and even Mandy and Bea, but there was no sign of Ben.

"You've got him to thank for your rescue. Him and me," George said. That explained the self-congratulation. "You got picked up by an ambulance and whisked off to a hospital."

"Hospital?" Nate's stomach sank. Ma and Pa had been vehemently against taking either of their sons to a medical professional. Now he knew that he wasn't entirely human, Nate could understand why. "Did—"

"While their treatment probably saved your life, the longer you stayed in the hospital, the more risk there was of your true nature getting exposed," George said.

"Whatever that is." Aki had evidently decided that Nate was in no danger of immediate death and sat next to him on the floor. He poked Nate in his ribs. "Maybe we should have left you to be identified as a dryad and settle this once and for all."

Nate swallowed. "They didn't—"

"Give me the credit I'm due." George picked up a file that Nate hadn't noticed and brandished it. "I didn't just swipe you, I swiped all the files relating to you. There's probably a record of you getting picked up by the ambulance, but nothing more than that."

Nate breathed out. It was a huge relief—or it should have been. "But where's Ben?"

"First things first." Charlotte pressed her fingers to his throat. "The ambulance crew got the weed killer off you, and you were treated for burns and put on a drip at the hospital. Knowing your other nature I completed the cure with a cleansing ritual to rid you of any lingering poisons, and on Aki's suggestion we, um—"

"Put you in the sun and watered you." Vazul sounded far more amused than he should be.

"I told you it would work. And it did." Aki crossed his arms.

It was a strange feeling, picking himself off the floor, knowing that his friends watched his every move. "Thanks. I'm really touched you guys came to my rescue."

"Anytime." George shrugged.

"It was no inconvenience," Charlotte assured him. "Mandy, Bea, and I were meeting tonight anyway, and we've been looking at the uses of cleansing rituals so it worked out well."

"I crashed your coven meeting?" That explained why Mandy and Bea were there.

"We don't mind," Mandy assured him immediately. "As long as you're feeling better, that's the important thing."

"And you weren't the only one." Bea snorted. "At least you have a good excuse. Vazul just likes being obnoxious."

Vazul drew himself up indignantly. "The practice of covens is a sexist institution that should have ended long ago. I'm here to voice my opposition to a practice that excludes—"

"You're not a witch! You've got no reason to want to be here at all!" Aki immediately cut him off.

Nate put his hand out to steady himself against the wall. "Not to sound ungrateful or anything, but you mind if I sit down?"

The bedroom opened onto the living room of the apartment Charlotte shared with her mothers. Modern art with a natural motif dominated. Charlotte pulled a chair up by the window so that he could soak up the last of the setting sun, and Nate found himself admiring a framed photo of a fern bud unfolding.

Grant placed a glass of water on the table beside him. "I don't want to push you, Nate, but there's a lot we need to get to the bottom of."

Nate remembered their last conversation with a lurch. "Yeah. I guess you're all waiting for an explanation?"

"Not waiting," Charlotte said. "But it would be appreciated."

Vazul rolled his eyes. "You're as curious as the rest of us, witch. The hunter told us it was the necromancer. That can't be right, can it?"

"Ben's not acting like himself." Aki sat on the sofa, his arms curled around him. "He attacked me. Twice. He fought Nate to try to get to me. If he's willing to do that..." The gesture exposed the Band-Aids on the underside of his skinny arm.

Nate winced. It would be a long time before Aki got over that experience, and who could blame him? Just thinking about what could have happened made him sick. "This—the attack on me—wasn't Ben."

"We all know that if Ben was in his right mind he would never act in such a way," Grant said. "But that doesn't mean we can overlook—"

"When I was attacked, Ben was in Saltaire's custody, across town," Nate said. "And there was someone with him who can confirm he was there. I was talking to them on the phone when...when I was attacked."

Aki's mouth fell open. George smirked. The others reacted with varying degrees of alarm.

"But if it wasn't Ben," Grant said slowly.

"We've got two lunatics to worry about?" Aki groaned. "Just great."

Grant sat beside him on the sofa, placing a hand on Aki's arm. "Elaborate."

"Sure." Nate sucked in a deep breath. "I don't know how much you guys know about Peter, but—" He gave them a quick summary of Peter's grudge against Ben and Saltaire, his drive for revenge and power and his combination of a vampire's blood magic with the necromantic arts. "The recently deceased files were deliberately removed from Department Seven so no one would realize that the victims weren't drained of their blood by a vampire. They were vampires drained of their blood by a necromancer. And that's when I was attacked. When I found the files in the Department Seven storeroom."

Grant frowned. "And you're sure Ben was where he said he was?"

"Even if Ben was lying, there's no reason Godfrey would be," Nate said. "He's Saltaire's servant and is totally loyal to him."

Grant still hesitated. "Don't take offense at this but the last time we saw Ben he was—"

"A rabid mess, intent on destroying me," Aki cut in.

Grant bit his tongue, shooting a worried look at Aki. "Not exactly in a frame of mind I'd be inclined to trust."

"When I spoke to him on the phone, he was himself. The old Ben." Nate felt his chest warm at the memory. "Calm, analytical, collected. It was his idea to check the recently deceased files instead of just concentrating on missing persons."

"That doesn't necessarily prove anything."

"I met up with him in person," George said. "The guy was himself and made no attempt to maul me or anyone else I saw. And you can trust me. I have no interest in sleeping with the guy."

Thanks, George. "You saw Ben last, right? Do you know where he is now?"

George shook her head. "We split up at the hospital. Our plan was Ben would create a diversion, drawing the guards after him, and I would go in and get you out while their backs were turned. It worked perfectly. I got you back to the RV without any problems, and by the time we got outside, there was no sign of anyone, Ben or police."

"So he's still out there on the run?"

"Not anymore." They turned to see Vazul, standing in front of the flat-screen TV mounted to the apartment wall. "Look."

The sound was muted, but a headline scrolled across the bottom of the screen. *Breaking News: Department Seven Confirms Bennet Hawick in Custody.*

Charlotte hurried over, grabbing the remote to turn the volume up.

"Hawick is the individual at the center of The Final Register theft," the reporter announced, standing in front of the Registry building. "A number of serious allegations have been made against him. He will be tried on those later, but the council will be convening here shortly to discuss what actions they will take in response to Hawick's actions involving the Register. Many citizen groups will be hoping for swift and decisive action to put an end to the threat of violence which has gripped the city since news of the theft broke."

Nate found himself on his feet with no memory of standing. He gripped the back of the chair to steady himself, trying not to give into the dizziness that had swept over him. *This is really bad.*

"Here's the Chief of New Camden City Police. Chief Jacobs, what do you have to say about these developments?" The reporter thrust her mic at Jacobs.

He looked dead at the camera. "The council meeting will send a clear message to all our citizens that New Camden is a city ruled by law—and that no one is above the law. We don't care whether you're a senior vampire or a senior citizen. If you commit a crime, you're going to be charged with it." With a cursory nod, he strode up the steps.

"Strong words from Chief Jacobs. And here is another representative of the council—"

"Senior vampires." Nate swallowed. "He's talking about Saltaire." He'd known this would happen. Ben was not going to get a fair hearing. He was going to be used as a weapon against Saltaire.

"I know I'm new to New Camden's supernatural politics and all," Mandy said hesitantly from the armchair she sat in, "but why is Saltaire so important?"

"He's been in New Camden since before New Camden was a city. He saw the potential of the colony way back when it was a handful of settlers with big ideas, and he wove himself into the very foundation of the city." Grant shook his head. "I've been doing a lot of research into how the Register works. It turns out that way back when the settlement first realized that the undead walked among them, they took the unusually advanced step of consulting magic-users to advise them on potential defenses."

"Not so unusual." Vazul sneered. "Many of the early settlers had supernatural links themselves and hoped to establish a colony sympathetic to their existence."

"Whether that's true or not is a matter of speculation. The only supernatural public records of that time are Saltaire's. Most of the supernatural citizens of New Camden were afraid to be open about what they were then." Grant paused a moment to collect his train of thought. "Anyway, the magic-users were stuck because they had come up with a spell that would defend New Camden from negative supernatural influence, while allowing its magical residents to continue to live in the city. The problem was powering the spell. No one could sustain casting it for more than twelve hours at a stretch, and the spell was so draining that even on a roster system the magic-users would be burned out within a few months. Then Saltaire sent word through the magic-users to New Camden's council that he had a solution to their problem. He would donate the power necessary to run the spell, investing it in a book. That book would be used to power New Camden's defenses."

Nate swallowed. "The Final Register?"

"The source," Grant corrected. "It only became the Final Register when Wisner decided to adapt it to his purposes."

"How come we've never heard of this before?" Charlotte asked. "I've been studying magic my entire life."

"It's been a closely guarded secret. Saltaire and the original council had a gentlemen's agreement," Grant explained. "Nothing was signed, but it was understood that if Saltaire didn't like the way the defenses were managed, he could take his power back. Naturally, successive councils were very keen to keep him happy. The defenses evolved with the city. The different class levels were introduced for supernaturals, each with their own levels of restrictions. It wasn't perfect—no system ever is—but each successive generation made their own refinements. And then Wisner came along."

Vazul rolled his eyes. "Your stepfather would care as little about keeping Saltaire happy as he would the rights of any one not his pack."

"Actually, I think he knew better than to cross Saltaire. He waited until Saltaire was in Europe to put his idea for the Final Register before the council. He probably left out the fact that Saltaire and the Register were still connected when he did so. Or maybe the panic he created with his allegations against me convinced them to risk it. Anyway, Saltaire's not happy that he wasn't consulted, which, in the eyes of the mayor and chief of police, is further grounds for getting the Register out of the hands of the supernatural."

"And that's why there have been riots at the Registry?" Bea's question surprised Nate. He'd almost forgotten she and Mandy were there. The two women listened closely to Grant's words.

"Yeah. Many supernaturals aren't happy with the registration system, but they're willing to go along with it because they know there are supernaturals involved in running it: Saltaire and the Magic-Users Guild. If you remove them from the equation, then you've got a system applied to supernaturals with no supernatural involvement—wide open for abuse. We've seen how an individual can twist public opinion to pursue his own agenda."

Mandy shuddered. "Stop. It's too grim."

Nate couldn't help but agree. He sank back in his chair. The situation was hopelessly tangled, like the roots of a plant with nowhere to grow. *I don't know what to do.* With the council and Saltaire involved in a tug of war over the Register, Ben was never going to get the trial he deserves.

"It might be grim, but it's not hopeless." Grant spoke slowly. "Look. Call me crazy, but I know the supernatural community. I know the majority of us want nothing more than to go about our lives without causing harm to others. Julian's vampires and Ronald's pack don't represent us. If we went to the Registry to show our support for the law, for just representation for the supernatural community, I think we could show New Camden that the majority of us stand with the city." He straightened, his expression taking on resolve. "Vazul, call your friends. Charlotte, you do the same with your guild. Mandy and Bea, this isn't your fight, but if you wanted to join us—"

"We'd be honored," Mandy said immediately. Her face was flushed and her eyes shone. The alpha-werewolf effect? Or had she simply noticed that Grant was an extremely handsome man?

Bea's nod was less enthusiastic but just as fervent. "We want to help."

"I'll let the guys at Century know," Aki said. "It's a slow night. They might be able to get time off."

"I don't know what good a hunter will be, but why not. It's not like I have other plans." George shrugged.

Grant nodded. "And I'll put the word out to my contacts. It's time we did this."

Nate felt his heart beating rapidly. Grant's speech had stirred hope. He didn't know if his idea was possible or not, and he was afraid to find out, but he had to find out. He waited until Charlotte had sent an email to her contacts. "Hey, Charlotte? I've got a question for you."

She closed her laptop, turning to him. "Yes, Nate?"

"If you saw a circle left after a spell, would you be able to work out what that spell was intended to do?"

"Possibly," Charlotte said. "If it was a type of magic I was familiar with."

"I've seen the magic circles the necromancer left his victims in. If I showed you a picture of the circle and you identified the spell, it might give us a clue to what Peter is up to."

Charlotte frowned. "Won't Department Seven already have done that?"

"The only magic-user on Department Seven's roll is a sorcerer. She's been pouring over Peter's books a lot, but the fact she hasn't found anything...I don't know. Maybe sorcerers don't get trained in this kind of magic."

Charlotte frowned. "It's worth a try."

"Here." Nate brought up the photo and handed his phone to Charlotte. "What do you think?"

Charlotte drew in a breath. "This is a real patchwork. I can definitely see the witchcraft influence, but some of these elements are really obscure... The thing about witchcraft is that it's not a prescribed science. The meaning comes from the caster, so while there are certain universal components, the actual practice is highly individual. I'd need either Peter's notes or someone who knew him to even attempt to figure this out."

Was that why Tremaine was struggling to make headway? Nate knew there was no chance of getting Charlotte access to Peter's notebooks. But there was one other alternative. "And if you had someone who knew him working with you?"

Charlotte nodded slowly. "It's worth a try."

"Then let's go. I—" Nate became aware of Aki standing very close beside him. "Aki?"

"I'm coming too," Aki told him. "Don't even think you can talk me out of this."

AS THE SUN set, Nate, Charlotte and Aki stood before the doors of Royal—New Camden's most exclusive club. As the doorman took up his position, Nate approached him. "Excuse me. We need to get inside."

The man met his eyes in a clear challenge. "No one gets inside. Especially not the likes of you." He ran his eyes over Charlotte and Aki scornfully, before turning back to Nate with a faint sneer.

"Look," Nate said. "I can't compel you, but I've been here before. Please, let us in?"

The man's sneer increased. "Nothing doing."

Aki drummed his heel against the pavement. "I told you that wouldn't work."

"This is really important," Nate continued. "I'm sorry, but if we have to go through you to get inside we will."

"What are you going to do, fight me?" The man shook his head. "You don't have the guts."

"Actually," Charlotte said brightly and unhelpfully, "I'm a pacifist. I abhor violence in any circumstances—"

Nate saw the man's lip twist contemptuously. "There's nothing wrong with working out problems through talking them out. But if you don't feel like hearing us, that's fine." After a full day of lying in the sun, his throat was sore but the rest of him was ready to go. Vines rippled, emerging from his arm and stretching toward the belligerent doorman.

His eyes widened and he stepped back. "What kind of freak power is that?"

"You think that's bad?" Aki smirked as he stepped forward. You don't let us in, and we won't just leave you tied up in vines. We'll leave you tied up in daisy chains."

"I must protest. My servant has been stubborn, but he surely doesn't deserve that." Nate felt a chill as if a wet towel had been draped over his shoulders. He turned and saw that the nondescript door to Royal's second, secret level was open. Standing in the doorway, looking as if he'd been awake for hours and not just the minutes since the sunset, was the third member of Saltaire's vampire family.

"Hunter."

"Hello, Nathan. This is an unexpected pleasure. The last I heard you'd been badly poisoned."

Nate took a deep breath. They had a mixed history, but he knew that Hunter cared about Ben as much as he did. "Ben needs your help."

Hunter's smile twisted. "I am not sure what you think I can do, but come in."

Hunter took them, not to his apartment, but to a meeting room attached to the main assembly room the vampires used for the balls and Senate meetings. He seated himself at the head of the table, and motioned for the others to take a seat. "Well?"

Nate took a deep breath. "Ben's not behind the murders. The third one happened while he was with Godfrey at Saltaire's house, making it impossible for him to have committed it. Not to mention that the first one happened while he was still on the Final Register. There's no proof connecting him to the crimes. Not only that, the victims were all vampires."

Hunter stiffened. "You're sure of that?"

"Positive. Ben and I worked it out together. The victims' files were removed from Department Seven's records, but they're still there in ARX's database, meaning that Peter must have possessed someone in Department Seven to help him. They attacked me—"

"Which could also be taken as further proof that you are on the right track with your investigation." Hunter's eyes glittered. He leaned forward. "Has the department been informed of this?"

"I don't know I trust them," Nate admitted. "Someone in the department's working for Peter, I know it. The poison—I could have died. If I hadn't been on the phone to Ben when I was attacked, I might not be here now."

Hunter frowned. "There is a certain truth in that. What do you want me to do, Nate? Saltaire has forbidden me to go near the council or the Registry. He hopes to avoid any accusations of using influence to sway their decision-making."

Watching Aki carefully inch his chair closer to Hunter, Nate could see the sense in Saltaire's decision. Whether deliberately or not, the vampire had a strong effect on those around him. "I've got a photo of the circle that the victims were found in. Between Charlotte's understanding of magic and your knowledge of Peter, I'm hoping the two of you can figure out what he's up to."

"Ah." Hunter turned his gaze on Charlotte. "I had wondered who this lovely young woman was."

"C-Charlotte Everett." Charlotte took a deep breath. Clearly this was the first time she'd been face-to-face with a vampire of Hunter's vintage and was finding it a challenge. "I'm a witch—obviously. I—that is to say, my coven—"

"Everett—of Everett's magic-based security?" Hunter raised an eyebrow.

"My mother."

"I am familiar with her work," Hunter purred. "It is an honor to assist her charming daughter."

Charlotte turned bright pink and shot Nate a pleading look, but it was Aki who came to the rescue.

"I'd better stay and supervise to make sure that actual work gets done," he said, planting his elbows on the table. "Well, Nate? Where's this photo?"

After one glance at the photo, Hunter disappeared to fetch his magical reference books from his apartment. Charlotte had brought her own with her, and within a few minutes, they were hard at work, deciphering the circle.

Nate breathed out. *This might actually work.* He couldn't allow himself to think what would happen if it didn't. More victims, each one increasing Peter's power. He might take control of the city a second time, leaving chaos in his wake. And Ben, held prisoner by Department Seven—or worse. Nate gulped. *If whoever attacked me is still at Department Seven, what is to stop them going after Ben now? He's a sitting duck.*

Nate glanced at Hunter and Charlotte, their heads bent over the book they were examining. Charlotte was talking quickly, as she pointed to a symbol on the page. Hunter nodded, a thoughtful expression on his face. *We could be here a while—*

"Just go." Aki had kicked up his feet on the table, obviously resigned to a long wait.

Nate blinked. "What do you mean?"

"You're worried about Ben. I can feel the tension radiating off you from here." Aki spoke quietly so that they wouldn't disturb the others. "You're no help. In fact, you're only a distraction. Go find your vampire boyfriend. You know you want to."

"You're sure it's fine?" But even as Nate asked, he knew that he wouldn't have any peace until he knew for himself that Ben was unharmed. He patted Aki on the shoulder. "Thanks. I— You'll let me know the moment you find anything useful?"

"At once." Aki said. "But Nate? Make sure Ben's not going to eat anyone before you do anything stupid, okay? I don't think I'm up to a third near-death experience."

THE TOUR OF Department Seven that Nate had received had been brief. Nate retraced his way down a shadowy corridor in the basement, fighting a rising sense of panic. While he'd something to do, he'd been able to keep the fear at bay, but on the journey to the station it had come back full force. *If anything's happened to Ben—*

"Was wondering when you'd show up." Gunn's voice was as flat as a headstone. "I'm not sure if this is dedication to duty or your ongoing infatuation with the world's worst vampire, but I'm impressed. From the description Leanne gave of you dying, I was pretty sure we wouldn't be seeing you for at least another day."

Nate stepped toward the patch of shadow he was pretty sure was Gunn. "I was attacked in the storage room with weed killer! And the victims were vampires. The files—"

"Hidden. I know." Gunn always sounded annoyed, but this was next level. Nate took a step back as Gunn emerged from the shadows, his teeth grinding together. "But before you get on my case about someone from my department being involved, there's something you need to know. I'm a *lemur*. There's no fucking way one of my staff gets possessed and I don't smell it."

Nate stared at him. The pungent smell of moldy leaves and smoke filled the corridor, mingling with Gunn's favorite brand of tobacco. *Is there a polite way to suggest that maybe he can't smell it because the scent is drowned by his BO?* "Um, you know you—"

"Impossible," Gunn said flatly.

"But it's got to be Peter. Ben's innocent. We both know there's no way he could have killed the third victim while he was in Saltaire's custody!"

Gunn reached out, grabbing Nate by his throat. He dragged Nate down to eye level, fixing him with a hard stare. "Front with me. You're not in this together in some misguided attempt to clear his name, right?"

Nate stared at him. "You know I'd never—Ben would never! There's no way!"

Gunn continued to size him up. Nate felt an uncomfortable feeling settle over him, like being draped in spiderweb. "It would explain a lot that doesn't make sense."

Nate shut his eyes and resigned himself to the search. *I've got nothing to hide.* "Ben would never murder anyone to clear his name—or at all! He spent most of his life working to protect people. That's what I love about him—one of the things I love about him. If he was a murderer, I wouldn't help him. I'd try to stop him. That's why I took him to Saltaire. Not to help him escape, but to protect others."

Gunn snarled. "Spare me." He released Nate abruptly. "I suppose it was unlikely, but it would have solved everything."

Nate carefully tugged his shirt straight, breathing through his mouth. "The situation's bad, right?"

"The council doesn't like the fact you were attacked here, or the evidence of Department Seven meddling. We've been taken off the case. The police are guarding the Registry, and you can imagine the mess they're making of it. But until we can prove that no member of staff is possessed, we're barred from doing our job."

Doing his job was the one thing Gunn cared about. "But if it's not possession, what is it?" Nate felt a sudden wave of fear overtake him. "Peter's back?"

"Sometimes dead means dead."

"But if the circumstances of death are traumatic, it can happen, right?"

"He died in sunlight. That's one of the most powerful purification agents there is. No way is Peter coming back from that."

"What if he left a spell behind? There was one in Ben's apartment, a booby trap. Ben thought it was there so that Peter could possess him, but if he'd left others, maybe he possessed someone else and used them to bring himself back…"

"It's possible," Gunn allowed. "If extremely unlikely."

"More or less unlikely than one of your staff getting possessed?" Nate was suddenly aware of a trail of goose bumps travelling down his arms.

Gunn snorted. "You've made your point. But the council aren't going to be convinced without actual proof."

"I'm working on it. Charlotte and Hunter are looking at the circle's used in the spells—"

"Sharing confidential police information with civilians? I don't know whether I'm appalled or proud. We'll make a Department Seven officer of you yet. After we work out a suitable punishment for your disobedience."

Nate breathed out. "So if Hunter and Charlotte find proof of Peter's plans, you'll listen to them?"

"I'll listen," Gunn said. "I can't guarantee the council will—" He cut himself off midsentence. "Saltaire. What brings you to my humble department?"

Nate found himself struggling to breathe. The goose bumps were back in force. Saltaire was there—and from the feeling of dread that had settled over him, he'd been there some time.

"You waste your time." Saltaire ignored Gunn's greeting. "I have come from the Registry. The council agrees with me that rather than the work of a necromancer, these deaths are a campaign against the city's defenses, designed to incite chaos and fear. After all, necromantic rites are designed to gain power and we have not seen any noticeable rise in power among those suspected of the attacks."

Gunn growled, clearly resenting Saltaire's presence as much as his words. "All the more reason my people should be out there, preserving the peace! You know what the presence of an all-human police force will do to the protestors!"

"I have the situation in hand." Saltaire's voice didn't allow for any argument—no. His entire being didn't allow for any argument. "The council agrees that until Department Seven can clear themselves of the allegations made against them, they should not be responsible for the city's preservation. I come to inform you of their decision—and to let you know that Bennet's fate has been decided."

Nate caught his breath. He couldn't imagine Saltaire seeking them out to share good news.

"Bennet has been found guilty of damaging the Final Register and thus endangering the city's defenses. In light of his behavior, there is no prison in the city that can hold him, so I have agreed to take him into custody—"

"No!"

Saltaire turned his gaze on Nate. "This time, he will not leave. I will make him anew as a vampire. It will be a fresh start, free from the pernicious influences that have proved so detrimental to him."

"You're not going to wipe his memory again?" Nate felt fear clutch in his chest. It was one thing to surrender Ben to Saltaire for his own good—but there was nothing good about Saltaire's plans.

"There is no need." Saltaire smirked. "Not now that I have made sure that he knows it was his lover responsible for his capture."

Nate stared at him. *He told Ben I betrayed him?* Ben would have nothing to help him resist Saltaire's ruthless control, no friends—he would be entirely alone.

There was a grinding sound, like metal being dragged along stone—Gunn's teeth. "Every time I think you can't possibly surprise me, Saltaire, you find a way to sink even lower."

Saltaire's tone was chillingly matter of fact. "The city must be made safe. Bennet's skills are too valuable to lose. I will ensure that he is once again a servant the city can be sure of."

"By breaking him? I always knew you were inhuman, but I deluded myself that you had some limits—"

Nate put out his hand, cutting off Gunn's rant. "Where is he now?"

Saltaire's mouth twitched. "The holding cell here is pitiful, but it will do while I establish order. I have forbidden him to leave, so do not think you can free him."

Nate turned his back on the senior vampire and continued down the corridor. They could argue centuries and not change Saltaire's mind. Every second spent with him was a moment wasted. *I have to find him.* "Ben!"

He leaned against the wall of the cell, looking like a shriveled autumn leaf. His head was lowered, and his arms wrapped around himself, as if he needed the protection.

Nate gripped the bars of the cell, feeling utterly helpless. "Ben..."

Ben's shoulders jerked. He paused before he raised his face, taking control of his reactions. "Nate?"

Fear stuck in his throat, mingled with shame and the knowledge of just what it was he was losing. "Ben. I'm so sorry." It was too hard to look at him knowing what he'd done, and Nate sagged against the bars, looking down at his feet. "I thought—"

He felt the cool touch of Ben's hand on his arm. Looking down he saw he'd managed to slip his arm through the cell bars. "You're recovered? The weed killer—"

"Forget about that." Nate drew a deep breath. "You saved my life—and all I did was deliver you to Saltaire! I know saying sorry won't make up for this, but Ben—if I'd had any idea it would come to this—"

Ben lifted Nate's chin so that he looked directly into Ben's eyes. They were unusually dark in the dimly lit cell, but they were steady. "You'd have had no choice, but to do it anyway."

Nate stared at him.

Ben's smile was just as Nate remembered it—thin and rueful—and marvelously expressive. "Saltaire decided to tell me all."

Nate couldn't take his eyes off Ben's mouth, captivated by that smile. *I never thought I'd see it again.* Ben's words registered, and he looked up in alarm. "He didn't—"

"I know that when you delivered me to him, I was in a violent blood rage, and that you'd tried and failed to restore my reason." Ben's tone was even, but he lowered his gaze. He took his hand from Nate's arm, using it to steady himself against the bars. "He emphasized how I'd given in to my hunger, and that I couldn't be trusted around civilians. He tried to make me believe that I only owe my current state of consciousness to his power, but I know better. I remember everything now. Attacking Aki, the cat bringing me its catches, the revenants at the cemetery—"

"The cat?" Nate started. "I never even thought about that." One more example of how he'd failed Ben. "I didn't believe in you. I should have known better than to think—"

"Listen to me." Ben squeezed his hand through the bars. "You kept your promise to me. You stopped me from hurting anyone."

How was it possible that Ben's words, delivered in an awed whisper, could hurt so much? "I gave up. I turned you over to Saltaire—" He felt a cool but gentle pressure against his hand. Nate's eyes flew open in surprise. Ben had kissed him?

"You made the most difficult decision anyone could make," Ben said, still holding Nate's hand. "And you made it, thinking about what was best for me."

"You don't"—Nate heard his voice crack but forced himself to continue—"hate me?"

Ben smiled, reaching up through the bars to stroke Nate's cheek. "I rely on you to keep me human. If that's not love..." He gripped the bars, bringing himself as close to the bars as he could be.

Nate took the invitation at once. Kissing through the bars was not easy, but it was as if the touch was the final ingredient that made Ben's words true.

Chapter Sixteen

BEN KISSED BACK, the cold metal of the bars a sharp contrast to Nate's generous warmth. He'd never needed a touch more—and never been more cruelly denied it. *Maybe this is for the best.* He was going to have to learn to feel without Nate there beside him, to be strong without Nate to lean on... *But some part of Nate will always be with me.* Saltaire couldn't erase him from Ben's heart, any more than he could fully exorcise him from Ben's memories.

Nate gasped, a breathy moan that directly threatened Ben's composure. "Ben." He opened his eyes, looking at Ben as if he still couldn't believe he was real. "You really mean that?"

How long had Nate carried the burden of fear for them both? Ben reached again for his hand. "I'm sure. More certain than I've been of anything else." It was strange. The month of forced isolation had driven him to despair many times over—but he'd always come back to his certainty in Nate. Standing before him, being seen by him, and seeing the sheer emotion in Nate's eyes as he swallowed, was validation of the rightness of his faith. "You remembered when it was impossible for you to remember. And then you never gave up."

Nate's eyes were fixed on Ben's. Trying to store them in his memory? Or making up for a month's lost time? "I'm not giving up now. There's got to be a way to overturn this decision."

The discordant blare of an alarm sounded. Red light pulsed down the corridor leading to the holding cells in time with the noise.

"What now?" Nate turned aside from the cell doors but left his hand clasped around Ben's.

The fact that Nate chose to stay with him, even then, meant more to Ben than any of his apologies. "We'll find out soon enough."

"You don't think it's whoever attacked me come back to finish the job?"

Footsteps sounded in the corridor. Someone was making their way toward them. Ben removed his hand from Nate's. "If it is, you get out of here. I'm not risking your life a second time."

Nate positioned himself against the bars in front of Ben. "Nothing doing."

Gunn emerged from the shadows. "Nate! How do you not hear the fucking alarm?" He waved a hand toward the flashing light. "Red means I need you upstairs now."

"What's happened?" Ben pressed himself against the bars.

Gunn snarled, the pulsing light making his teeth look as if they were bloodstained. "This is your fault. You and your fucking bad example. Some unoriginal bastard's gone and fucking stolen the Final Register—again."

Ben's eyes widened. "Wasn't it restored?"

"The interim power source is still in place at the Registry. Given the amount of interest in the actual Final Register it was deemed in the city's best interests to have the Final Register moved to a more secure location. Here." Gunn glared at Nate. "I gave strict orders that no one was to tell you about it."

"No one did," Nate said at once. "This is the first I'd heard of it. But if it's been stolen does that mean the classifications are gone?"

"The temporary source is still powering the city's defenses?" Ben took Gunn's grunt as an affirmative. "Suggesting that the goal isn't an attack on the city, but a personal bid for power."

"I've got no time for another round of pointless speculation." Gunn growled. "The council's freaking out, and the vampires and wolves are going to lose their fucking minds over this." He narrowed his eyes at Ben, stepping back so that he could get a better look at the cell.

Ben rolled his eyes, holding up his hands so Gunn could see they were empty. "I don't have it. I took the Final Register with one goal—to get myself off it. I left it with the most responsible person I knew."

Nate's fingers found his through the bars.

Gunn groaned. "Not sure you quite understand the meaning of 'responsible.' Damnation! Just once I would like you to be the criminal. Once would be enough!"

"I'm not committing a crime just to prove you right."

Gunn narrowed his eyes. "Nate. We're going."

Nate didn't move. "Gunn. Think about this. You know Ben's innocent."

"Innocent is such a vague term—"

"You know he didn't steal the Register—this time," Nate said. "And he can help. He's got ARX training, and he knows all about the Final Register. We need him."

Ben winced. Gunn would rather disembowel himself than accept Ben's help.

From the look Gunn gave him, he was contemplating solving two problems at once by disemboweling Ben. "Not happening."

"So you are going to leave him here to be attacked by someone with a grudge against us? Someone who has already infiltrated Department Seven and severely injured an officer—me, in case you'd forgotten."

"I hadn't forgotten." Gunn rubbed his forehead.

Nate persisted. "If we leave Ben behind, he's a sitting duck! And he's got every reason to want to help. If he assists in securing the Register, it'll prove to the council he wants to protect the city, not destroy it!"

"You know damn well Bennet can't leave the—" Gunn came to a sudden halt. "Actually, I can't think of a good reason not to take you with us," he said slowly. "Benny, I will forever regret doing this but...you in?"

Ben nodded. It was odd but he'd also assumed he would not be able to leave. Almost like there was a restriction beyond the prison in place. "Absolutely." He stepped back as Gunn pulled a key out of his pocket.

Gunn put the key in the lock but didn't turn it immediately. "Let's get a few things clear first. This is my case. You take orders from me. Should be obvious, but knowing how good the two of you are at creating confusion, we may as well be clear. You can't follow my orders, you'll be back in here. Understood?"

"Understood." Ben stepped out of the cell, still half expecting to meet with resistance. He looked up to find Nate watching him with a baffled expression. "Nate?"

He shook his head and pulled Ben into a hug. "I'm not complaining or anything... I just didn't think you could, you know. Do that."

Ben gave Nate a lingering squeeze. All he wanted to do was to stay wrapped in his arms, but the city wasn't going to wait. "Let's not give Gunn time to change his mind."

Nate reluctantly released him. "I was thinking more about vampire restrictions, you know?"

Ben cocked an eyebrow. *Vampire restrictions? He did know Gunn was a lemur, right?*

"We're wasting enough time." Gunn started back down the corridor. "Go, go, go!"

The office was organized chaos, with Kenzies pushing protective vests on those department members who were present. "The situation's bad. Word is out that the Registry is protected by the police, not us, and naturally our two groups of idiots interpreted this as an open invitation to help themselves to it. The latest reports are that Julian's vampires have succeeded in forcing their way into the building. They may have hostages."

Ben listened grimly, pulling on a battered SWAT vest. It was two sizes too big, but he couldn't complain. Without his vampire strength, he was going to need all the help he could get. As he glanced around the room, his misgivings increased. Department Seven was much smaller than he'd realized, and all the staff had the look of being stretched too thin.

"I know you're all tired," Kenzies told the gathered crew. "I am too. But our city needs us and we have never let her down."

Clay raised his hand. Ben remembered him from Peter's arrest. He'd seemed far too chirpy then. Now his upbeat manner seemed positively unnatural. "What's the plan?"

"We force the vampires out of the Registry, secure the city's defenses and stop the werewolves from doing the same damn thing," Gunn said. "Any questions?"

Simeon raised a trembling hand. "Shouldn't we be looking for the Final Register?"

Kenzies put her hand on Gunn's arm before he could snarl at Simeon. "He's got a point. What do we know about the theft?"

"It was here. And then it wasn't," Tremaine reported. "Kenzies and I can confirm it was still here yesterday afternoon. My guess is that it was taken in the chaos surrounding the attack on Nate."

So the attack might be unrelated to Nate's discovery? Ben cast a look at Nate to see how he was taking the news.

Nate frowned as he listened to the discussion. "If that's the case, then whoever took it is long gone."

"We'll find them," Gunn promised. "But before we do, we have a city to save. Once we're inside the Registry, our first priority will be securing the temporary power source, a book invested with power by..." He frowned. "By...whoever the hell invested the original Register with its power—yes, Nate?"

Nate lowered his hand. "Are you okay?"

It was the last straw. Gunn levered a glare at Nate that made everyone in the room take a step back. "No, I am fucking not okay! If Julian manages to figure out how to dismantle the spells surrounding the Register and use that to his own ends, this could be the end of New Camden. No more questions. We're moving out!"

IT WAS JUST as well Department Seven was a short walk from the Registry building. A sea of police cars surrounded it, their flashing lights making the scene look like the worst disco in the world.

Chief Jacobs saw them approach but made no move to stop them. "You're not supposed to be here."

Gunn turned his back on him, barking out commands. "Clay, Simeon. Do a perimeter check. Tremaine, see what you can detect about the status of the wards. Kenzies, see that there's a watch kept for Wisner's kicked puppies. Nate and Ben, stay where I can see you. The rest of you, make yourselves useful." Only when he had seen his staff scatter in obedience to his orders did he turn back to Jacobs. "What, you thought we were going to miss the party?"

Jacobs frowned. "I don't know what to make of you, Gunn, but I'm glad you're here. We had a brief skirmish half an hour ago, when another group of vampires tried to join those already inside. We ran them off, but they threatened to return in a bigger group."

Gunn lit a cigarette. He took a long drag and exhaled thoughtfully. "Tremaine?"

She threw a salute. "They must have gained access to the library. They're using the classification system to lock everyone but their group out of the building. If I had to guess, I'd say they've locked the building against categories—people, police, werewolves—rather than listing individual names."

"Better hope they've overlooked a few." Gunn nodded to Nate. "Try the door?"

"Me?"

"You're an unknown. It's worth a shot. You too, Benny."

Jacobs' eyes widened. "Bennet Hawick!" He reached for his gun. "He should be in custody—"

"We got a bunch of homicidal leeches sitting on the city's defenses and you want to split hairs about legalities?" Gunn shot him a look.

Ben decided they didn't have time to lose. "Come on, Nate." They stepped up to the doorway, but as Ben tried to step through, he encountered an invisible barrier. "No luck."

"Me either." Nate planted his hands square against the invisible wall and pushed. "I guess Julian remembers us from our last meeting."

Gunn snarled. "Almost makes you wish for the good old days when no one complained if you torched a historic building. I guess this is up to me."

He climbed the steps and tried the barrier. To no one's surprise, it didn't give. Gunn stepped back, eying the building. "You got a map of the interior, Jacobs? Where is the point closest to the library?"

Jacobs frowned. "There. By the parking lot. But there's an outer corridor between the wall—"

"It'll do." Gunn turned back. "Tremaine, you're going to be on standby. Soon as they rush out—"

Nate looked startled. "Why will they rush out?"

Gunn shot him a look. "Trust me. They're going to come charging out this door like their afterlives depend on it." He turned back to Tremaine. "And when that happens, I want you inside—taking control of the Register and fixing whatever those living corpses have done to it. Nate, you're in charge of securing those idiots so we can stop this happening again. Benny, you make sure he doesn't stuff up. Happy?"

Nate had gone a pale shade of green. "Me? But—"

"If even one of them gets away, I'm holding you personally responsible. I know you can do this. So do it." Gunn tossed his cigarette on the ground and stalked off in the direction Jacobs had indicated.

Ben ground the cigarette out under his shoe. The police chief had retreated, and his men had drawn back, leaving himself, Nate, and Tremaine on the steps. "What was that about?"

Nate looked despairingly at the doorway. "My first night on the job, there was a situation here. Gunn put me on crowd control and I fucked it up."

"No one has a good first night," Tremaine assured him. "You did fine."

Nate shook his head. "My vines didn't talk to me. And when I did manage to control them, I remembered what happened to Peter. My magic killed him."

Nate was still hung up on Peter's death? Ben opened his mouth to reassure him and stopped. He'd already assured Nate that what happened wasn't his fault. That it still bothered him meant this was deeper than simple regret. "You mentioned you'd seen Peter. Was that when?"

Nate shook his head. "No. The first sighting was the next day, when we were at his apartment."

"I remember," Tremaine said. "You've seen him since?"

Nate nodded, wiping sweat off his forehead. "When I was at a cemetery. The same cemetery the first murder took place at."

When did Nate go back there? With a start, Ben remembered the crypt. *The revenants!* He took Nate's hand and discovered it was clammy. "You were using magic then, too?"

Nate nodded. "I just—don't trust myself to use my magic. I don't want to kill anyone, but I don't know what I'm doing. Nobody knows what I'm doing! Gunn's relying on me, but there's every chance I'm going to screw up again."

Ben squeezed his hand. "Look. All the times you've seen Peter... They were moments of doubt, right? Of fear?" Nate nodded. "That's the clue there. That's not Peter. That's your own fear, Nate."

"But I saw him! The words he said—"

"Your subconscious," Ben said firmly. "Trust me. Think how far you've come from when we first met. Back then you would never have thought in a million years that you'd be capable of standing up to Wisner in front of an entire crowd of wolves."

Nate's eyes widened. "How did—? You were there?"

Ben nodded. "I was there. And Nate? I couldn't have been prouder of you." Also terrified that he was about to be shredded by a hundred angry wolves, but still proud. "But when we met, there's no way you could have done that."

Nate shook his head. "I was too afraid to admit I was different, even to myself."

"Exactly." Ben let go of Nate's hand and thumped him on the arm. "Now look at you. You're wearing a Department Seven uniform and you're doing your best to protect the city. You've grown so much, in such a short time. It's no wonder your subconscious is trying to slam on the brakes."

Nate stared at the empty doorway in front of them. "You think this fear is normal?"

"Absolutely," Tremaine assured him. "All magic-users know that fear affects their ability to cast spells. Maybe your fear's taken a more direct route by manifesting as someone you know, but that doesn't mean you have to listen to it."

Ben shifted, looking over his shoulder. He couldn't blame Nate for being afraid. He felt on edge, like he was being watched.

At the same moment, Tremaine drew a sharp breath. "Get ready. They're not far away."

Ben swallowed. He could taste it now, an unpleasant undertone in the air, like rusting metal. "Of course! We can't go in, so Gunn's driving them out."

"With fear." Nate took a deep breath and knelt, pressing his palms flat against the surface of the steps. "Yeah. Say what you like, but I'm not listening to you. I've got your number now."

Ben looked around sharply, but there was no one there. *He's seeing Peter again?* He stepped forward, putting his hands on Nate's shoulders. "He's not real. *You* are—and so is your magic."

A scream filled the air and continued. It was a frenzied sound, growing more and more hysterical before it was roughly silenced.

"Any moment now." Tremaine shifted.

Ben gave her a steady look. He didn't remember her, but there were a lot of Department Seven members with whom he was unfamiliar. Her eyes were fixed on the door, and she seemed confident in whatever Gunn was doing. *Clearly a professional.* He'd ask Nate about her later. For now, he simply tightened his grip on Nate's shoulder, giving him a tactile reminder that he wasn't going anywhere.

There was a loud bang inside the Registry and suddenly the sound of feet pounding down the corridor. The door flew open and the vampires ran out in a mass. There was nothing dignified about them now. With their fangs prominently displayed and their eyes wide and terrified, they looked like cornered animals, desperate to escape.

"Now!" Tremaine flung her arms out, releasing a bright flash of light. The vampires slowed their escape bid but continued to stagger toward Nate.

They never reached him. Instead, the pavement cracked. Brown branches pushed up from the ground, becoming twisty briars that tripped the vampires, catching their clothing on their thorns. While they struggled to free themselves, the plants wound around them. The vampires cried out in alarm, but their fangs were no use against wood, and the plant was a match for their inhuman strength.

"A million curses on you, freak!" Julian's face was pale—normal for a vampire—but his usually immaculate hair stuck to his damp forehead. He gave up his attempt to grapple one-handed with the vines, clutching the book he held to his chest. His eyes were fixed on Nate as he snarled. "You will regret angering New Camden's vampires, you deluded upstart! We will be back, stronger than ever!"

He didn't see Ben step up behind him and, pausing to summon his vampire strength, bring his hands down on his skull. He subsided into unconsciousness.

Ben shook his hands, letting Julian pitch forward. The vines stopped him from falling all the way to the floor, but the book slid out of his grasp. He picked it up. "I've got the interim source!"

Tremaine waved a hand through the doorway. "The restrictions are down. We can restore the defenses."

Ben handed her the book. "We'll follow you. Be careful. There may be some still inside."

Tremaine grinned at him. "Not likely. Gunn's an expert." She actually sounded proud.

Ben shook his head as he watched her hurry into the Registry. Gunn was high on Ben's list of most disliked people. The fact that his staff actually liked him was hard to believe. *Maybe like is too strong a word. Took satisfaction in him?*

"Who do you think you are, Poison Ivy?" Another vampire was making a spirited attempt to free herself from the vines surrounding her. "What are plants in a city? They'll be dead in a few hours. And so will you!"

Unable to free themselves, the vampires had realized their hope lay in striking at Nate's weakest point. His feelings. Did they sense his fear? Ben hurried over to join him. "Don't listen. They know they're beaten, they're desperate."

"I know." Nate levered himself onto his feet. He wiped his hands on his jeans, looking at his work with the satisfaction of a craftsman. Eight vampires were hopelessly tangled, snarling as they fought against the branches. "I've got this. Go see if Tremaine needs help."

Ben hesitated, but the jangle of handcuffs being readied behind him made up his mind. *And what better way to show Nate I have confidence in him than by trusting him?* "All right." He jogged up the stairs and into the Registry.

The usual smell of musty books and inadequate ventilation was overshadowed by the riper smell of vampire. Ben's nose wrinkled, but he stepped over a toppled chair and into the library. The vampires had clearly made this their base. It was a mess with toppled chairs and torn books, and the walls had been spray painted with crude graffiti, most of it crude speculations about the relationship between Gunn and Kenzies.

The circle of books was broken. They lay limply, their pages still. A few rested on their desks, but most were upended on the floor among a sea of broken glass. Tremaine brushed broken glass off the desk at the center and placed the interim source on it. Ben helped her right the other desks, laying the appropriate books on them. "Can you fix this?"

"Now all the components are in place, it's simply a matter of recreating what the original caster did." Tremaine raised her hands. "Luckily, I took over as source after you took the Register, so I was here to see exactly what he did."

Ben tugged at his collar. He was never going to hear the end of that. Fortunately, Tremaine didn't seem to hold on to grudges the way her boss did. She was totally focused on the task in front of her. In a few moments, the books rose on their desks, the library filling with the sound of turning pages.

"The sight of you in the Registry makes me profoundly uncomfortable. Get out of here, Benny." Gunn swaggered into the library. His snarl lacked its usual bite. He seemed smugger than usual. Or was he always this insufferable, and Ben was only noticing now?

"There," Tremaine pronounced. "We're back in business. All we need to do now is restore any changes those idiots made to the system. Fortunately, they don't seem to have realized how it works. They wrote all their spells in the source." She began patting her pockets, presumably searching for an eraser.

Ben felt Gunn glaring at him and decided that now was as good a time to check on Nate as any.

Nate was actually whistling as he lifted vampires into the waiting police van. "Kenzies said I did a really good job," he told Ben. "And she wants to talk to you."

"She does?" Ben looked around the scene. Now that the vampires were secured, the police were happy to take over. He scanned the sea of blue uniforms, spotting Kenzies's distinctive red hair among the crowd.

When he joined her, it was to find her standing on the scene perimeter, scanning their surroundings. "Officer Kenzies? Nate said you wanted to speak to me."

She turned a very toothy grin on him. "No need to be formal. This isn't the first time we've met."

"I guess not." Ben studied her. He was more familiar with Gunn than with his deputy. Kenzies seemed friendly, but what did he really know about her?

"Heard the pep talk you gave Nate," she said, turning back to her self-appointed role of watchdog. "Not bad. You wouldn't be available to speak to our new recruits, would you?"

Ben's eyes widened. Of all the things he was expecting, that wasn't it. "I hadn't thought about it."

"We can't offer to pay you much," Kenzies continued. "But we'd be very grateful. And your coffee and snacks would be on us. Gunn's treat."

Ben raised an eyebrow. Something about the offer didn't add up. The sound of raised voices caught their attention.

"This is police brutality. I object. My rights as a supernatural are being trampled!" Julian had recovered enough to project injured vampire dignity.

Gunn wasn't buying it. "Your right is to shut the fuck up. Kenzies, get over here!"

Kenzies thumped Ben on his shoulder. "Duty calls." She waded through the crowd. Ben cast a look at the empty streets around them and followed.

"We can take it from here, Gunn." Jacobs was doing his best to seem as though he hadn't left the actual solving of the situation to Department Seven.

Gunn gave him a flat look. "Nothing doing. You don't know vampires like we know vampires. Any chance to turn this situation around and they'll take it. That's why you want one of my people with them at all times." He nodded to the two vans. "Kenzies, you ride with this winner. See that he gets all the special treatment he deserves. I'm sending Simeon with the rest."

Kenzies narrowed her eyes. "But the wolves! As soon as news of this gets out, they're going to make an attempt of their own."

"And we'll be ready for them. Right, Jacobs?" Gunn grinned at the man's obvious alarm. "But we don't want the situation complicated by suggestions of ill-treatment of supernaturals at the hands of human law enforcement. You're going because you're the only one in this entire department with manners." He paused. "Except maybe Nate."

"Thanks, Gunn." Nate had found Ben in the crowd and was standing beside him. Ben automatically reached for his hand.

Gunn rolled his eyes. "I don't want to hear it. Do something about your impromptu garden."

He turned back to Chief Jacobs, leaving Ben and Nate free to retrace their steps to Nate's briars. Ben experimentally ran his hand over a vine. The hooked thorn pricked his finger. "You did a really good job of these. I've never seen you summon anything like this so quickly." There was no reply and he turned to see Nate staring down at the screen of his phone. "Nate?"

"Twenty messages from Aki and five missed calls. Fuck. This isn't good."

Ben put his hand on Nate's arm, leaning in so he could see the screen.

—Hunter snapped. Seriously trying to eat us

—Help us, please! So going to die

—In magic circle in bathroom. Always knew I would die in a bathroom

Ben's eyes widened. Hunter was a three-hundred-year-old vampire, Aki a barely trained psychic. It was an uneven match in every way. As they stared at the phone a new message appeared.

—Promise me you'll toss everything in the bottom drawer of my dresser without looking at it please Nate v. important

"He's still alive." Ben put his hand over the phone forcing Nate to look at him. "Do you know where they are?"

"Royal," Nate said. "That's only a few blocks. We might be in time."

"Let's go." Grabbing Nate's hand, Ben pulled him along. Ignoring the startled shout of a police officer, they dashed down the street.

Royal was located in the heart of New Camden's downtown area, only a few blocks from the Registry. Ben wove expertly through the pedestrian traffic, his thoughts racing faster than he could move. *What on earth could cause Hunter to lose control?* You didn't survive three centuries as a vampire without learning how to prevent situations like this. Hunter had no shortage of willing donors, and Aki had made it abundantly clear that he would donate at the drop of a hat. *Hunger's out. Did he get injured?* A fight with another supernatural might leave him so exhausted he was unable to contain his inner vampire. *But then why wouldn't Hunter have called for help?* He slowed to a halt outside Royal, the steady beat emanating from the nightclub downstairs echoing the pounding of his heart. He stared at the dark windows of the rooms above the club. Hunter was there. He could sense him.

Ben swallowed. If they didn't stop him, then every life in the club beneath them was at risk.

THE DOORMAN TOOK one look at Nate, scowled, and held open the second door to the rooms above. Ben frowned but didn't comment, leading the way up the twisting staircase. He could get to the bottom of that later. For now, they had lives to save.

The room used for the vampire assemblies was still, only illuminated by the light spilling in from the meeting room. Ben strode across the room, looking in the doorway. The table was spread with a variety of magical tomes and notebook pages. He scanned them, noting that most of them seemed to be related to ritual and blood magic. "A rite gone wrong? I can't smell any magic."

"Charlotte and Hunter were looking into the meaning of the circles that Peter used in the murders." Nate wiped his hands on his jeans and stepped into the room. He carefully sized up every corner and possible hiding place before he turned back to Ben. "Aki decided he'd stay to help."

Aki was not likely to be any help at all, but that was a concern for another time. *Charlotte's here, too?* He hadn't seen her magic in practice, but he knew she had a good grasp of protective wards. *All of which take time—and a vampire doesn't give you time.*

Nate's phone hummed again. Another message. He glanced at it. "Aki said something about the bathroom."

"This way." In the silence, Nate's footsteps were incredibly loud. Ben winced, but tried to tell himself that there was no chance of them sneaking up on a vampire anyway. Hunter would have been aware of their presence the moment they stepped into the hall. *So where is he?*

Light spilled out from beneath the doors of the ladies' room. Ben paused, his hand on the door handle. "Nate? Stay back." He took a deep breath, bracing himself—

And a snarling form leaped at him, knocking him to the floor before he could open the door.

Ben rolled, using the jolt of hitting the floor to loosen his assailant's grip on him. He rolled to his feet, the stinging in his arm keeping time with his racing heart. His eyes were locked on a shadow in the dark. His inner vampire stirred, recognizing a fellow predator. Ben growled.

Not again.

Still, if his inner vampire was predictable, it was useful. With the vampire's night vision, he could see Hunter lever himself to his feet carefully, barely giving Nate a second glance. All the vampire's attention was focused on Ben.

Just like the revenants. Hunter prowled to one side and Ben shifted away from him, maintaining the distance between them. *Defending against a threat takes precedence over feeding.* The thought made him sick. "Hunter? Tell me what's going on. This isn't like you."

The only response was a snarl.

"Emeric?" He tried again. "It's me, Ben. Your brother." No response. Ben felt a wave of horror steal over him. He hadn't totally believed Aki's report that his clever, charming, vampire brother could ever be reduced to this, but the evidence before him was too much to ignore. "Please— You're better than this!"

He was vaguely aware of Nate moving away but didn't dare take his focus off Hunter. He knew firsthand how volatile an out of control vampire could be. With the recent memory of his time as a revenant in his mind, Ben continued to circle Hunter, trying to think of a way to defuse the situation.

Light flickered, illuminating the hall. Nate had found a light switch.

Ben blinked, his eyes needing a moment to adjust to the light. That was Hunter's chance. The vampire leaped a second time.

Ben staggered back, not from the force of Hunter's blow but from the horror. His fangs distorted his mouth into a gaping hole, his eyes were devoid of anything but mingled fear and hunger, an animal torn between disparate instincts. He was beyond thought, beyond restraint, beyond anything but instinct—and his instinct was telling him to strike first. This wasn't Hunter. This was his shell.

"Jesus!" Nate was clearly shocked. "Ben, are you—"

He couldn't think about Nate now. Ben brought up his hand to block Hunter's swing and then lashed out, aiming at the vampire's sensitive eyes. As Hunter stumbled backward, Ben got in his face with a snarl that Gunn would have been proud of. "Don't you dare attack me! You're nothing—I'm everything!" It wasn't the words, so much as the power behind them, and Ben had pulled out all the stops on his inner vampire. He growled low, twisting Hunter's head so that he could see Ben's bared fangs. "You understand me." Behind the threat was the power, layering his words with compulsion.

Hunter whimpered, sinking to his knees.

"Secure him."

Nate did as he was told. Hunter stayed on his knees, his head bent, his long hair masking his expression as Nate tightly bound his arms to his side with his vines.

Ben stood, staring at Hunter. His jaw ached, and he could feel a slow trickle making its way down his arm. Had Hunter drawn blood? He couldn't look, unwilling to risk taking his eyes off his brother.

Hunter... Ben swallowed. It was painful to see him reduced to this. As a child, Hunter had been his hero, as a teenager, his first crush. Even now, after finding his other half in Nate, his feelings for the vampire were complicated. *This is wrong. He should never be reduced to this.*

He took a deep breath. *I'm not leaving you like this, Hunter. One way or another, we're getting to the bottom of this.*

Chapter Seventeen

"HEY." BEN TURNED his head to see Nate standing behind him. "Are you all right?"

Ben felt his mouth crease into a smile. Even at a moment like this, Nate thought of him. "It's such a shock, seeing him like this."

Sensing that Ben's focus had shifted away from him, Hunter snarled. He tested the vines, and a look of cunning distorted his usually handsome face.

Ben shuddered. *This is all wrong.* He stepped toward him, raising his arm.

"Wait."

He turned to Nate. "If we leave him, he'll work his way out of those vines. This is necessary. And it spares him pain and fear."

Nate patted his arm. "I know. But there's no reason it has to be you." He was businesslike about it, ignoring Hunter's hiss as he approached. His arm connected with the back of Hunter's head in an almost clinical way, only the wooden thud indicating that this was not normal. Hunter slid to the floor motionless.

Ben winced. "Thank you." He could have done it, but he was grateful for Nate's desire to spare him that pain. "I've got even more appreciation for what you did for me now."

"Don't mention it." Nate raised his hand over Hunter, more vines adding themselves to those already securing the vampire in place. "So, what now?"

"Nate? Oh my god—Nate!" The bathroom door opened. Aki stood in the doorway a second, his eyes quickly sizing up Ben and Nate and Hunter's prone form on the ground. Then he launched himself at Nate, colliding with him in a hug. "I thought we were dead!"

"Easy." Nate's voice was warm. "We got you. Where's Charlotte?"

"Here!" She swayed in the doorway, her eyes wide. "Is he dead?"

His inner vampire wanted nothing more than to stride over to Aki and peel him off Nate. Ben took a deep breath, suppressing the impulse. "Unconscious. Don't worry. We won't let him threaten you or anyone else." He walked over to her, leading her out of the doorway. "Sit down."

Charlotte let him guide her to sit with her back against the wall and her head resting on her knees. "I don't know what happened," she said without prompting. "One minute, everything was fine, and the next, he just doubled over. Like he was in pain. I went to help him, and he waved me away, snarling at me. He said we should run, that he couldn't guarantee our safety if we stayed and then he just leaped at me! If Aki hadn't pulled me out of his reach, I'd be dead!"

Ben glanced over and saw that Aki was still attached to Nate. His head was buried against Nate's shoulder, and his legs wrapped around Nate's waist. Despite himself, he was amused. "But you managed to escape?" He stood, glancing into the bathroom. He could see that candles burned in an impromptu circle, and he sensed the presence of salt. "You did well. There's not many who would have the presence of mind to create a barrier against a ravenous vampire."

"God, am I over vampires." Aki's voice was muffled. "Give me a nice, sane werewolf any day of the week."

"That's the spirit." Nate thumped him on the back, but Aki was still reluctant to release his death grip on Nate's torso. "What happened to Hunter? This isn't normal, right?"

"No. In fact, it's the opposite of normal." As Ben stared down at their captive, he felt the hairs on the back of his neck rise. "He's not injured, and just looking at him, I can tell that he's fed recently, so there's absolutely no reason for him to lose control like this unless he was the subject of a magical spell, or—" He caught his breath.

"Or what?"

"Or something happened to a vampire he has strong links to. His sire, for example." But Hunter was three centuries old! If it was rare for a vampire to live that long, it was even rarer that they did it without taking steps to extricate themselves from their sire's control. If Hunter's sire was still in existence, there was no way Ben wouldn't know about it. Ben wracked his memory for the identity of Hunter's sire. *Why do I feel like something's missing? Something big and obvious, something just out of my reach...*

"Aki, get off. I am going to need to move at some point."

Ben's frown increased. *Think! You were obsessed with the guy at one point. You must have looked this up!* He knew Hunter's place of birth, every alias he'd used in his three-hundred-year existence, but he couldn't remember the name of the man who had turned him. "Why can't I remember?"

Nate snorted. "If you ask me, forgetting Saltaire's a good thing."

A chill shot through Ben's skin, all the way to his nerves. He stiffened. "What did you say?"

"Forgetting Saltaire's a good thing," Nate repeated. "After everything he's done to you, I'd say you're perfectly entitled to just scrub him out of your mind. Yeah, I know he's not entirely to blame for everything that's happened and he has done a lot of good but—"

"Nate," Aki said. "What the hell are you on about? You're talking about this...saltine guy... like we're supposed to know who he is!"

"Well, yeah." Nate's expression was plainly baffled. "Yes, he's an asshole... But he's an almost all-powerful asshole..." He trailed off, looking to each of his friends in turn. "You really—you've got no idea who he is?"

Ben's blood froze. "The Final Register's been used again."

AKI OPENED THE kitchen cupboards of Hunter's apartment one after the other. "Come on, come on—ah ha! Wine! Now all I need are some glasses..."

Ben watched him wordlessly. *Is this really the time to indulge?* At the same time, he couldn't blame Aki. His head was still reeling from the implications of Nate's bombshell. *If everything he said about...the master vampire...is true, then we're in a lot of trouble.* He didn't like that his name had already vanished from Ben's memory. It was like trying to hold on to a live fish...

"Here." Aki put a half glass of wine in front of him.

Ben was grateful. "Thanks." He sipped the wine, hoping it would ease the tension running through him.

Behind him, the apartment door flew open. Charlotte held the door while Nate carefully carried Hunter, still wrapped from head to foot in vines, into the apartment. He'd recovered enough to thrash violently, and Nate's T-shirt was torn, evidence of the struggle getting him upstairs had been.

Nate readjusted his hold on Hunter. "You said there's a bedroom?"

Aki waved a hand. "Over there."

Ben opened the door, turning on the lights. He saw a lightly disturbed king bed and heavy-duty blackout curtains. While far from the traditional crypt, the room was an adequate protection against sunlight. "He'll be fine if we leave him here."

Nate heaved Hunter onto the bed. "There." He looked around the room. "Not bad. Trust Hunter to take care of himself."

Ben stared down at the trapped vampire. He couldn't help but remember how it had felt to lie in his coffin, the lid lowered over him, while the presence of other vampires was a niggling threat at the urge of his consciousness.

"It's all right." Charlotte's hand on his shoulder was a surprise. "I'll place a protective circle around the bed. He won't be able to leave, and no harm will come to him within the circle. Aki and I will remain here until you return or we're sure that Hunter's returned to his usual state of mind."

Ben breathed out. It felt wrong to leave him at all, but knowing Hunter would not be entirely alone went some way to soothing his conscience. "Thank you, Charlotte."

Back in the living room, Nate was on the phone. "Why would I call you if we'd decided to ditch? Aki was in trouble. Vampire attack. We're coming back, and we've got bad news. The Final Register's been used." He paused. "You wouldn't believe me if I told you. Where are you?" He bit his tongue. "Sure. We'll make our way back to the station now."

"Gunn?" Ben asked as Nate returned his phone to his pocket.

"Who else? He accused us of trying to skip out on them." Nate looked to Aki. "Are you sure you're okay staying here?"

"Between staying here where there is company and I can see for myself that Hunter's tied up and going home where I'm entirely alone and I have to take someone else's word that he hasn't escaped?" Aki shook his head. "I'm staying put. Also, Hunter has wine."

As they made their way through the streets, Ben couldn't shake off the feeling that he was taking the easy route. *I owe him so much. When I lost my mind, Hunter stood by me. He taught me how to keep the vampire in check, how to use it without ever being controlled by it...*

Ben frowned. Hunter was centuries more experienced than Ben. So how was it possible that Ben was walking around now, still in command of his senses, while Hunter had seemingly reverted to a base revenant? *It doesn't make sense... Unless this master vampire deliberately cut me off from his power—or is this because I'm living?*

Nate's hand found him. "You okay? I know how important Hunter is to you."

Ben squeezed his hand. "We'll get him back. Just like you got me back."

The footpaths were all but deserted, but there was still some traffic on the road, and light and noise spilled out from the clubs and bars. As they turned out of the nightlife area and toward Department Seven, the sound stopped as abruptly as if the volume had been turned down. Ben resisted the urge to shiver. "Tell me again about..." *This is getting tiresome.*

"Saltaire?" Nate took a deep breath. "He's old, no—ancient. He's really...I don't know how to put it. Rigid? Really locked into one way of thinking. Gunn says that the stick up his ass has been there so long it's petrified—which kind of says it all."

Ben's lips twitched faintly. "Gunn's not a fan?"

"I don't think anyone is, except Hunter and maybe Godfrey—shit, Godfrey!" Nate came to an abrupt halt. "Do you think he's okay?"

"He's a witch, not a vampire. We don't have to worry about him attacking anyone."

"Yeah, but he's old. Older than anyone gets to be normally. You told me once that was because of his association with Saltaire."

"All that means is that deprived of his employer's presence, Godfrey will slowly start to age again." Ben squeezed Nate's hand. "So...Saltaire...has a lot of enemies?" A thought occurred to him. "Could Gunn be behind this? The Final Register was in Department Seven's protection."

Nate was silent. Ben glanced at him and was relieved to see that rather than being outraged, Nate was considering the question. "I don't think so. In a really weird way, I think Gunn enjoys hating Saltaire. Without him around...well, there'd be an emptiness. There's no one he hates like he hates Saltaire."

Ben wasn't convinced, but he decided that Nate knew Gunn—and, at this moment, Saltaire—better than he did. "And me? You told me he's my sire. Do I like him?"

To his surprise, Nate blanched. "Fuck me. You've got more reason to want to get rid of Saltaire than anyone else."

"I hope you don't think I'm responsible for this."

"No, but everyone else will! This—" Nate had stopped stock still again.

Ben took his hand and pulled him into an alleyway—usually a terrible idea in New Camden, but he was confident that he and Nate were more than a match for any lurking predators. "Explain. Why do I hate Saltaire?"

"It's not so much you hating him as him having it in for you." Nate sounded as though every word escaped him reluctantly. "You've escaped his control twice. You've got no idea what that means to a control freak like him. You... He was determined that you weren't going to do it a third time. He threatened you in front of Gunn. I heard him! And it was totally legal. The council remanded you to his custody!"

The chill traveling Ben's skin had nothing to do with the cold shadows of the alley. "That's why you were surprised when I walked out of the cell. This...person...ordered me to remain there?" As Nate nodded, Ben's thoughts raced ahead. "Meaning that whoever put him on the Final Register did it before then."

"Shit!" Nate's eyes widened. "Gunn and I saw him only minutes before I came to you."

"Department Seven's at the center of this." Ben looked down the street. "We have to be very careful, Nate."

"I know." Nate sounded miserable.

Are we walking into a trap? Ben's mind raced through various scenarios. *If Gunn is in possession of the Final Register, he wouldn't be calling attention to the fact with an all-out hunt for it. And it's hard to imagine him taking revenge on anyone this way.* Hard, but not impossible. But Gunn wasn't the only member of Department Seven. *There's Kenzies. She's risked her life for the city many times over and is dedicated to her job—and her werewolf freedoms. She's defied Wisner, defied countless alphas to keep her integrity, and she even puts up with Gunn on a daily basis. Does she feel as strongly about the city's freedoms as she does her own? And then there was Simeon, Tremaine, even the suspiciously cheerful Clay.* Ben shook his head. Until they had some facts it was all speculation.

Ben ran through his memories. He couldn't remember...his sire...but he could remember around him. While he no longer remembered specific words or actions, the feelings lingered. He felt again the queasy sensation that always accompanied the realization that dawn was approaching and it was time to return to the house. The confining, suffocating house.

Ben's stomach rolled just at the thought of it. *How is it possible that even when not present, he affects me so strongly?* The visceral reaction of his body was reflected by the tension building in his mind. He could feel a persistent throb that would soon become a headache. "And you said the council, even Department Seven, let him make the majority of decisions?" At Nate's nod, Ben's stomach twisted further. "How did he get away with this?"

Nate's reply was unhappy. "Even though nobody likes him, everyone knows the city needs him. He's just that powerful."

GUNN, WREATHED IN a cloud of cigarette smoke, waited for them outside the station. He snarled tiredly in greeting, the action purely reflexive. "We're going in the back door. This way."

A warning sign if there was ever one. Ben reached for Nate's hand. *I'll pretend to stumble, whisper in his ear. Even Gunn will struggle with Nate's vines—*

His hand closed on thin air. Ben watched as Nate stepped through the back door without any hesitation. *Naturally.* He owed Nate everything, loved him more than he loved life, but sometimes he wished he'd just think a little more.

"Hurry, Hawick. There's something you've got to see." Gunn's tone was strained.

Ben decided that was sufficiently unusual for the *lemur* to justify the risk. "I suppose you can't tell us what?"

Gunn grunted. He paused, scanning the main corridor. "Look," he said, speaking quietly. "Only myself and Kenzies know about this. Kenzies because she hasn't had a moment to herself all day, me because I would know if it was me, and you will just have to take my word that it's not."

Ben felt Nate press against him, and he couldn't blame him for seeking reassurance. The implications raised by Gunn's words were not good. *He suspects a possession then, or worse. One of his staff deliberately doing this.*

Kenzies stood on guard outside the door. Like Gunn, she was clearly ill at ease, only managing a shadow of her usual smile for Nate. She glanced around before she let them into the briefing room and then followed them inside, closing the door behind her.

Ben couldn't fault their caution. The briefing room table had been thrust to one side, and a circle outlined in chalk on the floor. "Is that—"

"Just like the other circles," Nate said immediately. "Fuck me." He looked at Gunn. "But where's the body?"

"There was none." Despite smelling strongly of tobacco, Gunn's fingers twitched as if he were longing for another cigarette. "Look. See how the chalk is smudged? Someone lay here."

"Saltaire," Nate said immediately. "He's a vampire. And if the same person took the Final Register, that'd explain why no one remembers him to notice he's gone."

"He's not there now?" Gunn waved a hand to the circle. As Nate shook his head, his frown increased. "This Saltine guy. Powerful vampire?"

"A master," Nate said promptly. "Thousands of years old."

"But they didn't kill him." Ben crouched by the circle to take a closer look at it.

"Don't touch it!" Gunn snapped. "If you wreck it before our expert takes a look at it..."

Nate looked around the room. "Tremaine hasn't seen this? Where is she?"

"Remained behind at the Registry," Kenzies said. "I've left a message on her phone to get here as soon as possible."

Gunn waved his finger at Nate. "In the meantime, tell us everything you know about this Krispy guy."

Ben continued to study the circle, listening to Nate's explanation as he did. He was amused to discover that although mostly the same, Nate left out the part where Ben had been declared the man's prisoner. *Always looking out for me.*

"Sounds like a real winner." Kenzies shifted restlessly. Probably finding being in confined quarters with Gunn a struggle. Ben's eyes were watering, and he didn't have her werewolf nose. "Well, Ben? Can you tell us anything about the circle?"

"The spell worked was a transfer." Ben pointed to the runes establishing the spells direction. "Not power. Energy."

"Energy? From a fucking vamp?" Gunn's snort was explosive. "That's like trying to fill a bath with a sieve. You're stealing stolen energy—"

"Which is why there were multiple victims," Nate said slowly. "Because whoever did this needed more."

Gunn stuck his hands in his pockets, looking down at the circle. "Would a powerful vampire keep someone going longer?"

Nate held up his hands. "Don't ask me! I'm not the magic guy."

"Which itself raises questions," Kenzies said. "How come Nate remembers—and none of the rest of us do?"

Ben nodded. The same question had been puzzling him. "Do you have any...I don't know...link to Saltaire?"

Nate shuddered. "No. And that wouldn't explain it if I did. I mean, if I could forget you and you mean everything—"

"No," Gunn said. "Not when I'm present. Please. Think of my stomach." He narrowed his eyes at Nate. "You lying to us?"

"About Saltaire?" Nate shook his head. "I've got no reason to make this up."

Ben frowned. He knew Nate wasn't lying. "What did you do when you found the Final Register?"

"I panicked," Nate said promptly. "I mean, everyone in the city was looking for it and there it was, in my room. Obviously, I didn't remember you until I opened it."

"And then?" Kenzies saw where Ben was going.

"Like I said, I panicked. I wanted to get you out of there as soon as possible, so I ripped a page out. Only that didn't work. So I called Diya, and she told me I had to erase the name—"

That was it. Gunn stiffened, and Ben knew he'd seen it too. "Nate. Do you still have that page?"

"Let me check." Nate patted his jeans pockets. "Yeah. It's right here. Good thing I didn't have the chance to do laundry. Wait—*that's* how I remember while the rest of you don't? Because I have a page of the Final Register?"

"Give that here." Gunn tried to wrestle the paper out of Nate's pocket. There was a tearing sound. Gunn wound up clutching a scrap of paper while Nate slid the rest of it out of his pocket.

"You tore it!"

"Does it still work?"

Nate frowned as he concentrated. "Yeah. I still remember Saltaire—although I wish I didn't." He glanced nervously at Gunn.

Ben had seen Gunn angry before, but never like this. His face was contorted with fury, his knuckles white as they clenched around the scrap of paper. "Fucking hell, Nate. You weren't exaggerating."

"I couldn't make him up if I tried." Nate's smile was worried.

"I take it you remember now too, sir?" Kenzies's tone was unimpressed. Clearly she didn't have time for these dramatics.

Gunn's expression indicated an intense internal struggle. "It'd be so easy, just to burn the fucking page..." He sighed, reaching into his pocket for a cigarette. "Divide it up, Nate. Let's get them in on this."

Nate seemed to take an excruciatingly long time to fold the paper and carefully tear it into three pieces. "Here."

Ben took the scrap. Immediately, Saltaire's influence crashed down on him like an avalanche, knocking the air from his lungs and leaving him staggering under its weight. He stretched out a hand to steady himself against the wall. *This—*

But even this was only an echo of Saltaire's true power. Ben weighed it against his memories of being under Saltaire's influence and discovered that he could think clearly, not swayed by his sire's wishes.

Gunn exhaled, sending a fresh cloud of smoke into the room. "We don't *have* to rescue him."

"Gunn!" Nate was shocked, Kenzies disapproving.

Gunn was unrepentant. "Think about it! Yeah the guy's powerful, but is having him around really worth all the grief? Clearly his power still works even when no one remembers him, so the security of the city's not at stake."

Kenzies frowned, mulling it over. "What do you think, Ben?"

Ben was silent. *The chance to be free of him.* Leaving Saltaire's vampire family had enabled him to build a new life, explore new possibilities, but through it all, he'd known it was only a matter of time before Saltaire found him again. With the fear of Saltaire's retribution an ever-present threat, he'd never really been free.

"We can't leave him on the Final Register," Nate said. "No one deserves that. Even if it's Saltaire. Yeah, he's a pain, but we can handle him. We've handled necromancers, werewolves, even an actual demon. Why should Saltaire be any different?"

Gunn sighed. "Your misplaced optimism—"

"Nate's right," Ben said slowly. "Saltaire's overshadowed everything I've done. It's hard to see him for what he is—not a force, but a single individual. But I know that no one deserves to be on the Final Register. If we leave him there, we're no better than—than Wisner."

"Agreed," Kenzies said fervently.

Gunn scowled. "Have it your way, you bunch of pussies. I'm just saying, we could have made life a lot easier on ourselves. Nate, where do you think you are, fucking preschool? You have something to say, put your hand down and fucking say it."

Nate lowered his raised hand. "Shouldn't we be taking one of these papers to Hunter? That'd bring him back to normal, right?"

Good question. Ben frowned. "If Saltaire exists only to himself, then remembering him won't necessarily bring Hunter back."

"If Emeric hasn't developed enough self-control to hold his shit together in three-hundred years, then he's going to be a hindrance, and I got more than enough of those in this very room—"

"Our first step," Kenzies said loudly, talking over Gunn, "is to figure out who took him." She motioned to the circle. "Obviously, he was lured here."

Gunn sniffed. "Now that I remember him, I can recognize his foul odor. I'd know that stench anywhere."

Ben bit his lip. *Gunn's complaining about smell?*

Nate was not quite as successful, smothering a cough.

Kenzies simply stared at her superior officer in disbelief, her expression making her skepticism clear.

Gunn glared at her. "How about you make yourself useful? You're not going to catch any clues with your mouth wide open."

"Permission to check the security footage, see who was last in this room?" She saluted.

"Go on then." Gunn waved her away, before turning back to Ben. He indicated the circle with the butt of his cigarette. "What can you tell us about this piece of work, Benny?"

Ben looked down at it. "It's an expert, that's for sure. Whoever drew this is familiar with Peter's repertoire, but they've expanded on his work. This is an innovation, as is this." He pointed to the symbols.

Nate shifted closer to him. "What's the difference?"

"Peter's spell was a balanced transfer. For something taken, something would be given. In his case, he took my vampire abilities and gave his humanity in return. A balanced spell is stronger and safer, but it has the side effect of leaving a bond between the caster and the object of the spell." Ben indicated the circle. "This one-sided transfer is weaker, meaning that more power is lost in the spell."

"Huh." Nate frowned at the circle. "I guess that makes sense. If you've got the amount of power that Saltaire has, you don't really care if you waste a bit."

"Exactly." Ben looked up to see Gunn frowning at him. "Anything wrong?"

"That explanation was really neat," Gunn said slowly. "You're like some fucking magical tutor or something."

Ben snorted. "Is that a compliment?" They were getting off subject. "Anyway." He took a moment to line up his thoughts, looking down at the circle. "We're looking for a magical expert with prior knowledge of Peter's work. I don't imagine that's a very big field."

Gunn scratched his chin. "It's a very small field. It consists of you and—no, just you."

Ben tensed. "I'm getting really sick of these allegations. You know I'm not behind these deaths and at the moment that Saltaire disappeared, I was behind bars! As far as we know the last person to see him was you!"

Gunn frowned. "Pity I didn't appreciate the moment for what it was."

"If Peter's possessed someone, they would have access to his memories, right?" Nate scratched the back of his neck hesitantly.

"For the last fucking time! No one is fucking possessed!"

"It's a good point," Ben shot back immediately. "If Peter possessed someone or managed to return, then he wouldn't be hampered by the fact that ARX has impounded all his books." He paused. "They are still locked up at ARX?"

"You're kidding, right? Of course they are. No fucking way anyone's getting permission to look at them."

Nate tensed. "Peter's books are here. In the secure research room."

Gunn's mouth dropped open. His face went first white and then red as the blood that drained out of him in shock rushed back. "What did you say?"

"Tremaine has his books here. To study them." Nate took a step back. "She got permission from ARX. Why are you looking at me like that? I thought you knew."

Ben drew a sharp breath. "And she's a trained magic-user?"

"Best in the entire fucking department."

"I thought she was looking better recently," Nate said. "Healthier. Do you think—"

"Not another word, Nate!" Gunn kicked the wall. "God fucking damn it! I'm going to tear her to pieces!"

Kenzies rapped on the door and stepped inside. Her expression was grim. "Bad news. Only one person's gone anywhere near this room tonight."

"Tremaine?" At his subordinate's nod, Gunn growled. He stabbed out his cigarette on the table. "Really wonder why I stick with this job. It's just one long series of getting stabbed in the back."

"But if she was possessed, then we're helping her—"

Kenzies shook her head, cutting Nate short. "If she'd been possessed, we'd know. This is deliberate, Nate. Tremaine knows exactly what she's doing."

Chapter Eighteen

"WHAT WOULD POSSESS her to do something like this?" Kenzies jogged after Gunn. "She was so pleased to be back on the job. Working with her was just like old times—she seemed happy."

"She was happy." Gunn walked with rapid, angry strides that left the rest of them hurrying to catch up. "Didn't pay much attention because I didn't want the indigestion, but there were no red flags, no indication... Damn it! At least a possession would have been understandable!"

Nate winced. It was hard watching two people he liked reeling under a blow like this. "There's got to be an explanation. It's just a matter of finding her."

"Oh, we'll find her all right." Gunn's voice was low and dangerous. "And when we do, she will not be happy."

Ben brushed against Nate's side, finding his hand. "You okay?"

Nate took a breath. "Yeah. Obviously I only knew Tremaine a short time, but she was cool. I liked her a lot. Hell, you heard her encourage me outside the Registry. She's not a bad person."

Ben bit his lip. Now wasn't the time to point out that there was no way a Department Seven officer coolly murdering the legal supernaturals she was sworn to protect was a good thing.

"Are you okay? You've been quiet ever since we left the station."

He'd forgotten how observant Nate was. Even in shock at the discovery of Tremaine's betrayal, he noticed that Ben was distracted. "I've been thinking." He took a deep breath. "It's not just Tremaine we're bringing in. It's Saltaire too." He'd come up against Saltaire's power many times, but never once overcome it head-on. The thought of facing him again was daunting. "Saltaire's power is what Peter was planning to take over the city with—and he very nearly succeeded. I don't know if we can stand up to Tremaine's magic with Saltaire's power behind it."

Gunn and Kenzies had already disappeared inside the Registry by the time Nate and Ben reached the stairs. The scene was still chaotic. The vampires had long since been removed, but evidence of the battle remained with police cars lying on their side, broken glass spilling onto the pavement, and a twisted mass of branches where Nate had trapped Julian's vampires. As they drew closer to the briars, Nate could see an officer struggling to close a pair of pliers around a particularly thick branch.

"You're hurting it! Look, let me." Nate stepped up to the plant. He placed his hands on the branches, running his hands over them. The thorns tickled, giving way before his touch. "You helped us out a lot, and I'm really grateful to you—we all are. I'm going to let you rest now." He shut his eyes, concentrating on undoing the growth he'd called up.

With a sound eerily reminiscent of a sigh the plant folded in on itself, undoing its tendrils, and sinking under the ground. Nate followed it all the way back to seed form, lying dormant until it was once again exposed to air and light.

"There." He patted the soil and stepped back, wiping his hands on his jeans. Looking up, he saw the police officer staring at him, the pliers dangling from her slack hand. "Sorry, about that."

She shook her head. "No, I—do you do private gardens? Because we got a hedge that is just impossible—"

"You can discuss your alternate career as a gardener later." Ben planted a hand on Nate's back, steering him toward the Registry entrance. "We need to find Gunn."

It wasn't hard. They could hear him cursing the moment they stepped inside the building. The profanities led them to the library. As soon as Nate stepped inside, he knew why. "She's not here."

"And she's taken the original Final Register and Saltaire with her. A slow death—roasted alive maybe—" Gunn looked like he was only just stopping himself from kicking the desks that held the component parts of the Register spell.

Nate frowned, stepping forward for a closer look. All the books were in their appointed places, and the central desk held the interim power source. All of the books' pages flickered in unison, indicating that New Camden's defenses were up and running. "What? She took the time to tidy up and restore the city's defenses before she left?"

"Insult to injury!" Gunn spat. "She knew we were on her trail—"

"From what I've heard, this sounds less insult, more like Tremaine's goal isn't to bring the city down." Ben's calm was even more welcome compared to Gunn's fury. He looked at Kenzies. "You know her best. What do you think?"

Kenzies chewed her lip. "Helen would be the last person to care about power. She got into the job because she genuinely wanted to help people. A rarity in our line of work, but a welcome one. And through her long years of service, she became jaded, but she still believed in our work. I don't believe that whatever she's doing, she would risk the safety of the city. Leaving the interim power source behind and the spell restored, that's proof that whatever her goal is, it's personal."

"But what the hell is it?" Gunn suddenly stiffened, drawing himself up. "This is an unexpected pleasure, Your Honor."

The mayor stood in the library doorway. Her angry expression was a clear indication that she'd overheard enough of their conversation to come to her own conclusions. Chief Jacobs flanked her, his expression indicating that he shared her dim view of the situation. "Keyword being 'unexpected.' I gather you have information about the theft of the Final Register you haven't shared with me?"

Gunn shot Nate a glare that clearly said *Don't say anything.* "We only just came into possession of this information ourselves ten minutes ago. We came here in the hopes of confirming our suspicions—"

"And Tremaine's absence confirms those suspicions?" Mayor Chandler crossed her arms over her chest. "I came here to get to the bottom of how the vampires were able to get into the Registry, and I discover that one of your officers is behind this outrage."

Gunn snarled. "The vampires got in because your human police force has no defenses against them! Tell her, Jacobs!"

The chief of police scowled. "It's true that we were unable to prevent the vampires from forcing their way into the Registry, and that the assistance of our Department Seven colleagues was instrumental in removing them. But—"

The mayor continued as if he hadn't spoken, addressing Gunn directly. "So you'd prefer us to trust your officers—who may or may not be working against the city?" Her eyes flashed. "The council made its orders clear. Your officers were to stand down."

"My officers got the vampires out of here and repaired the damage to the Register—yeah, even the one you're accusing of betraying the city!"

The mayor walked over to the spell, frowning. "Has anyone checked that the spell was not altered in any way?"

"We literally just figured out it was her." Gunn massaged his temple. "I know you expect us to do the impossible, but there's only so much magic can do about things like time and space."

"Chief Jacobs!" The mayor barked. "Summon the Magic-Users Guild members responsible for maintaining the spell. I want to be absolutely certain that Tremaine hasn't left us any unexpected surprises. And at the same time, I want a citywide alert. Any sightings of her are to be reported at once."

Jacobs saluted. "At once, Your Honor."

As he left, the mayor crossed her arms. "Don't think for a second that I've failed to notice that you're accompanied by a known criminal, Gunn. Did you think I wouldn't recognize Bennet Hawick, or that I'd forget he's meant to be in custody right now?"

Nate started. He'd entirely forgotten that Mayor Chandler wrote Ben into the Final Register. He glanced at Ben and saw that his expression was blank.

"He's with me, isn't he?" Gunn said with complete shamelessness. "That's custody."

The mayor's lip curled. "I'm not sure my colleagues on the council would agree. No, you need to watch yourself. You've been walking a thin line for a very long time. Your department's reputation is still recovering from the werewolf debacle."

"Our reputation? Wisner took us off the case so he could make a clean sweep of the city! You're just lucky I was there to stop him."

Nate didn't feel like now was a good time to remind Gunn that he'd helped. There was an edge to this encounter that he didn't like.

The mayor stood at the Interim Register. "You're on dangerous ground, Gunn. You've disobeyed a direct mandate twice, and you don't appear to regret your actions."

Gunn snorted. "Really."

She narrowed her eyes. "No one's above the law—not even the representatives of the law. You show a reckless disregard for authority that endangers the city. I consider myself perfectly justified in entering you into the Final Register."

Nate gasped. "You can't do that!"

Kenzies stepped forward, her fists clenched. "Yes, he's reckless, but he's done what no one else in the city can do! Control a team of varied supernaturals—"

"I don't consider allowing one of his department to make off with a powerful magical object 'controlling.' If anything, it's further proof that Officer Gunn has overstepped his capabilities."

"But we need Gunn now, more than ever! With—"

Ben stepped on Nate's foot. He caught Nate's eye and shook his head.

I shouldn't tell the mayor about Saltaire? But if she doesn't know how serious the situation is... Nate turned back to the scene unfolding before them and his heart sank.

Gunn swaggered up to the mayor, his insolence in full force. "Threatening me? I think you've overstepped your capabilities, mayor."

"Think I'm bluffing?" She pulled a page out of her jacket pocket, tucking it into the book. "Think again. As I said in my campaign, vote Chandler for action—not empty promises."

The air in the library seemed to vibrate. Energy rippled through it, the endlessly turning pages of the books in the Register spell speeding up for a second.

Nate looked around. "What did you do?"

Ben swallowed. He'd gone white around his lips. "Please tell me you didn't make a second Final Register?"

"I congratulate you on your quick grasp of the situation, Mr. Hawick. I hope that you have also grasped what a mistake it would be to continue to defy New Camden's laws." As she continued to talk, she smoothed down the page. "I never trusted Wisner. I suspected that he had an ulterior motive in the creation of the Final Register, so I took steps to ensure that if he did misuse it, the council would have the means to stop him. I removed the original diagram the Magic-User's Guild drew up in the creation of the spell. Now that I've placed it within the pages of the Interim Register, I have a second Final Register, and I can assure you that I am fully prepared to use it. You have a choice, Gunn. Obey orders—"

"Sit back and watch as Jacobs's people make an even bigger mess of the situation? Are you shitting me?"

The mayor narrowed her eyes, talking over Gunn's interruption. "Or be taken out of the equation entirely by being put on the Final Register."

"That's not a choice." Gunn stepped forward.

"Please, Gunn!" Nate stepped after him. "Even if you can't act, we need you here!"

Kenzies addressed her protest to the mayor. "Think about this! As much as it pains me to admit it—and it really pains me—no one else could run the department. We need Gunn."

"The mayor doesn't want words. She wants proof. I say we test this." Gunn strode forward, and before the mayor could stop him, he tore a page out of the Interim Register. He handed it to her. "Put this in your pocket."

She didn't move. "That's destruction of city property—"

He snarled, his voice dropping to the tenor of a nightmare. "Do it."

Nate stepped back. That low tone took him back to the nightmares that had plagued him in childhood, lying in bed, unable to move but knowing that with every passing second his death drew closer...

The mayor tucked the torn page into her jacket with trembling fingers. She realized what she'd done too late and took a deep breath, squaring her shoulders and staring directly at Gunn. "You've made a very serious miscalculation, Isaiah Gunn. If you thought I wouldn't do this"—she lowered her pen to the paper—"or that I wasn't fully acquainted with your full name."

"No!" Nate stepped forward. "You can't do this—the legality of the Final Register's in question! There's no way this is okay—"

The mayor scribbled quickly. "But nobody will remember."

Nate took a hasty step toward her. He had to stop this.

Before he reached the circle of books, they rose in the air, pages rustling as if turned by a tornado. The furious sound was accompanied by a barrier of wind so strong that Nate's collision with it knocked him back. As he regained his footing, the wind died away, the books returning to their usual speed.

The mayor relaxed. "I strongly suggest you don't try that a second time, Mr. Granger. There is room in this book for you and Gunn."

Nate frowned. "For who?"

An EERIE SOUND was heard over the rustling pages. It started low, but rose to forlorn heights, leaving a feeling of unease behind it as it faded away, only to break out again a few seconds later.

Nate gritted his teeth. Wolf howls were quickly overtaking sirens as his least favorite sound. "Not again."

The mayor appeared to share his feelings. She looked sharply at Kenzies. "If this is your doing..."

Kenzies needed a moment to recollect herself. She shook her head, seemingly struggling to return to the current moment. "Not me, Your Honor. You know I'm the only wolf employed by Department Seven."

As the howl was taken up by multiple voices, the mayor frowned in the direction of the sound. "Then who?"

"Wisner's pack," Ben said immediately. "They have the worst timing."

Kenzies saluted. "Permission to put together a team to protect the Register against a probable attack?"

"Permission denied," the mayor said. "Chief Jacobs's force will handle any security needs."

"But surely you see that the use of human police to suppress a supernatural force will be throwing gas on a fire!" Kenzies protested. "The situation is already tense—"

"This is one city, not two! We can't have one set of laws for supernaturals and another for humans," the mayor snapped. "New Camden's supernatural citizens need the reminder that they are not above the law, no matter what they might think." She pointed to Ben. "Case in point. You'll take Hawick back to the station and see that he remains in custody."

All the while leaving Tremaine out there able to do who knows what with the Final Register? Nate cast an anxious look at Ben. "We can't do that!"

As Ben frowned, the howls sounded again, directly outside. This time the sound was accompanied by a series of loud bangs.

Gunshots? Nate drew in a deep breath. *This is going from bad to worse.*

The mayor smirked. "As you can hear, Jacobs's forces have the situation in hand. Now—"

This bang was so loud the room shuddered. Nate flung out his hand, grabbing a bookshelf for balance. With his other hand, he tugged Ben toward him. Plaster and dust fell from the ceiling, and the books paused turning momentarily. "What was that?"

The mayor ignored Kenzies's offer of a helping hand and pushed herself to her feet. "I'm sure that's nothing to worry about. Perhaps the Chief—"

"Mayor!" Jacobs rushed into the room. "The Registry's under attack. I cannot guarantee your safety if you remain. We need to get you out of here at once."

"Don't tell me your men aren't a match for a couple of unarmed wolves!" The mayor's laugh was scornful. "The city is relying on you!"

Jacobs took her by her arm, propelling her toward the door. "The city hasn't seen a couple of werewolves pick up a patrol car and throw it into a building. I'm sure they'll understand."

There was another shudder. A team of officers rushed through the library door, immediately piling furniture against it to secure it. "We've lost the front door!" One of them reported. "We're falling back, as ordered!"

"Hold your positions as long as you can." Jacobs turned back to the mayor. "You need to get out now."

She hesitated and then grabbed the Interim Register, hurrying to Jacobs.

Could she do that? Yeah, she's mayor but... The pages of the books that made up the spell continued to whirl, but their pace had slowed noticeably. Unless the book was replaced, would they run out of power?

"Wake up, Nate!" Kenzies prodded him. "We have to move."

A second door connected the library with the back corridor. They hurried through it toward the back door. "There's an armored car waiting to take you to a secure location—" Jacobs flung open the back door and came to a halt. The armored car was upside down.

Ronald smirked at them from his perch on the underside of the car. "Maybe now you'll take us seriously." He jumped down from the car, sauntering over to them. "You know what we want. Hand over the Final Register now."

Jacobs drew his gun, leveling it at Ronald, but the werewolf didn't give him a glance. Kenzies's low growl as she stepped in front of the mayor did, but it only daunted him for a second. The growls of his pack members waiting at the back door with him reassured him. Ronald held out his hand to the mayor. "I'm waiting."

"Think twice about threatening me. I have access to the Final Register." The mayor's jaw was clenched as she refused to be intimidated by the werewolves. "If you continue to obstruct the law, you and your associates will be entered into it."

"See?" Ronald stabbed a finger toward the mayor. "Just like I told you. Humans using the Final Register as a weapon against supernaturals!"

"And the fact you just threatened her has nothing to do with it?" Nate clenched his fists. He was getting really sick of Ronald.

The feeling seemed to be mutual. Ronald scowled and locked eyes with the mayor. "Give it to us. Or we'll take it by force."

"Don't worry, Your Honor." Kenzies stepped forward. "We're not going to let that happen." She adopted a defensive position on the steps, between the mayor's party and Ronald's wolves. "Ben, Nate. Protect her."

One person against half a wolf pack? Nate had a lot of respect for Kenzies, but those odds were dire. "But, Kenzies, you—"

Ben dragged him back inside the corridor. "Kenzies knows what she's about. If anything happens to the mayor, we can forget any chance of democracy in New Camden. She's our priority."

Leaving Kenzies on the steps was bad, but hearing the door slammed shut behind them was like getting punched in the gut. Nate watched as Jacobs and Ben sized up the surrounding rooms before deciding on the most defensible.

"In here, mayor." Jacobs pushed her inside.

The office must have belonged to a magic-user, as there was a bag of salt on the shelves. Ben grabbed it, scattering it in a circle around himself and the mayor. "I'm going to do what I can with defensive wards. You stop them getting in. Okay, Nate?"

"Sure." Nate took a deep breath. Jacobs took up a defensive position, pressed against the wall beside the door. They could both feel the thump as a body connected with the door. The wolves had found them and were doing their best to break down the door.

Does that mean Kenzies is down? The thought wasn't welcome. Nate drew a deep breath. *I can do this.*

The door shattered, torn off its hinges. Ronald's wolves dropped it. There were three of them, bearded men with broad shoulders and well-muscled bodies. For a terrified moment, Nate thought they were in the process of transforming into their wolf form and then realized all he saw was excess body hair peeking through the rips in their torn shirts.

They clearly recognized Nate. "You're the guy who thought he could tell the wolves what to do!" The first one spat, his companions snarling. "So maybe you think you're a hotshot, taking down Wisner one-on-one. But Wisner was old. His time was coming. We're not letting some hairless wannabe get the jump on us."

The man behind him took a deep breath, his nostrils flaring. "We can smell your fear, freak. You don't fool us."

Damn it! Nate fought the urge to wipe his clammy hands on his jeans. No point confirming what the wolves already suspected. He didn't allow himself to step back or look to Ben. Taking his attention off the wolves, even for a second, could be fatal. *I can do this. I've done it before.*

But this time Ben wasn't with him. This time, he was all alone.

Peter snarled at him from the body of the first wolf. "You didn't think you'd seen the last of me, did you? Ben gave you a pretty explanation, but kind words are all that is. He's not here when you need him. It's just you and me—and three furious wolves."

No! Nate struggled to think past his rising panic. *I'm stronger than this. I've done it once.* He remembered the feeling of the branches rising from the ground beneath him, forming from nothing but a long-forgotten seed and Nate's force of will. *I can do this again.*

His magic came easily. The wooden walls of the Registry corridor grew branches, locking around the two wolves' waists. As they struggled to free themselves, more branches appeared, clamping around their feet and arms, until they were unable to struggle at all, pinned to the wall.

The first wolf had better reflexes than his companions, darting out of the reach of the branches as the wood first started to move. "What fresh fuckery is this?" He swung back around to face Nate. "You want to fight? Let me show you how a werewolf does it!" He swung.

A werewolf, even an untransformed one, had the strength of two-and-a-half men. And this guy was angry. Every instinct Nate had told him to duck, to try to block. *I am the tree.* Staying put and trusting his magic was the hardest thing he'd ever done.

The wolf's fist connected with his gut. The wooden thunk echoed throughout the office. The wolf dropped to his knees, doubling up as he cradled his hand. "You—you fucking—"

Jacobs brought the butt of his pistol down on the man's head. He slumped to the floor. "Granger, is it? Good job."

"Uh. Thanks." Nate took a deep breath, watching as Jacobs proceeded to cuff the unconscious werewolf. He stepped into the corridor. It was full of activity. The remaining police were strapping cuffs on dazed wolves or attempting to read them their rights. He spotted a familiar redhead and grinned. "Kenzies! You're all right?"

"Was there any doubt?" Kenzies's grin was cocky, but she had a red mark across one cheek, and a police officer was attempting to apply a bandage to her hand. "These boys talk a good game, but easy living's made them careless."

"I want a full update on the situation!" The mayor stepped into the corridor.

Nate looked up in dismay. *What is she doing? It's not safe!*

As the police turned toward her, a dazed wolf, slumped against the wall, shook himself. With a growl, he sank onto all fours.

Oh shit—transforming! Nate tried to step toward him. "Stop him! Don't let him change!"

As the police realized what was going on, they scrambled. Most ran for cover or to grab weapons. All knew that a transformed werewolf was one of the deadliest beings in existence.

Nate tried to step toward the wolf, but the sea of bodies blocked his way. He could only watch with horror as cracking bone and tearing cloth gave way to a gut-twisting howl. The transformation was complete.

The mayor backed away. "Do something!"

There was nothing Nate could do but watch as the wolf launched itself directly at her. The mass of bodies blocking the corridor was nothing to him, the werewolf just barreled through them. "No!" He saw Ben push the mayor out of the way, taking her place in the wolf's path. *What is he thinking? There's no time for any magic! He'll be ripped apart—*

Suddenly the wolf skidded to a halt. The corridor emptied around him as he pressed himself flat against the floor, his eyes rolling. His powerful body was racked with shivers, and the wolf whimpered as he slowly backed away, his tail dragging across the floor.

Afraid of Ben? Nate raised his gaze to Ben and saw an equally confused expression on his face. *But if it wasn't Ben...?*

"That's enough of that nonsense." Kenzies grabbed the transformed wolf by his ear. "I am going to put you in a secure van, and you are going to stay there. Understood?"

The wolf's tail wagged and he nosed her hand, pathetically grateful to be arrested.

Has the world just gone insane? Nate turned to see Ben checking that the mayor was unhurt.

Jacobs strode up to them. "There's no time to waste, mayor. We've got a car outside."

This time she didn't argue. Nate followed after them as quickly as he could.

The mayor pursed her lips as they walked through the Registry, taking in the fresh wave of destruction. "Have all the wolves been arrested?"

Jacobs led the way through the front doors onto the Registry steps. "Most of them. A few ran off, including their leader—" He came to an abrupt halt.

"Looking for me?" Ronald stepped out from behind one of the stone columns on the Registry front steps. "Hate to break it to you, mayor, but I'm going nowhere." He bared his teeth. "And neither are they."

A huge crowd was assembling before the Registry, completely blocking the road.

"Reinforcements?" Nate's heart sank.

Jacobs swore. "Just what we need."

THE FLAT SPACE after the steps but before the doors was a natural stage. Ronald swaggered to the center of it. "Supernaturals, look! You see before your very eyes another example of your brothers being mistreated at the hands of the humans who want to rule us! We've had days of empty promises and refusal to answer questions from the mayor, but tonight your mayor made her stance on the Final Register clear. She threatened to use it against me—a clear violation of the city's laws!"

The crowd booed loudly. Nate saw those in the front row shift restlessly and his heart sank. He could suppress a few werewolves...but an entire crowd? He looked at Ben, saw him shake his head. *Really bad then.*

"Wisner's pack has committed a serious crime," Jacobs said. "They forced their way into the Registry, attacking the mayor—"

"All in self-defense!" Ronald countered. "The Register should be in the hands of supernaturals, not their oppressors! Hand it over!" He turned to the crowd. "It's time we let New Camden know we're sick of being pushed around! We demand our rights—or else!"

"Rights are not won by intimidation and threats!" The new voice was audible even over the murmurs of the crowd. The crowd fell silent, making way for Grant. He climbed the steps, his eyes on Ronald, the tawny glow in them more than usually pronounced. Grant was furious. "You're setting the supernatural community back decades with your unlawful behavior. For our rights as supernaturals to be inalienable, we need the trust and cooperation of our human neighbors. This isn't two cities—it's one."

Nate's eyes widened. *Didn't the mayor say something similar?*

Ronald bared his teeth as Grant approached. "Have you lost your mind, you foolish pup? Stand aside and let your betters speak!"

"And there we have your self-styled defender's attitude to everyone who isn't a werewolf—or isn't pack." Grant turned to speak to the crowd. "You're here tonight because you want to show the city where the supernatural community stands on the issues of law and justice. You're here because you care not only about your future, but that of everyone in this city. You're here to see that justice happens."

The cheers from the crowd only incensed Ronald further. "There's one major flaw in your argument, Grant! Humans hate us. Or have you forgotten? What's going to stop them turning against us?"

"You're making a big mistake trying to use fear against us." Grant folded his arms. He seemed to have a natural amplification to his voice. Nate could see even people at the back of the crowd nodding. "The city hasn't forgotten how Wisner deliberately created an atmosphere of fear in order to take control of the city's security. You can't keep people afraid forever."

"You're a dreamer!" Ronald's lip curled and he turned to the crowd. "Let's put it to the vote! Not one of us hasn't suffered at the hands of humans. The classification system is plainly discrimination, a front to get our information. We need to wrest control back, and there's no way the humans are going to surrender their best weapon against us peacefully. There's only one way to secure our future." He pointed to the book the mayor was clasping. "Taking control of the Register."

"You really think that the city would hand over the Register to you?" Jacobs was outraged.

"We'd protect it!" Ronald sneered, turning back to his audience. "The humans have been attacked twice tonight. How long do you think they're going to be able to protect it—or even want to protect it?" It took a special sort of person to blame humans for getting attacked, especially when they were responsible for one of the attacks. Ronald was clearly that special.

"You won't protect the Register," Grant said flatly. "You'd hold it hostage. You've got no experience in dealing with non-wolves. You live in a gated community, surrounded only by your kind. You shun human and non-pack social contact alike. Your track record is one of bullying, intimidation and violence. You don't speak for us, so don't imagine you do."

Ronald took a threatening step toward Grant. "Are you saying you'd rather trust the humans with it than your own kind? Where's your supernatural pride?"

Out of the corner of his eye, Nate saw a police officer raise his gun, tracking Ronald's movements.

Jacobs extended a hand, shaking his head.

This is really unusual. Preparing himself to be ready for anything, Nate shifted, clenching and unclenching his fists.

"I can trust humans. And I do." Grant threw his shoulders back, staring down his step-brother. "New Camden's at a turning point. We've got a choice between fear and hope. If we surrender to our fear, we will never be free. Whether we have the upper hand or not, fear will always come creeping back. But if we resist it, if we refuse to let it dictate our actions, we free ourselves and others." The crowd was hushed. Grant turned toward it. "I'm prepared to put my future in the hands of New Camden because I know we're stronger than fear."

He stepped down onto the first of the Registry steps, speaking deliberately to the crowd. "I know there's difficult times ahead. Not every decision will go in our favor. There will be resistance from those still trapped in fear. It will be tempting to give in to easy solutions. But threats and violence can never overcome fear, only cause it. Our actions today can prove that fear won't win."

The crowd stirred. All faces were turned toward Grant expectantly. Nate felt the hairs on his arm rising. *I've got chills.*

"Join me in showing New Camden that we choose hope, not fear. We will form a ring around the Registry, protecting it from those who would turn supernaturals against humans. We will show all of New Camden that her supernatural citizens stand, not against her, but for her. For all her citizens."

The crowd surged forward as one. Grant made his way to join the human chain assembling around the Registry. The buzz of conversation filled the air with a palpable energy.

Nate found his heart beating fast. *What just happened?*

Jacobs approached Ronald, holding out a pair of handcuffs before him. "You got the choice of doing this with dignity or without."

Ronald hesitated, but as Kenzies appeared, evidently decided to accept Jacobs's offer. He was cuffed, and the crowd parted for him and his fellow pack members to be led to the waiting police vans.

Ben's hand clasped Nate's. "That was something else."

"Right?" Nate shook his head as he looked down at the crowd. "I can't believe it." The city might avoid a fresh outbreak of violence after all...

"The pup can talk." Kenzies admitted grudgingly. "But we've still got to find Tremaine." She looked at the mayor. "Your Honor, I request permission to—"

"Do whatever it is you want to do," the mayor snapped. She glanced around her, clutching the Interim Register to her chest.

Nate scanned the scene, but no one was standing near the mayor. "Is everything okay, your mayorness?"

She scowled. "Just go."

Nate hesitated. *There's something really odd about this...*

"Let's go." Ben took Nate's hand. "We need to find Tremaine before the mayor changes her mind."

Chapter Nineteen

A PHOTO ON the desk caught Ben's eye. He picked it up. A younger Tremaine, her blonde hair tied back in a ponytail, stood with a group of uniformed Department Seven officers. Her uniform was crisp and her smile proud. Kenzies stood beside her, looking similarly young and untarnished. "Tell me about Tremaine."

Kenzies growled. She knelt on the floor, rifling through the drawers of Tremaine's desk. "Until today, I'd have said she was one of our best officers. She was a shining example that humans can work with supernaturals. Her professionalism was unquestioned; she had the patience of a saint." She slammed the drawer shut and started on the next. "I've got no idea why she'd do this."

Nate returned with two mugs of coffee. He handed the first to Ben and then turned to Kenzies. "Putting your coffee on the desk."

"Now's not the time—"

"You've been on the go this entire night," Nate countered immediately. "You're supernatural, not superhuman. And that goes for you too, Ben. Drink up or else."

Nate never changed. Ben blew steam away from the mug and took a sip. It was strong, heavily doused with sugar. *Nate knows me well.*

With a sigh, Kenzies dropped into the seat, taking the coffee. "Maybe you're right. We need to think. Tremaine's not the type to lose her cool and make an impulse decision. There's got to be a reason for this, and whatever the reason, she's not going to leave it in plain sight."

Ben nodded. His impression of Tremaine was of a clever woman, one who made her plans in advance. *She is bound to have come up with a safe house, one far away from any friends and acquaintances.*

"Could this be health-related?" Nate asked. "She's really sick, right?"

Kenzies shook her head. "She was diagnosed with bowel cancer last year, but the doctors caught it early enough to treat it. It's in remission. She wouldn't have come back to work if she wasn't well."

Nate shook his head. "She passed out at her desk. That's not well."

Kenzies's eyes widened and she set her coffee down. "When was this?"

"The day before the second victim was found—shit."

Ben sucked in a breath. "She was taking the energy from her vampire victims to keep herself alive!"

"That explains why she looked so much better after the murder, and why the murderer didn't show up on the yoga studio video!" Kenzies slammed her hand on the desk. "Tremaine must have faked the emergency call, shown up at the studio with the victim and murdered her on the premises!"

Very well planned. Ben frowned. He didn't like their chances of finding Tremaine before she accomplished whatever her intended goal was. "The energy she takes from Saltaire would pretty much make her immortal."

"Just what we need," Kenzies growled. "Hang on. I'm going to confirm this theory with her hospital." She pulled the phone on the desk over to her. "Central Hospital? Officer Kenzies, Department Seven. This is an official request for information pertaining to an investigation. I need to talk to a doctor who can give me the details of Helen Tremaine, patient at your hospital." Pause. "Sure, I'll hold."

Every second we spend here waiting, Tremaine gets closer to her goal. Ben started as Nate's fingers brushed his arm. "What's up?"

Nate hesitated. "It's probably nothing...but do you feel like something—someone's—missing?"

"Saltaire?" Ben guessed. "We're probably so used to having him looming over us that being without his presence feels weird."

Nate frowned. "I don't know. You're probably right, but..." He sighed. "The mayor wouldn't use the Final Register again, right?"

"Not if she doesn't want a whole lot of legal issues," Ben said promptly. "It's currently undergoing review. Besides, after what Grant did just now? She'd be out of office faster than Aki runs out of hair gel."

Nate's chuckle gave him a warm glow. "You're right. Guess I'm worrying about nothing."

"No one in the cancer unit is responding to the phone? No, don't send someone. I'll investigate in person." Kenzies ended the call. "We're rolling out, team."

Ben put his coffee down. "Central Hospital?"

Kenzies nodded, leading the way to the door. "There could be a perfectly innocent reason why an entire hospital ward decided to stop answering the phone, but somehow I doubt it."

BEN BREATHED IN the clinical smell of hospital corridors as they stepped inside, his eyes scanning the reception area for any sign of suspicious activity. Kenzies flashed her badge at the desk and continued down the hall with the air of someone who knew exactly where she was going. A security guard shot Ben a dirty look.

Probably remembers my last hospital visit. He hurried after Kenzies and Nate.

"What are we looking for?" Nate asked.

"Any sign of Tremaine or He-Who-Must-Not-Be-Named."

Ben snorted. He wouldn't have pegged Kenzies for a Harry Potter fan. "Let's think logically about this. If Tremaine is here, she has Saltaire with her. There's only a few hours before dawn. She's going to need to put him somewhere secure from daylight—"

"The morgue," Nate said immediately. "What? Where else would you put a dead body?"

"Too obvious," Ben said and Kenzies nodded.

"We don't need to guess. I've got Saltaire's scent. Tremaine didn't account for us being able to remember him."

Knowing that Saltaire existed gave them a definite advantage. Kenzies led them through a twisting maze of corridors without any hesitation, barely needing to pause and sniff. The trail led them to a staircase leading downstairs toward the...morgue.

Nate opened his mouth.

"Don't say anything." Kenzies shot him a look as she removed her gun from its holster. "I'm going in. Nate, cover me. Ben, you hang back. If anyone hears the disturbance, you keep them away from the scene."

Relegated to crowd control? He nodded reluctantly. It made sense. Without his vampire powers he was little more than a civilian...

Looking up, he caught Nate's eye. He took a deep breath and nodded, holding Ben's gaze. Ben felt his own determination lift. This was it.

Kenzies kicked the morgue door open. "Freeze!" She scanned the room. "Clear. Get in here."

There was no need to wonder if Tremaine had been there. The metal tables in the center of the room had been shoved aside to make way for a complicated magical circle. The smell of vampire was overpoweringly strong. Ben covered his nose as he crouched by the circle.

"This doesn't look like the others." Nate looked over his shoulder. "What is she trying to do?"

"Taking the energy of the dead and dying?" Kenzies's mouth was flat.

Ben shook his head. "No. There's supposed to be a second circle over there—see? She'd only just started working on it. One circle to gather power, the other to dispense it." He stood, walking over to get a closer look at the unfinished sigils. "If I had to guess, I'd say she's planning on sending the energy out."

"Right first time." The door swung closed, revealing Tremaine, standing behind it. "You know your magic, Bennet. I could have used your help creating the circle." She looked years younger than the last time Ben had seen her. Almost no gray remained in her hair, and she looked fresh, despite the late hour.

"We're not here to help you." Kenzies lowered her gun. "Helen... It doesn't have to go down this way."

Tremaine shook her head. "Believe me, I hoped it wouldn't come to this. But I'm committed. I have to see this through to the end."

"I really don't want to do this." Kenzies brought up her gun. "I'm placing you under arrest—"

Tremaine raised her hand.

It felt like a wall collided with them. Ben was lifted off his feet and flung backward. He collided midair with Nate, landing in a tangle. "Oof—"

Kenzies rolled, grabbing her gun. She fired at Tremaine, the bullets ricocheting off an invisible barrier. "Defensive wards!"

"On it!" Ben scrambled to his knees. He shook his head and then sized up Tremaine. She didn't seem to be wearing any magical devices, besides the Final Register, which she held in her arms. He scrambled to his feet, feeling with his hand for the invisible barrier. Immediately, he felt the morgue grow colder. "It's Saltaire's power! She's channeled it into herself!" Touching the barrier left his skin cold, pins and needles starting to prick his nerves as numbness spread through his body. "He's close."

Tremaine's eyes widened. "How did you know?" She shook her head, taking a step back. "It doesn't matter. If you're aware of him, then he can hurt you." She took a deep breath. When she next spoke, her voice was laced with steel. "Saltaire. Stop them."

Behind him, there was a metallic creak. One of the morgue storage units slid slowly open.

Ben spun around. The chill had spread throughout his body, leaving him numb. *No...*

Saltaire heaved himself out. Being Tremaine's prisoner didn't seem to have diminished him in any way. If anything, his power was even more off-putting.

Ben was rooted to the spot, struggling to breathe. *All this time, when he said he was holding back, he wasn't exaggerating.* This was the full extent of a master vampire's presence. Ben felt like a worm compared to him, lower than dust. A thousand years of knowledge, of experience, of power, contained in one human form. *No wonder no one in the cancer unit answered the phone! It will be a miracle if anyone in this entire hospital is able to think right now...*

"Told you he was in the morgue." Nate's voice was barely above a whisper, but it was all him.

Ben could have hugged him. He drew a deep breath, drawing himself up. *We're not giving up now!*

"We're wasting valuable time," Tremaine said. "Stop them!"

Kenzies unloaded her pistol into Saltaire's chest, bullet after bullet. He didn't even flinch. The bullets bounced harmlessly onto the floor.

Blunted? Ben watched a bullet roll over to his foot. It was easier to look at it than at Saltaire.

The gun choked. Empty. Kenzies threw it at Saltaire's head. Again the vampire didn't react.

"We can't lose this fight." Kenzies began to unbutton the collar of her uniform. Her voice was strangely hollow. "We need the big guns. I'm gonna transform. You two are going to cover me. And if either of you look my way, I will know, and I'll rip your eyes out."

Ben drew a deep breath. *We're buying time for Kenzies to transform. Got it.* He glanced at Nate and returned his nod. *We're ready.* With a deep breath, Ben charged at Saltaire.

Nate moved at the same second, following his lead. *Together, this might just work—*

Saltaire moved fast, faster than anything had a right to move. He swept Ben's feet out from under him with a single kick. Ben slammed into the floor so hard, it was a moment before he could breathe again.

Nate was more successful. Saltaire actually had to grapple with him. A rush of ozone filled the air, and Ben knew Nate was leaning heavily on the plant part of himself.

Nate grunted as he strained, putting everything he had into his attempt to subdue Saltaire. Sweat beaded on his forehead, and he ground his teeth, locked in a competition of strength.

Ben didn't dare breathe for fear of distracting him. He heard Kenzies gasp, and the sound of bones cracking, but his eyes were glued to the battle in front of him. *Please, Nate—*

Saltaire's eyes were flat. He didn't look alarmed, or even annoyed. He didn't look anything. He especially didn't look as if this were a competition for him. He seemed to relent, but as Nate pushed forward, he used his momentum against him, twisting his arm and pulling him down, only to throw him bodily.

"Nate!" Ben jumped on Saltaire's back, locking his arms around his shoulders as he scrabbled for his eyes. Even a thousand-year-old vampire had vulnerable points.

Saltaire slammed backward against the morgue cabinets. Once was enough to knock all the fight out of Ben, and he slid down, dazed. Saltaire grabbed him, sending him flying across the room, straight into Nate, struggling to his feet. They collided with such force that they skidded back across the floor.

Nate grunted. Ben shifted extremely gingerly. His vision was flashing in and out, white spots dancing before his eyes. He moved and discovered Nate was curled protectively around him. "I'm all right. Let me go."

Nate released him. He tipped himself forward onto his knees, spending a moment there before he levered himself upright. He swayed on his feet. "Let's do this again."

Ben swallowed. There was no way this wasn't going to end in another abrupt failure—and who knew if they'd walk away from the next attempt? *There's got to be something here. Something we can use.* He scanned the morgue, but the only furniture was metal, offering no weapon, and no defenses. The entire room was decked out with sanitary metal surfaces. There was nothing organic, nothing Nate's magic could make use of. *We are screwed.*

The vampire. It was their only hope.

"Cover me, Nate." Ben shut his eyes, ruthlessly searching for his inner monster. He'd done his best to erase it, but it remained deep inside him. The vampire had survived a demonic attack and a month of forced starvation that would have killed him otherwise. Could it withstand Saltaire?

Not if I'm afraid of it. Maybe all this time he'd been fighting the vampire, he'd been blind to what it was. *Another part of me, one that is good or bad depending how I use it.* He bit his lip until the skin cracked and he tasted blood on his lips. He rolled the coppery liquid around his tongue, deliberately courting the ancient hunger inside him. *This time the revenant doesn't wield me. I wield it.*

His skin stretched uncomfortably tight as his fangs emerged. He snarled, raising his head to look at the scene before him. Nate grappled with Saltaire, but as he watched, Saltaire ended the encounter with a quick kick, followed by a gut punch that sent Nate reeling. He raised his head to Ben, sizing up the newest threat.

Ben hissed. *Predator to predator. Let's do this.*

Saltaire bared his own fangs in answer. He didn't move, letting Ben come to him. *Deliberate.* Even with his vampire instincts prominent, Ben found he could still observe Saltaire's actions. *Establishing that he has the power in this encounter.* He'd never thought so clearly in his vampire form, not since he'd returned to life. *Because this is deliberate?* Ben silenced the thoughts. He could ponder the implications later—if he survived.

My only chance is hitting a major vein. The time for subtlety had passed. Ben made a feint and then dove, trusting to the vampire's faster reflexes.

Saltaire blocked him—and blocked his second attempt. As Ben tried to sink his teeth into Saltaire's wrist, he dug his elbow into Ben's stomach, following with a sharp blow to the back of Ben's head. He grabbed Ben by the neck.

Ben's feet dangled above the ground and he scrabbled uselessly for footing, trying to free himself. He hissed, staring at Saltaire in anger. "Release me!" He dug deep, accessing the vampire's power of compulsion. "Release me, now!"

Saltaire's expression didn't even flicker. Instead, his grip tightened. *What was I thinking? My vampire power comes from him. I have as much chance of intimidating him as I do Nate's brother!*

Behind them, Ben heard the cracking bone and the sound of twisting flesh come to a stop, Kenzies's pained wail deepening into a full-fledged howl. *She's transformed!*

Saltaire turned to face the werewolf, casually tossing Ben aside. He scrambled out of the way. Getting caught up in a battle between a master vampire and a transformed werewolf was not an experience he wanted to be part of.

He reached Nate and turned just in time to see Kenzies leap. She was smaller than the male werewolves, but no less intimidating, at least twice the size of a regular wolf. Her fur was a rusty shade of red, and her body rippled with muscle. She leaped at Saltaire, her teeth bared.

Saltaire was pushed back by the force of their collision. He snarled as he fought to stay standing, pushing back against the wolf. "You dare?"

It was the first time he'd spoken, and his words were laced with all his centuries of power, and no feeling, none at all. *It's like he's an automaton.* The thought wasn't comforting. Yeah, Saltaire had very little good feelings for anyone, but even his usual curt tone was better than this...emptiness.

Kenzies didn't seem to care what he said. Her jaw locked around his arm and she shook hard, tearing the fabric of his sleeve.

Saltaire grunted as old blood spilled from the wound. It bled sluggishly, already half congealed. Clearly, Saltaire hadn't fed in days.

Old vamp. Doesn't need to. Ben swallowed. Did Kenzies realize that wound was negligible to a vampire of Saltaire's standing?

With a hiss, Saltaire grappled with Kenzies, succeeding in lifting the wolf bodily. He slammed her headfirst against the cabinets.

Kenzies lost her grip on his arm. She snarled, snapping her jaws as she twisted, seeking to find a new line of attack.

Saltaire didn't let her have it. Faster than Ben could follow, he slammed her into the cabinets a second time. Before she could recover from the blow, he whirled her around by one rear leg, launching her across the room.

"Kenzies!" Nate took a step toward her.

She didn't move.

Really bad. "I'll go to her," Ben scrambled across the floor. "You keep him off us."

"Right." He heard Nate swallow, turning back to face Saltaire, and his heart throbbed painfully. They both knew that Nate, for all his incredible strength, couldn't win this fight. The most he could hope for was to last long enough for Ben to get Kenzies back on her feet.

"Kenzies." Ben swallowed, forcing back his fangs. He needed a head not clouded with the vampire's lust for blood. "Can you move?"

She didn't respond. *Please tell me she's not dead.* Ben placed his hand over the wolf's nose and was rewarded by a faint tickle of air. *She's still breathing.* "Kenzies?" He placed his hands on her. Healing spells were among the first spells taught to magic-users, given the huge risks associated with the profession, but Ben was rusty, not having used his spellcraft in months. He took a deep breath, fighting to clear his head. *Calm. Focus. You can do this.*

Nate grunted, and it was all Ben could do not to look up. He heard Nate's labored breathing, followed by a metallic bang and a groan. *This is impossible! And every second this goes on, the risk of him getting seriously injured increases.*

Focus! We have to stop Tremaine! He placed his hands on Kenzies. He'd never attempted to use his magic on anyone not human before, and it was difficult to know where to start. He ran his awareness over the werewolf's body and realized that things were much more serious than he thought. Kenzies wasn't stunned, she was unconscious. In her fall, she'd broken a foreleg.

I can heal that. But even if I do, there's no way she's waking up in time. Ben bit his lip. *What do I do?* They were out of options.

He looked up, to see Tremaine's eyes on him. Her mouth was tight and her eyes sympathetic. She looked past him, her fingers digging into the skin of her arm.

A loud crash made him jump. He looked up to see Saltaire holding Nate pinned against the wall. Nate's eyes rolled back in his head, and as Saltaire let go, he folded gently to the floor.

Ben couldn't suppress his exclamation. "Nate!"

The sound brought Saltaire's attention back to him. With a curl of his lip reminiscent of his usual snarl, he stepped over Nate's limp body, advancing toward Ben.

It's over. Ben stood. It took all of his willpower not to turn and run. Instead, he stepped toward Saltaire. He returned his stare, hoping against hope that something of the man his father had served, something of the person he'd once admired still remained. "Saltaire. If you can hear me right now, you've got to resist this. You're the most powerful vampire in New Camden, probably this entire continent. You're not going to let yourself be commanded. You've got to fight this!"

"You're wasting your breath," Tremaine said. "I laid my plans very well. There's nothing you can do."

Ben spun around to face her. "Why are you doing this? Kenzies told us how devoted you were to the department—to the city! Why have you turned your back on New Camden?"

"I haven't. I'm doing this for the city!" Tremaine's fingers tightened around the book.

"You're doing this for you. Don't try to disguise it." Ben took a deep breath, trying not to think about Saltaire looming behind him. "Your cancer was never cured, was it? You read about the necromancer case in the papers and it made you think, what if you could use Peter's ideas to save your own life?"

For a long moment, Tremaine was still. Then she shook her head. "If that's what you think, I'm no longer surprised you're trying to stop me. But you won't succeed. My plans are too important to be stopped." She sighed. "I am truly sorry about all this. Nathan seems like a very personable young man, and Kenzies... I'll never have a friend like her again. I'm sure in other circumstances, I would have enjoyed getting to know you, but it simply isn't possible." She raised her eyes to Saltaire. "Hurt him as little as possible."

Ben felt a hand close around his shoulder. He struggled to free himself from Saltaire's vice-like grip. "Don't do this, Tremaine, please! For—"

Saltaire's fist slammed into his face. The world spun and then, abruptly, Ben was lying on the floor. The last thing he saw before his vision faded was Saltaire looking down at him, unmoving.

BEN'S HEAD ACHED. His eyes fluttered, but it was dark. *What time is it?* He stirred, discovering that he lay on concrete. Well, most of him did. His head rested on something warm that shifted beneath him. Ben froze. *That's not a pillow. Whatever it is, it's alive—*

"Hey." Nate's fingers stroked his hair. "Take it easy. I don't know what happened to you, but I know it wasn't good."

Ben felt a rush of relief sweep over him, as the memory of Nate, slumped on the floor, came back to him. "You're—" His voice was so raspy that Ben dragged his tongue across his lips, swallowed, and tried again. "You're all right?"

"Yeah. I mean, apart from being trapped in a dark place in some kind of circle or something we can't leave."

It was difficult to pull himself away from Nate's comforting warmth, but Ben sat up. "Some kind of circle?"

Nate grabbed his arm, supporting Ben as he sat. "I'd tell you more, but I can't see it. Or anything else."

Ben braced himself and looked around. There was little to see, even for someone with preternaturally good night vision. "I think this is a basement." It smelled of concrete and dust, not a good combination. Tremaine had probably chosen it as the place least likely for them to be found.

Moving didn't seem to be making his headache worse. He stretched out his hand, encountering the magical barrier Nate was talking about. "Yeah. Definitely a magic circle."

"Do you know what kind?"

"Not without looking at it." Was the darkness deliberate? If so, did that mean that daylight would not make any difference to their predicament? Ben bit his lip, trying to push the thoughts aside. He explored the barrier with his fingers. "I can't get specifics, but this is Tremaine's usual combination of blood magic overlaying a circle that's she's modified for her own purposes."

"Can you break it?"

Ben continued to poke. It was unlikely that a practitioner as skilled as Tremaine would leave a weak point, but if she'd been in a hurry, maybe... Eventually he sat back on his heels with a sigh. "Not without a lot of power. It's fuelled by Saltaire, and because of the unequal bond between us, that puts me at a huge disadvantage magically."

"Unequal bond?"

"The council decision that put me in his custody. That created a bond. One I will have to address if we're to have any chance at getting out of here."

Nate sighed, pulling him close. "Figured. No matter what situation we're in, Saltaire always finds a way to make it worse."

"I don't think we can entirely blame him for getting kidnapped and controlled by Tremaine."

"How was she even able to do that? I mean, he's all-powerful. Right?"

Ben frowned. "I'm going to guess that entering his name on the Final Register created another unequal bond that gave Tremaine all the power. There's simply so much we don't know about the capabilities of the spell and what it could be used for."

Nate tensed, gripping his arm. "Ben! The Final Register—that's it!"

"What do you mean?"

"We've got the pages from it, right? Can we write Tremaine's name on them?"

Ben's eyes widened. "It should work." He shuddered.

"Ben?"

Of course Nate would feel that. Ben shook his head. "It's the thought of subjecting anyone to that. It— It was quite definitely the worst experience of my life. And I don't say that lightly."

Nate squeezed his hand. "We wouldn't leave her on there. Just long enough to disable whatever she's trying to do."

"Right." Ben took a deep breath, trying to calm himself. "What will you write with? Do you have a pen?"

"This is really gross, but I figured blood..." Nate patted his pockets. "I can't find my paper. Look for yours?"

"You must have it. You remember Saltaire, don't you?" Ben slipped his hand into his jeans pocket and came up empty. He tried both back pockets, his front pockets again, even the little inner pocket. In silence, he checked the pockets of his jacket. "Nothing. Tremaine must have searched us after we were knocked out and figured out what had happened."

"But then how come we remember Saltaire?"

"Either she removed him from the Final Register"—which did not seem at all likely—"or she—" Ben felt a burst of cold through his veins. "She's added us to it."

Chapter Twenty

"It's going to be all right." Nate's arms were around him, holding Ben tightly. He rocked him, stroking his hair soothingly. "We're gonna get out of this."

Ben's whole body was racked by shivers. "This is not all right! Nate, you've got no idea! Day after day of people seeing through you, no one hearing you... You can't make anyone feel you, but they can bump into you, hurt you... And if we're on the Final Register, then no one is coming to our rescue."

"But you're not alone this time." Nate's arms settled around him. "I'm here and I'm not going anywhere."

Of course you're not. We're trapped! Ben bit his lip. Snapping at Nate would not make anything better. It wasn't his fault he didn't get it. He'd understand soon enough when days turned into weeks and they were still trapped.

He rested his head against Nate's neck, burying himself in the comforting smell of freshly mown grass that always seemed to hang around Nate. Even in the circumstances, it still made him feel better. *At least I'm not alone this time.* Even that thought made him feel sad. *Nate loves people. He's going to find this a thousand times worse than I did.*

"It's not as bad as it could be," Nate repeated. "Tremaine's not a complete dick. I'm sure she's not going to leave us here."

Ben bit his lip. Yes, Tremaine seemed like a much more reasonable woman than some of the enemies they'd faced together. But being a responsible Department Seven officer had not prevented her from the cold-blooded (literally) murder of three vampires, kidnapping Saltaire, and stealing the Final Register—let alone dousing Nate, who she claimed to like, with weed killer. "I'm not sure we can count on that."

He stroked his fingers over Nate's cheek. He didn't like the reminder of the weed killer. He'd come very close to losing Nate permanently, just as he'd found himself again. *If he'd died...* It didn't bear thinking about. Ben lifted his face to Nate's. "Kiss me."

Nate obliged, his fingers gently stroking Ben's face, finding his chin, and tipping it up. His mouth pressed against Ben's with care.

Ben smiled. He never needed to doubt how much Nate cared about him, not when he kissed like this. Sweet, careful, with all his concern for Ben. He wanted to give some of that back, sucking at Nate's lower lip. Nate responded as he always did. Eagerly.

He's alive. And he's not going anywhere. Ben wanted to prolong the moment, settling his hands around Nate's shoulder and shifting so that he straddled his waist. Nate's tongue skated across his lips and he tried to pull it in, humming as Nate took the invitation. He loved this, loved how Nate made this effortless.

Nate's hands slowly stroked his sides, forming circles. Beneath his touch, Ben felt his tension dissipate. He was sure that was deliberate. Nate always knew just how to relax him. His earlier headache was gone, replaced by a slow-burning flame that, if not checked, would grow to an inferno.

We should stop. This isn't the time. Ben pulled back. Immediately he missed his connection to Nate. He wanted to feel him intimately.

Nate's sigh was reluctant. His fingers continued to stroke Ben's back, lightly skirting over him in comforting circles.

I don't want to be comforted. Breaking the kiss had done nothing to stop the spread of fire through his body. Their forced separation, the uncertainty of their future, the simple fact that they were, against all the odds, together... His body caught the flame like timber doused in gasoline. "Nate..."

Nate trapped Ben's lip with his teeth, holding it for a moment. Not enough to hurt, just enough to make Ben shiver. He released him, running his tongue over the newly sensitized skin, before answering in a breathy whisper against Ben's mouth. "Yeah?"

A step ahead of me as usual. Heat pooled in Ben's cock, and he shifted in Nate's lap. "Do you want to—I mean, can we..."

"Fuck?" Nate's voice was low and amused.

Ben flushed. He was glad for the surrounding darkness so that Nate would not know how much he rattled him. *No chance of that. The moment we touch, he'll know.* His body reacted to Nate's suggestion by sending his blood and breathing racing. Ben gave up and rocked against Nate, the pressure of his warm body sending a jolt of need through Ben's stirring cock. "Yeah."

Nate's hands settled on Ben's ass, roughly squeezing his cheeks. In sharp contrast, his mouth was tender, and his tongue slipped between Ben's lips without encountering any resistance.

Only Nate. Ben moaned, rocking forward. He could feel the heat of Nate's own erection, and he shifted position so that when he rocked he brought them together. His cheeks flamed with heat as he suddenly realized how loud his exclamation had been. "If someone hears us—"

"They won't." Nate's tone was amused. "And if they do, that's a good thing." His fingers continued to squeeze Ben's rear. The rough rasp of the denim against his skin had never felt more erotic. Ben was so hard that his erection throbbed against the fabric.

Light flickered on the floor beside him. Ben's eyes widened. "Did you see that?"

Nate paused, clutching Ben tightly. "The light? What was that?"

"I don't know." Ben stayed where he was, breathing heavily.

"Should we stop?" Nate made as if to lift Ben off him.

"No!" Ben took a deep breath. "Wait." Very deliberately he undid the fly of his jeans, peeling his briefs off his cock. He ran his fingers over his cock. Nothing happened.

"What's going on?"

The sound of Nate's voice in the dark brought to mind many such moments. Ben's fingers tightened over his erection, and he imagined his cock in Nate's mouth. He felt heat pulse through him, his cock becoming fully erect—and the circle flickered again.

Nate gasped, leaping to his feet and pulling Ben with him. "What the fuck?"

Ben laughed. "Exactly!" He couldn't believe he'd overlooked this!

"You're going to have to explain." Nate's arms were around him. Ben could feel him move as he scanned the room for any threat.

Ben placed his hand on Nate's shoulder. "Blood magic! It works on blood, sex, and bonds!" He squeezed Nate's shoulder. "Sex, Nate!"

He heard Nate's sharp inhale of breath. "So the light just now. That wasn't a booby trap, that was us?"

"Yeah." The excitement in his throbbing cock was nothing to how Ben felt about this discovery. "The circle responded to our...um...arousal. That means there's a chance we might be able to use that to get ourselves out of here."

Nate's hands returned to Ben's ass and he squeezed. "You know I never need an excuse to fuck you, right?"

Ben grinned, leaning in to claim Nate's lips. They bumped noses, but Nate quickly realized what Ben was after, and their mouths met in a long, leisurely kiss.

Ben ran his arms down Nate's sides. He pressed against him, feeling the rough cotton of Nate's pants against his cock. Nate pushed his jeans down, exposing Ben's ass to the cool basement air. The light flickered, growing more constant.

"You sure you want to do this?"

It took him a moment to parse Nate's question. "Of course. Even without the circle, I'd want to." He ground against Nate, letting him feel exactly how much he wanted it. "I missed you so much, wanted you so badly. You've got no idea—"

Nate's mouth cut off that statement. He was aggressive in his need, a fact which turned Ben on even more. Nate was faultlessly thoughtful when it came to Ben's comfort. For him to let go this much said volumes about his own need.

Suddenly, Nate stepped back. The distance between them was like a physical ache, and Ben bit back a whimper. "Nate?"

"I just want to be sure I get this. We're doing this because we want to and it'll help us—not because the circle's making us, right?"

It was a good question. Ben released Nate, bending over to get a better look at the flickering runes. As he continued to stroke himself, the glow became steady enough that he could read them. "I'm not seeing any compulsion here... Or anything that we might trigger by um..." How was he still not over this? "Fucking."

"What do you see?" Nate stood behind him, gripping Ben's bare hips and raising his ass into the air. He rocked against him, the heat of his cloth-covered erection pressing against Ben's exposed skin.

The contrast between Nate's heat and the chill air was enough that it took Ben a moment to decipher the question. "Let me see." He scanned the glowing runes. "Um. I'm going to need to get down on my hands to get a better look."

"I'm not stopping you."

When Nate sounded that innocent, Ben was in trouble. Still, what choice did he have? He got down on his knees, feeling with his hands to check that there was no disparity between the energy of the runes he saw, and what he could detect by touch.

It was hard to concentrate, as Nate's hand drifted underneath his T-shirt, his fingers idly stroking the bumps of Ben's spine, but thankfully, Nate didn't do any of the things Ben was half expecting him to do. By the time he'd finished double-checking the circle, his need had increased and he was eager for Nate's touch. "Nothing that I could find. It looks like Tremaine didn't consider the possibility of us, um. Doing this."

Nate pressed his mouth to Ben's bared ass, making him gasp. "So, we just have to fuck to get out of here?"

Ben squirmed as Nate pressed his mouth back to his skin. "It's not quite that simple. It's a question of power. It's all about the energy amassed. You get energy by..." Nate's tongue ghosted over Ben's crack and he gasped, surprised at the need the sensation elicited. "By um, building need. Once you come, it's all over. The energy's released, and all the power you have is that which built up before you came."

Nate eased his jeans down, nudging Ben's legs farther apart. "So what do we do?"

Ben took a deep breath. He was surprised at the heat in his cheeks caused by their discussion, sure that all the blood in his body must be centered in his groin. His cock throbbed between his legs, angrily demanding attention. He couldn't remember ever being so hard. "Turn me on. But you can't let me come."

"Right on it." Nate's reply was cocky, supremely self-assured.

Ben felt relieved, and then instantly worried. His body was reacting to Nate like this was their first time. He had no reserves of cool, of restraint. He was powerless before the need that Nate evoked in him, powerless to contain his rapidly spreading desire.

"Hands up." Nate tugged at Ben's T-shirt.

Ben obediently raised his hands over his head, only to remember their location. "This is a public place—a hospital! We shouldn't—"

"It's for a good cause." Nate stripped him of the T-shirt and then dropped it to the floor. His hands roamed freely across Ben's skin, obviously relishing the feeling of him. He could smell arousal blending with Nate's usual scent.

The circle hummed. Ben took a moment to ground himself in what he was doing and then replaced his hands, one on each side of the barrier. He could feel it pulse in time with the blood in his angry cock. *This might actually work.* He took a deep breath, applying himself to deciphering the spell. A simple barrier sealed with Saltaire's magic.

Despite the heat of Nate's mouth, currently between his shoulder blades, Ben felt a chill go over him. *Saltaire's power.* Were they kidding themselves, thinking they had any chance against a thousand-year-old vampire? There was a reason no one contested his decisions, and it wasn't respect for the aged.

The circle flickered. Clearly, the thought of Saltaire had an adverse effect on Ben.

Ben gritted his teeth. *I can't think about what could go wrong.* It was like Grant said. He needed to reject fear. *Saltaire has chosen fear. He doesn't trust anyone except himself, and he closes himself off from all meaningful human contact. He is trapped by his world view into a life of emptiness. I don't fear him. I pity him.*

He felt the need pulse back, buoyed by his decision. Ben sucked in a fresh breath as Nate's mouth lavished his skin with care.

Ben shut his eyes, giving himself over to the sensations Nate's workings called forth. *Yes... I choose this. Living with hope.*

The circle crackled. It didn't just glow, it hummed. He could feel the energy in the air, feel it surrounding himself and Nate, adding another level to the sensation building within him.

"Ben?" Nate stopped, his fingers still on Ben's skin.

"Keep going." There was no hesitation in Ben's reply. If anything, the light show was proof that they were on the right track. "We've got this. I know we do."

He expected Nate's mouth to continue its leisurely exploration of his back. Instead, he felt his Nate's fingers urge his crack open. He gasped, feeling the warmth of Nate's tongue pressed against his sensitive skin. "Nate—"

Nate chuckled. "We got this." He returned to his work, his tongue deliberately trailing over Ben's entrance.

Ben gasped. They'd never done this before. He'd considered it once or twice but was too embarrassed to bring it up to Nate. What if he was dirty or something went wrong? He'd be embarrassed, Nate disgusted—

No fear. Ben spread his legs wider, hoping to give Nate better access. His legs shook, struggling to support his weight. Nate's tongue probing his entrance felt so right...

I trust him. The discovery was not a surprise; the depth of the feeling was. Ben felt warmth fill him, pooling in him. His penis ached, every delicate sweep of Nate's tongue across his entrance making his entire body shiver.

"Nate!" His cock jerked uncontrollably, precome spurting from its tip. His balls throbbed, almost painfully needy. "Oh god. You—" Did Nate know what he was doing to him? Ben's words gave way to a keening sound. How long was Nate going to leave him on edge?

"Fuck Ben." Nate sat back. Ben only had a second to regret his absence. The sound of Nate's zipper being roughly undone more than made up for the loss of his tongue.

Ben took a deep breath, leaning his elbows against the floor for greater balance. It made holding his ass up more awkward, but he needed the extra support.

Nate's fingers casually stroked Ben's ass as he freed his erection. "Give me a second. I need to find—"

"No condom." Ben took a deep breath. "Spell's more effective without it." He bit his lip, knowing how careful Nate always was. "Please. I need to feel you."

"You're sure?" Nate's fingers disappeared. "I don't want to hurt you. We can swap. I'm more used to this than you are."

"I'm sure. I want you in me." Ben took a deep breath. At this point, he wasn't sure if it was want or need, but he knew that, either way, he had to have Nate inside him. "Please."

Nate's grunt was pure need. He took Ben's hips, pulling him against his hard cock.

Yes. Please— Ben braced himself, ready for Nate to fill him.

But as Nate's cock rubbed against his crack, he felt a finger probe his entrance.

"Nate, please. I need you now."

Nate pressed a kiss to Ben's shoulder. "We need to build energy still, right?"

He'd entirely forgotten the spell. Ben gasped, spreading his fingers for a better grip, and turned his attention to the circle. It pulsed in time with the need circulating through him, sending a wave of power through him. *And this is only the start.* "More—"

Nate took his own damn time. It was slow torture, and Ben didn't want it to stop even as he burned for more. By the time Nate had added a third finger to his explorations, Ben was slumped against the floor, his arms no longer able to hold him up. The cold concrete was a welcome relief to the fire that had overtaken his body and his mind, and his cock absolutely burned. He couldn't say it throbbed, the need was all-encompassing.

"Ready?"

He tried to tell Nate yes, but his words were gone with the rest of him. The most he could offer was a heartfelt moan as he used his remaining strength to push back against Nate.

Nate gripped Ben's thighs tightly, spreading him further. He lined up his erection with Ben's entrance, pressing inside in one strong thrust.

Ben gasped. He hadn't been braced for the sheer intensity of it. He tried to hold on to the feeling of pain, knowing it wouldn't be long before the shock of intrusion became a different sort of agony...

Nate shifted experimentally, driving deeper into Ben. His cock pressed against Ben's prostate, sending sparks exploding across his vision. His neglected cock jerked, its rigid head bumping against Ben's stomach. "Please—" The discomfort was already fading, leaving him only with the intense satisfaction of having Nate inside him. The need was greater than ever before, and Ben felt entirely helpless to deny it. "God, Nate. I need it, need you—"

"Let me know how much you need it. Talk to me, Ben. Tell me that you like what I'm doing to you." Nate followed the words with a shallow thrust.

More! Ben scrabbled for purchase to push back, but his body wouldn't obey. He fought to concentrate on Nate's command. "You...you turn me inside out. I... You make feel— Oh god, Nate, I'm on fire."

The circle roared. The gathered energy was enough to start a breeze building, the cool air soothing on Ben's enflamed skin. He could feel the runes pulse beneath his fingers as the circle came into startling, vivid life. His cock jerked, his release gathering.

Too soon! Ben bucked wildly, panicking. "Nate, I'm going to—"

Nate's hand locked around the base of Ben's penis, roughly, preventing his release. Ben moaned, feeling his cock twitch, as if fighting the grip that encircled it. *I need this so badly.*

Got to concentrate! It was agony, tearing his mind away from the sensations that held his entire body prisoner and focusing on the runes. Ben scanned the spell, seeking a way to take control of it. His breathing was hard and fast, his body trembling with need, just barely held at bay. Nate's hard length within him pulsed, an energy that was hard to ignore.

So close. Have to find it quickly—

He spotted a clause he'd overlooked, turning his full attention on the sequence of runes. His breath caught as he took in the full significance of them. Tremaine hadn't powered the spell directly. She'd relied on the combination of her magic and Saltaire's power, through the medium of the Final Register.

We can't attack Tremaine. Not while we're in the Final Register and she isn't. Which leaves Saltaire. Forcing back the chill at the thought, Ben applied his mind to the problem. *Saltaire's too strong for us, and so is the Final Register. But if we attack the link between them...* After all, a forced bond was weak, and Tremaine must have forced Saltaire to do her bidding somehow. The vampire would never agree to being entered on the Final Register.

"Fuck, Ben." He felt a tremble as Nate shifted, adjusting his grip on Ben's hips. "How much longer?"

Nate wants this too. It was not a surprise, not with Nate's erection buried inside him giving firsthand proof that Nate wanted him, but it felt like one all the same. "Just a little more. I've got this." He gripped the link with both hands, finding it weak. *Of course! Saltaire couldn't have created the Final Register himself. He'd need a magic-user he could trust—Godfrey!* And with Saltaire's existence in question, Godfrey was considerably weakened. *This is it.* Ben smeared his fingers with the precome sticking to his chest, tracing over the signal for the link. "Ready. Nate, please—"

Nate grunted, plowing into him. Each thrust was frenzied, their short pause evidently doing nothing to slake either of their need. Ben cried out, as his desire immediately rocketed to desperation point. Every thrust rammed his prostate, sending sparks dancing across his vision. "Oh god."

Nate released his grip on Ben's base, stroking his fingers over Ben's length. That was all it took. Ben exploded from within, a wave of feeling that erupted out, sweeping everything with it in a dizzying rush. He saw the circle blaze up, the room filling with a light—

EVERYTHING WAS DARK. Ben's cheek was pressed against the gritty concrete of the floor, his chest heaving. He could feel Nate's weight on top of him, his rasping breaths ruffling the hair sticking to Ben's forehead. His body still throbbed with the aftershocks of his release.

"Holy crap, Ben." Nate's laugh was shaky. "That was like some kind of out-of-body experience. If I'd known we could do that..."

Ben's mouth twitched. It was hard to believe they were only discovering this now. He stirred, reluctantly uncurling from Nate's hold.

Nate sat up, letting Ben move. "Did it work?"

"I'll find out." His legs shook dramatically, but they held. Ben wobbled over to the edge of the circle. He stepped out, encountering no resistance. "We did it! Nate, it worked!" He turned toward what he thought was the door. "We've got to—" Abruptly, his knees folded.

Nate caught him before he hit the ground, gathering him into his arms. "Not so fast. We need time to recover."

"But the city— Tremaine—" Ben's protests faded as Nate's mouth found his.

The kiss was gentle, affirming their bond. Ben felt himself relax, his momentary panic soothed away. "Um."

The city could wait five minutes.

IF THEY NEEDED any confirmation they were on the Final Register, the fact that despite their disheveled appearance, no one gave them a second glance was it. Even knowing they were invisible, Ben was grateful Nate had insisted they take the time to dress before they'd made their way out of the basement. Fortunately, "existing only to yourself" meant that if no one else was present, they could interact normally with inanimate objects. It was only the crowded hospital halls and occupied wards that gave them problems.

"So what now?" Nate reached for Ben's hand.

They followed a nurse down a hospital corridor, using her as protection against the many carts that came their way. "Find Tremaine. Work out a way to get ourselves off the Final Register and then stop her from doing whatever it is she's doing."

Nate stepped out of the way of a busy-looking orderly. "Tremaine's gonna see us. We're not invisible to her."

"We need to find her first." The hospital was huge, and they couldn't ask a nurse for guidance. As the nurse turned off down a side corridor, Ben spotted the sign for the cancer ward. "Here."

Nate looked at the sign. "You think she's here?"

"It makes sense. Remember when Kenzies phoned the hospital? The woman couldn't get a response out of the staff in this unit."

"Because Saltaire was present." Nate looked around. "I don't feel him now."

"Dawn's approaching. She'll have had to stash him somewhere out of the daylight. He's probably back in the morgue." There was currently no one behind the reception desk. Ben clambered over the desk, grabbing the folder of patient files.

"You can't do that! Those are private!"

"Desperate situations, Nate. Also, you're technically Department Seven right now, so you might have the power to authorize this."

"Pretty sure I need a warrant. Which we don't have."

"You can turn yourself in after we stop Tremaine." Ben found her name, but the file attached to it was empty. All that remained was a room number. "Huh."

"What did you find?"

"Her file's missing, but she's got a room." Ben frowned. "She's here as a patient."

It wasn't long before a nurse walked out of the unit, the door swinging open behind her. Ben ducked through, Nate following behind him. They made their way down the corridor in silence. Ben held his breath. He didn't like this. The scent of chemicals filled the air but didn't mask the slow yet steady smell of decay beneath. For the first time, the reality of the place came home to him. *Everyone in this wing is fighting for their lives.* He felt like the worst kind of intruder.

Tremaine's door was open. Ben took a deep breath.

"You're sure about this?" Nate stood so close that his arm brushed Ben's side.

"No," Ben admitted. "But I don't see what else we can do. You?"

"The same." Nate stepped into the room. Ben followed.

The curtains were drawn, the rising sun casting a gentle light into the room. It was an ordinary hospital room, bare of any ornamentation except a photo on the bedside table, a copy of the same one Tremaine had on her desk at Department Seven. The Final Register was placed beside it, looking unusually benign in the commonplace surroundings.

Tremaine sat on the bed. She looked as faded and washed out as the walls, the veins in her neck standing out against her pale skin. Her cheeks were sunken, her eyes unnaturally bright. Her mouth was pressed flat together, and her expression gave no clue to her thoughts. "There's no possibility of mistake?"

"We need a biopsy to be sure, but the scan shows that the tumor has increased in size. The preliminary results of the blood test also show your condition is rapidly deteriorating." The doctor hesitated. "Would you like us to contact a family member or friend so you can discuss your options?"

"That's all right." Tremaine lay back on the bed, shutting her eyes. "I need to rest."

The doctor returned her file to the end of the bed. "The oncologist will be here in a few hours." Tremaine didn't respond. After a moment, he walked out, pulling the door shut behind him.

Ben was braced for Tremaine's anger. There was nowhere to hide in the small hospital room. Instead, she lay on the bed, her fingers buried in the thin hospital sheet.

Nate leaned in to whisper. "You think she doesn't see us?"

Ben gave Tremaine a second look, noting the hospital gown she wore. "She must have put the paper aside to have tests done. And once she put it down, she'd have no idea that we exist, not until she picks up the Final Register again."

He looked at the book. "We can't erase our names ourselves. And if we destroy the book, New Camden's classification system will run out of power. Innocent people will be put at risk." They were stuck.

"There's another way." Nate stepped past Ben putting his hand on the book. "Paper used to be trees, right?"

Ben's breath caught. The Final Register's pages fluttered, the sound more reminiscent than ever of the wind rustling through leaves. The fresh smell of ozone filled the air, and the crackle of paper crumpling became the rough rasp of bark. When Nate stepped back, in the place of the Final Register was a miniature oak tree.

Nate gently stroked its leaves. "It's still got all the power of the Final Register, but you can't write on a tree."

"It's beautiful." Tremaine's voice was calm. "You've got a rare gift, Nate."

Ben spun around, preparing for a fresh attack. With the dawn already here, Tremaine could not call on Saltaire again, but he was sure she had other tricks up her sleeve.

Tremaine put both hands on the side of her bed, lifting herself into a sitting position. She made no other attempt to move, placing her hands in her lap.

Her calm is a bad sign. Ben frowned at her, wondering what form her attack would take.

Nate took a step toward her. "You're not angry?"

Tremaine grimaced, shaking her head. "I'm angry at myself. I betrayed my colleagues, my city, my badge...all for nothing."

"Where's Kenzies?" Ben barked, hoping that the reminder of her peril would put Nate on his guard.

"She's in the room next door. I had the doctors set her broken arm and sedate her. She should wake naturally within the hour."

Implying Tremaine had used Saltaire's powers of compulsions on the doctors. It felt wrong to leave Nate and Tremaine alone, but Ben strode quickly to the door. "Be careful, Nate." He peered through the glass window of the door next door. Kenzies lay on the bed in human form. She was clad in a hospital gown, her arm in a cast. She appeared to be sleeping peacefully, the monitor at the end of the bed showing her vital signs were all steady.

Ben hesitated. He didn't have the medical knowledge to confirm or disprove Tremaine's status, but it looked as though she was telling the truth.

When he returned to Tremaine's room, Nate was sitting at the end of her bed. "You really care about Department Seven, huh?"

"It's not just a job," Tremaine said seriously. "It could never be just a job. It's a vocation, and like any vocation, it demands your all. That's why your colleagues become a second family."

"Then why would you do all this?" Ben wondered at the complete lack of judgment in Nate's voice. He sounded like he genuinely wanted to know. "Because of the cancer?"

"Yes. But not in the way you'd think." Tremaine leaned back against the headboard. She wasn't faking her lack of energy. Her skin was turning a shade of gray that left them in no doubt they were talking to a very sick woman. "I'm not afraid of death. I've lost my share of colleagues. The risks we take, it's just part of the job. I figured it would be a vampire or maybe a wolf attack. The cancer was a shock, but I was young and in good health. There was every reason to believe that I would recover. But while I was in the hospital I met other cancer patients, the ones that weren't going to recover. And..." She shut her eyes, taking a deep breath before continuing. "Some of them were children. Some were parents with young families, some—it doesn't matter. I spent months in this unit with them. It was so unfair. None of them deserved to die. And while they were in here fighting for another day, there were vampires out there, literally preying on society and prolonging their existence endlessly."

"And that's where you got the idea to harness their energy?" Despite his instincts telling him to treat Tremaine with extreme caution, Ben couldn't help taking a step toward the bed.

Tremaine shook her head. "I was in here when the news broke about the necromancer's arrest and what he'd been attempting. The thought suddenly flashed into my head that de Silver might have come up with something that could help every terminally ill patient in this city, maybe the world. I just had to figure out how to get his research."

Nate sucked in a deep breath. "Wait. So the first murder, the one in the graveyard, that was just to make everyone think Peter was back?"

Tremaine nodded. "From the files on the case at Department Seven, I knew you were significant to de Silver in some way and that you'd been instrumental in his defeat. No more logical target for his revenge, right? Of course, I didn't know about Ben then." She lifted her gaze to him. "I got the idea of using the Final Register from you. Until you stole it, I had no idea we had such a powerful magical source tucked away in the Registry."

Ben swallowed. "You can't blame me for your actions."

"I don't. If anything, I thank you. If I hadn't realized I could use the Final Register in place of vampire victims, there would have been more deaths." Tremaine's face darkened. "Believe me when I say I wish I could have avoided those, but I needed to test my theory. And it seemed to be working. The transfer restored my energy and life. But I didn't realize that magic fed the tumor as well. My benign tumor is now extremely malignant and growing fast."

Nate swallowed audibly. "I'm really sorry."

Tremaine smiled sadly at him. "This is no one's fault but my own. I forgot the first law of magic. What you give, you will receive. The more I took energy by force to sustain myself, the more harm I did."

"There're still options," Ben said. "You heard the doctor. Perhaps the oncologist—"

Tremaine held up a hand. "It's too late for me, and I know it." Very carefully, she grasped the side of her bed and levered herself onto her feet. "Take me to Department Seven. I should be arrested."

Nate pulled off his jacket and draped it around her thin shoulders. He carefully supported Tremaine toward the door.

Ben followed, holding the tree that had once been the Final Register. *We're going to need to find a pot for this.* He was conscious of a feeling of anticlimax. After the battle with Saltaire in the morgue, he was braced for another attack. Tremaine's surrender, though understandable, left him with an anxiety he couldn't quite dispel. *I should not feel sorry for her. She attacked Nate with weed killer!*

But he did.

I guess this is part of being human. They made much easier progress through the hospital now they could use things like doors and elevators. *Having mixed feelings.* Although he decried Tremaine's actions, he couldn't help but feel some pity. *Her motivation was good, at least.*

In a way, the very fact that he had mixed feelings was proof of his humanity. In Saltaire's narrow mindset, everything was right or wrong.

He stepped into the elevator with Tremaine and Nate. "Incidentally, where *is* Saltaire?"

"The morgue," Tremaine said. "Where else? He'll be fine there until nightfall. I borrowed his power of compulsion to make sure the technicians would not disturb him." She leaned heavily on Nate's arm.

"You sure you're up for leaving the hospital?" Nate asked.

"I'm just woozy. I had the doctors do a bunch of tests. I wanted to be sure my plan worked before I tried it on anyone else." Tremaine's face fell. "Good thing I did. If..." Her voice trailed off.

Nate's free hand rested on Ben's arm. Seeking reassurance, or giving it? The result was the same, a warmth that cut through Ben's feeling of lingering unease. This might not have been the victory he wanted, but they were together, they were alive, and the city was safe. He couldn't ask for more.

"There's one thing I'm curious about," Tremaine said. "How on earth did you escape from my circle?"

Ben stepped on Nate's foot quickly. "You, uh. Don't want to know."

Chapter Twenty-One

TREMAINE'S FUNERAL TOOK place two weeks later. The council had stripped her of her rank and the right to an official police funeral, but all of Department Seven turned out for it.

Nate watched them file out of the crematorium in silence. For the most part, the department staff had maintained a dignified and solemn silence, broken only by the occasional loud sniff from Kenzies. As she sniffed again, Nate felt sympathetic tears well and blinked rapidly.

"Here." Ben handed him a tissue.

"Thanks." Nate dabbed at his eyes, hoping no one was looking their way. "I feel ridiculous. I barely knew her."

"Don't feel bad about feeling what you feel." Ben patted his arm. "It's what makes you special, Nate." His hand found Nate's, their fingers fitting together like two connecting puzzle pieces.

Gunn was making up for lost time by lighting a cigarette on the crematorium doorstep. He caught sight of Nate and Ben and sauntered over. "Cry more, Nate." He smirked in greeting. "Don't you just love a good funeral?"

Anger pulsed through Nate. He ground the tissue in his fist. "Can't you at least show some respect? Tremaine was—"

"Excuse us." Ben took Nate's arm and hauled him away. "Your reaction is exactly what Gunn wants. You can't blame him for being what he is."

Nate struggled with his outrage. Eventually, his shoulders drooped. "I guess not. But it's still inappropriate." He looked over his shoulder, shooting a glare at the *lemur*.

Ben's presence was a soothing counterpoint to his irritation. "You've talked to the Department Seven staff, right? Does anyone know how Gunn got himself off the Interim Register?"

"No. But the day he turned back up to work was the day after the mayor had her big nervous breakdown and quit politics. It could be coincidence, but…" Nate shrugged. "We'll probably never get the full story." He wasn't sure he wanted the full story.

Ben nodded. "I can make an educated guess—" He broke off. "Godfrey! I didn't expect to see you here."

Godfrey approached, impeccably dressed as ever in a pristine suit. "I am paying my respects on behalf of Saltaire."

Nate frowned. "Saltaire?" Tremaine had placed him on the Final Register, used his compulsion against him, and stolen his power. "He wants to make sure she's dead?"

Godfrey peered at Nate over his glasses and shook his head. "Although Officer Tremaine's methods are to be deplored, her ultimate goal was a noble one. Once I am finished here, I will be making my way to Central Hospital to make a donation to the research department in Tremaine's name."

"A fitting memorial." Ben frowned. Clearly he wasn't buying Saltaire's generosity either.

"I was also hoping to see you here." Godfrey coughed. "Congratulations on your successful appeal. You must feel very happy, knowing that your conviction was overturned and that you are no longer considered a threat to the city's safety."

Ben's smile was rueful. "I take it you're speaking personally."

"I am… But I am sure if Saltaire were here, he would echo my sentiments." Godfrey absently tugged his suit coat straight. "It is not easy for someone trapped in a single way of thinking to admit they are mistaken, but I sense a change in Saltaire. It would be too early to say for sure that it is a change of opinion, but it is a change. I think he will make no further attempt to bring you under his control."

It was good news. Almost too good to be true. Nate looked anxiously at Ben, worried at how he'd take it.

Ben smiled thinly. "I don't think he could, even if he tired." He paused. "Hunter's doing better?"

"He's made a complete recovery and is extremely embarrassed by his lapse. He is anxious to thank you for your help in preventing him from harming others."

Ben nodded. "I'm sure we'll run into him at some point."

"Indeed. Well, I must be on my way." With a casual bow, Godfrey left them.

Nate watched him walk away. Once again he was astonished at how Godfrey showed so little signs of age. "I guess it's all back to normal then."

Ben nodded, his hand tightening around Nate's. "Yeah. Normal."

AKI LEANED ACROSS the back of Ben's sofa and snorted. "I cannot believe you fell for this. Babysitting is the biggest scam there is."

Nate leaned back on the sofa so he could stare him down. "Come on. Diya's a really nice woman, and Ben and I owe her a lot. Taking care of her daughter for one night so she can go out with friends is the least we can do. Can you believe she hasn't had a night out since the baby was born?"

"Yeah, I can. And there's a really good reason why."

"Children aren't that bad. Ben says the baby's really cute."

Aki rolled his eyes, drumming his fingers against the back of the sofa. "Yeah, sure. We'll see which one of us has the better night." He was dressed in a tailored shirt and a subdued (for Aki) pair of burnt-orange trousers and still smelled of shower gel.

Before Nate could ask, Grant emerged from his room. Nate sat up straight to get a better look at him. Wearing a suit that checked all the right boxes, Grant was definitely dressed for more than a night on the town with Aki. "Special occasion?" Nate guessed. "Fancy dinner?"

Grant shook his head with a smile. "A political event. We've got a panel of guest speakers talking about the importance of diversity in local government, followed by a question and answer session. Then we're going to get drinks."

Nate gave Aki a pointed look. "Sounds thrilling."

Aki stood. "It will be. You know I find politics fascinating." Before Nate could remind him that he'd never expressed any interest in New Camden's political scene before that night, he grabbed Grant's hand, towing him toward the door. "Enjoy your larva!"

As the door closed behind them, Ben stepped out of his bedroom. In his arms, he held the stray cat from the alley. Two weeks of regular meals and several trips to the vet meant she no longer looked as though she was on the brink of collapse, but that was it. With her single eye glinting balefully at Nate and her tattered ears, she would never be a cute cat. "Was that Aki?"

Nate stood. "You just missed him and Grant heading out." He motioned to himself. He'd put a lot of thought into his outfit, wearing his best pair of jeans and a clean sweatshirt with the logo of the football team he supported. "Do I look like a responsible babysitter?"

Ben smiled. He hooked his arm around Nate's neck, drawing him in for a kiss. "Perfect."

The cat did not agree. She hissed and dug her claws into Nate's arm.

"She doesn't mean anything by it," Ben said, as he dabbed the scratch with Neosporin. The cat sat in a corner of the kitchen, her tail flicking as she gobbled down her food. "Schadenfreude's been living wild for so long, she's not used to people. She'll warm up to you eventually, I'm sure."

"It's cool." He couldn't blame the cat for disliking him. After all, she probably remembered him as the guy who'd chased her twice and forcefully removed Ben from the alley. But given that her bringing Ben dead animals to eat had sustained him throughout his Final Register ordeal, he couldn't hold it against her. Thanks to Schadenfreude's help, Ben had been able to resist the temptation to attack humans averting his and Nate's worst fears. "She's a good cat."

"We'd better keep her in my bedroom while Anjali's here. She'd probably scare a little kid." And right on cue, the doorbell rang. Ben stood. "That will be them."

Off duty, Diya indulged her love of color to the max. She wore a bright-pink dress decorated with orange flowers and a purple wrap. Anjali sat quietly in her mother's arms, her hazel eyes wide. A cloud of wispy curls surrounded her head. "I cannot thank you enough for doing this. I haven't had a night to myself since my mother went home!"

"It's our pleasure." Nate smiled at Anjali, and she immediately held out her hands to be picked up. He took her carefully, noting that the baby's skin had the same chill to it that Ben's always did. No wonder. Like Ben, Anjali was a living vampire.

"This is Anjali's diaper bag. It's got her bottle, clean diapers, toys, snacks, everything you'll need." Diya handed the bag to Ben, pulling a laminated page from the back pocket. "I prepared some instructions. She'll go down for her nap in about three hours, and when you feed her, make sure you heat the bottle to room temperature first."

Nate was making Anjali giggle by pulling funny faces. He caught the last of Diya's words and looked up sharply. *We're feeding her blood?*

Ben took the instructions. "We'll be fine. Go. Have fun. You've definitely earned it."

"Thank you." Diya hesitated and then gave him a quick hug. She waved goodbye to Nate and blew a kiss to Anjali. "Mommy will be back to get you in a few hours. Be good for Uncle Ben and Uncle Nate, Anjali!"

"Bye, Diya!"

The door shut behind her. And as if that was the cue she'd been waiting for, Anjali sunk her tiny baby fangs into Nate's neck.

THE APARTMENT WAS quiet. Too quiet.

Ben sat on the sofa. *Should I see if Nate needs help?* But that might set Anjali off again. He bit his lip. *I have to trust Nate's abilities. If he needs help, he'll let me know.* But there was so much that could go wrong. An infant vampire was a complete unknown. He glanced at the clock. *I'll give him ten minutes more. Then I'll check on him.*

The door of the spare bedroom opened softly. With exaggerated care, Nate eased himself out the door, shutting it behind him.

Ben realized he was holding his breath. "*Asleep?*" He mouthed.

Nate nodded, a huge grin breaking across his face as he padded across the living room. He held up his hand, and they high-fived— flinching as the sound echoed across the flat.

There was no sound from the spare room. Nate placed the baby monitor on the coffee table. "I think we did it."

"You did it." Despite their rocky first start, Nate and Anjali got along to an almost alarming degree. Anjali cried the moment Nate tried to hand her to Ben. Nate was now covered in scratches and Band-Aids, but was no less triumphant.

"We're really good at this responsible adults thing."

"I don't know if one night of babysitting really qualifies us as good." As Nate resumed his place on the sofa, Ben hit play on the movie they were watching. He leaned his head against Nate's shoulder and felt Nate's fingers settle in his hair.

He wasn't sure how long after that he realized Nate was unusually quiet. Lifting his head, he saw Nate looked not at the TV screen, but at the floor, his expression solemn. Ben squeezed his hand. "What's on your mind?"

Nate looked up, startled. He hesitated and then clearly decided it was no good trying to fool Ben. He shrugged. "Tremaine. Yeah, she made mistakes, but she still tried to help people. And until she went off the rails, she did a lot of good. She left a legacy, inspired new medical research, and the way her colleagues talk about her..." Nate sighed. "I guess I want that. To do something with my life." He bit his lip. "I didn't tell you this, but I gave notice at Century."

"You did?" Ben sat up. "Why?" Nate loved his job, and he was good at it. "Because of me?"

"Not because of you, but you are part of it." Nate picked up the remote, hitting pause. He turned to face Ben. "Ever since I met you, I've wanted more for myself. I used to think that sex was the only thing I was good at. You've made me see that I've got a lot more to give. And after today... Well, the funeral made me think. I want a legacy. I want to be able to look back and know I've done something with my life. And I think..." He sucked in a deep breath, bracing as if he was afraid of Ben's reaction. "I think Department Seven's it."

Ben sat very still. "I don't think that's a dumb idea," he said slowly. "In fact..." There were many arguments against it. The job was risky. They'd be exposed to greater scrutiny. Nate's background—both their backgrounds—would be examined, and they would be held to impossibly high standards, while given little in the way of support.

But they'd be able to help, using the skills only they possessed. Ben looked up, meeting Nate's eyes. "The recruitment forms are on the website."

Nate reached for Ben's laptop before he got the implication. "Wait. You too?"

Ben nodded. "I couldn't let you do this *alone*."

GUNN SCOWLED AS he thumbed through Ben and Nate's job applications. "Let me get this straight. You've seen our methods firsthand, know we're understaffed, that we can't afford to pay either of you anything like the money you're used to getting...and you still want to work here?" He looked up, shooting a suspicious look at Ben. "What is wrong with you?"

Ben's mouth twitched. "I've been wondering the same thing myself."

"Come on, it's not that bad." Nate wiped his hands on his jeans. "You work here."

Ben bit his lip. Gunn's presence was not an endorsement—it was the complete opposite. Before he could think of the word he wanted, Gunn snarled.

"Pod people," he pronounced. "Only possible explanation—"

"Nothing in New Camden's employment laws excludes pod people." Kenzies whacked Gunn with her cast and snatched their paperwork out of his hands with her uninjured hand. "Quick!" She charged toward the reception desk. "Leanne, we need to file these before they change their minds!"

It was definitely not the most reassuring start to a new job he'd ever had. Ben felt a chill go up his spine and turned to see Gunn was still glaring at him.

"You're making a big mistake, Benny. I'm not going to go easy on you simply because you work for me."

Ben snorted. "I don't expect anything less from you."

Gunn scowled, jabbing a filthy finger toward Nate. "I blame you for this nonsense, Nate. Now get out of my sight. I want to enjoy the last of my time away from the two of you."

The sun was bright, the morning thrumming with activity. Without needing to discuss it, they found themselves heading to the park around the corner from Department Seven.

The trees were just starting to change color, and aside from a senior citizen walking a dog, the park was deserted. Nate's hand found Ben's as they settled on a bench. "I feel really good about this. Like we made the right choice."

It was as if Nate had given a label to the feeling that had settled over him. Ben smiled, squeezing his hand. "Yeah. I know." They'd accomplished a lot in a very short time. "We've put all our demons behind us."

"Not yet," Nate said. "I've still got to talk to Denise about my final day of work."

"I wasn't meaning literal demons." *Except for Sandy's master, maybe.* "You've accepted your supernatural gifts, faced your past, and worked out what you want to do with your life. That's huge, Nate. And me... I've faced my fears. I've made peace with my inner vampire. Saltaire doesn't intimidate me—and neither does living." He swallowed. "Or loving."

Nate draped his arm around Ben's shoulders. "I noticed." He planted a kiss on Ben's forehead.

Ben looked down, gathering his courage. There was still one more step he had to take. "Nate, I've been thinking about us." He licked his lips, worriedly. "Do you want to move in with me?" He felt Nate tense, but it was too late to take the words back. They spilled out of him in a nervous rush. "I mean, I know it's really soon, and we've got so many other new changes to adjust to, so I understand needing space or wanting to think about it—"

Nate gripped his chin, tilting his mouth up. Ben found himself being kissed thoroughly. He grinned, feeling the last of his tension melt away, replaced by a rush of joy. There was only one way to interpret that kiss.

"Um." When they finally pulled apart, Nate was flushed. "I mean—yes, I would like to move in."

"I guessed." Ben knew he must be glowing. He brushed his hair out of his face, unable to meet Nate's eyes. He wasn't sure what to do with such happiness. His heart beat fast. Once again, Ben had no idea what he was doing.

And that's fine. He looked up, finding Nate's eyes on him, and realized that he felt only peace. "We've got this."

About the Author

Gillian St. Kevern is the author of the Deep Magic series, the Thorns and Fangs series, the For the Love of Christmas series, and standalone novels, The Biggest Scoop and The Wing Commander's Curse. Gillian currently lives in her native New Zealand, but spent eleven years in Japan and has visited over twenty different countries. Her writing is a celebration of the weird and wonderful people she encounters on her travels.

As a chronic traveller, Gillian is more interested in journeys than endings, with characters that grow and change, becoming empowered to achieve their happy ending. She's not afraid to let her characters make mistakes or take the story in an unexpected direction. Her stories cross genres, time-periods and continents, taking readers along for an unforgettable ride.

Email: gillian.stkevern@gmail.com

Website: www.gillianstkevern.com

Mailing list: www.gillianstkevern.com/newsletter-sign-up.html

Facebook: www.facebook.com/gillian.stkevern

Twitter: @GillianStKevern

Pinterest: www.pinterest.com/gillianstkevern

Other books by this author

For the Love of Christmas!

The Ugliest Sweater
Ibiza on Ice
The Charity Shop Rejects—Live in Concert

Thorns and Fangs

Thorns and Fangs
Uprooted
Life After Humanity

Also Available from NineStar Press

Connect with NineStar Press

www.ninestarpress.com

www.facebook.com/ninestarpress

www.facebook.com/groups/NineStarNiche

www.twitter.com/ninestarpress

www.tumblr.com/blog/ninestarpress

9 781948 608183